Y0-CCB-721

Urban Love Is

Urban Love Is

Erick S. Gray

www.urbanbooks.net

Urban Books, LLC
300 Farmingdale Road, NY-Route 109
Farmingdale, NY 11735

Urban Love Is Copyright © 2021 Erick S. Gray

All rights reserved. No part of this book may be reproduced in any form or by any means without prior consent of the Publisher, except brief quotes used in reviews.

ISBN 13: 978-1-64556-367-9
ISBN 10: 1-64556-367-7

First Mass Market Printing September 2022
First Trade Paperback Printing August 2021
Printed in the United States of America

10 9 8 7 6 5 4 3 2 1

This is a work of fiction. Any references or similarities to actual events, real people, living or dead, or to real locales are intended to give the novel a sense of reality. Any similarity in other names, characters, places, and incidents is entirely coincidental.

Distributed by Kensington Publishing Corp.
Submit Orders to:
Customer Service
400 Hahn Road
Westminster, MD 21157-4627
Phone: 1-800-733-3000
Fax: 1-800-659-2436

Prologue

What is love, it's up and down, comes and goes round and round, it can be hard, difficult, even intimidating, and scary at times . . .

"Are you dead serious about doing this shit? Marriage?" Ash asked me.

He wholeheartedly felt that I was making the biggest mistake of my life. But what did he know? He wasn't in love, and I believed he was immune to it, like he had the vaccine flowing through his veins and being in love was a disease. Ash was ready to spread some of his twisted medication my way. But I wasn't accepting it.

I knew a good thing when I saw it.

On our way toward lower Manhattan, we were on the E train to the courthouse where my fiancée was waiting. I was really nervous. I had butterflies partying drunk in my stomach waiting for me to throw up. Those nervous butterflies were not ready to leave so soon, but I wasn't going to show my nervousness in front of Ash. It would give him more of a reason to try to talk me out of it. He didn't need any more ammunition to fire my way.

"Marriage is suicide," he uttered and shook his head in sarcasm. "Why? Why you wanna join that dull fuckin' club, huh? Yo, you know once you say, 'I do,' then the pussy train stops running. You gonna find yourself standing alone at the dry train station, holding ya dick in your hand, waiting forever for that next pussy train to come through and pick ya ass up. You gonna be taking cold showers and jerking off."

"You really believe that, don't you?" I replied to his vulgar statement.

"It's true. Fools who get married don't get sex. Yo, you might as well shoot yourself."

I laughed. The shit that came flying out of Ash's mouth be crazy. Like wow, pause, and rewind, did he actually just say that shit? It was hard to believe we'd been friends since the first grade. You got used to him, though. But he didn't care what he said, when he said it, who he said it to, or who was listening. Ash always found himself saying, "Yo, I'm just keepin' it real wit' you, son."

Yeah, keeping it real. It was his favorite phrase.

We both were snug tight among dozens of passengers on the crowded E train traveling into the city. I felt like a sardine. The pushing and shoving, the people on top of each other, it came with rush hour. The subways could be a melting pot of different ethnicities, attitudes, and urban sensibilities coming and going. Everyone was jumbled together in one train car on a hot summer day. It was a fight to get to where you were going that morning. Rush hour was a bitch, but where I was going, it was worth it.

"I ain't never gettin' married," Ash continued.

Ash always had to speak. He still had something to say, like a dictator on his soapbox standing in front of a po-dium. If it wasn't his way, then he didn't believe in it—a fascist. He wasn't going to let up, not until he heard me say, "I do." He was relentless in nudging me away from marriage. And sometimes he could say shit that went too far. "You really gonna marry this bitch, yo?" he said.

I cut my eyes at him. "Yo, watch your mouth. Don't call my fiancée a bitch. Shit, Ash, I'm about to marry this woman. She isn't one of these hoes off the streets. So I would appreciate it if you respect my wife-to-be."

"My bad," he apologized to me.

"Sometimes you go too far with what you say."

"Yeah, I know, but I love you, and I just wanna see you happy."

"And marriage ain't gonna make me happy?"

"It's like playing Russian roulette—you never know when that bullet is gonna come," he said.

I sighed.

"Shit, I'm still surprised you're making me your best man," he said.

"Man, it ain't a real wedding. We're just getting married at city hall by a judge, nothing special. I just need a witness to come along."

"Yeah, well, I'm here at your service . . . grudgingly. But yo, is her friend gonna be there? What's her name? That fine-ass Spanish shorty she is always hangin' wit'?" he asked.

"You mean Yasmin."

"Yeah. Shorty is fuckin' fine. She got the phattest ass! I wanna fuck her," he said.

His boorish comment made an aging white lady tighten her face, and she looked insulted by what she'd heard. She definitely didn't look too pleased with my friend's choice of words.

"Yeah, she gonna be there too," I told him.

Ash smiled. "Yasmin, now she can definitely get this dick," he carried on. "Like that shorty over there." He nodded to a young girl nearby.

The girl was petite, pretty, and young, and she looked sixteen. She was holding on to the above bar with one hand and reading her schoolbook with the other. She was focused on her book, and Ash's eyes were focused on her.

"She's too young for you," I said, trying to snap him back to reality. "She looks like she's sixteen."

"Age ain't nothin' but a number," he countered. "Besides, you know my theory—if they're old enough to walk, then she's old enough to fuck. Besides, it ain't like we some old men up in this bitch. I'm only nineteen."

"Ash, you robbing the cradle wit' that one," I said, taking another look at her, then looking back at him.

"C'mon, Terrance, you telling me that you wouldn't go after that?" He grinned.

She was wearing a pair of tight blue Levi's and a white T-shirt that accentuated her full, young breasts. Her hair was pulled back into a ponytail. I had to admit, her body was looking right in them jeans and that shirt. However, I wasn't a pedophile, and I was about to become a married man, and Ash was trying to corrupt me to the fullest. He just didn't quit.

"Yo, look at that ass. It's the best time to get at 'em at her age, while they're young and gullible. You ain't gotta deal wit' that woman shit 'til years later. But by then, they're already on your dick. These bitches will believe anything you tell 'em."

"Yeah, like Chanel," I mentioned, who was one of the two young girls he'd gotten pregnant. Chanel was only sixteen years old and four months pregnant. She was a high school dropout, a hood rat, and in love with Ash—so in love that she was willing to have his baby when he continued to cheat on her. And then there was Monica. She was only 15 years old and six months pregnant by him. But she was still in school and holding down a part-time job at a clothing store. She regularly bought Ash whatever he wanted from her check. She, too, was in love with Ash.

"You need to stop fuckin' wit' these young girls," I warned him.

"Ah, man, Terrance, pussy ain't got a name or age on it. It's just there for a nigga like me to fuck. I feel the younger, the better."

"How young?" I asked him. "Because you're starting to scare me."

"I ain't no fuckin' pedophile," he retorted.

"Yeah, okay. You already got two kids on the way by these young-ass girls. You need to calm your wild ass down."

"What? Make a mistake and get married like you, at nineteen? You know how I feel. You're still too young. There's always still time to play, and you only knew this . . ." He paused, watching his tongue. He looked at me and continued with, "Yo, you only knew this chick . . ."

"Sophia," I reminded him.

"Yeah, you only knew her for a year, and now you wanna go and marry her and shit. What, Terrance, pussy that good?"

"Excuse me, young man," the lady standing next to us interrupted, finally hearing enough of his foul language. "I would appreciate it if you didn't use that kind of language while you're around me. It's just so disrespectful."

Ash looked stunned by her remark, like, what gave her the audacity to correct him? But he grinned her way. "Oh, I'm sorry. My bad, ma'am," he said to her.

Then he leaned over to me, and he whispered in my ear, "She just mad because her old ass ain't been getting. any dick since the men came home from World War II."

I chuckled.

Ash, he was the epitome of a player, a dog, a man who liked pussy by the boatload. He would overdose on it if he could. He was 19, had been around the block too many times, and had been through many ethnicities, like a kid in a candy store. He didn't discriminate when it came to the ladies. He loved the ladies, and they loved him right back. He stood at six feet one inch, he had light skin with brown eyes and dimples; and he sported long cornrows. Ladies saw them eyes and his braids, and it drove them crazy. He literally was the panty dropper, a walking pussy magnet. The man never worked a day in his life. He was spoiled, from his mother down to the females in his life. They fed him, clothed him, fucked him, and had his babies.

We both went way back since the first grade. He lived up the street from me, with his Jamaican mother and younger brother, Sunny. Every summer, his mother, Ms. Patrick, would throw these loud and wild parties, where there would be over a hundred people present. Everyone would dance, drink, and carry on like it was New Year's Eve. There would be so many people at her parties that it would start to look like the West Indian Day parade. And then around three or four o'clock in the morning, the cops would show up, telling Ms. Patrick that she had to either shut the party down or lower the music. If she was in a bad mood, Ms. Patrick would curse the cops out, telling them to go fuck themselves in her heavy Jamaican accent. One year, she received a $1,000 summons from the officers because of her rude and loud party. But she didn't give a fuck, because every year, it was the same thing. The loud women and men, the liquor, the reggae, and the soca carried on. It made her parties among the best in the neighborhood.

We came closer to city hall on Chambers Street in downtown Manhattan, and I became more nervous. Like, my stomach was doing backflips.

"Look at you, Terrance. You know you ain't ready for this," Ash said, starting things up again.

"Why are you so negative?" I asked, somewhat perturbed and starting to regret making him my best man and bringing him along. His mouth just didn't stop.

"Man, I'm tryin' to look out for your best interests. I don't want you to be committing the biggest mistake of your life," he proclaimed.

"Yo, Ash, I love this girl. I know what I'm doing," I uttered with conviction.

He shook his head. "Ain't no pussy worth marrying," he returned.

"Ah, man, you need to shut up. I remember back in the ninth grade when Shanice had you open like the freeway at three in the morning. You were wet behind the ears. You used to be talking all this shit back in high school about that being your future wifey and shit."

"Yo, I was young. I've made my mistakes. And Shanice, she fuckin' played herself. She went out and got pregnant by that cornball Danny. And then she gonna tell me that she was sorry, that shit just happened."

"Yeah, that was some fucked-up shit."

"But see, I've learned from that. I've learned what Snoop's always been preaching. 'Bitches ain't shit but hoes and tricks,'" he sang.

Crazy!

We ascended from the subway station into the metropolitan noise and the skyscrapers that hugged the blue sky, and we walked toward the courthouse. A summer day in the city was hectic, with people and traffic everywhere. I stopped in front of a storefront window to inspect my attire. I hated to brag, but I was one handsome muthafucka and looked sharp in my black khakis, white button-down Polo shirt, black tie, and brand-new loafers. My waves were spinning like a record, and my little peach fuzz was growing in around my chin.

Ash came clad in a pair of baggy Guess jeans hanging low off his behind, a plain T-shirt, and a pair of beige Timberlands. He had a gram of weed in his pocket. He brought it for us to celebrate, though he was constantly spitting out negativity about my big day. Ash was a straight thug. I didn't gripe about his attire. It was him. And who was I to judge?

There we were, standing at the foot of the courthouse steps. And there she was, my wife-to-be, Sophia, looking marvelous in a white dress that hugged her lovely curves and showed off her long legs. Her long, sensuous hair fell down to her shoulders, and she lit up brighter than the sun above. I smiled. I was in love. I wanted to spend the rest of my life with her. She was standing next to her friend Yasmin.

Sophia's bright brown eyes turned and looked my way. We locked eyes, and we both smiled simultaneously. I took a deep breath and was about to climb the stairs to be with her, but Ash quickly gripped my arm and tried to halt me from going to her.

"Hold on, let me holla at you for a minute," he said.

"About what?"

"Yo, what's up wit' tonight?" Ash asked.

"What do you mean, what's up wit' tonight? I'm spending tonight with my wife-to-be," I quickly told him.

"Damn, man," he dryly responded.

"Why, what's going down?" I asked.

"Yo, I'm supposed to meet up with Miz and them over by the park. Shit 'bout to go down tonight. We got this connect."

"Man, Ash, it's going to be my wedding night, and I can't be fuckin' wit' them crazy-ass fools on my wedding night."

"Yeah, I feel that. But a nigga like me broke right now. I need to make that paper," he said.

"Ash, don't fuck with them dudes tonight. Chill out with Sophia and me for a minute. And you see Yasmin right there. Now's your chance," I pointed out.

"Yeah, she do look tempting right now, but I gotta get this money. And since you goin' through wit' it, I ain't tryin' to get in the way of y'all honeymoon. Get all the pussy you can get before it's too late."

I shook my head.

"I just needed you to have my back tonight," he added.

He picked the wrong night. There was no way I was going to fuck up today or tonight with Sophia. "Wrong night," I said.

"I'm good still."

"You sure?"

He nodded. "I'm always good. I'm a warrior."

"Okay, Shaka Zulu," I joked.

I took a deep breath and calmed my nerves. Looking at Sophia from a distance, how could I not marry her? She was my world and my heart. She was the bread to my butter, the sun to my earth, my resurrection, the breath inside of me. She was my life, and I couldn't live without her.

"You know there is still time for you to back out of this," Ash said. "We can run for the border."

"And you'll be alone," I said.

I fixed my tie, got my nerves together, and climbed the courthouse steps to become closer to my wife-to-be. Ash followed me. I was getting married. *Damn, I'm getting married,* I kept saying to myself. This was it for me. No more single life. From now on, it was the married life, supposedly the good life, right?

She was going to be my ball and chain. I chuckled. I loved Sophia, and I knew she loved me just as much. This felt right, and we connected on so many levels. She was smart, beautiful, charismatic, and funny. We had a lot in common, but then she also was the opposite of me.

We met a year ago at Yasmin's backyard party in Brooklyn, where there was plenty of food, liquor, good music, and women—plenty of women. But Sophia was the only one who stood out and caught my attention. She made my heart skip a beat when I noticed her. My friends and I had taken the train into Brooklyn because we didn't have cars. It was my cousin Trey, Ash, and I. We were looking to have a great time and mingle with some beautiful ladies.

I remembered what Sophia had on that day of the party—a pretty white skirt and a blue top that made her slim frame pretty. Her hair was in two long pigtails. Yasmin introduced us, and from then on, we couldn't be separated.

I reached the top of the courthouse steps, kissed Sophia lovingly, held her hands in mine, and stared into her eyes.

"Are you ready to be a husband?" she asked me.

"Are you ready to become my wife?"

"Mrs. Grey is the perfect last name for me," she said, smiling heavily.

I smiled. We then marched inside and wouldn't come back out of the building until we were husband and wife.

Later that night, Sophia and I spent our honeymoon in a Sheraton suite in downtown Brooklyn. The room was costly, but it was worth it. It was just us, married and in love. The sex was fantastic, and I couldn't get enough of her.

My cell phone rang while we were in the middle of having sex. I forgot to turn it off. I ignored it, but it rang again. I ignored it. But it rang again. It was my cousin calling, so I knew it had to be necessary. I apologized to my wife for the interruption, and answered his call.

"What?" I exclaimed. He knew I was on my honeymoon.

"Ash got locked up," he uttered.

"What?" I was shocked to hear it.

"He got locked up," Trey repeated. "Central booking for possession."

"Damn!" I uttered—and on my wedding day.

Chapter One

Terrance

What is love, it's something worth waiting for, and it isn't tricks for treats, but just you and me, building a future, engineering our dreams . . .

Seven Years Later

Sex in the morning. It didn't get any better.

"Aaaah, baby, right there. Don't stop. Yes, right there, Terrance. Oh, God. Oh, God. Ooooh," Sophia cried out lovingly. Her moaning was music to my ears.

I was primed between her thick thighs, licking and sucking on her clit with my mouth and tongue, playing with her pussy and tasting my wife's juices, lapping it up like water from a fountain. She squirmed all over our bed, moaning like a siren as her fingernails tightly seized the back of my head. She was in full heat, ready to explode. She couldn't let go, and she held my head steady between her legs, winding and lifting her hips. She huffed and puffed. "Oh, God. Umm, ugh. Umm, ugh. Yes!"

Eating pussy in the early morning was what I loved to do. Sophia didn't complain. The only gripe that came from her mouth was, "You gonna make me late for work!" But she didn't take the initiative to try to stop me. She panted and squirmed and praised my sweet gift as my tongue tunneled its way deep inside of her. Her tight grasps went from the back of my head to the bedroom sheets. As the sheets became scrunched inside her fists, she turned her head to the side and cried out, "Oh, shit! I'm gonna come!"

Her mouth was gaping.

Seven years of marriage and our sex life was still great, fucking exhilarating. On certain mornings, we would take turns on each other. I would wake up to a blowjob from her, and she would wake up to some sweet cunnilingus. It was like giving each other a unique wake-up call. And what a wake-up call we would give to each other. There was nothing better to start your morning off than having sex. Y'all twisting and turning sexually like a pretzel, and then coming like a geyser.

"I'm gonna come!" she huffed again.

I continued to eat and eat. Sophia's passionate cries echoed off the bedroom walls and traveled like thunder inside the room. She could get loud and wake the baby. Yes, we had a daughter. Her name was Zaire, and she was 5. Born in Jamaica Hospital—six pounds and eight ounces—she was my world, my bundle of joy. Sophia went through twelve long hours of labor trying to deliver her. We named her Zaire because it was a unique and beautiful name for a girl. I remembered looking at my newborn daughter for the very first time and falling in love with her. When the doctor gently placed her into my arms, wrapped in her receiving blanket, I smiled so widely that my ears had gotten wet. My fatherly instincts kicked it, and I wanted to love and protect my baby girl. I was a proud father, and it was the happiest day of my life.

I had kissed my wife and thanked her for the best gift in life—a daughter. She did great. She was exhausted and depleted from giving birth, but she was a mother and a happy woman. And finally, I felt that my family was complete. I kissed her once again with Zaire in my arms and said, "We did it, baby, we did it!"

Sophia had stared up at me and said, "I love you. I love us."

I never wanted the feeling to end. My wife, my daughter, they both were my world. And when I saw them together, I had said to myself, *heaven finally reached earth.*

Sophia finally came in my mouth, but I continued to eat, ensuring I cleaned my plate below. She couldn't take it anymore and tried to pull away from me, but I playfully grabbed her in my arms, and we wrestled naked on the bed. The morning was fun, and though she would be late for work because of me, it didn't matter. We were still in love, right? Our marriage was absolute bliss.

She finally managed to escape my hold and jumped off the bed. She had to get ready for work. "I hate you," she playfully said to me, and then she ran into the bathroom and closed the door.

I smiled, saying, "You know you love it. There ain't no man out there who can do you better than me."

"How you know I ain't been looking?"

"Please. And fuck up a good thing at home?" I said.

She chuckled. I knew she was kidding. *She'd better be.* I rested on my elbows, lying buck-naked across the bed. I was in an excellent mood this morning. I was off today, and Zaire was spending the day at her grandmother's, which meant that I had the place to myself. But that wasn't the only reason why I was in such a good mood. My boy, Ash, was getting out today. He'd done seven years in an upstate prison for possession and assault, arrested the night I married Sophia.

Fucking ironic.

But he was finally coming home.

Sophia spent thirty-five minutes in the bathroom, getting herself dressed and ready for work. She had to be at work at eight. She would usually leave the house around six forty-five or so, giving herself ample time to reach her job early. She worked at Chase Bank in downtown Manhattan. She'd been employed there for about two years now, and she loved her job.

I worked at the airport, American Airlines in JFK— John F. Kennedy Airport. I'd been working there for the past five years now. It was full time with excellent hours and attractive benefits including health, a credit union, and a 401(k). I loved my job. I loved working on the planes—loading and unloading cargo and luggage, cleaning the planes, and guiding them in and pushing them out. Sometimes I felt that I should have been a pilot. But I made a decent paycheck, and I lived a sober life. I supported and took care of my family to the fullest.

I'm a good man, right? I know I am.

While lying on my bed, I spun over and stared up at the ceiling. I thought about my life and marriage. At first it had terrified me. I remembered thinking that I had to commit to one woman for the rest of my life. Damn! Could I do it? Was I able to do it? Yes, I was scared. I was afraid of fucking it up. I was scared that she would leave me. Then she became pregnant. I nearly hit the fuckin' roof. We were about to have a baby. Were we ready for a baby? If we were or weren't, we needed to get prepared either way because this baby was coming in nine months whether we liked it or not. I was getting used to the married life, and now I was about to become a father. But it all was such a blessing, and I wouldn't have had it any other way.

Sophia came out of the bathroom dressed for work. She sported a white stretch cotton-poplin shirt with French cuffs and a shirttail hem, and a pinstriped skirt, wearing that businesswoman look. She looked great. Her hair was styled in a French bun, and she made me smile.

"Don't forget to tell all your male coworkers that you're a married woman," I jokingly said to her.

She chuckled, playfully saying, "Damn, that means I'll have to call off all of my affairs."

"Yeah, you gonna have me go down there to shoot some fool," I said.

I removed myself from the bed and walked toward her, naked, while she was applying some makeup to her already-pretty face and staring at herself in the bedroom mirror.

"Whatever, Terrance. You ain't shooting nobody," she said.

"Baby, for our love, you think I won't? I'll go Terminator on a muthafucka for fuckin' with mine." I pretended to have a machine gun in my hand and shoot up the room.

"Terrance, I don't need my husband and the father of our child in jail like your boy Ash."

"C'mon, Sophia, let's not go there. I'm not Ash."

"Yeah, well, I hope not. I know you're better than him."

"Baby, let's get off Ash right now, and let me get on you," I said.

I pressed my nakedness against her body, wrapped my arms around her slim waist, and held her petite figure snuggly in my arms. I never wanted to let her go.

"C'mon, Terrance, I don't want any wrinkles or pre-semen on my skirt right now," she said, trying to pull herself away from my grip.

"Well, can I get a quickie?"

"Now you're tripping. You're definitely gonna make me late for work, talking that foolishness."

"I ain't tripping. I'll just get at that sweet pussy after work."

"You're stupid. I'm out. I'll see you tonight," she said. She gave me a kiss goodbye. "Love you."

"Love you too."

Damn, tonight. I probably wasn't going to see her until late tonight. Ash was getting out today, and I knew I and the rest of the fellows were going to hang out with our boy.

I knew Sophia would understand, even though I'd forgotten to mention that Ash was being released today. It'd been a long time since we were all together and got to hang out like the old days.

I couldn't wait to see him again and catch up on things.

Chapter Two

Trey

A real man doesn't point and constantly blame, and he doesn't apologize repeatedly for the same damn mistakes . . .

My day couldn't get any better for me. I finally got my car out of the auto body shop on Farmers Boulevard—my prized burgundy 2000 Mercedes-Benz CLK 320, which I leased for $697 a month. Two weeks without my ride was torture for me. Some asshole had hit me from the back on Linden Boulevard, and then he had the nerve to try to curse me out, saying it was my fault. I'd wanted to knock his head off with the baseball bat I kept in my trunk. But I'd kept calm. I had insurance, and he had insurance too. So we handled the accident like gentlemen. There was no need to get into a fistfight in the middle of the street. Although having him hit my ride, smash up the back, it was like a man having sex with my woman. I was ready to go to war for mine.

But my insurance came through. It was excellent having full coverage.

Today was a bright, bright day for me. I had made up
with my girl this morning. For about two hours we fucked
our brains out, and she gave me some of the best sex in
the world. We'd had a massive argument about a week
ago—about what, I couldn't even remember. My girl,
Trisha, could be a bitch sometimes. But she was my bitch.
And after being with her for three years, I somehow felt
connected to her. She kept talking about marriage. But a
man like me wasn't ready for marriage. I wasn't prepared
to settle down. I was too young for that, right?

My day was the bomb so far: makeup sex with my
girl, I got my Benz back, and today Ash was coming
home. It felt like life was finally coming together for all
my friends.

I took the day off from work. In my occupation, I was
a CPA, a certified public accountant. It was great money,
I loved dealing with numbers, and I loved making money.
I'd gotten my bachelor's degree in political science and
business from NYU. I also had passed the Uniform
Certified Public Accountant Examination with flying
colors. I was America's worst nightmare. I was educated,
smart, handsome, and successful, and I drove a lovely
Benz. I was a hater's worst nightmare too. I had it all.
And on top of that, I had a big dick.

But I wasn't bragging.

It was a nice day. I had the top down and some Biggie
playing, and I cruised through Queens. I was on my way
to see this girl named Chica. We'd met six weeks ago
after I had my umpteenth fight with Trisha. I'd needed to
escape my girl. I went for a simple drive and came across
Chica walking to the corner store on Farmers Boulevard.
Before I could holler at her, some buster-ass nigga had
started a conversation with her. I had climbed out of my

Benz and noticed her looking my way as I entered the
store. I knew she was interested in me. She looked aloof
from the guy talking her ear off. I had purchased a pack
of Newports and walked out of the store. She wasn't
talking to that guy anymore. She was on the pay phone. I
contemplated, *should I or shouldn't I?* Wifey had really
pissed me off. We had broken up for the umpteenth time
this year. And shorty on the pay phone was a cutie with a
nice-size booty.

Why not? I said to myself.

I had approached her while she was on the phone. She
saw me standing behind her and curtailed her conversation with whoever by saying to them, "I'll call you right
back."

I asked for her name, and I told her mine. And from
there we conversed. Her eyes told me everything, I
had her undivided attention, and I had that pussy wet.
She saw the Benz, the clothes, the good looks, and she
wanted some of me. And I told her the truth about me.
I already had a girl. Though we had broken up that day,
Trisha was still my heart.

I wasn't looking for another girlfriend in my life,
just another shorty to kick it with here and there. Chica
didn't even care. She was down. I didn't play games
with sidepieces. I told them the situation straight up, no
equivocation, no beating around the bush. You see, that
saved me from the drama, letting these hoes know right
off the bat about Trisha so there wouldn't be any confusion about where they stood. She wasn't the primary but
the second in my life. Trisha would always come first,
whether we were together or not.

These women didn't care. They still wanted to fuck
with me after that. They always wanted a piece of me.

They were even willing to throw pussy my way, throw my dick down their throat, and appease me sexually. I didn't need to lie to these hoes.

I parked in front of Chica's grandmother's place on Murdock Avenue in St. Albans, Queens. It was a cozy three-bedroom house with a front porch, colorful flowers planted in the front yard, and a manicured lawn. Her grandmother was a schoolteacher who'd taught math and science for over thirty years at the same elementary school in Brooklyn. She wasn't home during the day. Chica would tell me to come by around eleven or twelve, and I would stay until about three that afternoon. It gave us ample time to do us—to fuck our brains out!

She was a young girl of 19. Her grandmother was a strict Christian woman. No boys were allowed in her house while she wasn't there, and no boys were allowed even if her grandmother was home. Of course, Chica broke that rule repeatedly by a mile. It was fun sneaking around.

I exited my ride and walked toward the front porch. It was a quiet neighborhood. Most of the neighbors were at work, somewhere else, or in school. Not too many people were home this time of day. I rang the bell. I couldn't wait to see Chica. I could only imagine what she would come to the door wearing this time. Last time she answered the door buck-naked wearing some pink house slippers. It turned me the fuck on.

I didn't have to wait long. The door unlocked, then it opened, and there was Chica, not letting me down at all. She was nicely clad in a white collared shirt, opened fully, exposing those soft, perky tits of hers and a shaved pussy. She stood in a pair of stilettos while twirling her panties in her hand.

"Damn, Chica! You don't be worried about the neighbors seeing you?" I asked.

"Fuck my neighbors. I'm a big girl," she said, moving to the side and letting me inside.

"Yeah, I can see that," I said, staring at her rawness.

Chica had it going on. She was a beautiful, freaky-ass young girl. She stood at five feet six inches and had long black hair. Of course, it was a weave, but it still looked good on her. She had a nice phat ass, soft, round tits that felt like cotton in my hands, and she had some of the darkest nipples I'd ever seen. She had thick brown thighs that felt like silk touching you. She was a soft woman with some good pussy. She also had the fullest lips I ever had seen on a woman with these enticing brown eyes. She had this sexy-ass attitude like, "I don't give a fuck, I want mine, and I want it now."

I walked into the living room, and before I could take a seat or do anything else, Chica jumped onto me playfully. She straddled me as I held her in my arms. She kissed me. Her naked skin felt so inviting, and I found myself growing hard.

"You know the deal, Trey," she said. "You didn't come here to talk. I'm so fuckin' horny right now. I was thinking about you all morning."

I grinned. "Damn, a brother can't have a seat first?"

"Only if you're sitting on my bed," she replied.

I carried her into her bedroom, and I hurled her light ass onto the bed. She giggled. She gazed at me hungrily. There was no denying it. She was mine from head to toe, my personal sex slave. She positioned herself on her back and spread her legs for me with her feet propped in the stilettos she wore, showing off how clean and wet her pussy was.

"You gonna get it," I playfully taunted. I started unbuckling my belt like she was about to get a severe butt whipping.

"You gonna spank me for being bad, Trey?"

"Yeah, with my dick," I replied teasingly.

I slowly dropped my pants, then my boxers, and let my dick hang there for a while. It was eight inches and better. These ladies were not fuckin' with me. I started stroking myself, and Chica loved that, seeing a man jerk his big, black, and hard dick.

"You like this?" I said, with my dick gripped in my fist. I gazed at her.

She stood up on her knees and moved toward me. "That's a woman's job, baby. Let me handle that for you," she said. She removed my hand, seized my big dick in her small fist, and continued where I'd left off.

"Oh, shit. Mmm, yeah, that feels so good," I moaned.

She jerked me off, unwavering. I moaned and closed my eyes, enjoying her touch, enjoying the way she slid her hand back and forth leisurely against my titanic erection.

"Lie on your back, Trey," she said.

She pushed me, and I fell against her bed. My dick felt like a missile ready to launch.

"Damn, you got a big dick," she complimented me.

I'd heard it plenty of times. It was still nice to know. She leaned into me, still working magic with eight inches of erection. I felt her devour me nice and slow. She was giving me some great head. I grasped the back of her head and raised my butt cheeks, trying to put the dick down her throat deeper. She was about to make me come.

"Yo, chill. Stop," I uttered, defeated. I didn't want to come yet.

Chica stood ready on her knees and smiled my way devilishly. Her freak was out and showing ultimately. I pushed her against the bed, onto her back. She spread her legs, and I wanted to fuck her raw. Every fiber inside of me wanted to feel inside of her without a condom. Lust was screaming at me, yelling, "Go ahead, nigga. One time won't hurt." But my conscience was telling me different. It would be stupid, idiotic. *You don't even know this girl like that. Think about AIDS and other STDs.* I definitely didn't want to bring anything back to Trisha. She would kill me. Seeing Chica in that position, her legs spread completely, and watching her massage her clit and finger her pussy, I went dumb and stupid. *Fuck it,* I told myself. *Just this one time.*

I climbed on top of her, ready to penetrate that sweetness. I suddenly heard her sigh.

"What's wrong?" I asked.

"How come you don't eat me out?" she asked.

"I told you, I don't do that shit. I don't eat pussy."

"I'm sayin' you can try it at least once," she said dejectedly.

"Nah, love. I don't even eat out wifey. No disrespect, but you ain't no different," I told her.

"But I be blessin' you lovely, and you know it, too. Why you can't return the favor?"

"Just be quiet and come here," I said.

I pulled her by her legs and brought her closer to me. I knew once the dick was inside of her, she'd shut the fuck up about the subject. Chica didn't resist when I thrust my big black dick into her raw, causing her to pant out and squirm underneath me. She clutched me tightly and shut the fuck up as I predicted. She was loud and chanting, loving the dick. We went at it for over an hour—doggie style, froggy style, her on top, sideways, the floor, the wall. Her bedroom became our sexual playground. Three times she came, and I was still working on my first nut.

It was great sex. It was so great that I didn't want to pull out.

"Fuck me, Trey! Ooooh, shit. Fuck me, Trey!" she chanted.

She held on to me tightly, working her natural body against me, digging her nails into my back—*damn it*—leaving evidence behind. *Trisha sees that and she gonna know another woman put them scratches there.*

"I'm 'bout to come again, Trey. Oh, God! Right there, right there!" she hollered.

I was right behind her, feeling my orgasm brewing. *Pull out. Pull the fuck out,* I told myself. It was right there, close to an eruption. And then it happened. I exploded inside of her, and my semen went swimming everywhere. I grunted and howled while coming, as both our bodies shook vigorously from the aftermath. I damn near broke the bed by arriving inside of her so hard.

Damn, it felt so good.

I removed my sweaty, naked body from hers and exhaled, lying on my back, and now feeling that post-coital moment. *Damn, I just came in this bitch. What the fuck!* Chica assured me that she was on birth control, but what about that other shit. I knew that I had wilded out and lost power to lust. Her beauty, her curvy, naked body, her sexy thighs and sweet womanhood, it was entrapment. How could a man like me resist?

Another deep sigh followed by another, *what the fuck?*

I got up and got dressed. I got what I came for, and there was no need for me to linger in her bedroom or in her grandmother's home. Besides, it was getting late, and

I had things to do. Chica wanted me to stay, but she knew the routine. We weren't boyfriend or girlfriend, and there was no romance. It was just sex, nothing else. If I started staying longer and getting comfortable, treating her any differently and having pillow talk with her after sex, then she was gonna start to think it was something else with us. I left. Deuces.

Today had been a great day so far, and tonight, I was going to chill and hang out with the fellows. Ash was coming home today, and we all needed to catch up on lost time.

Chapter Three

Devin

*Love is when you look into her eyes, and you just
have to smile, knowing that she's something you
definitely have to cherish . . .*

I couldn't decide between the white roses or the red
for my sweetheart, Danielle. Today was our first anniversary. It'd been one year now since we'd been together.
I felt that I was the happiest and luckiest man on earth.
Danielle was a sweetheart, my honey pie, and tonight, I'd
planned something so wonderful for her. I left early from
work just for this occasion so I could give myself ample
time to make our evening together perfect.

I bought her this nice platinum princess-cut engagement ring, which set me back $1,500. *But hey, she's
worth it.* Then I had the florist arrange to drop off a
bouquet of roses an hour after she got home from work.
I bought the Maxwell CD so it would be playing as she
walked through the door.

I wanted to ease her mind a little while giving her
the exotic foot massage, rubbing her shoulders, and
whispering sweet things in her ear. I was making dinner

tonight. It was a romantic candlelit dinner just for both of us. And after dinner, I planned to pop the question to her. I was going to get down on one knee at the dinner table, take her hand in mine, show her the ring, and ask, "Will you marry me?" while the Maxwell CD was still playing softly in the background. Sometimes I surprised myself. But I felt that tonight was the night, no kidding around. I loved this woman. I loved her so much that I wanted to grow old with her.

I couldn't help but feel a little excited. I couldn't wait to see the look on my lady's face when she came home from work to see what I'd put together just for her. After dinner, I planned on carrying my woman into the bedroom to make love to my fiancée from dusk to dawn.

I carried the gifts to my car and placed them carefully into the back seat. I drove off to my next destination, which was home. It was only four ten, and I had plenty of time to do what I had planned to do.

As I was driving down Sunrise Highway, I heard my cell phone go off. I looked at the caller ID, and it was Terrance.

"What's up?" I hollered.

"Yo, you still on for tonight, right?" he asked.

"Tonight?" I had not a clue what he was talking about.

"Ah, man, you done forgot, Devin? Yo, Ash is home today. We all plan to head out to Eightball around nine tonight, get our party and drink on," he said, sounding excited.

"Ah, man, T, tonight? Shit, I forgot Ash was out today."

"But you're coming, right? It ain't gonna be fun without the four of us being there, just like back in the day, dog."

Damn, not tonight. I had too much planned for tonight with my lady for me to just up and cancel everything. "Damn, T. I can't roll tonight. I'm sorry, man," I told him.

"What? C'mon, Devin. You can't drop out on us like that."

"I got shit planned with Danielle tonight. I plan to pop the question to her."

"You serious, son?"

"Yes. I'm about to make that special move just like you did, Terrance."

"You sure you got the balls to? I'm sayin' that shit's a serious step in your life. You sure about her? You think she's the one?"

"Yes, Terrance, I'm sure. You've been married for seven years now, and you turned out all right."

He chuckled. "She ain't pregnant?" he asked.

"No," I quickly told him.

"You sure?"

"Why does she have to be pregnant for me to want to marry her?" I was offended.

"I'm just tryin' to look out for my boy," he tried to explain.

"Terrance, she isn't pregnant, and I can look out for myself. And even if she is pregnant, I'm still going to take care of mine."

"Yo, I just don't want a sister trapping a brother, that's all," he said.

"Terrance, why do you have to go there? Danielle isn't trying to trap me. Shit, I knew her for a year now. Like you knew Sophia a year right after you did go out and married her, being nineteen and all. I didn't say anything negative about the girl. I told you to do you and be happy. Now I want to get married because I'm in love with her, and you're talking about Danielle trying to trap a brother."

"My bad, Dev. I ain't mean to say it like that."

"Well, don't say it then," I chided.

"Damn, Devin, just stop being so sensitive about it. I'm sorry. Marry the girl, be happy, and have a bunch of babies. All I'm saying—"

"Terrance, now you're being sarcastic. I'm hanging up right now. I'll talk to you later," I said, clicking off the phone.

Terrance was my best friend, but sometimes the wrong things just happened to come out of his mouth at times. I didn't know why. He meant well, but sometimes he got me upset. And before we started arguing and he ruined my day, I decided not to carry the conversation any further. I was happy that Ash was coming home today, but I could see him some other day. Tonight, my woman had my time.

It was six fifteen, and I had about forty more minutes until Danielle came home. The place was spotless. I took the time to tidy up things and prepared dinner. I had spaghetti cooking on the stove with some garlic bread in the oven. A bottle of white wine was set on the table, and my Maxwell CD was playing throughout the rooms. I called the florist to confirm my order and my address, and he assured me that the roses would be there by eight tonight.

I placed two lit candles on the dinner table, one by her and one by me. I then went into the bedroom to change for my special occasion. I searched through my closet and pulled out my charcoal-colored slacks, my slate blue stretch silk shirt, the one that Danielle bought me for my birthday last month, and a pair of loafers. I got my hair cut early this afternoon as soon as I left work. I sported the low-cut style, with the sides tapered and my goatee trimmed perfectly.

I stared at myself in the bathroom mirror. I purposely left my shirt unbuttoned, exposing my flat stomach, but I was still working on the abs. I'd been hitting the gym twice a week now. I was looking sharp. Everything was ready and in place. Now all I needed was for Danielle to arrive and be caught off guard by my special arrangement.

I lit both candles and raised the volume to the stereo system a bit, listening to Maxwell's *Urban Hang Suite* album with "Ascension (Don't Ever Wonder)" playing. Dinner was ready, and the wine was room temperature. I was feeling a bit anxious. I couldn't wait to dine, wine, and romance my lady.

I was sitting on the living room couch, listening to one of my favorite songs. The mood was set right, with all the lights in the apartment either dimmed or turned off. You could smell the aroma coming from the kitchen, and it was making my stomach growl because I hadn't eaten all day. Finally, I heard her keys dangling at the front door, and I knew it was her. I jumped up from off the couch and hurried into the kitchen. I heard the door shut, and I waited a few seconds before I would approach her. I wanted to have her take in the sensual environment alone before I showed my presence.

"Devin," I heard her called out.

I heard her making her way into the kitchen, so I hid in the corner. She passed right by me, and I crept up behind her and grabbed her playfully in my arms, picking my beautiful woman up off her feet and swinging her around good-naturedly.

"Stop it. Put me down," she said, laughing.

I continued to swing her around in my arms. I placed her down back on her feet, and she turned toward me and asked, "What is all this?"

"It's for you, baby. Happy anniversary," I said, cupping her in my arms. "It's been a year since we first met."

She smiled and stared up at me with her lovely brown eyes and honey brown skin. Her beautiful, silky jet-black hair was falling down to her shoulders. She was my angel. Everything about her was heavenly.

"Oh, my God, Devin. Why so much?" she asked.

"Because I love you, and you're the most beautiful woman on this earth," I proclaimed.

She tittered. "You're too much, Devin."

"Nothing but the best for my queen," I said.

I nimbly pulled her by her arms, leading her into the living room, where I continued to hold her. We began to sway back and forth to the soft music by my boy Maxwell. She nestled her head against my chest.

"How was work today?" I asked.

"It was cool," she said with her arms wrapped around me.

I looked at the time, and it was seven fifteen. *My roses should be arriving soon.* I broke away from her precious grip and stared at her attire. She was in a knee-length skirt, a pair of Hush Puppies, and a white blouse: the typical workwear for her every day. Danielle was a receptionist at some downtown law firm.

I shook my head, indicating that her wardrobe would not do for tonight. "Baby, you need to change into something nice."

"But I have nothing new," she told me.

"Look in your closet," I said.

"My closet?"

"Yeah, there's a surprise for you," I said, smiling broadly.

"Devin!"

She hurriedly walked into the bedroom, with me following right behind her. She didn't know that I'd purchased this fabulous dress for her last week in the mall. I had it hidden in the back of my closet until now. I had placed it in her closet early this evening.

She opened her closet door eagerly, pulling back clothes and dresses in search of what I'd left inside.

"Oh, my God, Devin," she uttered in shock.

She spotted the dress. It was a purple beaded silk slip dress that had a sheer layer with vibrant, beaded roses over a satin lining, A-line shape. It had a V-neck and slim straps.

She pulled it out of the closet, gazing proudly at it. She placed it neatly across our bed. "Devin, you shouldn't have," she said.

"Yes, I should. I give my baby nothing but the best," I told her.

I walked up to her, and we embraced each other, and then we tongued each other down for a moment. We were becoming so passionate that we almost got into doing some things that I wanted to wait to do after dinner and after my proposal.

"Oh, the dress is lovely. Thank you, baby," she said, about ready to try it on.

I started to walk out of the bedroom until I heard Danielle asked, "You're not gonna watch me try it on?"

"Nah, I'm gonna chill out in the living room and have you surprise me when I see you come out in it."

She smiled, getting undressed as I left the bedroom.

I took a seat on the couch and waited patiently. I couldn't wait to see my baby walk out here in that dress. I made sure that it was her size, and with her thin figure, it was gonna be the bomb on her.

Fifteen minutes later, Danielle stepped out into the living room in the dress and some heels as I was lying on the couch.

"So how does it fit me?" she asked with her arms extended, doing a little twirl.

I got up. "It fits you wonderfully. Heaven just stepped into the room."

She blushed. I walked toward her and pulled her into my arms. "I love you," I proclaimed.

"I love you too," she replied.

So far everything was going perfectly. I looked at the time, and it was eight ten. *The deliveryman with my roses should be here any minute.* Danielle was enjoying the dinner that I had made. We sat at the well-decorated dinner table, talking, laughing, smiling, and enjoying each other's company.

As I was about to take a bite of garlic bread, the doorbell sounded.

"Damn, who in the hell can that be?" I cursed, pretending to be annoyed.

"You want me to get it?" Danielle asked.

"Nah, I'll get it," I said, getting up from my seat and walking toward the door. It was the deliveryman with my bouquet of roses.

"I have a delivery here for Mr. Devin Park," he announced.

"That's me," I said. I took the roses and left him a $20 tip.

"Danielle, look what somebody left at the door." I held the bouquet of roses in front of me.

"Devin, I know you didn't," she said with joy.

"Oh, yes I did." I passed her the roses. And she couldn't get enough of me.

By eight forty-five, I was ready to pop the question. We had almost finished dinner, and we both had full bellies. I subtly reached into my pants pocket and pulled out the small black velvet case the ring was in. I stood up and coolly approached her.

"Devin, please, no more surprises. You're too much for me," she said, looking at me brightly. But she couldn't resist showing me her beautiful smile. I stood over her while she was still seated. I took her hand in mine, slowly got down on one knee, and showed her the ring.

"Danielle, you're my world, and I love you so much. Will you marry me and become my wife?"

She cupped her hand over her mouth, peering down at me with eagerness. She looked speechless.

"Say yes, baby, and I promise to do right by you until my grave and beyond," I added.

I felt her breathing a little heavily, like she was catching an asthma attack. I hoped that all this wasn't too much for her to handle—the gifts, the dinner, and the proposal. *I can't be having my lady passing out on me.*

She gazed at me, and then she said, "Yes!"

I slowly placed the ring on her finger and then kissed the back of her hand like a true gentleman. I then stood up and embraced her in my arms.

"I love you, Danielle," I proclaimed.

"I love you too, Devin."

We kissed each other fervently. Our dessert was going to be in the bedroom.

Chapter Four

Terrance

What is love, love is when she trusts you, and it's when she believes in you, love is when you turned that house into a home . . .

It was a quarter to eleven. I was on my way to pick up Ash. He was staying over at his mom's new place over on Merrick Boulevard. I couldn't wait to see my friend again. Tonight, it would be like old times, like how it used to be back in the days. But less one man though, Devin. He decided to bitch out and spend the evening with his woman. However, it was all right. I just felt that he was spending too much time with Danielle. He was always all up on her. *Damn, give the woman some breathing room.*

Anyway!

I pulled up in front of his mom's place. I smiled. I wondered how much he done changed. We had spoken to each other via collect phone calls over time, and we exchanged several letters. But I never went to visit him. I couldn't stand seeing my boy caged in some prison.

I went to the door and pushed the doorbell. I waited. Less than a minute later, I heard movement behind the door.

"Who is it?" I heard Ash ask.

"Your PO. Open the door so I can violate your ass," I joked loudly.

The front door swung open, and there was Ash. He quickly commented, "Nigga, that ain't even funny."

"Whatever. What is up?"

"What is up, my nigga?" Ash hollered, excited to see me. He gave me dap and embraced me with a brotherly hug.

"What's the deal?" I hollered back.

It was smiles and love. It had been too long.

We hugged each other for a good minute, and then he told me to come in. I stepped into his mom's new home. It was nicely furnished with big-screen TVs and plush furniture. It smelled lovely. His mom always had expensive taste in furniture and clothes.

"So what's good, T?" he asked.

"Living life."

"I feel you. I'm 'bout to get back to living my life too," he said.

He walked through the living room shirtless, and I noticed that his upper torso was swathed by tattoos. Ash was a little more ripped, too. He added a bit more mass and definition to his frame.

"Damn, Ash, what the fuck do they be feeding y'all inmates?" I asked, surprised that this once-slim dude gained like twenty-five pounds, looking muscular.

"That prison food ain't shit. A nigga like me been hitting the weights like every other day. You know, tryin' to get my swell on," he said, flexing his chest and biceps in front of me.

His features also changed. He went from having a baby face to growing a mustache and looking like he needed a shave. He had dreads now instead of braids, and they were shoulder-length. He had on a pair of gray sweats and was wearing some house slippers and tube socks.

"Yo, what's up wit' the tattoos?" I asked.

"I got bored," he responded.

"You sure they ain't no gang signs?"

"I was holding shit down in Rikers and upstate. Them fools wasn't fuckin' wit' me. You see this?" he said, showing me his knuckles, holding them up to my face. They were ashy, scarred, and looked like they had been through a lot. "I fucked up plenty of niggas who thought they were hard and tried to step to me on some bullshit. And I had some of my niggas locked up wit' me, too. You know we had it on lock. Yo, you remember Dee from high school?"

"Yeah, yo."

"He was up in there wit' me too. He is doing twenty-five years to life, son. He caught that murder charge," Ash told me.

"Word!"

"Yeah, and yo, you remember Pepper?"

My memory didn't recall that name. *Pepper, Pepper . . .*

"Yo, that nigga from the south side. He used to fuck wit' that fine-ass bitch who used to live across the street from you. He drove that blue Pathfinder."

"Oh, that little muthafucka with the braids," I suddenly remembered.

"Yeah. Yo, he is holding shit down inside too."

"Word!"

"Yeah, yo."

"Damn, son."

"Yo, T, I could run a list of names on niggas I done been locked up wit', especially upstate. But everyone is cool. You know, they doing they thing, reppin', yo, holdin' shit down, doin' their time and whatnot, ya know what I'm sayin'."

"I know you glad to be home," I said.

"Hell yeah, my nigga. I get to sleep in my own bed, eat Ma's cooking, and the best thing, the shit that I've been missing the most, yo, T, is the fuckin' ladies. I'm tight right now. I ain't had pussy in seven muthafuckin' years."

I laughed. "You sure it still works?" I joked.

"My dick is coming out of retirement tonight. I need some pussy, T," he said eagerly.

"Tonight, son. Eightball."

"Word, yo. I need to see somethin', some ass shake, and some tits bounce. A nigga like me been around too many ugly-ass inmates and COs too long."

"Vaseline ain't been holding you down?" I joked.

"What? I don't beat my meat. That's what we got bitches for."

"Stop frontin'. You know you whacked that shit off once or twice up in the joint."

"T, don't fuckin' play yourself. I've been keeping busy by creating this," he said, once again flexing the biceps.

"Whatever," I dryly responded.

He looked at me, trying to be all serious and shit. But then he cracked that smile and started laughing. "You stupid. You lucky you, my boy. All I have to do is go buck wild on that ass and fuck you up."

"Hurry up and get dressed. We are supposed to meet Trey there soon," I told him.

"My nigga Trey," he said, heading toward the steps. "Yo, is your cousin still playing these bitches? That was my equal right there."

"Yeah, a little somethin', but he got his girl now."

"Word, he tryin' to get locked down too?" I heard him echo down from upstairs.

"Something like that," I replied calmly.

"What is this world coming to?"

"Just changing, that's all," I said.

I took a seat down on one of Ms. Patrick's brand-new plush leather couches. She moved into this new home last year after she'd received an amicable settlement from her accident that happened several years ago. A city bus ran a red light and smashed into her car, pinning her to the steering wheel and breaking her collarbone, hip, and right arm. She had to have surgery twice and endured two years of physical therapy. But she got paid a lovely settlement from the city, somewhere in the range of $250,000.

Paid!

I waited twenty minutes for Ash to get his black ass dressed so we could hurry down to the club and get the night started. Typical Ash, he was taking longer to get dressed than my wife. I looked at the stereo system's time by the stairs and saw that it was getting late. I slumped down on the couch, thinking, *damn, we about to have a ball tonight.*

Hopefully not that wildin'-out fun! Still married!

Ash came down the stairs dressed impeccably in pair of black Sean John jeans and the fashionable T-shirt to match. He wore some fresh beige Timberland boots, and he had on a fitted blue Yankees baseball cap, tilted to the left a little with his dreads protruding from underneath.

"Damn, you just got out and you are already dressing better than me," I said, eyeing his new gear.

"Moms hooked me up," he said. "Check it out." He pulled out from under his shirt the gleaming diamond pendant and gold link chain that was draped around his neck.

"Yo, that shit is nice." I took his gold piece into my hand and gawked at it, "Yo, tell your moms to hook a brother up with one too," I joked.

"You know you're family. I'll bless you wit' it later on tonight, have the ladies all over you wit' the bling bling on, get you some pussy."

"You forgot I'm married," I refreshed his memory.

"Yeah, yeah, I know. But I know you still cheating out there on wifey," he said. "By the way, how is your wife, Sophia?"

"She's fine."

"Oh, I forgot, you got a seed, too, Terrance. Yo, I gotta see my little goddaughter, because you know I'm her godfather," he said.

Sophia and I hadn't established that yet, but Sophia had a problem with Ash being Zaire's godfather. She was never really that cool with him, and he had been in prison for seven years.

"You gotta make sure you come by and check my baby girl, Zaire. She's five now."

"I will," he said.

"Yo, let's roll before my cousin starts trippin'," I said, walking toward the front door.

"He can wait. Shit, I waited seven years for this," he joked.

When we stepped outside, Ash's eyes became fixated on my new ride. I was pushing a black Expedition with twenty-two-inch chrome dubs and an over-the-top sound system with TVs in the headrest.

"This you?" he asked excitedly.

"Yeah," I said. I grinned and deactivated the alarm.

"You slingin' crack on the side?"

"Credit union," I told him. "They hook a brother up."

"Oh, you working for that airline now," he said, checking out my dubs.

"American Airlines."

"They hiring?"

I laughed.

"You think I'm playing. I need a job and shit."

"I'll see what I can do."

He got into the passenger seat and praised the interior. I let it be known that I didn't need to sell drugs to drive a nice car.

We made it to the social establishment around eleven forty that night, and yet Trey wasn't there. Ash and I climbed out of my truck, and we proceeded toward the front entrance, where people were lingering outside. Eightball was a popular Queens club/strip club near the Van Wyck Expressway and Rockaway Boulevard. It was some underground shit, an impromptu strip club that some local hood guys put together. The ladies stripped, got buck-naked on the stage and off, and they were willing to do something strange for the right amount of change. You could call it a sex club where VIP was done in the basement: fucking, hand jobs, blow jobs, and threesomes. For $20, you had access to one of several private rooms below, where you could have some fun with the girls of your choice.

Tonight was a lively night. Ass, pussy, and tits were everywhere. The DJ was playing some old-school hip-hop, and there was a lot of bumping and grinding going on in various sections of the club. Ash and I sat at the bar and drank Coronas. A dancer was on the stage busting her pussy wide open and putting on a sexy show for the fellows. She had my attention. Ash's too.

"This is what I'm talking about," Ash said. "Yo, I want that bitch."

I chuckled. "Look at you, like a dog in heat."

"It's been seven fuckin' years. I'm ready to fuck."

I couldn't blame him. If I did seven years upstate, I would be ready to explode too. Drinks were on me. It was the least I could do for him. He took a few singles and went to the stage to tip the stripper. She smiled at him. He took a seat at the stage and started to do him, working his charm and trying to make something happen for free. Ash never paid for pussy. There were two things he used to say should come for free: water and pussy. I watched him start a conversation with the big-booty and big-breasted woman. She was buck-naked in clear stilettos, and whatever Ash was saying to her, it was working. He had her smiling and laughing.

From the bar, I watched him rub her butt and play with her tits. He sprinkled a few dollar bills on her and continued talking to her. Her eyes said it all. She was already interested in him. Ash made her completely stop dancing, and just like that, he made it all about him. It was his first day home, and he continued where he'd left off—becoming a pussy magnet and making girls' panties wet.

Yeah, she was going to fuck him for free.

Still waiting for Trey to show up, I ordered something more substantial: vodka. I tossed that back and ordered another one. I watched the party happening around me, but I barely participated. I placed a few dollar bills in strippers' G-strings, but I had to remind myself that I was a married man and I was only here because of Ash.

The night continued, and it was starting to look like one big orgy inside the place. Almost every stripper was walking around buck-naked, asking for tips and fondling men's crotches, and the men were grabbing ass and tits. Lap dances and wall dances were happening everywhere, and the stage had two strippers dancing naked, and the DJ had Luke blaring, "I Wanna Rock."

"Yo, T, I missed this shit, man," Ash said to me excitedly. He threw his arm around me and embraced me in a brotherly way.

"Welcome home," I exclaimed.

"What's up wit' Trey and Devin? Them fools still coming through or what?" he asked.

"Speak of the devil," I said as Trey appeared suddenly out of nowhere.

"My nigga!" Ash shouted, excited about seeing my cousin. He stepped up to him and gave him dap and a long, embracing hug.

"What's up, Ash? Long time," Trey hollered.

"Damn, you still a pretty boy," Ash said to Trey.

Trey replied, "Nah, you still the pretty boy."

My cousin was dressed in gray slacks and a black silk shirt, which was unbuttoned down to his chest. He sported a Cartier watch and wore lavish Gucci shoes. His golden brown bald head was glistering, as it had just been waxed.

"Ash, you know I got to be up to par," Trey said.

"I heard you got a wifey now," Ash mentioned.

"You know I needed a little companionship here and there. So what's up with you? Just got out and already you out here with the bling bling," Trey said, touching Ash's nice-size gold pendant.

"My moms copped this for me."

"Shit is hot, though," Trey said.

"Trey, you don't say, 'What up,' to your cousin?" I interrupted.

"Terrance, I see your ass every day. You ain't special," he said, grinning at me. "Yo, where Devin at?"

"He bitched out. He chillin' wit' his girl. Yo, he talking about he 'bout to get married to that chick Danielle," I told them.

"Get the fuck out of here. You serious?" Trey was taken aback by the news.

"Married? Damn, Terrance, what you got, some kind of epidemic spreading throughout here?" Ash said.

"Yo, why are we in here talking about marriage when we got all this pussy roaming around?" Trey said. His eyes were fixated on some big-bootie ho walking past him in a pink thong.

"Yo, it's my first day out. I'm wit' my niggas, got my drink in my hand, and pussy is lurking around. Yo, after seven fuckin' years of not having any, son, I'm 'bout to go bag me up a bitch and try to get some free head from a ho," Ash said.

He guzzled down the last of his beer, then placed it back down on the bar countertop, and then disappeared into the sea of pussy that was everywhere. Trey and I looked at each other and simply laughed. It was great to have him home again.

It was getting late, and I hadn't called home yet. I pulled out my cell phone and saw the missed calls from my wife. It was two in the morning, and we hadn't spoken to each other since early this morning. I had to call home. I walked away from the crowd only to hear Trey shout, "Where are you going, Terrance?"

"Gotta call the wife," I told him.

"Damn, Terrance. I'm the one who just got out, and you the one who gotta report in. And I thought that I was on parole," Ash joked.

"Fuck y'all," I quickly responded, throwing up the middle finger at them.

I walked away from the scene to somewhere a lot quieter. The music, the bass, the noise—it was all overwhelming. I couldn't even hear myself think. I had to exit the club to make my phone call.

I stood outside and dialed home. Three rings later, Sophia picked up. "Hello," she answered.

"Yeah, baby, what's up? You called me, right?"

"Terrance, where are you? It's two in the morning," she said, first with concern in her voice.

"Oh, I'm chillin' with the fellows. We over at this club on Rockaway."

"A club? I thought that you were going to be home tonight," she said.

"Yeah, I'll be home in a minute, baby."

"You didn't mention to me that you were going out tonight," she said, now sounding a little upset.

"Oh, I didn't tell you?"

"Tell me what?"

"Ash is home. He got out today. So we decided to celebrate."

"No, you didn't tell me this. I would have remembered, Terrance," she dryly said. "And the point is, you wait until now to tell me this after I've been sitting up almost all night waiting and worrying about your ass, calling, and you ain't answering your phone."

"Well, I'm telling you now," I said to her with a bit of sarcasm.

"Good night, Terrance!" she said, and it didn't come out of her mouth too friendly.

"I'll see you—"

Click. All I heard was silence.

She hung up on me. I knew she was upset. I should've told her, but I didn't think it would be that important to her. Anyway, there wasn't any harm in going out and having a few drinks with the fellows. She was upset now, but I knew tomorrow morning she would probably be over it.

I headed back inside, returning to my little spot at the bar.

"Everything cool, Terrance?" Ash asked.

"Yeah, that was just the wife. You know she is worried about me."

"Checking up on you, huh?" Trey uttered.

"At least my wife's home. Where your girl at, Trey?" I asked, trying to say I knew where my lady was probably twenty-four seven, and he didn't have a clue where his woman was tonight.

"I don't need to know where she be, 'cause when she comes home, she comes home to be with me. Trisha, she always says she's gonna leave me. But on the real, I got her heart so deep in my grip, my girl ain't bouncing nowhere," he said, talking shit like usual.

"Whatever. Tell it to the man she's lying up with now," I countered.

"You funny, son," he responded.

"Yo, y'all shut the fuck up wit' that wifey shit. I'm trying to get some pussy tonight. Y'all are fuckin' up my concentration," Ash hollered.

"Go ahead then. Dust the cobwebs off your nuts, and do you," Trey said to him.

I chuckled. Both these fools were stupid. But that was how we were when we got together. We always had a great time. We clowned around and talked shit to each other. It was good having Ash home. Being with him tonight made me feel alive. We had a lot of catching up to do. We were like the Three Amigos inside the place—one for all and all for one.

Ash met with the stripper on stage from earlier and continued to work his charm on her. She was definitely feeling him. It wasn't hard to tell. He threw his arm around her and whispered something in her ear. She was fully dressed. Subsequently, Ash came my way and asked if I carried any condoms on me.

"Nah, I don't have any need for them. I'm married now," I once again reminded him.

He sucked his teeth, shook his head, and replied, "Yeah, keep telling yourself that, Terrance."

"I got you," Trey intervened. Trey removed a pack of Magnums from his pocket and gave Ash two, saying, "I know you gonna need them."

"My nigga, you always lookin' out." Ash and Trey gave each other dap.

"You out?" I asked.

"Yup."

"How much she charging you?"

Ash looked at me like I was stupid and then reminded me, "Do I ever pay for pussy? Like I always say, water and pussy I'm gonna always get for free. Shorty lives two blocks from here. I'm comin' out of retirement tonight. I'll see y'all clowns later."

"Do you," Trey said.

With that, Ash made his exit with the girl.

Like old times.

Chapter Five

Ash

*She putting her lipstick in places y'all can't even
imagine, kisses on his neck like she adores him,
she's tearing away his clothes like she's a savage . . .
fuckin' 'n' suckin' that dick is what she mastered . . .*

Ah, man, last night was a trip. It was definitely something to remember for a while. I found myself waking up
in this girl's bed around eight in the morning with my big
dick against her big butt. The sex was great—so great
that I had to plant like three nuts into her. She made me
come like a geyser every time. I had this young ho calling
out my name, and we did things that they probably
wouldn't allow in porno movies. She was lying next to
me, still sleeping. She needed her rest after what I did
to her. We both were naked underneath the covers.

The bedroom was silent, finally. She was still sleeping,
but I was ready to go. I already had my fun with her. I
didn't even know her name. Or maybe she told it to me,
but I just forgot. Anyway, her name was irrelevant. It was
that body and that mouth that I completely remembered.
She was a quick fuck, easy pussy, something tight and

wet to hold me down until I could see one of my baby mamas. I didn't plan on seeing her again. I already got what I came for, and it was worth staying the night.

I climbed out of her bed and started to get dressed. My one-night stand was great in bed, I admit, but she was a sloppy woman. Her bedroom looked like a pig's pen—cluttered with clothes, shoes, and junk—and she had roaches everywhere. But I wasn't judging. I pulled up my jeans, and I went through my wallet, counting my cash to make sure it was all there. You never knew what a girl might do when a man was asleep. She could quickly go through your wallet and take some extra cash for herself. But my stack was all there—$500.

I fastened my belt, and she started to stir awake. She rolled over and looked at me. "What's up? You were leaving me already?" she grumbled.

"Yeah, I gotta go."

"Damn."

"It was fun," I said.

She threw back the covers and removed herself from her bed, naked. Her body was juicy, and her tits were excellent, but I got bored already. I wasn't in the mood to fuck her again. She reached for one of her old T-shirts that was scattered across the room. She had clothes everywhere, along with old plates of rotten food, shoes, strewn trash, and whatnot. I couldn't believe that I fucked this girl in her nasty-ass bedroom. But it was late, and I was horny.

She donned her T-shirt and looked at me. "You smoke?" she said.

"Not right now," I replied, being short with her.

I made her exercise her mouth last night. She stretched those corners of her jaw like a rubber band, and it felt so good.

She sat at the edge of her bed and lit a cigarette. In the morning, she looked a mess with her hair in disarray and makeup gone. I was ready to go. But she had something to ask me. She took a quick puff and asked, "Can you leave me a little somethin'?"

"Huh? What?"

"Can I get like a hundred from you?" she dared to ask me.

I chuckled. "You know I don't pay for pussy. We fucked for free."

She caught an attitude, sucked her teeth, and rolled her eyes. She was gullible. How was she going to fuck me and then want to charge me later? She didn't know that I was a pimp. I should have charged her for this good dick. She caught more of an attitude, but I wasn't hearing her. I pivoted and left her foul-looking room.

"Fuck you then!" she cursed at me.

"You already did . . . for free."

I had plans for today. I wanted to see my baby mamas and my kids. There was Chanel and my daughter Patrice. She was 7 years old. I was locked up when Patrice was born. Chanel sent me a couple of pictures of my baby girl, and she was beautiful. And being the wifey Chanel was, she even came to visit me upstate a few times, bringing my little girl, too, so she could get to know her daddy.

But lately, she hadn't been coming around. It'd been eighteen months since I saw or heard from her. Word on the streets was that she had hooked up with some cornball named Keith and had gotten pregnant again. She had this man's seed, a boy, and forgotten about me. It upset me. I was anxious to see her and my daughter. Chanel still lived at the same location, and Chanel was still that loud and obnoxious sexy-ass hood rat I loved having around.

Chanel was a ride-or-die bitch, but she was going to do her still. I was inside and she was free. I couldn't lock her down from upstate. We wrote to each other, and I gave her permission to do her until I came home. And now I was home, and I wanted Chanel to end whatever relationships she had with anyone. I wanted her to drop them before I did.

Now Monica, my other baby mother, was a different story. She gave birth to my son, Justin. He was 7 too, and that was my little soldier right there. I talked to him over the phone occasionally. And Monica came to check me also, once in a while, but she was doing her thing. She was in community college, attending NYC Tech over on Jay Street in downtown Brooklyn. She got a retail job, and she was trying to make her job into a career.

But this chick went out and got married to some ol'-school clown-ass fool living in Manhattan, which made me upset. To be real, Monica had her shit together. I could see myself being with her, and not just because she was my baby mother and the sex was fuckin' good. She was smart, and she would always talk to me on some intelligent shit. Monica would write me poems and send them to me upstate, easing my mind a little. She was a good mother to my son, and I loved that about her. Monica wasn't on that chickenhead shit. She wasn't ghetto. Sometimes I would ask myself, how in the hell did a shorty like that end up with me?

But it was good dick and my personality. How could she resist?

Monica and Chanel both knew about each other. They both sat in the same courtroom when the judge had sentenced me to prison. There was some tension between them, you know, "Bitch," murmured under each other's breath, and Chanel one time was quick to throw the hands at Monica, about ready to fight her ass in the courthouse, but security had stepped in between the two.

But that was little beef. You know, one being jealous over the other, and wanna be fighting each other over a nigga like me. But now they both had grown up and moved on. Well, at least Monica did. Chanel, she was still that around-the-way hood, gully chick, ready to throw down for a nigga, with her fine ass. She was lucky she had some excellent pussy, because it kept me coming around.

It was four that afternoon when I stepped up on Chanel's grandmother's raggedy porch, over on 164th Street by South Road. There were a few people I recognized outside, like my little homie, Peanut. He was looking at me oddly like he ain't know who I was. It was because I had dreads now, and I had a little more muscle to me. I wanted to holler at him, show my presence, but I thought, *nah, them niggas ain't gotta know that I'm out already.* If Peanut knew that it was me, he would have talked me to death and tried to get me into some shit. I just came by to see my daughter and baby mother.

I banged on her door, since her fuckin' doorbell didn't work, and her grandmother answered the door. *Damn, this woman doesn't stop smoking,* I said to myself. She came to the door in a blue cotton robe, with her hair in curlers and a cigarette in her mouth.

"What you want?" she asked roughly, looking at me like I was one of these young guys from off the block.

"What's up, Ms. Brown? Chanel here, right?" I asked.

She turned her head, looking up at the tattered steps behind her, and shouted, "Chanel. Chanel, you got some nigga asking for you down here."

I wanted to say, "Bitch, you don't fuckin' remember me?"

"Who is it?" I heard Chanel shout out from upstairs.

"Just come get the fuckin' door," her grandmother cursed, cigarette dangling off her lips.

It was the same ol' Ms. Brown, with a mouth like a sailor and smoking more than a chimney. Seconds later, I heard and saw Chanel trotting down the steps in a pair of blue sweats and an oversized white T-shirt. She cut her hair short, sporting that Nia Long–style hairdo, and she'd gained a few pounds. But she still looked good. Her ass had gotten much fatter, and her tits were looking plumper. Shit, she done gave birth to two kids.

She looked at me in shock, becoming wide-eyed. "Oh, my God!" she hysterically screamed out.

She lunged toward me with her arms extended, and jumped into my arms, straddling me. I embraced her tightly. I loved how good a woman felt in my arms.

"Baby, when did you get out?" she asked as I still held her in my arms. She kissed me and kissed me.

"Yesterday," I told her.

"Why you ain't call me?" she asked.

"I wanted it to be a surprise."

"It is! Yo, Patrice is gonna be so excited to see you."

We went upstairs to her room, where I saw my daughter watching television and sitting Indian style by the bed.

"Patrice, look who's home," Chanel said.

Patrice turned her head from the television, gazed up at me, and then smiled broadly. She leaped up and shouted, "Daddy!" She jumped into my arms, giving me the sweetest hug.

"Ooooh, I missed you, baby girl," I said, embracing my daughter with love.

"I missed you too, Daddy."

I held her in my arms for a few more minutes, not wanting to let her go.

"You not goin' back to that place, right, Daddy?" my little girl asked.

"No, sweetie, I'm out for good," I told her.

"Good, 'cause I hate that place."

"I do too, sweetie. I do too."

I looked over at Chanel. She was standing by the bed, smiling, looking so fuckin' good even in sweatpants and a T-shirt. I put my little girl down and walked over to her mother. I pulled Chanel into my arms. Being blunt and to the point, I whispered into her ear, "I wanna fuck you tonight."

She chuckled, "Damn, why you gotta be sayin' it like that?"

"Because there ain't no other way to say it," I told her. "You know me."

I grabbed her ass firmly. I squeezed that luscious booty she had as it belonged to me. I forced myself against her, and I was yearning for some affection. We kissed passionately in front of my daughter. I wanted her to see that her mommy and daddy still loved each other. Chanel felt so soft and inviting. Her full lips tasted like cherries. I wanted to undress her right there and fuck her.

Suddenly, her little boy came running into the room clad in a red and cartoonish sweat jumpsuit, surprising me. I almost forgot about her son by this other man. He ran up to Chanel, grasping her leg tightly and peering up at me with his wide brown eyes.

"Yo, who this?" I asked.

"This is my son, Ash. Timothy, say what's up to Ash. Say hi," Chanel said.

He just looked up at me, not even budging from his mother's leg. I extended my hand to him for a hand five and said, "What's up, li'l man?"

He just looked at me. I was a stranger to him.

"How old is he?" I asked.

"He'll be two next month."

"That's my li'l brotha," my little girl told me.

"I know, sweetheart."

I wasn't upset. You know, shit happens.

Chanel picked him up into her arms, holding him against her hip. He was still gazing at me awkwardly, remaining silent. I was wondering where his bitch-ass father was. I knew he had to be a pussy nigga. He had gotten my woman pregnant.

But anyway, Chanel still loved me, even better now that I had dreads and had a nice build to me. She was all over me the entire afternoon. I couldn't wait until tonight. I wanted some sex, and I wanted to make my presence known. I wasn't going anywhere. I was here to stay.

Chapter Six

Sophia

What is love, it's holding her when she gets cold, conversing with her when she feels alone, consoling her when she's afraid, and wiping away her tears when she's in pain . . .

I couldn't believe that Terrance tried to pull that shit with me last night. He knew he was going out. He probably had it all planned out, and the fact that he didn't tell me about Ash coming home was the thing that upset me the most. He wanted to wait until two in the morning to inform me about that shit after I had to call him to find out about his whereabouts. I was so mad that I wanted to scream and punch his face in. *My husband likes to play games? I can play 'em too.*

On my way to work, I was riding this A train, trying not to stay upset, but my husband had put me in a foul mood. He came home late, smelling like liquor and pussy. He went to the strip club with Ash. His friend hadn't been home for more than twenty-four hours, and he was already causing trouble. Terrance and I quarreled early in the morning. We had our moments, but we never fought like this. It had gotten so loud between us that we had woken up Zaire. I had to calm her down and put her back to bed.

The train was crowded, too crowded. I hated rush hour. There wasn't an open seat for a lady to sit in. I had to stand from Queens to Manhattan. I wanted to rest my legs before I went to work, but it wasn't possible. I was holding the handrail, trying to read today's newspaper. I couldn't concentrate on the paper. Terrance had pissed me off. I frowned and just stood there, counting the stops before mine came.

Seven years we'd been married, and during those seven years, I'd never cheated on my husband. I loved that man a lot. He was a great father and a great man, but sometimes I had my disbelief.

I always had men trying to talk to me on the normal. They flirted with me from Manhattan to Queens. I was a beautiful woman, and so many strangers would tell it to me. I pretty much would ignore their flirting and catcalls. I would tell them that I was a married woman, happily married. I often boasted about my wedding ring, shutting down many attempts. I wasn't that kind of lady. I wanted to have a happy marriage and love my husband.

But then something changed. It happened months ago, maybe longer. Maybe I had been lying to myself all these years. I was happily married, wasn't I?

I started to notice other men. My gaze would linger on a handsome face. I would find myself smiling their way when they smiled back at me. Sometimes I would be tempted to go over and say hi to a handsome stranger and get his name. But I kept reminding myself that I was a married woman with a child. Terrance was a good husband. But lately, we'd been bickering and arguing with each other. I found myself becoming annoyed over little things he would do around the house. He would chew with his mouth open, and he would smack at the table. He didn't compliment me enough. He watched too many sports or didn't give me enough attention. We had sex. It was good but it wasn't great! I wanted to have great sex again. I wanted to come so hard that I would melt. We didn't communicate. We had lost touch on so many things. He used to hold me affectionately and near, but now the only time he welcomed me with affection was when he wanted some pussy.

It felt like I wanted a break from him. I needed my space. We had gotten married young, and I had this urge to live life again.

I walked into Chase Bank at 7:55 a.m. I walked by everyone, chanting, "Good morning. Good morning." Sometimes coming to work helped ease my mind from certain things. I loved working in a bank, being a bank teller. It was like the first professional job that I had where a sister could be promoted. And after working here for two years, I felt that it was time for me to step up. I was thinking about going to college and earning a degree in business, maybe becoming a loan officer, a bond trader, or even better, a bank manager.

"Good morning, Sophia," Randy said, smiling my way.

Randy, he was a cute guy. But he was trifling. When I first started working here, he used to try to come on to me every day, knowing that I was a married woman with a child, and he had a girlfriend. But after two years of trying to hit it, he finally got the point, and he just became cool with me.

"Good morning, Randy," I said casually and walked on by.

All employees had to arrive an hour early before the bank opened at nine. We had to situate things, count money, open the vault, do a security check, run systems, blah, blah, and blah. I got a cup of hot coffee from across the street along with my usual bagel with cream cheese. I tried not to think about my husband or get upset that he was an asshole last night. I stayed focused on work.

There'd been talk that we were supposed to be getting a new bank manager. Our current manager, Mr. Robins, was retiring soon. He'd been in banking for forty years now. He was an old Jewish guy, a nice guy with a great sense of humor. He was always smiling and took his job quite seriously. Sometimes he wouldn't leave until ten or eleven at night, going over books, counting cash, or processing equipment.

Like usual, I found myself gossiping with my coworkers while we were working. Everyone was curious about who was taking over Mr. Robin's position. I hoped that he wouldn't be a stick in the mud. Working under Mr. Robins made the job relaxed. He made it pleasant to work here, and I couldn't think of anyone taking his place. Sometimes he would buy employees lunch. He got to know everyone personally. All he asked for was respect, that you came to work on time, and that you performed your job with efficiency. Honestly, he was like a father to some of us.

The day was going by fast with customers coming and going. I completed one transaction after the other. I smiled, greeted them casually, and made them feel welcome at the bank. I was at my window, finishing up this one transaction. A man just deposited $2,500 into his account, and I was logging it into the computer.

"Next," I hollered.

Subsequently, a well-dressed and tall man in a gray suit wearing a Rolex walked toward my window. He was very handsome, black, with a thick goatee. It was apparent he had money. My coworker glanced his way and smiled.

"Hello, welcome to Chase Bank. How can I help you this afternoon?" I said.

"I need to make a withdrawal," he said with his baritone voice.

Damn!

He took out his bankbook from the inner pocket of his suit and placed it in front of me. Then he passed me the withdrawal slip, and I saw that he was taking out $7,500 from his account. I opened his bankbook and wanted to gasp when I saw how much he was holding down—$250,000.

Oh, my Lord, I said to myself. I couldn't help but stare at his figures and then up at him. A fine man like him, dressed nice, and holding it down financially. *Calm yourself, Sophia,* I had to remind my hormones.

He passed me some identification, and I saw that his name was Rowell James. I began processing his transaction. He stood there. When I glanced up at him for the sixth time, he smiled at me. I smiled back. He had great teeth, luscious lips, and a nice build.

Everything cleared. He was good to go.

"How would you like that?" I asked.

"Nothing but hundreds," he politely said.

I pulled out a wad of hundred-dollar bills from my drawer. I completed the transaction and counted the money in front of him—$7,500 in cash. For once, I wished that I were banking the cash that I was counting out to him. Being a bank teller, you make decent pay, but damn, Mr. Right who was standing in front of me, whoa, he definitely had it going on, and he was rich.

I counted his cash twice, making sure that it was accurate, and then passed him his money inside a bank envelope. I smiled. I daydreamed about leaving out that door with him. Where he was going, I wanted to go too.

"Thank you," he said, snapping me out of my quick daydream.

"You're welcome," I said.

I watched him walk out the door. I wished that one day we could have dinner and some wine. His treat of course. I laughed it off. I felt one of my coworkers nudge me in my side with her saying, "So are your panties dry yet?"

"Shut up, Lauren," I laughed.

She laughed too. I uttered, "Next." I was still on my job.

"So are your panties dry now?" Lauren asked me again. We were having lunch across the street at this café on a warm, sunny, and lovely spring day. Lauren was a coworker and a really cool and loving friend. She'd been at the bank five years now and was receiving her degree in business management. Soon I might be working for her.

I laughed, telling her that she was silly.

"I ain't gonna front, homeboy was fine," she said. "Umm, umm . . . that's something I wouldn't mind taking home from work and playing with all night."

"Ain't that the truth," I said, giving her a high five.

I had a small cappuccino cup and a little turkey and cheese sandwich sitting in front of me. And Lauren had herself a light salad and a fruit punch Snapple.

"So what's up with you and Terrance? How are things going between y'all two?" she asked.

I sighed.

"It's that bad, huh?"

"No. It's just . . . I don't know, Lauren. I love him and all, but right now I feel that I need a break from everything—him, the marriage, and sometimes my daughter."

"Did you tell him this?"

"No. He's good to me. But something just isn't there between us anymore. I don't know what it is."

"It's because your ass got married so young, and now you want to be free. What are you, twenty-five?"

"Yes," I said. "I got married a week before my nineteenth birthday."

"See, and you married him when you were only eighteen, and he's the only man you have been with for the past seven years," she chuckled. "I understand you, girl."

"I mean, the sex is good. Don't get me wrong, he is doing his thing. But that chemistry between us, it's like it faded away. He doesn't even romance me anymore. The only romancing he does today is grabbing on my tits and kissing in between my thighs and then sticking it into me. I remember back in the day we used to foreplay for hours, and he used to say the nastiest and sweetest things to me. But now it's just getting his nut off, and that's it."

"You'll be okay, girl," Lauren said.

"I hope so, 'cause on the real, I'm thinking about other things," I said. I took a sip from my cappuccino.

"Other things like what?"

"I never cheated on my husband. But now I'm starting to get that urge, that desire, to just find me some sexy-ass man and have him fuck the shit outta me."

"Are you serious? You're thinking about cheating on your husband?"

"Lauren, you don't even know. I'm starting to find myself being attracted to a lot of men. Like that fine-ass man who came into the bank this morning. I had to compose myself, girl."

"How long have you been feeling this way?" she asked.

"Awhile now," I admitted.

"So why don't you just admit it to your husband, tell him the truth?"

"It's hard. Terrance likes being a family. He's a good father. I guess I'm just scared. I don't want to hurt his feelings."

"You gonna hurt his feelings a lot more if you keep this going. Tell him the truth now. It's better to tell him now than to have him catch you cheating out there. How you think he's going to feel then?"

"I know. I know."

"Sophia is looking for some new dick in her life. I guess the old one is about to expire soon," she joked.

"Shut up," I laughed.

But she was right. I needed to tell my husband how I was feeling. I couldn't just keep having him believe that everything between us was okay. I couldn't keep living this lie within myself. I loved him, but I felt that I just wasn't in love with him.

I got home around six that evening. Terrance was already home. He was lying in the bedroom in his boxers and a T-shirt and watching television.

"Where's Zaire?" I asked.

"Oh, she's still at my mother's," he said. He looked up at me casually when I stepped into the bedroom.

"But I thought I told you to pick her up. Why she always gotta be at your mother's? I would like to spend time with my daughter too," I told him, getting upset.

"Relax, Sophia. She a'ight. My moms don't mind watching her."

"But she's not your mother's child. That's our child, Terrance. I hate when you do this shit."

"Damn, Sophia, why you trippin'? I can get the child tonight. It ain't like she's over there all week."

"That's not the point, Terrance."

"Then what is?"

I sighed and stormed into the bathroom. I slammed the door behind me. I just got home, and I was already having an argument with him. I really wanted to see my daughter tonight. But Terrance was continuously taking her over to his mother's house knowing that I didn't have a car. I had my license, but he had the car.

His mother was cool. And I know she didn't mind watching her, but lately, this mofo be thinking he was slick. I knew what the fuck he was up to. He kept Zaire over at his mother's house purposely, thinking that he was gonna get him some quick ass tonight—fuck me first, then go get our daughter. He was always putting pussy first, and our daughter second. I wasn't in the mood for sex tonight. So he was shit out of luck.

I walked back into the bedroom, and he was still looking at the television. We were both quiet. I started to get undressed. He grinned, watching me slyly. Now he wanted to show me some minor attention. I went into my drawer and pulled out my sweatpants and an old T-shirt. I then went into the bathroom to change clothes. I knew what he wanted. *Not tonight!*

Subsequently, I went into the kitchen to make myself a snack. Terrance didn't cook. The most he did was breakfast and barbeque. I was the cook in this family. Would he survive without me, I didn't know. Not likely. His diet most likely would be fast food.

I was in the kitchen making a sandwich. Terrance didn't even ask me how my day was. Did he care? I didn't know. He was still in the bedroom watching TV, and I had a lot to think about. I wanted romance and great sex.

The phone rang, but Terrance wasn't answering it.

"Terrance, can you please get the damn phone? I'm busy in the kitchen."

The phone stopped ringing, and then I heard him shout out, "Sophia, it's Yasmin."

I cleaned off my hands and picked up the kitchen phone. "Hey, Yasmin," I said.

"What's up, girl?"

I sighed wholeheartedly and then said to her, "Nothing much."

"You just got home?" she asked.

"Yeah, like twenty minutes ago," I said.

"How's my little goddaughter doing?"

"She's at her grandmother's."

"Terrance didn't go pick her up?"

"No. And I told him to. But he's acting like a jerk."

"You want me to go and get her for you?"

"Can you? I'd appreciate that so much. You know Terrance is gonna want to get Zaire from his mother's house around nine, ten tonight. And I ain't trying to have my daughter come home that late."

"I got you, girl."

"So what's up for the weekend?" I asked, biting into my sandwich.

"You know me. I stay clubbing. There's this party Saturday night if you wanna come," she said.

"I'll think about it."

"Come, Sophia. Have Terrance babysit, and get your groove on."

I chuckled. "That sounds like a plan."

"That's because it is."

"I'll let you know when you come by with Zaire."

"A'ight then, girl."

I hung up the phone. I looked around the kitchen and griped even more. The sink was a mess, filled with dishes. My husband had been home all day, and he couldn't wash the dishes. It was another negative. So being the woman of the house, I started to wash the dishes.

Terrance finally came out of the bedroom and placed his arms around my waist, pressing his body against mine and kissing the side of my neck. Now he wanted to show me attention.

"What the hell are you doing, Terrance?" I said to him, annoyed.

"What do you think I'm doing? I'm trying to love my wife."

His words agitated me even more. I felt his hand reaching into my sweatpants and going for my goodies. I pushed him off me. He wanted to grab places that I didn't want him to hold.

"What's up, Sophia?" he said. Now he was the one looking annoyed.

"Nothing," I responded dryly.

He attempted to fondle me again, and once again, I pushed him away from me and caught an attitude.

"Can't you see that I'm trying to wash dishes here? Something that your ass should have done since you've been home," I barked.

"You're catching an attitude over some dishes? I always clean," he had the nerve to say.

"Whatever!"

"C'mon, Sophia, let me get mine real quick. It ain't gonna take that long," he said.

"Terrance, I'm not in the damn mood," I exclaimed.

"C'mon," he said, grabbing my butt.

"Terrance, what did I say? I got dishes to wash. Take your ass back into the bedroom and watch TV."

He griped and whined, but I didn't care. "Why you gotta be so stingy with it? Y'all be acting like y'all shit is gold."

"Fuck you, Terrance!" I shouted. Now I was irritated.

He marched toward the bedroom, upset. I didn't care how he felt. What about my feelings and my needs? He had some nerve expecting some pussy when he was becoming lazy and insensitive to his wife.

I needed some time to myself, so I went for a walk to the nearest bodega to buy a pack of Newports. It was a balmy night with a full moon above. I exited the bodega, placing a needed cigarette into my mouth. I lit up, inhaled, and enjoyed the nicotine coursing through my system. The neighborhood was quiet, and my marriage was quieter—or dull. What I wanted was a nice massage, some romance, and to make passionate love. I didn't want to feel like some truck-stop whore. My life, or my love life, needed some spicing up. It needed a spark.

I proceeded to walk home, and then out of nowhere, a black convertible CL600 came to a stop nearby, and he stepped out. He was six foot three with an athletic build, wearing cargo shorts and a wife-beater that highlighted his body. He was chocolate covered with a gleaming bald head and a thick goatee. He was gorgeous from head to toe. I stood there, fixated by his appearance. Where did he come from? Who was he?

He looked my way and suddenly came forward. I was rooted to the sidewalk, not able to move. He spoke to me. "You okay, beautiful?" he asked.

I was speechless at first, but then I got myself together and replied, "I'm fine."

"You sure are," he flirted.

I smiled.

He extended his hand to me and introduced himself, saying, "My name is Eric, and what's yours?"

"I'm Sophia," I said, shaking his hand and touching him.

"Sophia—beautiful name for a gorgeous woman," he said. "So, Sophia, what brings you out on a nice night like tonight?"

"Just walking," I said.

"Do you need a ride somewhere?"

"No, I'm fine. I live up the street."

"I wouldn't mind walking you home, then," he said.

"And leave your car behind?"

"It's a nice neighborhood, right?"

I smiled. "It is."

"So let's walk then," he said. "And besides, people know me around here."

"You are . . . known for what?" I asked with a raised eyebrow his way. I was curious to know why he was known and what he was known for.

He smiled and replied, "I play ball."

"Oh, are you in the NBA?" I didn't watch basketball.

"Nah, not yet. I play overseas, in China."

"China. Impressive," I admitted. "So why aren't you in the NBA?"

"I didn't quite cut it yet. But I'm nice. You have to come to see me play one day."

"I might."

We walked a block, but I didn't want him walking me home. The last thing I needed was for Terrance to see me with another man. I didn't need the drama. But as we walked down that block, he told me quite enough about himself. He was 25. He played college ball at St. John's University. He played point guard, and he was single, supposedly. And he spoke some Chinese. I was definitely intrigued.

"Why are you in Queens?" I asked him.

"I don't live too far from here. Well, my mom doesn't. I grew up here."

"That's nice. Mama's boy?" I joked.

"You can say that."

"And how long are you in town for?" I wanted to know.

"A few weeks. I'm on break."

We walked some more, and suddenly I found myself a block away from my house. I didn't want him to know where I lived.

"You're easy to talk to," he said. "I would definitely like to see you again."

I hesitated. I was a married woman, and he was too close to home. But I found myself saying, "I'll take your number."

He smiled. He wrote down his number and placed it into my hand. "Please use it. I would love to hear from you again. I want to take you out."

"I'll see," I flirted.

We talked for a minute, and it was getting late. Eric had beautiful eyes and a beautiful smile. I wanted to give him a hug and kiss, but he was still a stranger—though it was tempting. I started to walk away with his number in my hand. I then heard him say, "Call me, please!"

"I'll see," I said again, smiling broadly.

He finally turned and trotted back to his Benz. I went walking home, feeling like I was on cloud nine. It felt great to be wanted. I exhaled, thinking, *where will this go?* Eric made me feel refreshed and needed in that short amount of time.

I smiled all the way home.

Chapter Seven

Terrance

What is love, love is when you continue to love your woman a thousand different times . . .

I wanted to say, "Fuck her!" I was upset. I was so horny last night, and she didn't give me my dessert. I loved my wife, but I hated it when she pulled away from me, denying my manly needs. So I did the next best thing. I picked up a bottle of Johnson & Johnson baby oil and rubbed one out in the bathroom. I wasn't shy in pleasing myself.

I was supposed to meet with the fellows at Dreams bar on Sutphin Boulevard. But I was the first one there. I sat at the bar and ordered a beer. I watched basketball on the mounted screen behind the bar and waited for the fellows to arrive.

"Where's my drink?" Ash said, finally arriving and placing me into a playful chokehold from behind.

"Still behind the bar until your black ass pays for it," I quipped.

He sat next to me. He signaled for the bartender and ordered himself a beer too. It was on me. "So what's up?" he asked.

"Not much," I said.

"How's my goddaughter?"

"She's fine." I was dry tonight, not much excited.

"You good? Why the long face?"

"It's the wife," I admitted.

"What, she ain't give your ugly ass no pussy last night?"

"Just issues," I said.

"Yeah, she ain't give you no pussy. I know your dick feels like sandpaper right now." He chuckled.

"What, you find my sex life funny?" I uttered.

He tasted his beer and replied, "That's marriage. You say, 'I do,' and no more sex life. Yo, me, I'm gonna stay with more than one bitch in my life. If one starts acting up, then I'm seeing the next bitch, and if she starts acting up, then I'm moving on to the next bitch. Simple math, subtract and add."

"That's you!"

"Exactly. Y'all fools getting all bent up over one bitch. That's crazy. There are a million hoes in this city, and you know they ready to fuck. It's a new age, the pussy age, so get yours."

"She's my wife."

"So get you a side ho who will keep your dick coming," he suggested.

I shook my head at Ash and simply said, "You're bugging."

"No, you're bugging, 'cause you the one with the dry dick. And don't be acting like you innocent. I know you cheated on Sophia before. Don't front on me, nigga. This is me you're talking to."

"That's my business. I'm a good husband."

"Whatever." He waved me off.

I swallowed my beer and ordered another one. The bar was mostly empty, and the Knicks were playing the Celtics. I was rooting for the Knicks, being a diehard fan for years.

"Yo, I went to see my baby moms the other day," Ash said out of the blue.

"Which one?"

"Chanel. Yo, she got fuckin' thick, and she was lookin' good, Terrance. You know I had to run up in that pussy a few times."

"How's your daughter?"

"She cool. Missing her daddy, you know."

"So what's with Monica? You heard from her yet?"

"Nah, yo. I'm 'bout to check her mom's, though. I know she lives somewhere uptown, but I ain't sure. You know I gotta check up on my li'l nigga Justin."

"He's like seven now?"

"Yeah."

We sat around for another half hour talking and drinking. I watched the game. The Knicks were up by five points. Allan Houston just sank a three-pointer.

"Look at this fool here. About fuckin' time," Ash shouted out.

I turned around, and Devin was walking into the bar. He smiled. He came our way looking like he had just won the lottery. "Hey, Ash. How have you been?" he greeted him civilly.

"I thought you forgot about me," Ash hollered. The two embraced into a brotherly hug.

"No, I was spending some time with my woman. You know how that is."

"Yeah, pussy first, then your friends. I know how that goes," Ash replied, being sardonic.

"Same old Ash."

"And same old Carlton Banks," Ash quipped.

Devin was the proper-speaking and most well-mannered one in our crew. He was a good boy, a mama's boy, and he had been a one-woman man all his life. We used to joke on him about something: he wore his heart on his sleeve and quickly fell in love. We just wanted Devin to sow his wild oats before it was too late.

"Hey, Terrance, and how are you? How's the wife?" Devin addressed me.

"The same old thing—work, family, the wife. You'll be in the club soon," I teased.

He laughed.

Ash chimed in with, "So I heard you're pussy whipped now and got you a dime piece. I heard she's nice and shit, so nice that you went and got engaged. What's up wit' that?"

"Her name is Danielle. We're in love," Devin proclaimed proudly.

"In love. That's good. I gotta meet this shorty. Y'all living together or what?"

"Yes."

"Are you knocking the juices off that pussy every night?" Ash asked with no boundaries.

"I need a drink," Devin said.

"Yeah, you do. We all do," said Ash, signaling the bartender our way. "Give us three shots of vodka. We're celebrating tonight," he said.

The bartender nodded.

Three shots of vodka were poured for us. We downed those shots and slammed the shot glasses on the bar counter. "I gotta look out for my niggas," Ash said.

"Where's Trey?" Devin asked.

"He said he was coming," I said.

Ash ordered another round of shots, and we threw those back and laughed. Ash started to tell us some prison stories, telling us about fights and prison life. It was intriguing. I never saw the inside of a jail. He then stated that he missed us. We missed him too. I needed to get out, get away from the ball and chain.

An hour later, Ash exclaimed, "Look at this fool here."

Trey had finally arrived. Trey smiled and shouted our way, "My niggas, what's good?"

"I see your old lady finally let you outta the house," Ash teased.

"Please, my woman doesn't run me. I run her," Trey countered lightly. "And where my drink?"

"Late fools don't get drinks," Ash said.

"Fuck you. You buying," Trey said to Ash.

Ash laughed. Trey ordered a rum and Coke. We crowded the bar, watched the game, and talked shit. The four of us were finally together again. It was great.

Trey downed his drink and looked at Devin. "So you tryin' to die slow, huh?"

"What?" Devin replied, baffled by his comment.

"Marriage! You tryin' to end up like my cousin, the walking dead!"

"Ha-ha, you got jokes, cuz," I said.

"I see Terrance didn't hesitate to spread the word," said Devin.

"I couldn't resist."

"So what is this, an intervention?" Devin said.

"We need to prevent your ass and my cousin from being pussy whipped, from becoming the great lost hope," Trey continued to joke.

"Yo, I'll drink to that," Ash chimed.

"Fuck you, Trey," I said.

"Don't hate on us because we're in love with some wonderful women," said Devin.

"And what, you think I got an ugly duckling at home? My girl is bad too," Trey said.

"All black women are beautiful," said Devin.

"Yeah, only you would say some shit like that. Black is beautiful. Okay, Jesse Jackson and Dr. King," Ash said. "Hey, all black ain't beautiful. I have seen a few creatures out there lately."

We all laughed.

"But anyway, Devin, you gonna love everything. You always did, fuckin' 1960s hippies and shit. Love, freedom, and peace. Far out, dude. Shit, nigga, get some freedom away from the pussy and have some fun wit' your boys. Shit, the way you crowd pussy, you gonna fuck around and strangle the shit up on it so close," Ash said as a joke. "Give the pussy a break. She'll love you more."

Judging by the look on Devin's face, he didn't find the humor funny.

"Always the jokester you always are, Ash, and I hope you didn't drop the soap inside, and don't hate on me and mine," Devin said.

"Hate! I'm handling mine. I don't know about you."

"I'm handling my business too," Devin countered.

"I need some proof of that," said Ash.

"And why are you so worried about my sex life, huh?"

"Lighten up. Damn, we just fuckin' wit' you, Devin. Look at you gettin' all serious and shit. Damn, I definitely gotta meet your shorty, because you ready to fight me."

"I'm just saying I love her," he said.

"A'ight, and I love my bitches. So let's drink."

We all shook our heads and laughed. The night was still young, and I knew that there was still more to come. The four of us together—it was just getting started. Would I survive the night with these three clowning around? It was skeptical. But we all talked about good sex and our ladies and past experiences, and the more drinks we consumed, the more real it got.

But the sex talk made me think about home. I embellished my sex life, knowing that my sex life was lacking. I wasn't getting it like I used to. I could feel my wife growing distant from me for some reason, and I tried not to think about it, but it was getting more serious every day.

Trey ordered another round of beers, and I decided to focus on the Knicks game. It was the fourth quarter, and they were up by six points.

"Yo, what's good for the rest of the night?" Ash asked.

"Isn't you going to chill with your baby mother, Chanel?" I said.

"Yeah, but that pussy can wait. She's not going anywhere soon."

"A'ight, better be careful," I said.

"C'mon, Terrance, I got that pussy on lock. Chanel knows better. I'm fuckin' home now, so there ain't any need for her to be seeing no other nigga. I'll fuck that fool up. She fuckin' respects me. She knows I'll bury her face to the concrete if I catch her creeping out there."

"You creep too," Devin chimed.

"So what! She ain't me, and she can't be me. I do me, and I'm gonna continue to do me. That's how I get down. Y'all fools know that."

Devin shook his head. "You're so wrong, Ash. What goes around comes around."

"Bullshit! My fist gonna come around if that clown acts up. I'm doing me."

"So you don't love Chanel?" Devin asked.

"Yeah, I do a little," he replied.

"So why don't you show her that love? Be faithful to your woman. You just got out of prison, and you don't need to be going back in," Devin said.

"What is this? Devin is trying to preach to me right now," Ash said.

"Nah. I'm just trying to look out for my friends."

"This is Ash you're talking to. I can handle mine. I just love the pussy too much to stick to one. I need my pick of women, like that shorty over there."

Ash gestured to a beautiful dark-skinned female standing by the bar in a short skirt, revealing her meaty thighs. She had long, sinuous, thick black hair. She looked young, but not too young.

Damn, I said to myself. Her shit was looking right. I ain't gonna lie, looking at the girl caused a slight bulge in my jeans. I had a minor erection for some reason. Maybe because I was still horny from the other night. She was pretty, and if I weren't a married man, I probably would have flirted with her first. But Ash already had his eyes locked in on her.

"Go ahead, do you," Trey encouraged.

"Give it time. I'm 'bout to go work my magic," Ash said.

We all watched her closely, like a bunch of perverts by the bar. In a way, the girl, to some extent, resembled that actor Taral Hicks from head to toe. She walked away from the bar with a drink in her hand and took a seat with her friend. Her friend wasn't so attractive. She was a chubby girl with a broad nose. All of us just stared that way with no discretion.

"Yo, I'll be back," Ash said to us.

He got up, cocky and very sure of himself, and he coolly walked their way. I took another sip from my beer and thought about what his chances were. Ash had a very successful rate of picking up women.

"Yo, you think he gonna bag that up? Homegirl looks kinda wicked and shit," Trey said.

"I got fifty dollars that says he doesn't succeed with her," Devin said. He put $50 on the table. "She doesn't look like that type of girl to fall for his bullshit," Devin added.

"A'ight. I got your bet, Devin," Trey said. "You in on this, Terrance?"

"Nah, too rich for my blood."

We all watched closely. Ash made his approach. So far, he looked to be making a smooth landing toward the runway. He took a seat at their table and somehow made conversation with both ladies. So far, he was coming in nice and smooth, no turbulence. It was smooth for him to start talking to both girls. He treated them both as equal. Smart.

"I want my fifty," Trey said to Devin.

"He didn't succeed yet," Devin said.

"You already know what's gonna happen, Devin."

"No, they're just talking."

Trey laughed and said, "A'ight."

However, Ash went from talking to both girls to somehow talking to the pretty one, and she started to laugh and smile. His chair moved closer to hers, and his hand was against her back. Their eye contact was firm, and he had her undivided attention. It was clear. Ash was in there profoundly, and he wasn't coming out anytime soon.

"My fifty dollars, please!" Trey said.

"He didn't get her number yet."

"Devin, it's over with. He's already in there. Look at him. She's practically throwing the pussy at him. Oh, oh, look. She's touching his chest, and her hand on his leg. Oh, he's fuckin' her tonight."

The chubby friend suddenly looked like a third wheel at the table. She sat there nursing her drink and looking everywhere from the basketball game to around the room. She was lonely. It showed in her eyes. Her pretty friend had all the attention. Ash simply shaded her out and worked on her friend like a mathematician solving a mathematical problem.

Ash had her laughing like she was at *Def Comedy Jam,* and she was touchy with him. The deal was sealed, and they exchanged numbers with a promise to call each other. And Devin was out $50. He wasn't too happy about it.

When he was done chatting with the girl, Ash removed himself from the table and came back our way, looking like he won the lottery. His smile was golden.

"See that? Easy pickings. I'm fuckin' her tonight," Ash said smugly.

"It's that easy, huh?" Trey said.

"She wants me to come to her crib tonight," he said.

"Really?" I uttered.

"I'm the golden boy. Put me up on y'all walls and admire me," he joked.

"You stupid," I said, chuckling.

"And she is pushing a Lexus," he mentioned.

Ash done hit the jackpot. He got himself a fine woman with a nice car.

"Do you then," Devin said halfheartedly, breaking his silence.

I couldn't help but notice that it looked like Devin hated Ash's success with women. He drank his beer and didn't have much to say.

"What about her friend?" Trey asked.

"Fuck her friend," Ash said. "Why? You wanna fuck her friend?"

"Don't play yourself. You know I don't get down like that. I don't do fat."

"Why? Fat people need love too," Ash said.

"Yeah, but it won't be from me," Trey said.

During everyone's conversation, Devin got a phone call. He jumped up out of his chair, looking at the number, and he smiled.

"Curfew," Trey teased.

"Nah, that's my lady. Let me see what she wants. I'll be back," Devin said. He removed himself from his friends and the bar and walked toward the exit.

"You see that, Terrance? His woman calls him, and he goes running to talk to her. You better school your boy."

I shrugged. It was his business.

I finished off another beer. The good news was that my Knicks won tonight. They beat the Celtics by eight points. The night was winding down, and we were all about to go our separate ways. Ash was with his new girlfriend for the night, working his way between her legs. Devin was outside speaking to his woman, and Trey and I were hugging the bar.

It was a quarter to 1:00 a.m. We were all drunk and tired. Devin was the first to leave the group. Trey followed, and Ash left with the pretty girl in her Lexus. I was the last to leave the place. I guess I wasn't in any rush to go home. I was horny, and it felt like my dick was on strike. I was in the mood for some sex, but lately Sophia hadn't been.

I released a deep sigh and ordered my last beer.

Chapter Eight

Ash

She came to me in those "Come and fuck me heels," her smile sayin' come touch me there . . .

I opened my eyes and quickly looked at the time. It was almost noon. *Shit, I didn't mean to sleep that late.* But Shannon, the shorty I met from last night in the bar, she definitely put it on me. Everything about her was an A-plus. She had cute toes, a nice body, and could suck dick like the best of them. She was cuddled up against me, still asleep with her tits against my side. It was a new day with the morning sun percolating through her bedroom window, and that meant it was time for my exit.

It was fun, but I had other places to be.

I quietly slid away from her, got out of bed, and started to get dressed. The one thing I gave Shannon credit for was that her place was lovely. It was neatly furnished and clean, unlike the last girl I was with, where it felt like I was in a trashcan. I respected a clean and well put-together woman. The only trash on her floor were the discarded condom wrappers, and the used condoms were in the trash can.

I had my sneakers on, and I made sure my cash was right, nothing was taken, and I was ready to leave. I had her information. Maybe I'd call her this week. But they always managed to wake up before I went.

"Why are you leaving?" she asked.

"Gotta go," I said.

She sighed. "So just like that, you fuck me, spend the night, and was gonna leave without me knowing."

"Hey, it was fun, and you're mad cool. I'll be back around. I just got some things to take care of."

"So that's what you do, have sex with a girl and leave without her knowing?"

Her attitude toward me was manifested through her scowling eyes and frown. She felt used, probably. But what did she think this was? She got hers and I got mine.

"You know what? Lose my number. Fuck you!"

"Been there and done that." I laughed.

I swear, you give a bitch some good dick, and she becomes a sponge in 5.2 seconds. But good dick would do that to a woman. Those were good problems.

"Can you give me a ride home?" I dared to ask her.

She looked at me with that "nigga, you can't be serious" look. "Fuck you!" she cursed at me.

Hey, it didn't hurt to ask. Shit, we were in Canarsie, Brooklyn, and that was a long trip back to Queens by bus or train.

"Bounce, clown. The bus stop is eight blocks north," she said.

She was cute, and I already got what I came for. And I guessed it was the public transportation for me today. I left her place without saying goodbye or, "I'll call you later." I already knew Shannon had "leech" and "needy" written all over her. Girls like her were potential problems in the future. She seemed independent, having her own place and a Lexus, but there was a flaw somewhere inside her. She was already asking for time that I didn't have to give her. Today I had plans, and I wanted to get in contact with Monica. I wanted to see my son. I was away from them for far too long.

Monica. Monica. I couldn't stop thinking about her. She and my son were heavily on my mind. They were difficult to track down. Her family didn't want to tell me anything, not even her new last name. They saw that I was out of prison, and the look on their faces was of disappointment. If it were up to them, I would have stayed in there for life.

"You're a bad influence," they told me. "Monica's doing better without you in her life! She's a married woman now." *Yeah, right!*

I was still Justin's father. I didn't care who his new stepdaddy was. And I was determined to find her no matter what. And fortunately for me, she had a cool cousin, Jonathan. He pulled me to the side and told me where she was. I was grateful. Jonathan understood that I wanted to see my son, and no man should be kept away from his child. He was a father too, with three kids.

Harlem, New York, was her new location.

It was a sunny afternoon when I ascended from the train station on 125th Street and was in the midst of a bustling urban metropolis. 125th Street was the mecca for black America, but the place had changed over the years. More white people were in Harlem, and gentrification had taken over with a Starbucks nearby and a few other commercial businesses.

Though I was in Harlem, I was still quite a distance from Monica's place. So I hailed an unlicensed taxi and told him to go to 138th Street. I wasn't about to walk that many blocks in the sun and heat. It was a quick drive. He got me there instantly and sat double parked outside of a magnificent brownstone nestled in the middle of the block. I gave him his fare and climbed out of the cab. I stared at the place, and it was a beautiful residence on what appeared to be a quiet street. *Wow.* It was definitely an upgrade from her home in Queens. I climbed the concrete steps and rang the bell. I was a little bit nervous. It had been some time now, and a lot of things were going through my mind.

There was no answer, so I pushed the doorbell again. I could hear it chiming inside. I hoped Monica was home. I'd traveled too far to go back empty-handed.

Finally, I heard some kind of movement on the other side of the door. It had to be her. I hoped it was her. But if it was her husband, then what? He wouldn't scare me. I came in peace, and maybe soon to try to get a piece of Monica.

"Who is it?" I heard her say.

"A friend," I shouted.

"What?"

"I'm home! It's me, Ash."

The front door quickly opened, and she loomed into my view. I could tell she was utterly stunned, taken aback by my sudden presence at her front door.

"Oh, my God. Oh, my God, what are you doing here?" She looked shocked. Her hands were cupped over her mouth.

"What, you're surprised to see me? You want me to leave?"

"No, I mean, how did you find me? Oh, my God." She was at a loss for words. She didn't know what to do or say.

"You know I got my ways," I said.

"When did you get out?"

"A few days ago."

We stood in the threshold of the doorway, talking, and I wanted her to let me in. I wanted to see my son. And I tried to reconnect with her.

She looked good—really damn good. She was dressed simply in this red and white print dress, and she was barefoot. Her hair was still long and sinuous, and her brown skin looked smoother than ever. Her lovely, hypnotic brown eyes could always put a man into a trance. The way she looked at you did something to you. It made you want to love her and never let her go.

"So what's going on, Monica? Where's my son?" I said. "And why you got me standing out here?"

"It's just this visit is so sudden, Ash. My place is a mess, and look at me, I'm not even dressed."

"You look fine to me."

"Look at your hair. You grew dreads," she said.

"Don't sweat me. You know I'm still looking good."

She smiled.

"So what's up, you gonna have me waiting out here forever?"

"No," she sighed. "Come inside."

Gladly!

I stepped foot into her new home and took it all in. The place was three floors, neatly furnished with parquet flooring and decorated with some pricey artwork, from African artifacts spewed around to the painting on the walls. Monica gave me a quick tour of the place. It was her husband's. They lived on the first two floors and rented the third floor to a man and the basement to a single mother.

"Shit is nice, Monica. You like the Jeffersons. Moving on up and shit," I said.

"Thank you."

"So can I get a hug?" I said. "I came all this way to see you and Justin, and I get no love from you at all."

I opened my arms and waited for her to fall into them. I wanted to feel her against me again. At first she looked reluctant, but I wasn't taking no for an answer. It was a simple hug. That was it. And eventually, she came my way and fell into my arms and hugged me back half-heartedly. The touch of her again, damn, it had me feeling crazy. It didn't last long though. She pulled away from me. I then noticed the ring on her finger, proof of her marriage to some fool. It stung a bit, but I kept calm.

"Where's Justin?" I finally asked.

"He's in school."

"Oh. When will he be home?"

She looked at her watch and said, "Anytime now."

We had some alone time, I believed. But Monica was behaving standoffish toward me.

"You want something to drink?"

"Yeah, I'll take a Coke or Pepsi."

She disappeared into the kitchen, and I took a seat on the sofa. I looked around the living room. It was tastefully decorated. The pieces of furniture looked like they cost some money. On the mantle and walls were lots of framed pictures, large and small, of her and my son and her new husband. Curiosity got the best of me, and I removed myself from the sofa to take a look at a few pictures.

Monica looked gorgeous in every last one of them, and my son had grown up a lot, and he was handsome like his daddy. And then there was him, her husband, and he looked nothing like I expected him to be. In fact, he was the total opposite of me, looking like a slim and nerdy brainiac. He wore glasses and was dressed like a computer programmer. He was hugging and kissing Monica in a few pictures and being a father to my son in others. And in one image, they looked like a happy family, where he was holding my son in his arms, and Monica's eyes upon him looked like she was utterly in love with him.

I released a deep sigh. It was hard to see, hard to take in. *Seven years incarcerated and a lot done changed.*

Monica came back into the living room with my can of Pepsi, and I took a few gulps. She stood nearby.

"Beautiful pictures," I said.

"Thank you," she replied with an uneasy smile. "So where are you staying?"

"With Mom."

"How's she doing?"

"She's fine, missing her grandson," I said seriously.

She looked convicted of a crime. The comment sparked some guilt, knowing that she could have taken Justin to see his grandmother plenty of times. She didn't have an answer or an excuse for it. "Give her my love," was her reply.

"I will."

A half hour went by, and we had small chitchat. I was waiting for Justin to arrive home from school. My little soldier had a nanny. Can you believe that he had his own fuckin' nanny? The boy was growing up privileged. It was good and bad. I didn't want him to forget where he came from.

I sat there in the living room when he finally arrived home from school, accompanied by his aging Caribbean nanny named Lena. Monica quickly introduced us and she departed. Justin, however, looked up at me like I was a stranger to him. He knew who I was, but his stepdaddy was the more frequent man in his life.

"Justin, go and give your father a hug," Monica said to him.

His eyes were aloof, and he didn't smile. He hesitated. The reaction from him was far opposite from the one I'd received from my daughter the other day. He was handsomely dressed in khaki shorts, a T-shirt, and Transformers sneakers, and he carried a Spiderman book bag. He sported a low haircut, and he had my eyes and my nose.

"Yo, what's up, little man?"

His aloof stare at me continued. It was not the reaction I expected.

"Why are you acting so shy around Daddy, huh? You miss me?"

There was still nothing from him, not even a crack of a smile.

"He's shy," Monica said.

I didn't want my son to be shy around me.

"You're my son, and I'm gonna break you out of that shy routine. You can't attract the ladies by being shy all the time."

"He's fine," she said.

I already knew she was raising my son like some pussy. It was the last thing I wanted. And I wanted him to know me, and I wanted to teach him something. I had no idea what his stepfather was teaching him.

"Justin, c'mere," I said to him.

Still, he stood there like his feet were in cement. So I went up to him and picked up into my arms and hugged him. He didn't even attempt to hug me. He wanted to be put down. He struggled in my arms, and he was acting spoiled. I tried not to get angry, but his reaction was hurtful.

"I want Daddy," he said.

What! I was his daddy. That new nigga done infiltrated my son's mind, and he was turning him against me.

"I am your daddy," I retorted.

The look in his eyes said no, I wasn't.

"He gotta get used to you. You were gone for a long time," Monica said.

"If you had brought him to visit me more often, then I wouldn't be having this problem with him," I griped.

"I had a lot going on."

"Too much for me to get to know my son," I said.

I felt an argument brewing between us, so I dropped it. Monica held her tongue too, or there would have been a war with us already.

"Justin, go watch cartoons," Monica said.

He didn't hesitate to pivot and run off into the other room. It felt like he was running away from me. With my son out of the room, things felt awkward between Monica and me. She didn't have much to say. But I did.

"So who's the lucky guy?" I asked.

"His name is Patrick, and he's an English and history professor at John Jay College."

"Wow, you got you an educated man, huh? Mr. Feeny, *Boy Meets World,* huh?"

She didn't find my joke funny. "He's a wonderful guy, and he's great with Justin."

"I bet he is Mr. Cosby and shit," I replied dryly.

"Anyway, he should be home soon," she said.

"Oh, was that your cue for me to leave?"

She sighed. "No, I would love for you to meet him."

"Yeah, I would love to. Me and your husband, we can sit down and talk—"

"Ash, please don't embarrass me."

"What? Embarrass you? Why would I embarrass you? I mean, you're a married woman now."

"Exactly," she uttered. "And Patrick is a really nice guy. He keeps to himself, and he works hard."

"He got to, to afford a nice place like this."

Patrick. If it weren't for the pictures of him I saw on the mantle, I would have sworn he was a white boy with that name. What black mother would name their son Patrick?

I had so many questions to ask him and her. I wanted to know everything about him. And I wanted to see from her if he fucked her better than I did. I mean, how did she meet this man? From the pictures I saw, I couldn't tell what she saw in him. I figured that it had to be his money. He was well-off, and he provided financial security for Monica, because it damn sure wasn't physical security from the looks of him. The man looked like he couldn't break a pencil in half.

Monica and I spent some time reminiscing in the living room while Justin was engulfed in snacks and cartoons. I managed to make her smile and laugh. It was good to see her laugh. And she had the perfect smile and the perfect teeth.

Our eyes locked, and I proclaimed to her, "You're still beautiful. And I miss you."

I could tell that my comment made her very uncomfortable. She wasn't about to go there with me. She picked herself up from the chair and said, "Ash, you need to move on with your life and move on from me. Whatever you're thinking, stop thinking it. And if you came here for any other reason than to see your son and meet my husband, then you can leave. I'm happily married, and I truly love my husband. He's good to me, and I'm good to him."

She said everything practically in one breath, and her look was severe. Her eyes narrowed tightly, and she had her hands on her hips.

"I'm not tryin' to break up a happy home."

"As long as we have that understanding, you can stay."

"We do."

She quickly shut me down. I had to respect that. She definitely wasn't Chanel. I was fresh home, and all I was doing was catching up on lost time and reconnecting with friends. Sometime later, we heard movement at the front door and keys jingling. The door opened, indicating that her husband had arrived home.

Soon he loomed into my view, carrying a leather briefcase, and we immediately locked eyes. "I see we have company," he said.

Monica stood up and right away introduced us. "Patrick, this is Ash, Justin's father, and Ash, this is Patrick."

He smiled. He came over to me with his hand extended and said, "It's finally good to meet you. I've heard so much about you."

Really? From Monica?

I halfheartedly smiled and shook his hand, saying, "Same here."

I quickly sized him up. The man was of average height and thin with a faded haircut. He looked to be in his mid-thirties. He was dressed in beige khakis and a white-collar shirt and wore wire-framed glasses. My first impression of him was Steve Urkel without the suspenders. And it was hard to believe that Monica fell in love with him and gotten married.

I was on my best behavior. But I knew if I were challenged, I would wipe the floor with him.

"Ash came by to see his son," Monica said.

"He's a fine young lad," said Patrick. "Monica and I already have him reading at a fourth-grade level."

A young lad? Where did this guy come from?

"That's my son," I proudly said.

"Where is Justin anyway?" he asked.

"He's in his room watching cartoons," Monica said.

Me, I was still in awe at Patrick. How did he meet Monica?

"So, Ash, what are you doing for yourself? Are you working?" he asked me.

"Nah, I'm still looking. Right now, I'm just catching up on lost time, you know, meeting up with niggas I ain't seen in a minute."

He frowned at the word "nigga." "If you don't mind, we try to refrain from using that word in this house or anywhere else," he said.

"Oh, word."

"Yes. It's a very derogatory word."

"Hey, it's your palace," I simply replied.

"Well, if you're looking for employment, then maybe I could become of some assistance to you."

"Really? I'll keep that in mind."

I felt he was bullshit and only playing Mr. Nice Guy in front of Monica. Why would this fool want to help me out with a job when he didn't know me at all? It was all a ruse.

"Well, once again, it was nice to finally meet you, Ash. If you don't mind, I'll be in my study. I have some papers to grade and lots of work to catch up on."

Once again, we shook hands, and he left the room with his leather briefcase, but not before he came with an afterthought. "And Justin is a handsome young man. I see where he gets his looks from," he added.

Whoa, was he trying to flirt with me?

With him finally gone, it was Monica and me, alone again.

"Nice guy," I said. "But it's kinda hard to see you with him."

"He's my husband, Ash, and I love him."

"Yeah, I know you do. But anyway, I don't wanna overstay my welcome. It was nice seeing you again, Monica," I said.

"You wanna tell your son goodbye?"

"Nah, I'll let him be for now. I gotta run. It's a long trip back to Queens."

I started toward the door, and she followed me. I opened the front door and stepped foot outside. I turned around to see her standing in the doorway. God, she was so fuckin' beautiful. Just looking at her was making my heart flutter. I wanted to kiss her right there. I missed her.

"Ash, you be safe out there, okay?" she said.

"I will."

We hugged each other. It was an awkward and fast hug. I didn't want to release her from my arms, but Monica pushed herself away from me, keeping things appropriate between us. She flashed a quick smile and subsequently closed the door. I lingered for a short moment on the steps and sighed.

Damn it. Seeing her again, it was hurtful. I was still in love with her. I loved her more than I could ever love Chanel.

Chapter Nine

Trey

What is love; love is when you look at her and it's taking you back to that first date, when you gaze at her, it's like seeing her on that first day . . .

I was breathing heavily from the exertion of keeping up with my genuine sex warrior. I shuddered as I released myself deep inside of her. It felt like I was going to come forever. The sex was great, and Chica rode my dick like a porn star. A deep exhale, and I collapsed on my back with her still straddling me. Her body glistened with sweat from our hour-long tryst.

Shit! I said to myself. Once again, we had sex without any protection, and I came inside of her. What was I thinking? Why the repeated stupidity? It was like her pussy was crack cocaine, and I couldn't get enough of it. I was chasing this sexual high, and Chica was able to fulfill it completely. I didn't want to come down from it anytime soon.

It was the middle of the afternoon. I felt entirely appeased, and it was time for my exit—like usual. I removed myself from her naked grasp and climbed out of bed and started to get dressed.

She huffed at me. "You're leaving already?"

"Yeah, I got things to do."

She sucked her teeth, manifesting an attitude with me. "Fuck me and leave, right? That's our song?"

Her attitude after sex was becoming tiresome.

"You gonna let me out?" I said while buttoning my jeans, ignoring her nagging.

She slowly removed herself from the bed and followed me out of the bedroom and downstairs toward the door. She remained naked. Before I walked out, she hugged me from the back, pressing her tits against me with her hands moving underneath my shirt.

"Can I least get a kiss goodbye?" she said.

Why not? I turned and faced her, still so pretty after sex. She groaned as my tongue lapped across her lips and sank into her moist hole. Her petite body held in my arms, and we wrestled tongues heatedly. I could feel her reaching for my crotch and get ready to unzip my jeans and dig for my penis again. I had to pull away from her. Things were getting hot and heavy between us. That quickly, she had my dick hard like concrete.

She laughed. "See what I can do?"

Damn, she was dangerous. I had to rush out the door before I fell victim to her enticement again.

"Call me," she hollered at me.

I would. Her pussy had me hypnotized like a good Biggie verse.

Later that night, I planned on meeting up with Trisha at Juno's restaurant in Freeport, Long Island. I was planning on spending some quality time with my girlfriend. We were on good terms again. We hadn't had a severe argument for fourteen days. I wanted to keep it like that.

Trisha lived in Baldwin, Long Island, and it was a reasonable distance from Queens, and it gave me some room to play around. I was a cheater. I admitted that, and the feel and touch of a beautiful new woman was my weakness. Like potato chips, I couldn't have just one. But that didn't mean I didn't love my woman. I did greatly. But I was still young and wanted to sow my wild oats, and at the same time, I didn't want to lose the best thing that ever happened to me, which was Trisha.

So I was always careful, like a spy in enemy territory.

The plan tonight was a nice and intimate dinner at Juno's, a classy and elegant restaurant near the lake, and then we would go out dancing. We both were looking forward to it.

But first I had to go home and wash the smell of Chica off me. I was on vacation from my job at the accounting firm in Manhattan. I was on the fast track to making partner. I was good at what I did—numbers. When dealing with tax consulting, assurance services, or audits for publicly traded companies and many private companies, I was the man—the top-notch CPA to go to. I worked hard and I played harder.

It was early evening when I finally arrived home after a busy day. The plan was to relax until my night out with Trisha. I was going to drink a cold beer and catch up on some ESPN.

I drove home in my Mercedes listening to music and replaying my afternoon with Chica in my head. I pulled into my neighborhood and slowly drove down the quiet street, looking at the neatly manicured lawns and brick homes. Laurelton, Queens, was a middle-class neighborhood, and I lived in a three-bedroom home with two bathrooms, a sizable backyard, and a front yard with a manicured lawn and a garage. It was my castle.

I pulled into my driveway and exited my Benz. And the moment I stepped foot onto the ground, I noticed my neighbor, Janice, coming out of her front door. She was back in New York. Janice had been my neighbor for a little over a year. She was a middle-aged woman in her early forties with grown children and some grandchildren. She was a career woman who traveled often. She was in pharmaceutical sales. Her job required her to cover certain territories, which involved lots of traveling from different cities. She was rarely home, but we'd developed a good friendship.

Janice was a beautiful and well-endowed woman, shapely and thick, and sophisticated and classy, sporting a high puff hairstyle. When she was home, we had intelligent conversations about everything from politics, movies, and history to sports. She was a Steelers fan, and I loved my Giants. She was a divorced woman of two years now, and she moved to Laurelton from New Jersey for a fresh start away from her ex-husband. She had a strong personality and a tasteful sense of humor.

Now, was I attracted to her? I definitely was. What man wouldn't be? Janice had it going on. She would playfully flirt with me, but I didn't want to shit where I ate. Trisha sometimes spent the night at my place, and I didn't need that kind of headache. And besides, Janice was a relationship kind of woman. She didn't bring men to her home, and she lived a bachelorette's lifestyle.

"Hello, Trey," she acknowledged me from her front steps.

"Hey, Janice. I see you're back from Chicago. How was the trip?" I asked.

"It was lovely, but it was strictly business. I didn't get the chance to paint the town red," she said.

"Maybe next time."

"I guess."

I started walking toward my front door, and she began to come my way. "Trey, I need a favor from you," she said.

"What's that?"

"I have this new entertainment system, and it's becoming a problem to put together. You know I'm all thumbs when it comes to stuff like this."

I smiled. "I got you. Give me a moment to settle in, and I'll come by."

She smiled. "You're a lifesaver, Trey. Thank you."

"Don't thank me yet."

She turned around and strutted back to her house. I caught myself lingering on her ample backside for too long. I went into the house. I closed the door and exhaled. I knew electronics and technology, and my home was set up like a concert hall. I liked high-end things, especially stereo equipment, and Janice knew that about me.

I brushed my teeth, washed my face, and was knocking at Janice's door fifteen minutes later. She answered with a smile and stepped aside. I passed over her threshold with virtue. Just one friend helping out another, right?

Janice's place was neatly furnished with that woman's touch. It had wood floors, a great room, a fireplace, and there were many pictures of her family, from her kids to her three grandchildren, placed everywhere.

"Where's the problem?" I asked her.

"Right over here."

She took me to where her attempt at putting together an extensive home entertainment system was failing. There were wires and pieces of equipment everywhere.

One look at the trouble, and I saw that she wasn't even close. "Okay . . ." I uttered.

"I guess that's why it's good to have a man around, huh?" she said.

"Hey, you tried."

"Did I make things worse?"

"Nah, I got this. I'll have you listening to Jodeci and Keith Sweat in no time."

She smiled. "My knight in shining armor. Do you want something to drink?"

"Nah, I'm good."

I got down on my knees and went to work on her home entertainment system. It was going to take me a moment, but everything was feasible. Once you did one, you did them all.

While I worked on her system, she disappeared into the next room. I glanced at the time, and I had three hours before my night out with Trisha. There were six speakers and a fifteen-inch powered subwoofer in total, one amp, the DVD player, her large TV, and many wires to deal with. I took my time and connected it all together. While I did so, Janice was keeping busy in other rooms. I didn't mind. It was my forte, entertainment.

After an hour of connecting wires to speakers and amps and checking things accurately, I pushed the power button, and it all lit up and came alive. I tuned into Hot 97, and there was a commercial on. I needed a music CD. I found Jodeci's debut album nearby and decided to play that for a start. Once it was in the CD drive, I cranked up the volume. "Forever My Lady" came alive, blaring through the surround-sound speakers. It sounded like we were at one of their concerts in Madison Square Garden.

Forever, Forever, Forever
So you're having my baby
And it means so much to me
There's nothing more precious
Than to raise a family

The song came through clearly and so clean, the bass bumping, and it brought Janice into the room with a massive smile on her face.

"Oh, my God. I love it! And you put the right song on to bless it. I love Jodeci," she said with enthusiasm.

She had changed into something more comfortable, wearing an ivory soft fleece knee-length polar-bear hooded bathrobe. Her hair was slightly wet. It appeared she had just taken a shower.

"I'm happy to be at your service."

"You're the best, Trey."

I smiled.

I watched her dance slowly to Jodeci. Her eyes were closed, and she was feeling the music completely. She swayed to the music, her hips moving rhythmically as the beat echoed through the system. The way she moved her hips, it was mesmerizing. I stood there and simply watched her enjoy her new entertainment system and a Jodeci song.

"Come dance with me, Trey," she said, extending her arms to me. "C'mon, I know you got some nice dance moves."

"Maybe next time."

She sucked her teeth lightheartedly and replied, "Don't be a party pooper."

I chuckled. *Me, a party pooper?* I exhaled and said to myself, *oh, why not?*

I moved closer to her and took her hands into mine, and we began to move as one. She continued to smile at me. We started to dance beautifully and slowly together. She moved closer to me, and we slid around her living room in perfect step, correctly anticipating each other's every move. Soon our bodies were pressed tightly together, and she looked into my eyes with a flirty smile on her face. My arms wrapped around her waist, and hers wrapped around my neck.

With her breath against my neck, she asked, "Do you find me attractive, Trey?"

Of course I did. "You're a beautiful woman," I said.

"Thank you. I miss this with my husband. We used to dance like this all the time," she said.

I wondered where it went wrong with them. She spoke of him sometimes, and when she did, I could see the nostalgia in her eyes. But they were divorced, and she was supposedly moving on from him. My assumption was that he cheated on her.

I had her shapely curves in my arms, and they were too enticing. She smelled like roses on a beautiful spring day, and her womanly flesh pressed against me was starting to make something grow.

Before I knew it, we were slowly tongue kissing each other. It just happened. And as we danced closely, our tongues danced with each other too, entwined like roots. My hands, as if they had a life of their own, went from holding her waist to cupping her succulent ass cheeks. I began to moan while feeling her hands moving downward and reaching for the buttons of my jeans. She quickly undid them and slid her manicured nails inside my jeans and started stroking my complete erection. With our hearts racing and the deep kissing, it didn't take long for her to shed her robe to reveal her nudity underneath.

"All I want is one night with you," she said to me.

And she was about to get it. We weren't about to turn back now. The heat was turned up, and our bodies started to melt for each other. She undressed me, and I found myself contorted on the living room floor with her. Her body was naked and ready for me, and I was stiff and big, and she was impressed. The look on her face said enough.

"You got condoms?" I asked.

She nodded. She stood up and went to her purse and removed several Magnum-style condoms, the perfect fit for me.

"Allow me," she said.

Not a problem. Janice rolled back the latex against my thick and giant erection, and the Magnum-sized condom was still a snug fit for me. And for the moment, Janice wanted it missionary. I mounted Janice and penetrated her slowly. Her eyes opened wide as my dick slipped deep into her body and I sucked on her dime-sized nipples. She moaned with her legs wrapped around me, and I groaned. *Shit!* I felt that suction of her pussy already, like a deep, gulping throat. She was wet like a running river, and each stroke inside of her was fierce and rhythmic. Our dance went from vertical to horizontal against the carpeted floor. Her nails clawed against my back as I pounded inside of her, and I could feel her leaving marks against my skin.

"Oh, shit, Trey. Oh, God. Oh, God. Oh, God," she moaned into my ear.

From missionary, we transitioned to her riding me nice and slow. The Jodeci album continued to play. The song "Stay" blared through the speakers, and I stayed deep inside of her as her meaty thighs crushed against me. Her naked brown flesh tumbled all over mine, and she happened to leave a few bite marks against my shoulder and on my neck. She was a freak for real. And it didn't take long for her to announce those magical words, "I'm about to come!"

I was running really late for my date with Trisha. I called Trisha and gave her an excuse for arriving at her place at a quarter after 10:00 p.m. instead of our scheduled time, 9:00 p.m. My time with Janice had run over. The sex was so good that I'd lost track of time. I had to hurry up and shower, dress, and make sure I looked extra sharp for my woman tonight.

I was out the door like the Flash.

Luckily, tonight there was no traffic. I did eighty miles per hour on the Southern State Parkway and came to a halting stop in front of Trisha's place in Baldwin, Long Island.

Her condo was newly built, and it came with the latest amenities, including a gym room, pool, and spa. And Trisha liked the finer things in life. She wasn't materialistic, but she worked hard as a legal aid. She lived a good life and always dressed impeccably. She was also frugal with her spending, and she was outgoing. There were so many things I loved about her that I could quickly lose count.

I hurried from the car and rang her doorbell. She made me wait. I figured she would be upset. I hollered from the steps, "Trish, c'mon. I'm sorry I'm late. I plan on making it up to you."

She hated CP time—colored people time. Trisha was a very punctual woman. She was organized, smart, and always on point. I stood outside her front door, clutching a bouquet of flowers and begging for her to give me a chance tonight. For a moment, it looked like all hope was lost, until she finally opened the door and frowned at me.

"What the fuck, Trey? Will I ever be a priority in your life?" she barked at me.

"You are a priority in my life," I said wholeheartedly.

"Actions speak louder than words, and lately, your actions suck!"

"I'm sorry, okay? I had a busy day today," I lied.

"Busy." She chuckled at my comment and then said, "Busy with who? I know for a fact that you're on vacation. So you're definitely not busy with work."

"C'mon, Trish, let's not do this tonight. I wanna have a good time with you," I said.

She continued to frown my way, but she looked impeccable in an animal-print minidress and a pair of braided-detail wedges. Her hair was sinuous and long, and she was breathtakingly beautiful. Myself, I had to cover up the scratches and marks Janice left on my body. I had a hickey near my neck and shoulder area and deep scratches on my back. I was a walking confirmation of my infidelity. So I wore a white shirt with cuffs, a stylish tie, and black slacks, with hard-bottom shoes. But for extra measures, I covered the hickey with a bandage. If she saw it and asked, I would lie and tell her it was an injury.

Finally, I escorted her from the door and to my car. I opened the passenger door for her for good measure, and she slid inside—not a thank-you from her. She was quiet toward me, but I was okay with it. She could have canceled on me.

Juno's was the perfect place for my girl and me to eat. It had a spacious layout with customers having their own intimacy, and the artwork on the walls made it feel like you were eating in a museum. There was nothing worse than staring at a bare wall. But what took the cake were the pianist and the breathtaking view of the lake nearby. The decor and the music were great, and I wanted to impress Trisha with the best.

For starters, we dined on strawberry sushi and mango sushi, very tasty. We sipped white wine and conversed about different things. I had the beef bourguignon for the main course. Trisha had the lamb and whitefish in a tomato and black olive sauce, smashed red baby potatoes, and vegetables.

Everything was delicious, and the night was going good until she noticed the bandage underneath my collar and asked, "What happened to your neck?"

"Oh, this? I was playing ball with the fellows earlier, and the game got a little rough," I lied to her.

Her look at me was dubious. "Let me take a look at it," she said.

"I'm okay, Trish."

My resistance made her more suspicious, but she also knew my basketball games with the guys could get a bit physical. We played to win, and sometimes we pushed and shoved each other around. And sometimes we did get hurt.

"I just want to see it," she insisted.

"For what?"

"Why don't you want me to see it, Trey? You sure that's an injury from playing basketball?"

Here we go with this shit. "Why I'm gonna lie for?"

"Because that's what you do. You lie!"

"We're having a nice time tonight. Don't ruin it, Trish," I said.

"You're worried about ruining tonight. I'm worried about this relationship." Her voice got a little elevated.

We went back and forth for a moment, and the waiter had to come to our table and say, "Dessert?"

"Not right now," I told him. I waved him off.

He was being polite. Trish and I were starting to make a scene in a nice restaurant.

He walked away, and I hunched over with my elbows on the table and said to her, "Why are you fuckin' with me, huh? I can't take you anywhere without you trying to start some shit."

"*I'm* trying to start some shit?" she retorted. "Are you kidding me? If you knew how to keep your fuckin' dick in your pants and stop fuckin' cheating on me, then we wouldn't be having this problem."

"I'm not cheating on you," I lied.

"There you go again, lying!"

Trisha never physically caught me cheating, but she knew something was wrong. She saw the numbers on my phone, and there was the condom she found in my car, which I put on Terrance. In a court of law, it would be circumstantial evidence, nothing direct.

I huffed. I was upset.

She continued with, "You must think I'm stupid, Trey. You expect me to believe that you got an injury on your neck playing basketball, and you tried to hide it from me by wearing a button-up and tie. I swear that better not be a fuckin' hickey on your neck."

"It's not, okay?" I continued to lie.

I sighed and sat back in my seat. I felt defeated. I was tired of fighting with her. Tonight was supposed to be unique, but it ended with a fight between us like always.

"I want the truth, Trey," she said.

I chuckled. She wasn't going to stop. "You know what? This is hopeless. I swear you make it impossible," I said.

"I make it impossible? You have some nerve."

I pushed my chair back from the table and stood up. I was done for the night. I took out my wallet, removed a few hundred dollars, and dropped it onto the table. "There. That should cover dinner tonight and your cab ride back home. I'm done! I'm out."

"So you just gonna leave like that?" she hollered.

I had nothing else to say to her. I pivoted and marched toward the exit.

"Trey, seriously. You gonna walk out just like that? Fuck you!" she screamed at me.

I love that woman, but fuck her too!

And our fourteen days without an argument or an incident went back down to one. Our record was gone.

Chapter Ten

Devin

What is love . . . you love her because just the touch of her takes you to a better place, just the warmth of her melts any doubt away . . .

I walked into the kitchen and stared at my wife-to-be. She was a beautiful woman, and I couldn't wait to marry her. She had the kitchen lit up with a lovely smell, preparing spaghetti, shrimp, and garlic bread, one of my favorite dishes.

Clad in a long white T-shirt and house slippers, she was a dime piece to me even in the simplest garb. I watched her work her magic on the stove, turning our kitchen into a feast of love. Everything she did turned me on.

I walked up behind Danielle and placed my arms around her slim waist and kissed the side of her neck. Holding her in my arms was blissful. There wasn't anything better than the affection of my woman while being held in my arms.

She smiled. "I'm trying to cook you dinner."

"I know, but you look so damn good doing it. I just wanted to hold you for a minute."

She giggled in my arms. "So I guess you're not hungry yet?"

"I'm hungry, but I'm starving for you," I said.

"Oh, so you're starving for me, huh?"

"Yup!"

"You didn't get enough of me this morning?"

"I can never get enough of you."

She turned around while in my arms and looked at me. We had matching smiles and a deep love for each other.

"Why are you so good to me, Devin?"

"Because you deserve it. You deserve the best, baby," I replied wholeheartedly.

She displayed a big, wide smile on her face. Our lips neared each other, and we started to kiss passionately. I picked Danielle up into my arms with her legs straddling me. I was horny again. She was the only woman I wanted. She was my sun, my moon . . . Danielle meant everything to me.

We quickly forgot about dinner on the stove, and I carried her into the bedroom. I was ready to make sweet, passionate love to her. I was prepared to fulfill everything. She removed her T-shirt and tossed it aside, and her nude body always left me in awe. Subsequently, she approached me and draped her arms around my neck.

"You want me, Devin?"

"Of course I do," I replied undoubtedly. "What kind of question is that? I'm always going to want you."

"Then fuck me, Devin. I don't want to make slow, grinding love to me. I want you to fuck me long and hard. No foreplay or lovemaking, I want you to take me like a beast and ravage my body," she proclaimed.

I'd never heard her say that before, but I definitely liked it. I also liked romance and lovemaking. And I loved foreplay. It got the blood moving inside of me. But she wanted to have rough sex.

She kissed me aggressively and started to unbuckle my jeans. We'd been together for a year now, and I'd never given it to her like that before. We didn't have quickies like that. I always took my time with her, kissed her nice and slow, massaged and caressed her body, and got things stimulated with romance and slow jams. I was that type of man to hold my woman all night, after sex or not having sex. I didn't see myself as a freak. I saw myself as old-fashioned.

I remember when Danielle wanted to do it in the car's back seat while parked in the parking lot, but I shied away from the idea. I was afraid of being caught. She was kind of upset with me. There were other freaky moments I'd shied away from. I don't know, having sex outdoors just seemed inappropriate to me. I believed that sex should be inside the home and inside the bedroom. And as for oral sex, it really wasn't my thing. We tried it on each other on a few occasions. I was okay, I guess, but she was so much better performing it on me.

Danielle finally removed my pants and fisted my erection. She kissed me aggressively again and then exclaimed, "I want you to fuck me, baby. Just take it!"

She pushed me against the bed and mounted me, sliding my erection into her womanhood. She arched her back, and she started to ride me, and it all felt too glorious. I huffed and puffed, feeling the beauty of her insides stimulating me entirely, and then it started to happen. I felt myself coming already.

"Oh, shit," I grunted.

"No, baby, don't come yet," she said nervously.

But it was too late. I exploded inside of Danielle and quivered with glee underneath her from the intense orgasm she bestowed on me. I got too excited and ejaculated prematurely. It was embarrassing. Things happened too quickly, and I felt I would have lasted longer if I took my time.

"I'm sorry, baby," I said.

"It's okay. I enjoyed it," Danielle said with a faint smile.

She climbed off of me, and I saw the disappointment on her face, even though she said she enjoyed it. She was trying to make me feel better. I got mine, but she didn't get hers.

"I guess I'll go finish making dinner," she said.

She donned her long T-shirt again and left the room. I heaved a sigh, knowing that wasn't my best sex. But it happened, right? I had to make it up to her. I couldn't go out like that, not after I initiated things.

The sex didn't go as planned. I wanted things to last longer than half a minute. I sighed again, and I didn't leave the bed anytime soon. I could smell Danielle's cooking coming from the kitchen. She was a good woman, and I wanted to please her by any means necessary.

As I was about to depart from the bed, my cell phone rang. I wasn't in the mood to talk to anyone, but I answered anyway. It was the nice guy in me. "Hello?"

"Devin, what's up?"

"What up, Terrance?"

"Chilling, yo," he said. "Yo, the fellows and I are thinking about going down to the club tonight."

"What club?"

"The strip club. You wanna roll?"

I wasn't really into places like that. I'd been there a few times with the fellows before, but ever since I'd met Danielle, I just found myself wanting to be more with her every day. And besides, I felt that it was a waste of money and time giving these females money that I'd worked too hard for.

"Nah, I'm good. I'm just gonna relax with my woman tonight," I said.

"You need to get out of the house more often, Devin," he said.

"Strip clubs aren't my thing."

"We just hanging out and gonna have a few beers. Nothing wrong with that," he said.

"Maybe next time."

"A'ight. Peace out."

"Bye." I ended the call. *Why go to a strip club when I have the finest woman in the world?*

I finally removed myself from the bedroom and joined Danielle in the kitchen.

"Who was on the phone?" she asked me.

"It was Terrance."

"Oh, everything okay?"

"Yeah, he wanted me to go out with the fellows tonight."

"So why don't you go?" she said.

"I don't feel like it, and besides, I got you here to keep me company all night," I said. I hugged her again and added, "Let me make it up to you. I was too excited."

"Well, I'm cooking dinner right now," she said.

"Okay. I love you," I said.

"I love you too."

We kissed, and I went into the living room to relax and watch some TV. Danielle and I were meant to last forever. I knew it deep in my heart.

Chapter Eleven

Sophia

Love is knowing that things will never be perfect, but you try your best to make it be . . .

"You're beautiful," he told me.

I blushed from his words. I was beautiful to him, and he looked like a god to me. We were having a superb dinner, drinks, and a fluid conversation at this eloquent restaurant on City Island. It was expensive, but Eric didn't mind. He was spending money on me like I was his woman, and this was our first date.

I'd lied to my husband and told him that I was going out with Yasmin.

"Out with Yasmin doing what?" Terrance had questioned.

"Doing girl stuff," I'd replied. "We're gonna get a few drinks and talk. I need it, Terrance. And I might stay the night."

"Okay, just be safe."

And then I called Yasmin, explaining to her that I was out with a different man and that I needed her to cover for me just in case. She was okay with it, shocked at first, but she encouraged me to have fun. I didn't plan on having too much fun.

"So use me as your scapegoat to cheat on your husband," Yasmin had uttered. "But don't worry. I got your back. Just be careful."

"I will."

Eric was eye candy in his casual wear of blue jeans, a collared shirt, and Hush Puppies. His bald head gleamed nicely, and his goatee was precisely trimmed. His jewelry wasn't flashy, and his smile was white. He was a flawless-looking man, but he was funny, too, having a great sense of humor, and he wasn't conceited. He wanted to know everything about me. I talked, and he patiently listened.

I had the lobster, and he had the shrimp and biscuits.

"How's the lobster?" Eric asked.

"It's good. Why, you want a bite?"

"I don't know, maybe. How big of a bite can I have?" he smiled.

"Just don't be too greedy," I teased.

"Then just a taste for now. I want to save some room for dessert," he countered.

I came out looking my finest for him. I didn't want to overdo it, but I wanted him to see me, see my sexiness. So I decided on a black halter top with the self-tie back, my silver bangle set, a pair of jeans with crocheted side panels, and peep-toe heels with ankle straps. My hair was long and black, and I wore my hazel contacts for him.

"Were your eyes this pretty when I met you?" he said.

"Contacts," I said.

"You're pretty with or without them."

I smiled and said, "What are you trying to do, get some tonight?"

He laughed. "I'm just having a good time with a lovely woman and complimenting her at the same time."

"And do you treat all the women you meet like this?"

"No, only the special ones, and I haven't met anyone special in a very long time," he said.

Once again, I smiled and blushed. Why was I so giddy over him? We just met, and he could be a player for all I knew: a man talking that game to try to fuck me. But it was working.

"So what's on the agenda after dinner?" I asked.

He shrugged. "It depends on what you feel like doing."

"I want to go dancing."

"Then dancing it is."

I hadn't been dancing with my husband in months. And I loved to dance. And thinking about Terrance for a split second, I knew that I had to be totally honest with Eric. I hadn't told him about Terrance yet. He still believed that I was a single woman.

I tasted the alcohol and looked his way with some gravity in my eyes.

"Eric," I started, taking a deep breath, "there's something I have to tell you. I have to be honest with you."

He looked at me. He looked like he could be very understanding already. At least I hoped he was.

"I'm married. And I have a five-year-old daughter."

"Oh," he simply uttered.

"Before we get into anything else, I thought you had the right to know."

"Well, I'm glad that you're honest with me. Truth, I suspected that you probably were seeing someone. A beautiful woman like yourself, I figured some lucky man had to have snatched you up already. But the marriage thing, now that caught me off guard."

"Why?"

"You're young."

"I'm not that young," I said.

He tasted the alcohol. "So you and your husband, is it separation, or are the two you still together?" he said.

"Yes, we're still together," I hated to say.

"And do you still love him?"

I took in a deep breath. "I mean, we've been married for seven years now, and I still love him. But I feel something is missing between us. I don't know, Eric."

"So do you feel that you need a break from him?"

"Probably a very long break," I said.

"Like how long?"

"Probably a permanent one."

He smiled. "So is it safe to say that I'm more than just a rebound?"

I smiled and then let out a slight titter. "See, now that's too early to tell. You're fine, and you're cool, funny, too, but we have to see about that. I'm just taking things slow right now."

"Does your husband know about you dating other men?"

"Honestly, no."

"I see," he said. He took a sip from his drink.

"Are you nervous?" I said, noticing his expression.

"I don't want any crazy and jealous man coming for me with a shotgun. I don't need that in my life."

I laughed. "Please. It's nothing like that."

"Okay. I believe you. But I'm still going to watch my back," he said, subsequently glancing over his shoulders.

I laughed. "You're stupid."

"Nah, just cautious," he said.

"I understand. If you want this to end right now, just let me know," I said.

"What? Hell no!"

I wanted to kiss him. Probably do more than kiss him, probably get a room with him for the night. But I wanted to take it slow. I was still married and had a child.

After dinner, Eric and I drove into the city, and we went to this nightclub on the Lower West Side called the Shadow. It was a place with good music and a good crowd. Inside, he bought me a drink and then led me onto the dance floor, where we danced to Amerie's "Talkin' to Me."

We danced for what felt like hours, and he was an outstanding dancer. He was able to keep up with me, and it didn't matter if it was hip-hop, rap, or reggae, Eric had moves and rhythm. He was impressive, and I was enjoying him more and more. Eric took control of my body on the dance floor wildly when dancing to the reggae songs. I could have sworn that he had some West Indian blood in him. The way he grabbed my hips and ground against me and swayed side to side with me . . . We were so close and so intimate that it felt like we were making passionate love on the dance floor. He wasn't scared to hold me correctly. He was confident and I liked that.

We took a quick break from the dance floor, and he bought me another drink.

"Who taught you how to dance like that?" I asked.

"I've been dancing since I was eight."

"Really?"

"Yup. I was even in a few music videos when I was young."

I sucked my teeth. "Stop lying."

"Nah. I'm for real."

"Which ones then?"

"A'ight, I was in a Mary J. Blige video. Um, SWV, Soul For Real, Bobby Brown, R. Kelly, and New Edition."

"You're full of it," I said. I didn't believe him.

"Sophia, I'm serious. When I was eleven, my mother had me get down with a talent agency for kids, like modeling and dancing. I've been around."

"You serious, aren't you?"

"I don't lie. I don't have a reason to lie to you."

I was impressed. Damn. The man was going places.

"You want to hit the dance floor again?" he asked.

"Give me a few more minutes. Let me finish enjoying my drink."

He smiled. "Take your time, beautiful."

"And when we do get back on, you better start keeping up with me. Because I'm about to put it on you, you hear?"

"Excuse me, Janet Jackson. We'll see."

"That's right. We will see." I laughed.

I didn't want our night together to end, but it had to. And I hadn't thought about my husband all night.

It was five in the morning when he pulled up in front of Yasmin's place in Queens Village. I told Terrance that I would be spending the night at her home. He didn't care. Zaire was at her grandmother's, and he was probably hanging out with the boys.

Eric and I lingered for a moment in his car. It was evident that I didn't want to get out right away.

"I had a really good time tonight," I said.

"I did too."

He stared at me.

"What is it?" I said.

"I just wanna kiss you right now," he said.

"So what's stopping you?" I found myself replying to him.

We fixated our eyes on each other, and I already felt myself doing the unthinkable. Eric made it easy with his concentrated gaze upon me and his hunger for me.

So he leaned closer and neared his lips toward mine. The moment our lips connected, it felt like fireworks exploded inside his car. I melted as he stuck his tongue into my mouth, his tongue swirling.

"Oh, God," I moaned. The inside of his mouth felt like a gateway to heaven. Subsequently, his hands started to move about, with things becoming hot and heavy between us. I felt his touch between my inner thighs, his grope increasing between my legs.

His lips and his touch—it all felt exhilarating. His touch groped the inside of my shirt, and he suddenly had one of my tits out. He cupped it. His lips brushed my neck, and then he sucked behind my ear, swirling his tongue. He nipped at my neck, then swirled his tongue against the hollow of my throat. His tongue subsequently teased my nipple, flicking over and around it, and then he took it into his mouth, concurrently shoving his hand into my pants and reaching for his paradise—my pussy. I felt his fingers move to my pussy, and then two glided between my lips, inside of me, fingering me nice and slow.

Shit. I felt myself approaching unadulterated stimulation and the abyss of an orgasm without him fucking me or eating me out. I felt this flame ignite inside of me. His hands were all over me, and I wanted to return the favor. So I reached for his crotch and started to unzip his jeans. And then it came out, his growing erection, and it was thick, big, black, and very impressive. I took it into my hand and started to jerk him off. His moaning blew against the side of my neck. His big dick felt like a lead pipe in my tiny fist.

Oh, God, I was about to fuck him on the first date. Something was coming over me. I wanted to feel him inside of me. I was tempted to ask Yasmin for a massive favor: if she had an extra bedroom for me to use.

He continued to finger me and kiss me everywhere, and I continued to jerk him off. But what stopped everything so suddenly was his cell phone ringing. It was like a bell going off to end a boxing round. Hearing his phone, I pulled away from him and removed his hand from my pants.

"I can't do this," I uttered, breathing heavily from excitement.

"What's wrong?"

"I just need some time," I explained to him.

He sighed. I knew it was wrong to lead him this far and stop abruptly, but I didn't want to regret tonight. Everything was perfect, and sex—I couldn't go through with it even though my body yearned for it.

"It's cool. I understand," Eric said.

"You sure? I apologize."

"No need to apologize. We just met, right? And besides, I want to see you again."

I nodded.

He put that anaconda he called a dick back into his pants, and we collected ourselves in the front seat of his CL600. Everything was back in place, and my body temperature went back down to normal.

I smiled his way. I praised him for being so understanding.

"So when am I going to see you again?" he said.

"I'll call you."

"Please do."

I gave him a hug and kiss and exited his car.

"Good night, beautiful," he hollered from the driver's seat.

"Good night."

I knocked on Yasmin's door, and she answered. I hurried into her place before I changed my mind. Yasmin tried to get a glimpse of Eric before he drove off at the doorway, but it was too late. He was gone.

"So that was him, huh?" Yasmin uttered.

"Yes."

"You fucked him?"

"No!"

Yasmin gave me that look like, "bitch, why should I believe you?"

"I want to know everything, and I do mean everything," said Yasmin. "What is going on with you?"

She wanted to know everything about the man in the CL600 and why, after seven years with Terrance, I was suddenly stepping outside of my marriage. I didn't know where to start. There was a lot to tell her.

I could feel him trying to wake me with his oral pleasure. He was trying to arouse me early Sunday morning by touching my body and grabbing places that I wanted to be off-limits for now. I knew what he wanted, and it'd been a while since he had some. His dick was hard.

Terrance tugged at the booty shorts that I slept in, desperately trying to remove them. But I gave him lots of resistance, keeping my legs closed and saying to him, "Baby, please, not this morning. I'm not in the mood."

His look toward me was of heated frustration. He frowned. He continued to try to undress me and go down on me, and I continued to fight him. I didn't want to be bothered with him, and I especially didn't want any kind of sex this morning. I roughly nudged him away from me.

"Really?" he spewed at me with loathing in his voice.

"I'm just tired, baby."

"Tired? You slept for like eight hours. What are you tired of?"

I sighed. "I'm just tired."

"Fuck it and fuck you!" he cursed at me.

"Terrance, is that shit fuckin' necessary? You ain't gotta curse at me," I retorted.

"Fuck you fo' real, Sophia!" he cursed louder.

He jumped up from the bed and stormed out of the bedroom, slamming the door behind him. He was acting like a damn child, like I was the toy that he couldn't play with. He done woke me up entirely and had me upset. But why was I upset? Was it toward Terrance, or because it had been three days since my night out with Eric and I hadn't spoken to him? I called him several times to no avail. He wasn't returning any of my phone calls, and I was worried.

Terrance and I hadn't had sex in three weeks. I wanted to please my husband and make him happy, but I wasn't pleased, and I was thinking about Eric.

I released a deep sigh and removed myself from the bed. It was a sunny and warm Sunday morning, and the day was already starting wrong. My husband wanted to please me this morning, and I rejected him. I was wrong, right? I was thinking about another man while lying in bed next to Terrance.

I donned my house robe and knew that I needed to go and apologize to him. Cook him breakfast, fuck it, suck his dick, and enjoy my husband today, because he was still my husband. But before I could do any of that, Terrance was already gone.

Chapter Twelve

Terrance

What is love; it's the simplest things, washing her feet, making her smile, stirring up laughter . . .

Where was my marriage going? Did Sophia still love me? What was I doing wrong? Was she seeing someone else? There were so many questions swimming around in my head that I was drowning with upset and worry.

Sunday morning, I was pissed off. We hadn't had sex in three weeks, and yet she was still denying me mine. It felt like I was about to explode, and there was just so much jerking off that a man could do. I wanted my wife, but did she still want me? I stayed gone all day. I didn't want to go home. I wanted to be far away from her, and I needed to cool off. And I did that by hanging out with Ash that Sunday and throwing back a few drinks at the bar.

Monday morning, Sophia and I left for work, with Zaire at school, without saying three words to each other. How was she upset with me? I guessed she was mad at me for staying gone all day yesterday. But I didn't care. She didn't have to speak to me at all. The bitch was acting like her pussy was platinum.

I worked hard all day in the hot sun loading and unloading luggage and cargo from various planes. JFK Airport was a bustling place with national and international flights coming in from all over the world, and American Airlines felt like it got the bulk of the flights. I helped my crew unload an Airbus A300 from Barbados and confessed my marriage crisis to an aging coworker. Larry was in his late forties, and he had been married for twenty-five years and had been with the airline for longer. He suggested I make it up to my wife, but I didn't do anything wrong.

"Terrance, when it comes to a woman, especially a black woman, they gonna always be right. Maybe she's going through something at the moment. It'll work out. Buy her some flowers, and apologize even if you didn't start the argument," he advised me. "But communicate with her."

"Is that your secret for staying married for so long?" I asked.

"Hey, a happy wife, a happy home."

I was trying to make my wife happy, so what was I doing wrong? All I wanted was a happy home.

After work, I followed my coworker's advice and bought Sophia some flowers and candy. And I decided to take things a step extra and cook dinner tonight. I stopped by the supermarket to pick up a few things and then picked Zaire up from school.

That evening, the house was scented with the sirloin steaks cooking in the oven, rice, and shrimp, and vegetables cooking on the stove, one of Sophia's favorite dishes. I cleaned up and had Zaire chilling, watching her cartoons in the living room. The plan was to put Zaire to bed early and make it all about my wife tonight. I wanted things to be perfect because I wanted to have sex tonight.

My body ached for it. I didn't know how much longer I could go on without having sex with my wife.

Sophia and I had our good days and bad days, but lately, it felt like we were having more bad days than good. The fights, the arguments, and the bickering were definitely strangling our marriage. And I wanted to breathe again. I was tired of the fighting.

Two hours passed, and I fed Zaire and put her to bed, yet my wife hadn't arrived home from work. I blamed her lateness on rush hour. She would be home soon, home to enjoy the meal I cooked for her and the arrangements I made. The house was clean, and it all felt perfect.

The evening grew late, and I was starting to worry. My wife wasn't home from work yet, and her cell phone was going straight to her voicemail. I sighed with concern and sat in my La-Z-Boy, trying not to exaggerate the worst in my mind. Dinner was ready hours ago, but it was getting cold. I made another call to her cell phone and received the same result: her voicemail. I left her a concerned message, hoping and praying that she called me back very soon.

Another hour went by, and the day was almost gone. I was edging toward full-blown panic mode. My next move was calling her best friend, Yasmin. She hadn't heard from Sophia all day. Next, I called her cousin, Nancy, and unfortunately I received the same results from her. I called her mother in Yonkers, and she hadn't seen or heard from her daughter, and my phone call put my mother-in-law in worry mode too.

"Call me if you hear from her," she said.

"And you do the same."

I hung up and kept busy on my cell phone. I was desperate to find my wife. Call after call, there was nothing. Where was she? I could no longer sit. I started to pace around the house with the cell phone glued to my hand, always looking out the window, hoping to see her approaching.

"Daddy, I want Mommy," Zaire said, coming out of her bedroom in her pajamas, clutching her small doll. "Mommy always kisses me good night."

"I know, sweetie. Mommy will be home soon to kiss you good night. I promise," I said.

I picked my daughter up into my arms and carried her back into the bedroom. I placed her comfortably back into her bed and kissed her good night. "Daddy loves you," I said.

"I love you too, Daddy."

I smiled. I loved my daughter and my wife deeply, and I would have died if anything happened to them.

When my cell phone rang, I hurried to answer it, believing it to be Sophia calling me back. Unfortunately, it wasn't. It was Yasmin calling.

"Is she home? Did you hear from her yet?" she asked me.

"No, she isn't home yet. Did she tell you that she was going somewhere after work?"

"She didn't tell me anything."

I let out a heavy sigh. The worries and emotions started to go into overdrive. "Damn this woman!" I shouted.

"I'm sure she's okay, Terrance," Yasmin said.

I couldn't think straight.

"Call me if you hear anything," said Yasmin.

"I will."

Her call ended.

Two more hours went by, and it was after midnight. I started to fear the worst, and I was tempted to call the police and file a missing person report on my wife. So many emotions were inside of me—worry, anger, concern, regret, and panic. I was trying to keep things together, but I kept thinking about rape, kidnapping, and murder. Fortunately, Zaire was sound asleep and not awake to see Daddy going crazy. But I was on the verge of calling my mother to have her come watch Zaire, and hopping into my truck to search for Sophia.

Sophia's cell phone was going straight to her voicemail, which meant either her phone was off, or her battery went dead. It threw more fear and panic into me.

Yasmin called again, hoping for some good news. "You heard anything yet?" she asked frantically.

"No, nothing."

"I'm coming over there," she said.

"No, don't. I'm fine."

"How's Zaire?"

"She's sleeping."

"I'm thinking about calling the police," she said.

"I thought about it, but I'm gonna wait another hour," I said.

We both felt helpless. We didn't know what to do next. I prayed sometimes, but tonight I was ready to drop down on my knees with tears spilling from my eyes and pray like I never prayed before. I wanted God to protect my wife wherever she was. I strongly felt that something was wrong.

"Call the cops if she's not home in the next hour," said Yasmin worriedly.

"I will."

The next hour was about to pass, and I was about to call the police. It was the last thing that I wanted to do, but I had no other options left. I was growing more hysterical. I went back and forth to the window and had my phone in my hand. Sophia's mother called, but I had no good news to give her. I could hear the panic in her voice over the phone. Where was her daughter?

It was ten minutes to 1:00 a.m. when I finally heard a set of keys at the front door. I knew it had to be Sophia. I stood in the middle of the living room, lights off, and gazed at the front door, waiting for it to open and waiting for Sophia to loom into my view, coming home finally.

She walked in, and I looked at her. God, I didn't know if I should give her a long, loving hug, knowing that she was home and safe, or punch her in the face and slam her against the wall for putting her family and me through this meaningless worry. She walked into the room as if it weren't the wee hours of the morning and she hadn't been missing since work.

She stared at me, deadpan. We both stood quiet, looking at each other, feeling like strangers toward each other. It was like I didn't know her.

I coolly asked, "Are you okay?"

She nodded.

"You're nodding. I don't want a nod. I want a yes or no answer," I exclaimed.

"I'm fine, Terrance," she replied sharply.

She had the attitude. *Seriously?*

"Where the fuck was you all this time then? It's damn near a new fuckin' day, and you come home now! You had me and everyone else worried about you," I shouted. I was no longer peaceful.

"Terrance . . ." she started to say, but paused.

Looking at her, it looked like she had been crying. Her clothes were wrinkled and in disarray. Something was wrong or off with her.

I continued to shout. "I've been calling your phone all damn night, and you don't answer it. What the fuck is wrong with you? You don't have the courtesy to call home and tell your family where you are? I'm here stressed the fuck out about your safety and whereabouts. I was so close to calling the police!"

"I'm sorry, Terrance, believe me. I'm truly sorry," she apologized.

"Nah, fuck that. Sorry ain't gonna cut it. I want an explanation. Where the fuck was you?"

The tears started to trickle from her eyes like the floodgates had opened. Her eyes showed great sadness and trouble. What was going on with my wife?

"Terrance, we need to talk," she said. "It's serious."

"Talk about what?"

"It's about us," she replied sadly.

Where was this going? I was upset with her, and she looked like she was going through a crisis.

"What about us?" I said, fearing where this was going.

There was more sadness in her eyes. There were more tears. Today was supposed to be perfect, from flowers and candy to dinner, but now everything was in turmoil.

"I'm not happy, Terrance!" she exclaimed.

"You're not happy with what?"

"I'm not happy with us, with this marriage, with everything!" she cried out.

Now everything changed, and I went from pissed off to, *what the fuck is she talking about?*

I stepped closer to her. I wanted to hug her, console her, but she didn't want any part of me. She stepped backward, stretched out her arm, and held her hand out to prevent me from coming any closer. "Don't!" she uttered.

"Talk to me, Sophia. What is going on with you?"

"I need a break."

"You want a divorce from me?" I said gruffly.

"I don't know. Maybe."

Such anguish was on her face. Did she not love me anymore? She had been distanced from me for a while with no sex. And her words started to cut into me.

"Let's just take a deep breath and talk," I said coolly.

"Terrance, I love you, but honestly, I'm not in love with you anymore. I've been feeling this way for a while now," she said.

"How long is a while?"

"Close to a year now."

Wow. I was utterly taken aback. It was a hurtful announcement, and I didn't know what to think.

"Sophia, you know I love you so much. I'll do anything to fix us. I love my family, and I don't want to lose it." I started to cry myself. And then I asked the most wounding question that I feared the answer to. "Are you fuckin' someone else?" I went from feeling like a ferocious pit bull with anger toward my wife to feeling like a damn Muppet.

"No, I'm not fuckin' anybody else," she said straightforwardly, looking directly at me.

I wanted to believe her, but it was hard. How does a woman entirely fall out of love with someone? It felt like my heart was decaying. We had seven years of marriage, and I always tried to give her what she wanted.

"Why now? What brought this on?" I asked her.

"It just happened."

"Shit don't just happen," I shouted.

"I didn't want to hurt you. I didn't want to continue this lie any longer."

"So our marriage was a fuckin' lie?"

"No, it wasn't. You're a wonderful husband and a great father—"

"So what is it? If I'm so wonderful, why do you want a fuckin' divorce?" No matter what she told me, there was no reasonable explanation. In my mind, there had to be someone else.

"Let's just try to make this easy on both of us, Terrance," she dared to say.

"Make it easy? Make it fuckin' easy?" I shouted. "You come in here after I was worried sick about you for hours, and we ain't fuck in like three weeks. And now you tell me that you don't love me anymore, you want a divorce, and you fuckin' talking about making it easy!"

I snapped. I turned quickly and put my fist through the wall several times, leaving behind several gaping holes in the living room wall. My hand was bleeding, but I didn't care. I was hurt more inside than anything else.

"I love you! I always loved you!" I strongly proclaimed. "I don't wanna lose my wife."

She looked at me with her teary eyes and proclaimed, "I'm already lost."

"And Zaire, what about her?" I said.

"She can stay with me. I love my daughter."

"But you don't love me."

"I do."

"Liar!" I shouted.

"I'm sorry," she said sadly.

I didn't want to hear that she was sorry. I wanted her to love me, to be in love with me. But looking into her eyes, I saw that they were so distanced from me that not even light speed could take me back to her.

"You know what? I'm out. I need to get the fuck away from you!" I growled.

"We need to really talk," she said.

"Fuck you!" I cursed at her.

I dried the few tears trickling from my eyes, hurriedly collected my things, and rushed toward the door. The sad thing, though, was that Sophia didn't even try to stop me from leaving. She was allowing my departure at such an early hour of the morning. What I wanted most was her to prevent me from going. I wanted her to call out my name and say that we could work things out. But I got nothing but silence from her.

My final words to her were, "Enjoy the dinner that I made for you. I cooked one of your favorites."

I slammed the door behind me. I got into my Expedition and sped off. I had no idea where I was going. I just wanted to get away from home.

I was utterly broken inside. I cried and cried like a baby. It was embarrassing because I was a grown man, and I was flooded with tears, my vision was cloudy, and I felt sick to my stomach. I couldn't see life without her.

There had to be someone else. I wasn't stupid. Sophia was a liar.

I went to my mother's place in St. Albans and used my key to enter without disturbing her. I went into my old bedroom and closed the door. I continued to dry my tears and huff and puff. I asked God to bring her back to me. I wanted Him to make my wife fall in love with me again. I always felt that she was my soul mate. Yeah, it hadn't always been easy, but we still had each other. And I tried to be the best husband and father I could be. I wasn't perfect, but who was?

I prayed and I prayed. I wanted to wake up and find my wife beside me. I wanted it all to be a bad dream.

"Bring her heart back to me, Lord. Please do. I know that I've made mistakes in the past, but I love my wife and my family, and I'll do anything for them. Amen."

Chapter Thirteen

Sophia

Love . . . love is having her lay her head against your chest so she could feel that you're just a heartbeat away . . .

The truth hurt, but the truth shall set you free, right? I knew Terrance was crushed, but I couldn't hold things in any longer. I instead had decided to tell him now rather than keep living a lie every day. I wasn't happy. I wasn't in love, and I wanted out of my marriage.

He didn't want to talk about it. He stormed out of the house like a crazy man after punching holes into the walls. Two of my problems with Terrance were his anger and his lack of communication most times. We only talked when he felt like it, but most times, he was busy with sports, his friends, work, et cetera, and he put me second. I only came first to him when he wanted sex.

I went into Zaire's room, and she was still sleeping peacefully. I was glad that our argument hadn't woken her up.

I sighed. Why was this so hard? When I went into the bathroom to go change, I looked into the bathroom mirror and suddenly started crying again.

Damn this.

I wasn't sleepy. It was the early hours of the morning, and I needed someone to talk to. Yasmin was my first option. She was always the first person I called when I needed to chat. I dialed her number.

"Hello?" she quickly answered.

"Hey," I somberly uttered.

"Girl, where in the hell have you been? You had Terrance going crazy looking for you. We both were calling everywhere, trying to look for you. You okay?"

"Yes," I replied feebly.

"What's wrong, girl? You sound upset."

"I told my husband how I was feeling. I told him that I wasn't in love with him," I said matter-of-factly.

"Shit! How did he take it?" she asked.

I sighed. "Not good."

"He didn't hit you or nothing?"

"No. He just stormed out of the house cursing and carrying on."

"You'll be a'ight, Sophia."

"I wish. I feel so wrong right now, Yasmin. Why I gotta be feeling like this?" I said, tearing up, my voice choking.

"It just happens, girl."

"I mean, I still do love him. But at this point in my life, I just feel I can't be together with him like that anymore."

"You need me to come over there?"

"No. I'm okay."

"Where were you all this time?" she asked.

I kept quiet for a moment, deciding if I should tell her the truth. Yasmin was a good friend, but I didn't want to give her the wrong impression if I told her my actual whereabouts. But I needed to tell someone.

"I was with Eric."

"Did you fuck him?"

"No. It wasn't even like that. All we did was talk all night, and he held me."

It was the truth. And I lied to Terrance. I was seeing someone else, but we weren't having sex—not yet anyway.

"All I got to say, Yasmin, is that I definitely do feel something for him."

"But you just met the man," she said.

"I know. But there's something there with him."

I heard her chuckle.

"What's so funny?" I asked.

"I know you feel for the man, but don't rush into anything else so fast. You just told your husband that you weren't in love with him anymore. I don't think he's going to like you falling in love with another man so quickly."

"I understand."

"Think it over, Sophia. You're my girl. Don't do or get into anything stupid."

"I won't."

"You sure you don't need me to come over there?"

"Yasmin, I'm fine," I assured her.

"Okay."

"So I'll see you tomorrow, or this weekend?" I said.

"Of course. We definitely need to talk about this in person."

I smiled. "Okay."

"You be a good girl."

"You too. Love you."

"Love you too."

I hung up.

I was feeling a little better. It was always good having a friend to talk to. And no matter how bad or severe the situation was, Yasmin had always been there for me. I'd known Yasmin since junior high school, and we'd been friends ever since.

I tried calling Terrance, but his phone was going directly to his voicemail. He was upset and probably needed to cool off. I understood that. And he was still my husband, and I always loved him and cared about him. I hoped that, wherever he was, he was safe and wouldn't do anything stupid.

Chapter Fourteen

Trey

Love is . . . when you crown her your life, give her that divine . . .

"You're so stupid," Trisha laughed, watching me dance around in my blue and white silk boxers with the smiley faces. We had the stereo playing rap music. We were back on good terms with each other again.

We had great sex again—really great sex, with her having multiple orgasms. Good dick would always give women amnesia. I apologized to her and confessed my undying love for her. I told her that she was the only one for me, and that easy, I was back with her having great sex, and she was my woman again.

I had my shirt off and attempted to do the C-walk. It was a dance innovated by the Crips in LA that included shuffling, the V, and heel-toe. I stumbled a few times trying to do it, but it was fun. It was making Trish laugh, and that was all that mattered to me.

"You think I'm silly. Watch this," I said. I attempted to do a backflip and fell flat on my face. Trisha was in tears.

"You okay, Trey?" she said, laughing like she was at *Def Comedy Jam.*

"You think it's funny, huh?"

"No." She continued to laugh.

"A'ight. I see you still laughing."

I jumped up and ran toward her. I grabbed her in my arms, tossed her on the bed, and started tickling her. She squirmed and laughed harder. Trisha had always been ticklish. It was one of her weaknesses.

"Trey, stop it, stop!" she hollered and laughed. I was giving her something to laugh about.

"Nah," I taunted. I had her pinned to the mattress and held her wrists flat against the bed. Trisha was staring up at me, still smiling. "I'm funny to you, right?"

"No," she said.

"You sure?"

"You're sexy to me."

"I'm sexy, huh?" I said.

"Yes."

"Oh, really? A minute ago I was hilarious to you. Now I'm sexy."

"You're both."

"Really?"

"Yes."

We looked at each other. Trisha was unquestionably looking sexy in her white signature cami and panty set, with her skin looking sleeker than ever. She'd just gotten out of the shower and oiled herself down from head to toe with some baby oil.

"Kiss me, Trey," she said.

"Now you want me to kiss you." I smiled.

"You better right now."

I leaned closer and pressed my lips to hers. They were soft, like cotton. She shrouded me with her arms and let me fall in between her legs. Things went from joking to sexual that quickly. I was going for her panties when I heard the fuckin' phone ring. At first I tried to ignore it, but Trisha told me to answer it, and after the seventh ring, I thought it might be necessary. I frowned. Whoever it was, they were ruining my moment with Trisha.

"Yo, who this?" I answered with fret.

"Trey, it's Terrance. I ain't mean to call you so early in the morning."

"Damn, Terrance, you a'ight? You sounding all upset and shit. What's good?"

I heard him sigh. "Yo, man, shit is fucked up."

"What happened?"

"How my wife gonna come home and tell me that she ain't in love with me no more?"

"What?"

"Yeah. She told me that dumb shit last night."

"What does she mean, she ain't in love with you anymore? Y'all been married for like seven years now. What kind of dumb shit is that?"

"You tell me."

"Trey, is everything all right?" Trisha asked me.

"Yeah, everything's cool, Trish."

"I don't know, man, this shit got me buggin' the fuck out," Terrance said.

"Where you at right now?"

"I'm at my mom's crib."

"Damn, man, you moved out?"

"I had to leave," he said.

"Yeah, I feel you."

"Yo, I don't know, man. Sophia told me that she ain't fuckin' any other nigga, and that she ain't seeing anyone else, but I don't believe her."

"Yo, ain't no woman gonna tell you some shit like that unless there is some other man involved," I told him. "Yo, she fucking some other man."

"I know, right."

"You don't know who it is?"

"Nah. I've been there for her always, and now she on some ill shit. Fuck her."

"Yo, Terrance, where you gonna be at today?" I asked. I had to go see my cousin, and we needed to talk. I needed to be there for him.

"I don't know. I took the day off today."

"A'ight. I'll come by Auntie's place in like an hour or so."

"I ain't going anywhere," he said in a gloomy voice.

After that talk with my cousin, Trisha was all into my business. "Trey, who was that, Terrance?" she asked me.

"Yeah, and I gotta go see him."

"Why? What happened?"

"He and Sophia had a fight. I think they might be getting a divorce."

"What?" She was totally shocked by the news.

I started to get dressed.

"They were like perfect for each other," she said. "They were happy."

"I don't know. I'm going to my aunt's place to talk to him."

"I wonder what he did," she uttered without thought.

Her remark caught my attention. "What he did? Why he gotta be the one at fault?"

"Because men always fuck up. It's in y'all DNA," she said.

I sighed. It was a biased statement, because females fucked up too. I didn't want to argue with her, so I kept my comments to myself.

I was dressed and ready to leave. I kissed Trisha good-bye and left her place on Long Island to drive to Queens.

I arrived at my aunt's place half an hour later. It was a quaint and comfortable home with a manicured lawn. She had a flourishing garden in the backyard and flowers growing in the front yard. I remembered Terrance and I used to run rampant everywhere while growing up. And I felt some guilt because I hadn't been by to see my aunt in months. I'd been busy.

I knocked on her door, and Terrance answered. I gave him a manly hug and walked inside. My cousin looked like he hadn't slept in days. He looked unhinged from his fallout with Sophia. His attire was sloppy, and he was always well put together, like me.

"You good, cuz?" I asked, knowing that he really wasn't.

"I'm okay," he lied to me. "You want something to drink?"

"Nah, I'm good."

He sat on the couch. I sat opposite him. "Talk to me. What happened last night?"

He spewed a deep sigh, looking upset all over again. He then said, "Sophia comes home around one in the morning after I've been calling her phone constantly with no answer. She had me worried sick about her, but she tells me that she's not happy with me, with our marriage, that she's not in love with me anymore. We argued. Man, I just had to leave."

"That's crazy, yo," I said.

"I don't know what to think, Trey. There's gotta be some other man she's seeing."

"I know Sophia's a good woman, but damn, I'm thinking the same thing."

"She's probably fuckin' this dude right under my nose and acting all polite with it," he exclaimed.

"You can't trust these bitches fo' real," I said.

"You trust Trisha?" he asked.

"Not like that. She's wifey and all, but I'm gonna keep an extra ho or two on the side just in case. So when wifey starts acting up, fuck it. I got pussy elsewhere. You know what I'm saying?"

"You think Trisha ever cheated on you?"

"Yo, I'm gonna put it like this: a woman gonna do what she wanna do. Ain't no stopping that shit. She gonna fuck who she wanna fuck and be with who she wanna be with. But my shorty knows what she's got at home. But trust? Shit, nigga, I don't even trust myself sometimes." I laughed

Terrance didn't laugh with me. "I trusted my wife," he voiced.

"I know you did. Yo, truth, you always gotta keep a woman entertained. Don't ever let a woman get bored with you. That's when the problems start."

"So you saying I'm boring?"

"Nah, I'm just saying keep a woman on her toes, and keep a woman intrigued with you. If shit starts to get redundant and mundane, then you risk your woman creeping out on you." It wasn't the best advice, but it was the truth.

He sat there, deadpan. I had to comfort him some other way.

"Terrance, don't stress it. I know you love her and you would do anything for her, but fuck her, cuz, and do you. Let her know what she's gonna be missing. I understand that's your wife and all, but if she's saying that shit to you about not being happy and whatnot, then there's gotta be a reason behind it. Like I said before, a female gonna fuck who she wanna fuck, and neither you nor me is gonna stop that from happening," I proclaimed.

He nodded his head.

"Where Auntie at?"

"She went out."

"You told her?"

"Yeah. She says that she's going to have a talk with Sophia."

"Man, these bitches today be losing their damn mind. They have a good man like you at home, doing what he needs to do to provide and take care of his family, and yet they still ain't happy and want something else. They don't appreciate shit! That goes to show that you can't please any bitch out there," I said without a doubt.

"I did my best with her," he said.

"I know you did, Terrance."

I stood up. *Fuck it. No more of this moping around and talking about our supposed better halves.* I needed to cheer my cousin up, and I knew the perfect remedy.

"We are going out tonight," I said. "I'm going to call Ash and Devin, and we are going to the strip club or something. You need to get that shit off your mind, cuz. You know my motto: the best way to get over a bitch is to fuck with a new bitch."

He laughed.

"You down?" I asked him.

He looked at me for a moment and then replied, "Fuck it. I'm down."

"We gonna get your dick sucked or something tonight," I said.

I spent the afternoon with my cousin, cheering him up and getting his mind off Sophia and his marriage. I felt like the male version of Dr. Ruth. I gave Terrance some solid advice. I didn't want him moping over his wife and falling into depression. It was sad to see any man depressed over a woman when there was plenty of pussy out there.

I called Ash and told him everything. Of course, he was ready for tonight. He wanted to wild out with his friends. Devin, however, was a different story. He would rather stay home with Danielle than hang out with his friends. I was continuously warning him about that, crowding his woman and ignoring his friends. He was becoming a lost cause.

After talking with my cousin, I wanted to go back to Trisha's place and finished where we'd left off. I was ready for some great sex. I was about to call her until I realized I made a big mistake by rushing from her place to see Terrance. I left my cell phone there.

Shit! I had numbers in my phone and a few text messages. If Trisha went through it, she might see some shit that I didn't want her to see. I pushed down on the pedal and accelerated to seventy miles per hour. This was a matter of life and death.

I walked into Trisha's condo and ran right into her stern glare at me. Fuck, something was wrong. If it weren't, she wouldn't be looking at me like this. And the first thing out of her mouth was, "Who's Chica?"

Fuck me!

I had to get ready for another battle with her.

"Who?" I looked dumbfounded by the name. "I don't know any Chica."

"Muthafucka, don't lie to me!" she screamed. "I went through your phone, and she sent you a text talking about she misses you. I guess you forgot to delete that one, huh?"

"That's some old shit," I lied.

"Sent a few days ago," she angrily countered.

"I ain't fuckin her!"

"Who is she then?"

"She's a friend from work, a client of mine."

There goes sex with her and our rekindling. Days without incident or an argument was back down to none. And I was upset with myself for leaving crucial evidence behind at her place—my damn cell phone. Now I had to get back into repairing mode once again and lie my way out of a bad situation. It wasn't the first time Trisha saw a woman's text on my phone. One time, she'd seen some naked pictures of a woman, and she was furious. So I knew if I could get her back after the nude picture incident, a text from Chica wasn't shit.

"I swear, I'm not fucking with you anymore, Trey! We're fuckin' done!" she threatened.

I'd heard it all before. Blah, blah, blah, blah!

Chapter Fifteen

Terrance

What is love . . . it's willing to be that man by your woman's side until the end of time . . .

It was my third night out with Ash, Trey, and even Devin. My friends were doing their best to help me cope with and forget about my ordeal with Sophia. And it was somewhat working. I was thinking about Sophia that night less and less.

Sophia and I hadn't spoken in three days. She was calling me, but I refused to talk to her. I was angry and hurt. I didn't want to hear her voice or her explanation. I wanted some time to myself. I felt that I deserved it.

The four of us were at this bar on Merrick Boulevard called the Tipsy Angel, an amusing name for a bar in Queens. It was a regular night with a regular crowd. The Knicks were playing and losing by fifteen points in the fourth quarter, and I was watching it on TV and enjoying my friends.

"Fuck these bitches!" Ashes exclaimed. "Cheers, my niggas!"

"Cheers," we all shouted together, except for Devin, and downed our beers.

Every last one of us had issues with our ladies. Devin too, surprisingly. He and Danielle had a minor spat the other night. God knows about what, because they both felt they were perfect. But if it took a little confrontation to get my friend out of the house and to drink and hang out with us, then I was thankful for small favors.

Ash threw his arm around me and pulled me closer. "Yo, Terrance, don't sweat that shit. You got plenty of hoes out there to choose from," Ash said. "You see me. I ain't ever stressing one bitch that hard."

"Damn. I never thought that Sophia would say a thing like that to you," Devin said. "I thought you and her had y'all shit together. Y'all look good together."

"Yo, I'm good, though," I said, drinking my beer.

"I know you good, Terrance. You family," Trey said.

"See, you can't trust these bitches out here today. One day they are feeling a nigga, all in love with you and, shit, 'bout ready to marry you, and then the next thing, bang. What the fuck happens? Your woman gonna come up to you and say some shit about her not being happy and this shit ain't working out. She's probably out there fucking the next nigga," Ash proclaimed earnestly. "These bitches don't know what the fuck they want today. I'm telling you, son, don't get caught out there with that shit again. I feel the more you disrespect a shorty, the more love you get."

"You really feel that way, Ash?" Devin asked.

"Yeah! These bitches out here don't want Cliff Huxtable anymore. Nah, they want a nigga like me, a fuckin' thug, a roughneck muthafucka who's gonna fuck 'em long, hard, and great, and blow they fuckin' back out, nigga. Them the niggas who get the respect from a bitch. Shit, you know what they say—nice guys finish last."

"Listen to him, cuz," Trey said.

"What about me?" Devin chimed. "I'm a nice guy, and I'm not finishing last. I've been with my girl for one year now, and she still loves me. We love each other."

"Listen, you need to stop being under your woman too damn much before your woman stops being under you, if you know what I mean," Ash said.

"Devin, you tell your girl everything?" Trey asked.

"We don't keep secrets from each other," he said.

"Ah, man, you fuckin' up!" Trey said mockingly. "You don't tell your woman everything you do. I'm telling you, son, that shit is gonna fuck you up down the line."

I expressed amusement. I couldn't lie to myself. I used to tell Sophia a lot of the things that we did. We rarely kept secrets from one another. That was how our relationship was. It was intense. At least I thought it was. And I was never insecure about our marriage. She had male friends, and I had female friends. She went out with her friends. I always knew that she was coming back home to me. I was giving her room to breathe.

What went wrong?

"Yo, Dev, let me tell you something. Playing that fuckin' choir-boy, good-man role today, that shit don't work. All a shorty is gonna do is see that shit and use you, step all over your punk ass like concrete. See, you gotta let a ho know upfront, 'I ain't the one to game. You ain't gonna play me the fuck out like that,'" Ash said.

"Man, listen, my mother has been married to my father for thirty-five years now, and my pops still is a good man. And anyway, I feel that there's too much shit going on today for y'all men to be bragging about jumping from woman to woman," Devin replied firmly.

"Man, listen, we all gotta die someday. I'd rather die in some pussy than without it. Shit, I went seven fuckin' years without no ass. I'm gonna do me, Devin. They throw it at me, shit, I'm gonna take it. But hey, that's me," Ash said.

We all laughed except for Devin.

"True that," Trey blurted out, giving Ash dap.

"What you gonna do if Danielle just up and left you like that and told your ass that she doesn't wanna be with you anymore?" Trey asked Devin.

"That's why you keep more than one shorty in your pocket," Ash chimed.

"If Danielle decided that she didn't want to be with me anymore, then I feel that's her loss. I've been good to her since day one, and that mistake would be on her conscience, not mine."

"Fool, you'd probably break down and cry like a bitch, with your weak ass," Ash said.

"I would be a man about it," Devin countered.

"Whatever, man, stop lying," Ash exclaimed.

"Terrance, you all right? Why you so quiet?" Trey asked me.

"Probably thinking about the wife," Ash said.

"Nah. I'm good. Just listening to y'all talk, that's all."

"We 'bout to get you some new pussy tonight," Ash said excitedly, clapping his hands together. "How do you forget about old pussy? By getting you some new pussy."

I chuckled and took a swig of my beer. The truth was, I was thinking about Sophia. No matter how much I was trying to forget about her, I was deeply missing her. But I refused to show any emotions in front of everyone. I hid it deeply, burying that feeling underneath the concrete and hard rock. I would never hear the end of it from Ash and Trey if I showed emotions like that, tears and pity.

"What's really good with you, Terrance?" Trey asked.

"You know, shit is pissin' me off. But what I'm supposed to do? She felt what she was feeling, and I can't change that, right?" I said.

"Just give her some time, Terrance. I feel everything is going to be all right between the two of y'all," Devin said.

"Fuck that shit. Don't listen to him, T. He pussy whipped," Ash scoffed. "Like I keep telling you, what you really need to do is grab you up one of these fine-ass ladies in this bar tonight and do your thang. The only thing that will get your mind off of old pussy is being in some new pussy."

I swear, that was his slogan—new pussy.

"Yo, Terrance, check that shorty over there in the blue skirt," my cousin pointed out. "You need to go over there and push up on that."

"Why is y'all asking the man to cheat on his wife?" Devin uttered. "He's still a married man."

"Man, fuck that shit. His wife said that she don't wanna be with him anymore. I ain't trying to have my man sit here all night and be looking depressed."

"No matter what, Terrance, you are still committed to your wife. You still wear that wedding ring on your finger. I believe that this is nothing but a phase that Sophia is going through," Devin said.

"Terrance, go over there and do you," Ash encouraged me, "or I will do it for you."

The woman in the skirt was cute and definitely curvy and thick in the right places, and she appeared to be alone. I gazed at her for a moment. But I wasn't in the mood to talk to another woman. I was still stuck on Sophia.

"You ain't gonna fuck wit' shorty?" Ash said.

"Nah, I'm good."

"Man, y'all fools is crazy," Ash griped.

"He's doing the right thing," said Devin.

"Fuck it. Both y'all fools can have the dry dick tonight. Me, I'ma stay into something nice. Shit, I might holler at her myself."

As the night progressed, we all got drunker, and we all continued to talk about our problems, pussy, and women. Ash came with my cousin, and I was driving. Devin left a half hour ago. He probably went home to make up with his woman and have himself a good night. Ash had continued to ridicule Devin, mocking that his woman had him on a tight curfew and schedule.

By midnight, we were leaving the Tipsy Angel. I stumbled to my truck, drunk but not hammered, and contemplating if I should go home to my family or head back to my mother's house for the night. I missed my family. It had been three lonely nights without them.

I climbed into my truck, started the engine, and made a choice. Love was fucking me up. It was painful. My wife had broken my heart, and if a woman could have you in tears, then that was love, right?

I'm going home to be with my family and to see my little girl, I reasoned. Three days away from her was long enough. And besides, I wasn't about to give up so easily on us. *No way! Be a man about it, and fight for your marriage. Your wife tells you she's not in love with you, then as a man, her husband, you need to find a way to make her fall in love with you again.*

I parked my truck in our driveway like usual and marched toward the front door. I hoped Sophia didn't change the locks on me. Would she make it that kind of party already? I doubted it.

My keys jingled, and I was nervous for some reason. I took a deep breath and tried my key in the lock. I turned the key, and the door opened. Thank God. I entered my home. It was dark and silent. It felt like I was a stranger inside my own home. I had the crazy thought, *what if I find my wife in bed with someone else?* I didn't know what I would do, go mad and kill the bitch?

I took a deep breath, and I proceeded toward the bathroom, where I heard the shower running. I figured it had to be Sophia. I wanted to go into the bathroom and surprise her, but I turned and went into the kitchen instead. I started some coffee and raided the fridge. I needed something to eat to combat the liquor in my system.

In the kitchen, as I munched on a few snacks, I suddenly heard, "So you just gonna come up in here and have nothing to say? Where were you? Three days you've been gone, and I was calling you. I was worried."

She looked angry. She glared at me, clad plainly in a towel with her arms folded across her chest. I didn't care for her attitude.

I smirked and sarcastically replied, "Now you know how it feels."

"Terrance, I was gone for a few hours. You were gone for three fuckin' days. Did you forget that we still have a daughter to help raise?" she angrily proclaimed.

She moved closer to me, looking fabulous in her blue towel, hair wet and body looking right. Damn, I missed her. But I was still hurt. I was angry, and I wanted to make her pay. I wanted her to feel the same pain I felt.

"No, I didn't forget. I just had to get away from you, that's all. Sorry if you were worried, but you don't fuckin' love me, so why worry?" I replied vehemently.

"You're so damn immature, Terrance," she spat at me. "I swear."

"I'm immature? How do you think I'm supposed to act? My wife comes home and tells me that she's not in love with me anymore! You want a divorce from the man who loved you unconditionally for seven fuckin' years. I loved you more than anything else, Sophia! I wanted to spend the rest of my life with you, and you fucked that up!" I shouted.

"Don't curse and yell at me, Terrance!" she retorted.

"Don't tell me what to do!" I shouted.

I scowled and clenched my fists. Looking at Sophia was hard to do because I was still heavily in love with her. But to know the feeling wasn't mutual, it was crushing.

"And how do you think I feel, huh? You think that it was easy for me to say that to you? I wrestled with myself every day, Terrance. I cried every time I thought about us, and telling you how I really felt about this marriage was the hardest thing for me to do," she rebuked. "I've been struggling with these emotions for too long now, and it was time for you to know."

"What did I do, huh? What did I do to you that was so bad that you stopped loving me? Why don't you want this family anymore? I mean, I did everything I could for us, Sophia. Everything!"

"You think I don't know that?" she replied in a lower tone. "I don't know about us anymore."

"How can I fix it? How can I fix us, baby?"

"I don't know. I don't know if we can be fixed, Terrance," she replied coldly.

"You serious? Are you saying there's nothing I can do to make us work again? Eight years together, married seven, and just like that we're done?"

Sadly, she stared at me, her eyes watery, and I saw no love for mc in her gaze. This was a completely different woman. Her look was compassionless when I was desperately searching for a glimmer of hope for us.

"I'm sorry," she said weakly.

"Fuck your sorry," I retorted. "I swear, Ash and they be right. Your bitch could just wake up one day and piss you off. Ain't no place in the world for nice and weak fools. A bitch gonna dog them regardless."

"So I'm a bitch now?"

"If the shoe fits," I returned coldly.

"You know what, Terrance?"

"What?" I dared her to continue.

"Never mind. You're so ignorant," she said.

"You fucking somebody else? Just be honest with me," I blurted out.

"Is that what you care about? If I'm fucking some other man?"

"Are you?" I wanted to know badly.

My eyes never left hers. They were locked into Sophia's eyes, waiting for an answer. And my heart beat so fast that it felt like it was going to tear out my chest. What if she said yes? How would I react?

"No, Terrance, I'm not fucking anyone else. You happy?"

Was I happy? Seriously! I was bitter and angry. I didn't know what I was going to do. I strongly felt that she was lying.

"I don't believe you," I exclaimed.

She shook her head at me, looking irritated. "You're so damn pigheaded," she said.

"Whatever, Sophia. Do you. I don't give a fuck anymore," I lied.

I did, but I was angry and frustrated with her. And the thought of someone else seeing her naked and having sex with my wife, it took me somewhere very dangerous—like psychotic.

"So what's the situation now?" I asked. "You want me sleeping on the couch?"

"You sleep where you wanna sleep, Terrance, because it ain't gonna be with me," she replied matter-of-factly.

Wow, it was a really low blow. I almost wanted to hit her for that cruel comment.

"So we're really doing this?" I said. "You really want this?"

"I just need to do me and live again, Terrance. Maybe we got married too young. I was only eighteen. And we had Zaire soon after. Everything just happened too fast. I need time to think and know what I really want."

I wanted her to want me.

"What about Zaire?" I asked her. "You're still her mother, and there ain't no changing that."

"I know. I'm gonna always love my daughter regardless. And I'm never going to abandon her."

"But you can abandon me," I shot back, throwing jabs below the belt.

"I love you, but—"

"I don't want to hear it! It is what it is. You want a divorce, fuck it. Let's get a divorce," I said dryly.

I was done talking. I was done trying. Sophia had made up her mind, and there was no changing it. I marched out of the room, angrily leaving her in the kitchen to contemplate whatever.

Fuck love! The only thing I was going to love was my daughter. But love for another woman, especially my wife, wasn't happening.

Why was love so hard? Love was supposed to be a wonderful and exuberant feeling, supposed to make a person feel high and exceptional. But it quickly wounded me and brought me down to this intense and dangerous feeling. It made folks do things without thinking, flew them over the edge and made them do things that they'd probably regret later. I knew it was taking me places, and it was changing me—for the worse, I felt. I loved her, and she made me feel like shit.

Chapter Sixteen

Ash

The sex is gettin' ugly, fuckin' her like her soul is being taken . . .

It was two in the morning, and I had Chanel face down in the pillow and ass up, legs spread with my hand around her slim neck and my hard dick inside of her. She took it in the ass—off-limits for many. Still, I was a man with no limits. I smacked her ass, pulled her hair, and treated her like a whore, and she loved every minute of it. She groaned and moaned. She couldn't get enough of me. Fresh out of prison, and we started right where we'd left off, and it was the best.

My daughter and Chanel's son slept in the next room, and it was Chanel and me, taking advantage of the early hour and some privacy. Chanel was my freak. She had qualities in the bedroom room that you wouldn't believe. She had the perfect resume to handle a big-dick nigga like me.

Small sweat beads formed on my brow, and I announced, "Damn, shorty, you 'bout to make me come!"

"Come in me!" she dared.

She threw her ass back on me. It moved like a wave with my nuts, smacking it from behind. She came a few times earlier, and it was my turn now, and I was ready to release. I needed a good nut. I was seven years overdue for some great sex, starting with Chanel and many others. I had a lot of catching up to do.

"Come for me, baby," she said.

"Oh, shit, I am. That's right, make me come," I growled excitedly, feeling my orgasm brewing while inside of her.

For almost an hour now we had been going at it, sucking and fucking each other until we were dry and exhausted, if that was even possible. A few more forceful thrusts into Chanel's gaping asshole, and I felt that needed stimulation about to discharge from me.

"I'm 'bout to come!" I announced.

Soon after, I gripped her naked frame firmly and ejected my semen like water rushing out from an open fire hydrant. She was able to do that to me—make me come like a racehorse. I quivered and moaned, and I pulled out. I collapsed on my back, breathing like a man who had just run a race. Chanel collapsed beside me and nestled against me with a satisfied smile.

"Damn, that was good, baby," she said.

I knew it was.

She wanted to be close to me. I'd been staying over her place mostly. She gave me shelter, food, and pussy—the three basic needs for me so far. And I got to spend more time with my daughter. It was too bad I couldn't get the same thing from Monica.

I closed my eyes and relished the moment, and Chanel continued to lie next to me. The room was quiet and dim. We tangled our legs around each other. The opened window brought in a nice breeze that was needed. Sex made things hotter inside.

"Was it good, baby?" she asked me with her fingers dancing across my chest.

"You know your pussy is platinum," I said.

"It better be, and don't you forget it."

I chuckled. "I won't. Now take your ass to sleep."

She laid her head against my chest and continued to touch me in placcs pleasingly. My baby mother was a hood rat, but she was cool peoples. And I had much love for her. I closed my eyes and tried to get some sleep, but something made my eyes opened back up. I heard a buzzing sound that echoed and interrupted the silence, and I realized that her pager was going off against the dresser.

Chanel immediately leaped up from me and hurried over to her pager to see who it was.

"Yo, who fuckin' paging you at this time of the night?" I said.

"Nobody," she replied.

"What the fuck you mean, nobody? What nigga tryin' to get at you?" By now, I'd propped myself up against the headboard with my eyes fixated on her.

"Ash, it's nobody."

And I'm supposed to believe that.

"Nah, fuck that. Who that?"

She sucked her teeth with annoyance at my questioning. "Ash, just go to sleep."

"What?" Now I was off the bed and on my feet. "Don't tell me to go to sleep."

She was hiding something. I was a second away from snatching the pager out of her hands and looking at the number myself. And I was going to take it a step further and call the nigga back and find out who was trying to get at my baby mother.

"Bitch, I'm 'bout to knock you the fuck out," I threatened her with my fists clenched.

"It's Keith!" she finally admitted.

"Who?"

"Keith. Timothy's father. My son's father. You forgot?"

"Why he tryin' to hit you now?" I asked with a frown.

"He's my son's father."

"So! I'm your baby father. Fuck that nigga! I was here way before that punk-ass nigga came around and got you pregnant. And best believe that shit only happened because I was locked up."

"You sound stupid right now, nigga," she shouted. "He's my son's father. What, you just want me to ignore him and cut him off because you home now?"

"Hell yeah! I don't want that nigga around my daughter."

"And you gonna help take care of Timothy? You don't even have a fuckin' job yet," she came back at me. "You ain't paying any fuckin' bills around here, and you ain't bought your daughter shit yet. You just a bum nigga shacking up with his baby mama."

That quickly, things went from paradise to hell between us, and we were in a full-blown argument in her bedroom.

"Bitch, who you talkin' to like that?" I shouted and glared at her.

"I'm talkin' to you, nigga!" she rebuked with a matching glare.

She got up in my face, naked and all. She was ready to fight me, and I was prepared to fight her. Chanel and I were no strangers to domestic abuse—physical violence. I lost count how many times we tried to tear each other's heads off and how many times she called the cops on me back in the day.

"Your ass shouldn't have gotten pregnant by him anyway! You fuckin' ho! I get locked up, and the first thing you do is spread your legs and have some other nigga's baby."

"I'm a fuckin' ho, nigga! Fuck you!"

"No, fuck you! And I'm telling you I don't wanna see that nigga around my daughter. Don't let me see that nigga at all!" I screamed at her.

"You ain't shit, nigga, but some dick. At least Timothy takes care of his," she shouted heatedly. "And what you gonna do?"

She was now deep in my face, with her hands moving about wildly and daring me to strike her. I was on paper, and Chanel was trying to get me locked back up.

"Fo' real, Chanel, you better step the fuck back!"

"Or what?" she challenged me.

"I'm gonna fuck you up! And I'm gonna see that nigga, too!"

"You so stupid, Ash! We ain't fuckin'."

"So why he paging you?"

"I don't know!"

Her pager went off a second time during our heated argument. She glanced at the number again. I knew it was him trying to reach her. It was a booty call that he wanted. I wasn't stupid.

"Yo, give me the damn pager." I tried to take it from her hands, forcibly.

"No!" She resisted.

"Chanel, I ain't fuckin' playing with you. Give me the fuckin' pager. I'm 'bout to call this nigga and tell him don't be calling you no fuckin' more."

"This is my business, Ash, not yours."

"Yo, you are gonna get fucked up tonight."

She was ready for me, like a thorough hood-rat bitch would be.

"You a weak-ass nigga," she shouted. "You don't control me, and if I were fuckin' him, what? You ain't my man. Did you put a ring on this finger? No! So I can fuck whoever I wanna fuck, you bitch-ass nigga!"

Her words had me boiling like hot lava, and I lost control. I smacked her. She came back at me with her fists, swinging my way violently, and caught me with a few hits. I punched her in the face, blacking her eye, and she fell to the floor.

"I told you, bitch, step the fuck back from me," I yelled.

It was on.

"You muthafucka!" she yelled.

It seemed like the iron out of the blue appeared in her hands. She stood up raging, scowling at me heavily. She was poised with the tool, ready to strike me with it.

"Yo, I swear, Chanel, if you hit me with that fuckin' iron, I'm gonna kill your ass up in this bitch."

She didn't care for my threats and threw the object at me heatedly, I ducked just in time, and the thing crashed into the wall behind me. I was even more pissed off. Before I could get my footing, Chanel charged at me. She was ready for war.

She yelled, "Get the fuck out of my house! Get the fuck out, nigga! I hate you! I fuckin' hate you!"

We fought. Chanel hit me with a few things, and I bloodied her lip and gave her a black eye. It became a battle in her bedroom. Chanel was a fighter. Nigga or bitch, she could bring the pain, and she wasn't going down without a fight. But the fighting woke up the kids, and my daughter was crying and screaming, and her son was crying louder.

Urban Love Is 175

"Daddy, stop. Stop it, Daddy," my daughter yelled out.

The room became a mess, torn apart, and things were spewed about as if a hurricane had hit it. I soon heard her mother yell at me, "I'm callin' the fuckin' police. You put your fuckin' hands on my fuckin' daughter, nigga!"

That was all I needed to hear. I quickly got dressed and hurried out of the bedroom, flew down the stairs, and went out the door. The side of my face ached from where Chanel hit me with a broomstick and then the house phone. Some blood trickled from my bottom lip, and it felt like old times between us. But I had to hurry out of there. I couldn't afford to go back to jail—not tonight, not ever!

A few days after my fight with Chanel, I expected police to show up at my mother's door and take me into custody. I was nervous. I couldn't lie. I fucked up. I let my anger get the best of me, and things got carried away. But I was a jealous man. I hated to see my baby mama with somebody else. She was my woman, and I didn't want to share her with anyone.

After three days without Chanel, I felt lonely. She was always my ride-or-die bitch, and although it wasn't our first fight and probably wouldn't be our last, I couldn't get enough of that girl.

But as if on cue, my pager went off. I didn't recognize the number. I called it back, and I was shocked. It was Monica paging me. It had been two weeks since I saw her, and I would be lying if I didn't say that I yearned to see her again.

"Ash, you awake?" she asked me.

"Yeah, what's up? You miss me?" I joked.

"Don't flatter yourself," she replied.

I wondered why she was calling me. "Is my son okay?" I asked.

"He's fine. I'm calling to see if you were interested in a job."

"Maybe. What kind of job?"

"My husband knows this guy in Brooklyn who does bodywork on cars, and he put in a good word about you."

"Why would he do that?"

"Because he cares, despite that you don't. He wants to see my son's father turn out okay," she said.

"Oh. A'ight," I uttered faintly.

"But the manager there is looking for new guys to work part-time. It's good pay with decent hours. I can give you the number and the address if you like."

"Yeah, I guess," I said to her halfheartedly.

She gave me the information, and I jotted it down. But I wondered if a job was the only reason why she was calling me.

"I want you to clean up your act," she said.

"Clean up my act? What do you mean by that?"

"Like I don't know you, Ash. You're probably out here running the streets and fucking everything that moves."

"Oh, so you know me now," I replied with resentment. "Please. You don't know me, Monica."

"Tell it to someone who wasn't with you for two years."

I sighed. "Whatever. Maybe if you and I got back together, I wouldn't be out here like that."

"I'm not that person anymore, Ash, that naive little girl you took advantage of."

"You think I took advantage of you?"

"You did."

"What? You was in love with me."

"The keyword is 'was,' and that was a long time ago," she protested.

"Yeah, your life is good now, right? You forgot about your past 'cause you married a college professor, you're living in an expensive brownstone, and you got some other nigga taking care of my son," I griped.

"His name is Patrick."

"Yeah, whatever! Do you love him?"

"What kind of question is that? I'm married, right?"

"Yeah, but do you love him?"

I swore I heard hesitation over the phone, and then she replied, "Yes, I do."

I had my doubts. I loved Monica, and I wouldn't hesitate to proclaim it.

"Listen, I called to help you find a job, not for you to intervene with my personal life," she scolded slightly.

"I'm sorry. I just wanted to talk."

"We have nothing to talk about except for your son."

"How's he doin'?"

"He's doing fine."

"I wanna come by and see him again."

"We can arrange something," she said.

Her attitude toward me was direct and brief. She didn't want to linger on anything personal. Seven years went by, and it felt like we were strangers again. I hated that feeling.

"So are you going for the interview tomorrow morning?"

"I'll think about it."

"No, I need a yes or no answer from you. I don't want you wasting my husband's time with your bullshit. He called in this favor for you, and you can't embarrass him."

A favor for me. The man married the woman I loved the most, and he was trying to do me a favor.

"I'll go if you come with me," I said.

"This is your life, not mine. Don't play games, Ash. You need to move on and do something with yourself. I did."

"Oh, that's cold."

"You know what? I don't even know why we're wasting our time. I'm just going to tell them that you're not interested."

"I'll go!" I blurted out.

"Don't embarrass my husband, Ash."

"I won't."

"Remember, the place is in Park Slope, on Third Avenue, between Sixth and Seventh Streets. It's called UV Repairs, and the manager's name is Jim Jackson. I'll call him today and tell him to expect you tomorrow before ten a.m."

"A'ight."

I wanted our conversation to linger, but Monica had different plans.

Once again, she repeated, "Please don't embarrass him, Ash. My husband went through a lot to look out for you when he didn't have to. But he's that kind of guy."

"My husband." "My husband." I was tired of hearing about her husband. Fuck her husband!

Before she hung up on me, I had to ask, "Monica, do you ever think about us?"

"No. That was a different chapter in my life," she replied coldly. "Goodbye, Ash."

She made it clear to me that she didn't want to reminisce about us. I did. Of all the girls I'd been with, Monica was remarkable, and Chanel was number two. She was a good woman, a good mother, and a great fuck.

After my talk with Monica, I spent most of the day smoking weed and in the house. I hoped this job didn't have a mandatory drug test.

It was early morning, and I was leaving the house. I took a gypsy cab to the subway and got on the F train to Brooklyn. I had to deal with rush hour and people.

A job in a mechanic repair shop. I started to have second thoughts. But all I had to do was show up and meet with this Jackson guy. I was doing this because of Monica. I wasn't a nine-to-five type of guy, but I wanted to impress my baby mother.

I got off the F train at Park Slope, Brooklyn, and followed the crowd toward the elevated subway exit. I walked two blocks on Fourth Avenue, clad in a red and white Enyce suit and a pair of white Nike Uptowns, and my dreads looked fresh. I didn't wear the traditional tie, shirt, and shoes for this job interview. I came being myself.

I soon reached my destination, and I hesitated at the gate. The job wasn't that needed. I wasn't desperate to find work. My moms gave me cash when needed, and I had ladies looking out for me.

The repair shop looked like a repair shop, with banged-up and smashed-up vehicles scattered everywhere. The area was mostly stained with grease or oil spots, and men who wore dirty, filthy blue coveralls were working on cars. And the job was in the industrial part of town.

"You looking for something, son?" this man asked me.

He looked like he worked there.

"Yeah, I'm looking for Jim Jackson."

"Jimmy's in his office. You go through there, through the garage, make a left, and his office is right there," he directed.

"A'ight, thanks," I said.

I walked past the mess of cars that cluttered the place and into the garage. Inside the garage, you heard nothing but tools and machinery going off as mechanics worked on various vehicles. It was deafening inside. I was surprised that these niggas could listen to themselves think. They even had the nerve to have a radio playing rap. I noticed a few guys staring at me as I walked by them. But I paid them no mind and continued along.

When I came close to Jim Jackson's office, this shorty caught my eye. She must have been his secretary or something. We locked eyes for a moment. She was on the phone, staring up at me while she was talking to whoever was on the phone. She gave me a quick smile and then averted her eyes. Shorty had brown skin and chinky brown eyes, and she sported her hair in a short bob style. She had a nice figure. And she had on this tight white T-shirt, and I couldn't see her from the waist down because she was sitting behind her desk. But I knew she had a body.

"You here for Mr. Jackson?" she asked, hanging up the phone and finally directing her full attention over to me.

"Yeah," I said.

"What, you here for a job?"

"Why you need to know? You're hiring me?" I good-humoredly replied.

She sucked her teeth. "You ain't gotta get all sarcastic. I was just asking."

"He here?"

"I'll let him know you're here to see him. What's your name?" she asked.

I saw her eyes catching an attitude with me. "Ash."

"That's your real name, Ash? That's what people call you?"

"You don't need to know my real name."

"Why not? You hiding something?"

Off the bat, she was a headache, but I liked her. She appeared to have this spunky type of attitude toward me.

"I got a two o'clock appointment with him."

"I'll let him know that there's a Mr. Ash here to see him."

"It's Kirkland."

"Excuse me?"

"My real name is Kirkland."

"Oh. Okay, Kirkland."

"You're making fun of my name?"

"No. It's cute," she replied.

She contacted Mr. Jackson over the intercom like we were in some lavish corporate building like a multimillion-dollar company. It was nothing but a filthy, smelly junkyard where they repaired cars.

"Okay," I heard her say. "He'll see you. Just go right in."

"Thank you."

"You're welcome," she said, sounding short with me.

Our eyes quickly locked together as I started to head into his office. I chuckled slightly. Maybe it wouldn't be so bad working here after all.

I walked into Jim Jackson's office, and it was a mess, cluttered with paperwork and files from his desk to the floor. There were even car parts scattered everywhere. What looked like day-old coffee sat on the window ledge, and his chairs looked like they needed some tough upholstery. Shit, it just looked like he needed new fuckin' chairs and a new office.

"You must be Kirkland, Patrick's friend?" he greeted me, shaking my hand.

I wasn't his friend. He was some fool married to my baby mama.

"Yeah," I replied dryly.

He was Black. I kind of figured he would be, with the name Jim Jackson and all. He was stout, dressed in blue jeans and a T-shirt, like he would be in a suit and tie working here. His hair was low cut, he had razor bumps underneath his chin, and he had big bug eyes. *Not quite the ladies' man.*

"So," he started, taking a seat in this big, tattered leather chair behind his cluttered desk, and then he gestured for me to do the same. "Have you ever worked on cars before?"

"Honestly, nah."

"Um, okay. Well, the job pays $8.25 an hour, and it's only six-hour shifts, Tuesday through Saturday. Your hours would be seven to one or one to seven. And you'll mostly be doing minor work, like buffing down and washing cars, or banging out dents. None of the major stuff yet," he said.

Damn, he was offering me a job just like that. He wasn't even going to do a background check. Shit.

"So what do you think? We do need the help. As you can see, we are swamped with cars."

"Yeah, I'll take the job," I told him.

But the only reason I took the job was that cutie he had sitting outside his office. I wanted to get with that, and I thought the best way was to start working here. It gave me a better chance with her. Other than that, I would have told him to kiss my ass. I wasn't desperate like that. But I was going to do it for a minute, probably until I fucked shorty, and then I thought I might quit.

"Good. You can start next week. Tuesday good with you?"

"Yeah. I'll be here at seven o'clock in the morning, right?"

"You got it."

We both stood up and shook hands. *Fuckin' pushover.* I'd come up here and probably run this shop. I figured these guys in here was soft. But at least I had something to work on Tuesday when I come to work—new pussy.

I stepped out of his office, and I saw shorty glance up at me.

"So you got fired before you even got hired?" she joked.

"Much you know up in here. I start Tuesday," I told her.

"Oh. We'll see."

"Oh, you don't want me up in here?" I said.

"I ain't saying that. But you don't look like the type who can hold down a nine-to-five like that."

"For your information, I'm not working nine to five. I'm working seven to one. Get it right."

"Whatever! Part-time, ooh, now you're making money," she said, mocking me.

"Yo, is your mouth always this fuckin' smart? Word! I'm gonna have to put that attitude in check."

"What, you are talking like you're my man now?"

"Shit, if I was—"

"But you ain't," she quickly cut me off.

"Please don't sweat a nigga now, 'cause you know I'm soon to be your coworker up in this bitch."

"Please. I don't like men with dreads anyway," she said.

I laughed. The first sign to let you know that a woman is interested in you is if she acts like she isn't interested.

"I'm too pretty for you."

"Whatever," she said, then rolled her eyes at me and turned her head.

"See you Tuesday, love."

I started to walk out. I then heard her voice call out something to me.

"Um, Kirkland, Ash, whatever you like to be called, a little advice. When you come in here on Tuesday, try not to be looking so stylish. Wear something less expensive and stylish because you will be getting your hands dirty, okay?"

"Yeah, I guess I'll go shopping where you get your clothes at," I quipped.

"Okay, then you'll be looking silly, and you ain't funny."

"You know I am. That's why you're smiling."

"Just leave."

God, I wanted to fuck her. She was turning me the fuck on. There was just something about her that I loved. Maybe it was her attitude and her fuckin' mouth, and she was fuckin' gorgeous.

I left the shop and went to the nearest McDonald's for a quick bite to eat. I laughed at myself. I was a working man now.

Chapter Seventeen

Sophia

What is love, it's when you tell it to her again and again; I love you, because those three words will always feel fresh coming from you . . .

The last place I should have been after having an argument with Terrance was at Eric's home. But I needed to escape, and I needed someone to talk to. I was looking for comfort. Unfortunately, that talk and comfort exceedingly turned into something else. And Eric took me to a place that only my husband should have been taking me. But I didn't want Terrance. He was something old, and I wanted a sober experience from a new kind of lover. And I found myself sliding into infidelity.

From the waist down, I was naked, my legs spread and wrapped around Eric's head and his face between my thighs as he licked and sucked me adeptly. He had my body tingling. He tasted me like I was ice cream on a summer day to him, strawberry and chocolate mixed into his mouth. He molested my clit and buried his tongue deep into me. It caused my legs to quiver and my fists to clench the bedsheets beneath me. I was afraid if I let go, I would be sucked into his vortex of ecstasy and held captive by him absolutely and endlessly. My back arched, and my mouth opened wide with a pleasurable moan echoing like surround sound.

"Oh, God. Ooooh, shit," I moaned. "Damn. Oh, shit!"

He swallowed up my pussy.

He was treating me like something special, and I was enjoying him too much. I didn't want him to stop. I blocked out my marriage and my family, and tonight I became a single woman for him. I didn't want to think about my husband at all. I closed my eyes tightly and allowed him to enjoy me. I came correct for him, completely shaved and waxed and smelling like a rose garden. He made my butt cheeks clench and my body squirm. At the rate he was going, I was about to cover his face with plenty of juices. He was going to make me squirt again. I'd never squirted before, and it was an extraordinary feeling.

Eric was naked as he ate me out. His dick was hard and big. I told myself that we were not having sex, simply oral. He initiated it, and I didn't put up too much resistance. I wanted to wait until my husband and I were separated before having sex with anyone. But at this point, it looked like I was about to contradict myself. My pussy was throbbing, and he was making it unbearable to deny what my body needed.

Twenty-five minutes was spent of him going downtown on me, and finally he came up for air, wiped my juices from his mouth, and asked, "You want me to get a condom?"

He left me breathless and spent. Shit, if his oral sex was that good, I could only imagine what the dick would feel like.

A part of me wanted to continue this later—no sex, but I was profoundly yearning to feel him inside me. I wanted it sooner rather than later. In fact, I wanted him right now. I came several times, yet my pussy was still throbbing. Why let a good erection go to waste?

He looked at me, waiting for my reply, and I nodded yes. He smiled and removed himself from the bed, went into his drawer, and removed a latex condom from it. I had butterflies in my stomach. In the past seven years, the only man I'd been with was Terrance. Now another man was about to enter me, and part of me was ambivalent. Was this right? It was feeling like it. I was nervous, though.

I got comfortable on my back and had my legs spread and was ready to give him my most treasured gift—inside of me. My attention was transfixed on his every movement. He came toward me. His penis was dangling and swinging in front of him impressively. He tore open the Magnum package and smoothly rolled the latex back against his thick and long growth. There was no room for slack. I had to admit that he was much larger than my husband. Would I be able to handle him? I was about to find out.

He mounted me slowly. I was nervous. This was it. It'd been three weeks since we'd met, and already I was giving him some pussy. But I made my husband wait nearly three months for it.

Funny thing though, I could count the men I'd been with on one hand—three, including Terrance. I lost my virginity a year before I met my husband. His name was Michael, and he was five years my senior. We had a brief thing. After Michael, there was Dennis. He was a one-night stand. Finally, Terrance. Now Eric was going to become my fourth.

Gently, Eric entered me, opening me up below like a good book. My legs quivered against him as I felt every inch of him gradually penetrating me. Eric made sure to take his time with me. I guessed he read my apprehension and saw the look in my eyes.

"I got you," he whispered to me.

Already, his dick felt like it was concrete inside of me. I felt him in my stomach. He coolly started to thrust, trying to find his rhythm inside of me. I moaned. I grabbed hold of his lean, muscular, and chocolate frame and closed my eyes. Our bodies became passionately entwined in the missionary position. We kissed fervently, and he fucked me vigorously.

I moaned, "Ooooh, God. Mmm. Mmm."

There was definitely no turning back now. Eric quickly found his rhythm with me. Nearly nine inches of hard dick thrust in and out of me as he made my eyes roll into the back of my head. I had my legs up vertically and spread around him, quivering against him, and my manicured nails attacked his skin. I couldn't help it. I had to leave marks on him. The dick was vicious. It crowded my pussy—no vacancy here.

From missionary to doggie style, I was like a ragdoll to him with my legs spread and tits flopping around as he fucked me from behind, ass up and my face down. He played with my clit and gave me the business, making me come instantly. I had so many orgasms with him that I lost count.

My body was weakening. I wanted him to come already. He definitely had stamina. He was like the Energizer Bunny. He kept going and going. I had to finally say, "Please, baby, come for me already."

"You want me to come?" he taunted.

"Yes." My pussy wasn't going to hold out any longer.

We fucked everywhere in the room, and he twisted me into every position. It was the most incredible sex. And then I finally heard those words from him. "I'm gonna come!"

"Yes, come! Come!" I hollered.

And after a few hard, repetitive thrusts inside of me, I felt his body jerk against me and react to what my pussy did for him. I felt his massive erection pulsating in between my walls. I could feel his semen filling the condom completely. I knew it was a huge load. If it was released into me, he might have gotten me pregnant. And that was the last thing I needed.

Subsequently, we both were breathing heavily. It felt like an intense workout.

"That was special," I said.

"Special?"

"Yes, it was great."

My body felt like it had been massaged in a thousand different places. My pussy felt complete. I was very much satisfied. It felt like a thirst had been quenched after going thirsty for months.

The unique part was that he pulled me into his arms and held me lovingly. We nestled, my head against his chest with his arms around me and our feet touching. Our bodies were covered in slight perspiration. I closed my eyes and found myself falling asleep in his soothing grasp.

But that tender moment between us was soon interrupted by my cell phone ringing.

"Is that you?" Eric said.

"I think so."

I removed myself from his arms and went to answer my phone. It was already late, going past midnight, and the caller ID indicated that it was my husband calling. I sighed and hesitated to answer the call. There was some wild guilt swimming inside of me. I was still a married woman.

"Hello?" I answered softly.

"Sophia, where the fuck is you?" he shouted and cursed abruptly.

"Don't yell at me, Terrance. I'll be home soon."

"Home from where?"

"I'm with Yasmin. I needed to talk to her about something," I lied to him.

"I hope you ain't telling that bitch our business."

"Don't be nasty. We're just talking, and I'll be home soon," I said.

"You know what? Fuck it. Stay the night where you at. I don't give a fuck!" he yelled. "You dumb bitch!"

He hung up. I was stunned by his words, his disrespect. He was upset, and I became a cheater and a liar. But for him to call me a dumb bitch, those were words that lingered and upset me.

"Is everything okay?" Eric asked me.

"Yeah. I'm fine."

"So that was him? Your husband?"

I nodded.

"Why don't you come back to bed?" he said.

"No. I have to go."

"You can stay the night. I would like that," he said.

"I would love to, Eric, but I still have a family, and I need to go home to them. Especially my daughter."

He sighed deeply and replied, "I understand."

I started to collect my things from the floor, and I began to get dressed. Eric remained in bed, watching me dress. I would have liked nothing better than to stay the night and enjoy his company, but playtime was over for the night. It was back to my reality.

Before my exit, he hugged and kissed me good night. It was a lingering and passionate kiss, a kiss that got me aroused again. It was hard to pull myself away from him, but I needed to, and I did.

"I gotta go," I said with a warm smile.

He chuckled. "I'm gonna miss you."

"I'll call you," I said.

"You better."

I left his place feeling alleviated. I was 25 years old, and I wanted to live again. I wanted to live life fully. I wanted to have some fun. With Terrance, I was starting to feel like an old maid. Life was becoming redundant doing the same shit and feeling the same way. I didn't know, maybe I wanted to become someone's whore, have good sex, party with my friends, and feel young again. I didn't want to be anyone's wife anymore.

I arrived home twenty minutes after my husband's phone call. The house was dark and quiet. But I knew my husband would be awake and waiting for me. It felt like stepping onto the battleground, knowing what was coming. But I was armed and ready.

I walked into the bedroom to find Terrance sitting in the chair near the bed watching TV. Immediately, we looked at each other, and it wasn't a good look. It was a look of disdain. He didn't say anything to me. He averted his eyes and looked back at the television.

"You don't have anything to say? You're not gonna apologize to me?" I said. He'd cursed and yelled at me, and he called me a dumb bitch. I was highly offended by it.

"For fucking what?" he spat my way.

"You called me a dumb bitch," I exclaimed.

"And? You think I'm stupid? You should be home at a decent hour instead of out there fucking whoever," he griped heatedly.

"Fuck you!" I retorted. "You're a childish and stupid asshole, nigga! And as for your dumb bitch, I'll show you a dumb bitch!"

"You are a fuckin' liar. That's what you are!" he yelled at me. "You wasn't over at no damn Yasmin's house. Be fuckin' real, bitch." He leaped from the chair and charged my way with an intense scowl and some tougher words.

"What, you're stalking me now?"

"I'm not stupid, Sophia!"

"Nobody said you were."

"You are a fuckin' dumb bitch. Fuck you! You fuckin' cunt!" he screamed madly at me.

He angrily pushed his way by me, almost knocking me down to the floor. He stormed down the hallway and went into the bathroom. He slammed the door. I was in awe. He'd pushed me aggressively, cursed at me, and called me a dumb bitch again, followed by a cunt, and I wasn't about to take that shit. I charged down the hallway after him and banged and kicked on the door. I demanded he open it up. He wasn't opening the door. I cursed and yelled, and I called him every despicable name I could think of. I threatened him with violence and more.

"Fuck you, cunt!" he cursed at me from behind the door, shielding himself from my wrath.

I charged back into the bedroom and was ready to destroy whatever he owned. It was on. But turning around to see Zaire standing in the doorway prevented me from being that bitch. Our fighting had woken her up.

"Mommy, why are you and Daddy screaming at each other?" she said in her tiny voice.

I quickly went to her. "Oh, baby, we're sorry. We woke you up?"

She nodded.

I hugged her into my arms. I sighed deeply. It was terrible to fight with your spouse, but it felt a lot more terrible to do it in front of a child.

"Everything's okay, baby. Mommy and Daddy just had a small disagreement. C'mon, let's get you back to bed."

I picked her up into my arms and carried her back to her bedroom. Zaire was the one who calmed me down and saved the bedroom from absolute destruction. Because I was about to create serious havoc.

I tucked her back into bed, talked to her for a moment, made her say her prayers, and kissed her good night. I left her bedroom and exhaled. I went back to the bathroom and knocked gently.

"Terrance, how long are you going to be in there?"

I received no answer from him at all, so I knocked again harder. "Terrance? We really need to talk."

He remained silent—nothing. He was being childish. He was ignoring me, and I hated to be ignored. But I kept my calm and tried to be the grown-up in the situation.

"Terrance, I understand that you're upset, but I gotta pee. Can you come outside so we can talk?"

There was still no response from him.

"Terrance," I desperately called out again. "Please, I gotta pee."

I banged and banged on the door. I started doing the bathroom dance. I was about to kick down the door. He was making me upset again.

"Terrance, I swear, if you don't open this door in another minute, I'm gonna kick this door down, and believe me, you're going to see the true bitch in me tonight."

After my threatening remark, I heard the bathroom door finally being unlocked. Terrance walked by me, uttering, "Fuck you!"

I glared at him. He didn't know when to stop. But looking into his eyes, I saw that he'd been crying. He was upset. I went into the bathroom to pee, and he went back into the bedroom. When I was done using the toilet, Terrance was fully dressed and leaving.

"Where are you going?" I said.

"Why the fuck do you care? Go, do you."

"Terrance, we need to talk seriously."

"I don't feel like talking. Go talk with Yasmin or whatever nigga you was with tonight. I'm fuckin' done!"

He left the house abruptly. I was left standing there, feeling guilty. I wanted to tell him, but how? And would he go out there and do something stupid, like have sex with someone else? Tit for tat?

I heard his truck peeling out of the driveway. He was gone. I went into my bedroom and sat at the foot of my bed. I sat there in silence, pondering. This marriage was definitely over. *So where do we go from here? What next?* I felt a multitude of emotions, and out of nowhere, the massive tears came.

Earlier, I'd had another man inside of me, and my husband was falling apart. He was angry. He was hurt. And I didn't have the treatment for his pain, although I knew what his treatment should be. I knew what he wanted, and that was me, but I didn't want him to have me because I didn't want him.

This wasn't the end of our bickering. I knew more problems were coming our way. I felt that it was going to get much worse before things got better. Because I wanted to see Eric again.

Chapter Eighteen

Terrance

Love is . . . when you turned her heart into your home, and you make her your wife because she's priceless . . .

The morning sun percolating brightly through the windows of my truck had woken me up. I had fallen asleep in the front seat, with my head slumped against the window. I was parked near the park, and I slept underneath the stars. I yawned and looked around me. It was still early and warm, looking like it was going to be another peaceful and warm summer day. But I felt no peace in my life. I had cried myself to sleep last night.

Last night with Sophia was tragic. I had to leave the house urgently before I did something that I was going to regret. I knew she was lying to me. Something wasn't right. But it was still hard for me to swallow that she wanted a divorce. That pain I felt, knowing she was with someone else and wasn't in love with me anymore, felt never-ending. I couldn't get rid of it, and seeing her always made it worse. I was emotional. I was an absolute wreck.

God, why was this happening to me?

I wanted to get as far away from Sophia as possible.

I was the best man I could be for my wife. When she became pregnant, I didn't miss one appointment with her at the ob-gyn. I would sit there with her and wait for what felt like forever. I was there for her first sonogram and making runs to different stores late at night to satisfy her cravings. And I was there through the mood swings and the nervous temperament. And when she went into labor, I was there right by her side, doing my best to appease her and hold her hand, and help her get through the birth of our first child.

I was there through her unemployment and funerals, and her ups and downs, and whatever life tossed our way. Seven years together, and I was always there—until now, when she didn't want me there anymore. When she didn't need me. And now she wanted to throw me away, for what or who? Would they be there like me?

I should've stayed single. Maybe Ash was on to something.

I had to go somewhere and talk to someone. I knew I couldn't ride around in my truck all day. I picked up my phone and dialed Devin's number. Though we had our differences sometimes, we understood each other.

It was early Saturday morning, and I figured he would still be in bed. His cell phone went to voicemail, but his home phone was the one he finally answered.

I heard a faint, "Hello?"

"Devin, hey."

"Terrance, what's up? You know what time it is?"

"I just need to talk," I said.

"What's going on?"

"I had another fight with Sophia. I think she's fucking someone else," I admitted.

"What?"

"I'm fucked up, man. I slept in my truck all night," I said.

"Come to my house. We'll talk," he said.

I sighed. "A'ight. I'll be there in about a half hour."

"Just be safe, Terrance, and come see me. I'm here, bro."

I ended the call. Immediately, I had second thoughts about going to see Devin. I dealt with intense and raw emotions, and I didn't want to start crying in front of him, looking like a bitch. But something inside of me told me to go and talk and let it all out. And Devin was the right person for that. He wasn't Ash with his womanizing and negativity. He wasn't my cousin, who probably had more issues with his woman than myself.

I arrived at his place an hour later, and Devin stepped out of his front door and greeted me at the sidewalk. He embraced me with a dap and a brotherly hug and said, "Talk to me, Terrance. I'm here for you, man. What's going on?" He showed genuine concern for my problems with Sophia.

I took a deep breath. I looked at him. The tears had been wiped away, and I did my best to keep any more from leaving my eyes.

"It's my wife. She doesn't want me anymore. She wants a divorce. She doesn't fuckin' love me. And I'm sure she's having an affair. I know she's having sex with someone else. I can feel that shit. C'mon, I'm not stupid. The coming home late, the lying to me and using her friend as an alibi. I could see it in her face. She's hiding something or someone!" I proclaimed with heavy emotions.

"And are you a hundred percent sure about this? You have proof she's having an affair?" he had the nerve to ask. "You know what they say—it's not what you know, but what you can prove."

I looked at him and irately replied, "I know my wife, Devin!"

"I know you do. I'm sorry," he said.

"Man, I don't have physical proof, but I feel it. I love this woman, Devin, and she's tearing me apart right now. She fucked me up."

I could feel the tears welling inside my eyes as I spoke about Sophia. I wanted to stop the flood, but it was becoming difficult. "I don't know what I would do if I found out that she's having sex with someone else. What if she's leaving me for him? Is this nigga the reason why she's ending our marriage?" I continued with grief in my voice. Now the tears started to trickle down my face. I couldn't hold them back any longer.

"There's got to be a way for you and her to talk and work something out," he said.

"I've been trying everything, Devin. I'm willing to do anything to fix us, but how can I fix us when she wants us to continue to be broken?" I proclaimed. "I swear, if I ever see this nigga—"

"Terrance, don't be foolish. Don't go out there and do anything stupid. Despite everything that's going on with your wife, you still have a daughter to raise and support," he said.

"I know, but this bitch got me going crazy right now."

"Don't let her, man. Don't let this situation control you. You control it, Terrance. I know Sophia. She's a good woman. Maybe she's just going through something."

"What, cheating on me? Fuckin' some other nigga?" I uttered angrily.

"Look, how long have we known each other? Since we were kids. We've been through a lot, all of us. Terrance, just take a deep breath, and take this one day at a time. You keep fighting for your marriage, for your woman, and live your life, man. This is just some turbulence while you're on your way to paradise, man. Every flight to paradise isn't going to be smooth, but at least you're flying first class," he said.

"What? What the fuck are you talking about?" I said.

He laughed. "I know, I'm just saying marriage isn't easy. And I go through it with my girl too."

"What, Ms. Perfect?" I managed to joke.

He chuckled. "Yeah, I know. Being in love is tricky. I mean, the best feeling in the world is being loved back by the person you love. But look, you're a good man, and she's going to realize that. Hopefully, she'll come to her senses and come running right back to you."

"I don't know, Devin," I said, being pessimistic.

"I sound like Ash saying this, but do you, Terrance. Enjoy your life and your daughter, go to work, and try not to think about her so much. And when I mean do you, I don't mean become a whore and start having sex with everything that moves. That will make things even worse. But go mingle and have yourself a good time. I mean some clean, honest fun. Hey, go to church even. That might work."

I took a deep breath and replied, "I need a drink, Devin."

He smiled. "I got you."

I followed him into his home. He had a beautiful place—three bedrooms and two bathrooms, a front porch, and a sizable backyard. Devin worked hard for everything he owned. He was into sales and managed several high-end clothing stores in Brooklyn and Queens. The man knew how to save money and invest, understanding the stock market, too. He had always been frugal with his earnings.

We sat in the living room, and he poured me a glass of Grey Goose. We sat back and continued to talk. I threw back the liquor and wanted more.

Out of the four of us, we always figured Devin would be the first to get married, but I beat him to the punch. He didn't sleep around. He wasn't a player or whoremonger. He always had a girlfriend and was continuously in a monogamous relationship. In our eyes, the man was a saint. I didn't think he ever cheated on any of his girlfriends. Devin respected females while the three of us had our fair share of fun and games with the girls.

That morning, Devin and I reminisced about old times. We joked and drank, and he was helping me get my mind off my troubles with my wife. He was a good friend, one of the best.

I asked where Danielle was, and he said she was with friends.

I spent the entire morning and early afternoon with Devin. He asked me a question, and he wanted to know if I ever cheated on my wife. Our conversation was deep into relationships and our spouses, and as a friend, I admitted yes—twice.

"The first time it happened, it was during our first year of marriage," I said, sighing. "She was an old girlfriend of mine. I was going through problems with my marriage and ran into Megan by chance on the street. We talked and connected again, and one thing turned into another, and I ended up in a motel room with her. The affair lasted a month, and Megan left town."

"And the second time?" Devin asked.

Reflecting, I realized it was stupid. "The second time was with a girl named Bree. She was friends with my cousin's sidepiece who Trey was heavily involved with. Trey brought me along with him one day, and I met Bree. We went on a double date, dinner, movies, et cetera. Bree and I talked. We laughed, and we joked, and afterward we fucked, more than once, for a few months. And then things just faded between us. She went her way, and I went mine."

"We make mistakes," said Devin.

"But not those kinds of mistakes anymore," I replied.

Early in my marriage I was a fool. I made mistakes. I was weak and stupid, and I realized that cheating on my wife was idiotic. I didn't want to lose the best thing that ever happened to me. So I got my shit right, and I'd been faithful to my wife since then. I loved her too much to lose her.

But then the thought came, *what goes around comes around, right?* So did Sophia have the right to cheat on me too?

Chapter Nineteen

Devin

*Love . . . love is when your actions toward her
are louder than just the words you speak because
your character is no lie, and your love is no lie . . .*

Danielle was cooking for me again, and I appreciated
it. A woman cooking for her man and vice versa was one
of the beauties of a healthy relationship.

I stepped inside my home after a hard day of work.
Retail sales were down quarterly at one of the Brooklyn
stores. They were thinking about closing it, which meant
laying off nearly a dozen employees. And I would be the
one to give the employees the bad news unfortunately.
Some had worked there for years, and I'd grown close
with them all.

So all I wanted to do was sit back, relax, and be with
my woman. Danielle had Mary J. Blige playing in the
house. "My Life" was one of Danielle's favorite songs.

*Life can be only what you make it
When you're feelin' down
You should never fake it
Say what's on your mind*

I loosened my tie, unbuttoned my shirt, and called out for Danielle. She came from the kitchen, looking eye-catching to me in her plain gray sweats and a wife-beater tied up in a knot against her stomach.

I went into the bedroom to change clothes. I got comfortable in a pair of jeans, house slippers, and a T-shirt. I came back out to the living room, and Danielle had dinner already set at the table.

I could get used to living like this. But then I started thinking about Terrance and his problems with his wife. What if Danielle just started feeling like that one day? What if all of a sudden, she just came to me and hit me with the most awful news that she wasn't in love with me anymore? It would be crushing news.

For seven years, Terrance and his wife have been together. It was shocking news of an impending divorce. I always felt that marriage was supposed to last forever. It made me nervous to know that sometimes it didn't. But what could you do but still love and have faith? And I had faith. And I wasn't scared to show my affection. I told my woman every day that I loved her. And I would do anything for her. But then I would ask myself, *is she truly happy with me?*

We'd been together for a year now, and that one year had been perfect. I had some of the best moments of my life with Danielle. Yes, there were arguments and disagreements, but not too many. In fact, I could count on one hand how many arguments we had. I spent the majority of my time with her, and our lives were comfortable. I was in my mid-twenties, and already I owned my own home, drove a nice car, and managed stores in two boroughs. On top of that, I had a lovely woman I was engaged to.

"What you thinking about, baby?" Danielle asked, coming toward the table.

"Huh? Oh, nothing," I replied.

"It looks like something's bothering you."

"Nah. I was just thinking about Terrance."

"What about Terrance?"

I sighed. "You know, him and Sophia might be getting a divorce."

"What, are you serious?" she said. She sat down at the table.

"Yeah, I don't understand."

"Why? What happened? He cheated on her, right?"

"No. And why is it when a couple breaks up, it's always because the man had to cheat or do something wrong? It could be the woman too."

"But they looked so good together, and they have the cutest little girl."

"Yeah, I know. But it's Sophia. She doesn't want to be with him anymore."

"Are you serious? She just came out and said that to him?"

"Yes."

"Damn, who would have ever thought?"

"You can never tell with women," I commented.

"Never tell what with women?" Danielle said, raising her eyebrow.

"I mean, their true feelings deep inside, how they really feel. Sometimes it's just so hard to tell what y'all want."

"So what are you saying about us, Devin? We've been together for a year. We're engaged. So you're telling me that I might just up and leave you like that, so quickly? You should know me better than that."

"I know, baby. But sometimes y'all can be so complex."

"And men can't be?"

"All I'm saying is that a woman can be in love one day, and then she'll wake up one morning and be out of love the next."

"No, sweetie, it takes time for that to happen. I'm not just going to wake up one day and fall out of love with somebody. Sophia was probably feeling that way about him for a while now. Maybe she just couldn't bring herself to tell her husband so soon the way she was feeling."

"But why? Terrance is a great guy. I grew up with him. He's a good man. I feel Sophia is making a big mistake."

"Well, that's her life and her mistake. Personally, I feel the girl got married too young. How old was she when she married him, seventeen?"

"No, eighteen, right before her nineteenth birthday."

"See, and now she's probably regretting getting married so young, feeling trapped. She probably just wants to live out her life and be that free woman again. I know if I got married at eighteen, I'd probably be unhappy too. And then there's having Zaire. That's the problem with couples today. They want to get married so young and don't comprehend what a marriage is all about. They think it is all about sex and love. But marriage is an understanding. It's about having responsibilities and devotion, and it's about respect and being honest with each other. People rush into getting married and yet don't know the person. People get fascinated with that man or woman over a few months, and they think that's love."

"I'm glad you feel that way," I said.

"I do."

"So we're more than just an infatuation? This is the real thing, right? You love me?"

"Do you even have to ask me that?"

"No. I'm sorry."

"You know I love you so much. And you know that I want to be with you. We've been together for a year and have been living together for five months now. I do want to marry you and become your wife."

I smiled. I got up out of my seat, went over to Danielle, and gave her the most passionate kiss. "I love you, baby."

"I love you too. Now finish eating your dinner before it gets cold."

"Yes, ma'am."

Danielle was indeed a wonderful woman. I was just blessed to be with such a charismatic and promising woman like her. I was so lucky to even meet a woman like her.

I met Danielle most strangely. It was because of a minor fender bender on Merrick Boulevard. I was stopped at a light, listening to the radio, and waiting for the red light to change. It was raining. I was on my way to work, and I was running late. I suddenly felt my car jerk forward. Someone had hit me from the back.

"Shit!" I had cursed. It was turning out to be a bad day.

I turned around and saw that this green Accord had smacked into me. I was about to have some words with the driver of the car. I had stepped out into the rain and approached the Accord. That was when Danielle stepped out, apologizing, "I am so sorry. My brakes slipped and it's raining."

I was stunned. She was beautiful. She had on this long-sleeved, long denim dress and a pair of black knee-high boots. Her sinuous hair fell over her shoulders, and the rain cascaded off her beautiful brown skin.

"It's okay," I had said, gazing at her beauty. "You okay?"

"I'm fine," she had replied. "I don't know what happened. My car just suddenly started sliding after I pressed on the brakes."

"Don't worry about it."

I saw my back bumper. It was nothing major, just some minor damage, nothing a body shop couldn't fix.

"As long as you're okay, I'm okay," I had said to her. I was in complete awe over her.

She had smiled. That was good. "You're so nice. I appreciate you not blowing this out of proportion."

"That's me."

"Look, at least let me give you something for the slight damages," she had said. She began reaching into her purse.

"No, no. I got it covered. I mean, I was planning on getting a new car anyway."

"You sure? Because it's nothing to me. I feel I owe you that."

"You know, you're truly a beautiful woman. I'm sure many people always tell you that every day."

She had smiled. "Are you coming on to me?"

"No. I just thought that I should let you know."

"Thank you."

"Look, I'm already late for work. And it's kind of silly for the both of us to be out in the rain like this. Would you like to get something to eat, or coffee maybe? My treat."

She looked at me, hesitating. "No. I can't."

"Okay." It was the only thing I could say, feeling rejected. "Well, at least I tried."

"See, you didn't let me finish," she'd suddenly said. "No, I can't let it be your treat when I'm the one who ran into you. It's on me."

I'd smiled.

There was a quaint diner a few miles away, and we went there and had breakfast and coffee together. We talked and we laughed. And we really got to know each other. She was single, and I was available, and I felt that the accident was fate. And fortunately, we didn't just have breakfast together. We ended up spending the rest of the day together. For me, it was love at first sight. We became inseparable after that.

After dinner, I helped Danielle with the dishes and thanked her for the meal, always showing her my appreciation.

"Devin, since we're always honest with each other, I have to tell you something," she suddenly mentioned.

"What is it?" I asked. I felt nervous unexpectedly. What did she want to be honest about? Whatever Sophia had, I hoped Danielle wasn't catching it too.

She leaned against the kitchen counter, staring at me and wiping her hands at the same time. "I ran into an old friend today," she said.

"I see."

"Actually, it was an old boyfriend of mine from back when I was living in Chicago. And he's in town on business for a few weeks, and he asked me if I could show him around town while he's here visiting."

"Oh. And how long is he in town again?"

"He told me three weeks."

"So long?"

"He's here on business. He's in the music business, basically a concert and club promoter."

Damn, what was a man to do in this kind of situation? Should I tell her okay, or put my foot down and say, "Hell no?" I didn't like the idea of those two being alone together. Suddenly, I felt some trouble in paradise.

"Baby, how do you feel about this?" she said.

"You know what? I'm cool with it. I trust you. At least you were honest about it and didn't go sneaking behind my back."

"You're the best, baby," she said.

She gave me an intimate hug and a lingering kiss. Was she excited about seeing an old boyfriend or that I trusted her? Anyway, we continued to talk. I wanted to know some more about this ex-boyfriend. She wasn't shy in explaining her past with him to me. They had a thing for six months, and it didn't work out. She ended it.

"I promise you, baby, we're just friends, nothing else. He went his way, and I went my way. And now I'm here with you, about to become your wife. So you have nothing to worry about," she proclaimed wholeheartedly.

I believed her and I trusted her. She had a good thing at home. I loved her unconditionally, and I was faithful, so there wasn't any reason for her to step outside our relationship. I treated her like a black Nubian queen twenty-four seven. And if that wasn't enough for a woman to love you, then I didn't know what else there was to do.

Chapter Twenty

Trey

Love is when she becomes your primary, your best friend, your woman, your mate, your muse; your art . . .

Trisha kept saying that we were over, but I didn't believe her. She ignored my calls, but I continued to call her. I was relentless. She was still mad, but I wasn't giving up on us. I made a mistake. It happens. It had been over a week since my mishap with her, and I did miss her. But I figured all Trisha needed was more time alone, and I would give it to her. She would soon come to her senses and miss me too, like she always did. But still, I was a man with needs.

To pass the time, I spent it with Chica. I'd promised to take her out to the movies and dinner, and later we would get a motel room. She was excited. I was nonchalant.

I arrived at her place sometime after 9:00 p.m. It was another balmy summer night, and I was looking forward to the sex rather than my date with Chica. She perpetually begged me to take her out somewhere, and I relented.

I was expected to meet her grandmother for the first time, and I was uneasy about it. I didn't do well with parents and grandparents. There was always something about me that the elders didn't like. But I shook off the trepidation and was ready to put on my game face. Why was I nervous anyway? It wasn't like I was marrying the girl.

Dressed in Sean John jeans, a stylish T-shirt, and a pair of new white Uptowns, I approached her front door and pushed the doorbell. It rang and I waited. First, someone looked through the blinds at the side window, and then I heard the door unlocking. It opened, and there was Chica's grandmother glaring at me and already sizing me up.

"I guess you're here for my granddaughter!" she said.

"Yes, ma'am," I replied politely.

"And how long have you known my granddaughter?" she asked.

"About a month." I still stood on the front porch, not invited inside yet, even though I'd been inside dozens of times.

"I see that you're a pretty boy," she continued.

"Nah, I'm just your average Joe."

"Are you trying to get smart?"

"No, ma'am."

"I don't like pretty boys. All of y'all are too damn sneaky," she stated. "All of y'all got a girl or two on the side probably pregnant or even married. You married?"

I chuckled. "No."

"You find that funny, young man?"

"No, ma'am."

"You have any children?"

"No, ma'am."

Chica's grandmother was a hard woman. She was asking me twenty questions. It felt like I was in an interrogation room and she was ready to lock me up for a crime—probably fornication. I was there to see Chica, and our relationship wasn't serious.

Her grandmother was a hefty woman with a round face and gray strands of hair on her head. She had on a sundress and looked intimidating. But that didn't get to me.

"What do you see in my granddaughter?" she asked.

"I like her," I answered.

"I don't trust any of y'all young pretty boys. What is your name anyway?"

"Trey."

"And, Trey, how old are you?"

"I'm twenty-seven."

"Well, you know my granddaughter just turned nine-teen, and she's still a baby."

"I understand that, ma'am."

"And if she comes back pregnant, I'm gonna twist your dick off and shove it someplace not nice," she threatened.

Wow. This lady was serious. Yo, I wanted to laugh, but knowing her, she probably would have slammed the door in my face. So I just stood there and kept my composure.

"I'm serious, you little nigga. I know what all of y'all young guys are about—pussy. And that's what you see in my granddaughter, right? I don't play that shit, you hear me, dammit? I love Chica, and I don't want to see her hurt because some young, horny nigga can't keep his fuckin' dick in his pants. And you look like that type of nigga! I've been around, Trey. You can't fool this old lady."

I thought grandmothers were supposed to be sweet, innocent, and loving. Nah, not Chica's grandmother. She was acting like a straight-up OG or something.

"Trey, Chica better not come back pregnant. Because if she does, God help you, I'll take this shotgun right here," she said, suddenly producing a shotgun in her hands and threatening me with it, "and I'll blow that pretty face of yours right off . . . and your dick!"

I was fuckin' speechless.

"Okay," I muttered.

Where the hell was Chica?

She continued to glare at me. I saw that she was a serious old woman.

"Grandma, leave him alone," I heard Chica say.

Thank God.

"Hey, Trey."

"What's up, Chica."

Chica loomed from behind her angry, bitter grandmother, smiling and looking outright sexy. *Damn.* She had on a tight, sexy leather miniskirt, sandals, and this tight white T-shirt that stopped just above her belly button.

"You ready?" she asked, stepping outside.

"Yeah."

"Bye, Grandma," Chica said to her grandmother, following me to my car.

I turned around and saw her grandmother still glaring at me, and then she hoisted up the shotgun and did her best to intimidate me. It was working.

"Chica baby, don't you think that outfit is a little too much for a date? You need to wear something more conservative," her grandmother hollered.

"I'm okay, Grandma. I'm comfortable," Chica hollered back.

When we got inside the car, I asked Chica, "Yo, what's up with your grandmother?"

"Don't worry about her. She just be trippin' like that since I'm her youngest granddaughter."

"But the shotgun? Who does she think she is? Rambo in a dress?"

"Trey, she doesn't even keep that gun loaded," Chica informed me.

I shook my head, sighing, and then started up the car.

"So what's good for the night?" Chica asked.

"You know. We talked about it over the phone," I said.

"Well, you know what? I don't want to even see a movie tonight. I just straight want some dick," Chica uttered candidly.

"Wow. What about food?" I asked.

"We can get it to go."

"What are you, a nympho or something?"

"I just like to fuck. You see how my grandmother gets down. A girl can't have any fun with her being on my back. I'm tired of sneaking around. So let's just get a room for the night and do our thang."

"Damn, you need a sex toy or something?"

"Trey, I know you ain't frontin'. What, my grandmother got to you?"

"Not even."

"So c'mon. I wanna fuck you."

I had no other words. I just drove away.

I drove to a twenty-four-hour fast-food joint where we could pick up a meal and head straight for the motel. Chica was ready to suck my dick in the front seat. That was how eager for sex she was. She massaged my crotch and was lusting for me. But as I was about to help her unzip my jeans, my cell phone rang. The caller ID said that it was Trisha. Damn, she had terrible timing. I ignored her call. It was a hard choice, but Chica had my undivided attention. She finally unzipped me and pulled it out and shoved my dick into her mouth. I was quickly thrust into absolute bliss.

"Oh, shit," I moaned.

I kept control of the car and drove toward the motel. It was a few miles away, but Chica almost had me wanting to pull over and enjoy her oral skills outright. But soon after, my cell phone rang again, and it was Trisha. I sighed. Chica stopped what she was doing and lifted her face from my lap.

"Everything okay?" she asked me.

"Yeah, everything's cool."

"Who keeps calling you?"

"Listen, I'm not worried about her, so you don't need to worry about her. We're separated," I said.

"Oh, really? Y'all are?"

I nodded.

That bit of news made her day. She was excited. She smiled widely and then leaned her face back into my lap, opened wide, and continued what she started—sucking my dick. I was thrust back into total bliss.

My cell phone went off a third time, and it was Trisha calling. I knew that I was wrong for not answering her calls. She probably wanted to work things out between us and have a lengthy talk, but sex had consumed me or possessed me, and the only thing I could think about was an orgasm. So to make sure there weren't any more interruptions, I turned off my phone and focused on Chica giving me head, and arriving at the motel.

The motel on Rockaway Boulevard was seedy, cheap, and vile. And for $50, I had the room for several hours. It was plenty of time to get into some nasty and lewd shit with Chica. I had a bottle of champagne, some condoms, and some uncontrollable hormones.

The moment I stepped into the room, she was all over me, undressing me, kissing me wildly, and ready to suck my dick again. I didn't even get a chance to close the door. She immediately came out of her clothes and made herself comfortable on the bed. The only thing missing was me on top of her. So I undressed, tore open a condom, and joined her on the bed. We kissed fervently and became tangled up on the bed.

"Fuck me, Trey," she said.

"Hold on, let me put on the condom."

"Nah, fuck that. I wanna feel that dick raw."

"Nah, Chica. I've been doing that too many times already."

"Trey, please, just this one time again. We ain't got to worry about my grandmother or anybody else. We got all night, baby. Just fuck me raw this one time, and then we can use the condom. Just pull out when you feel yourself about to bust."

I hated myself. I must not have cared about myself, because if I did, I wouldn't be doing what I was doing and having sex with Chica without any protection. But once again, I felt her glorious insides without a condom, and I closed my eyes and let her pussy take control of me.

We were in the missionary position, and she groaned and moaned underneath me. I felt her nails against my back, and her legs tightened around me. It was good for both of us.

"Ooooh, fuck me, Trey," she cried out.

Suddenly, there she was—her grandmother. I could see her standing over me with the shotgun pointed at me. She was heated and angry. She was ready to kill me. And a deep, frightening chill came over me. I stopped mid-thrust, quickly pulled out, and released myself from Chica's soft and tender hold.

"Trey, what happened? Why did you stop?" Chica asked. "C'mon, I wanna come."

"I can't do this, Chica," I said.

"You can't do what? You forgot how to fuck me?"

"This needs to end."

"Stop playin' wit' me, nigga, and come get this pussy. Finish what you started."

"I can't do this with you anymore, Chica," I said heartily.

I didn't know what it was, but it felt like I suddenly had a conscience and felt guilty being with Chica. Trisha had called me three times tonight. I knew she wanted to reconcile, and I ignored her calls because I was rushing to have sex with a girl I didn't see a future with.

"Don't tell me that my grandmother got you scared. You pussy now? Huh? You scared to take this pussy? A sixty-year-old woman gonna tell you what to do? What, you a fuckin' faggot now?" she hollered.

She was upset. I got it. But looking at Chica and knowing I ignored Trisha to be with her, it was foul. And her grandmother did embed something into me that led me to have second thoughts. I didn't know what it was.

I went into the bathroom to get a moment away from Chica. She was cursing and hollering at me, carrying on like a madwoman. I looked at my image and said to myself, "Trey, you wilding out, having sex with this girl without a condom."

I feared an unwanted pregnancy, or worse. The thought suddenly crept up on me like the flu. Trisha was a great woman, and I was dogging her out with this stupid young girl. I couldn't help myself though. I loved sex. I loved a beautiful woman. I had a weakness, but I had to conquer this weakness before it started to destroy me.

I splashed some water on my face and exited the bathroom. Chica was still livid. I began to get dressed. I needed to go for a walk and call Trisha back. I needed to apologize to her, too.

I grabbed my phone and said, "I'll be back. I need some air."

"Fuck you!" she cursed at me. "You're fuckin' weak, Trey! Fuck you!"

I ignored her and left the room. I trotted down the hallway, through the lobby, and outside to smoke a cigarette. I took a few pulls from the Newport, lingered underneath the stars, and enjoyed the warm night. I tried to call Trisha, but her phone was ringing and going to her voicemail. I called again with the same results. After the fourth time, I figured she was upset with me too and not answering my calls. I finished off my cigarette and flicked it away.

Fuck it. I wanted to see Trisha in person, and that meant taking Chica back home.

I entered the room again. Chica was dressed. When she saw me, she smirked. "You changed your mind?" she said.

"Nah, I'm taking you back home."

"You ain't shit, nigga, fo' real." She was upset again.

"It was fun while it lasted, right?"

"Fuck you," she yelled. "But guess what." Chica looked at me like she had a nasty little secret to reveal. I wasn't in the mood for her shit. But she continued with, "I spoke to your girl."

"What?" I had no idea what she was talking about. Who did she speak to? "What are you talking about?"

"Trisha. I called her," she said.

Impossible! How could she call Trisha when I had my cell phone the entire time? I didn't believe her. She was lying. But then she confirmed it by saying, "While you were in the bathroom, I took down her number and called her from the motel we're in."

My eyes went wide with shock.

"You wanna play games? I can play games too," she barked. "I told her everything."

"Are you fuckin' crazy?" I screamed heatedly.

I went after her. I was ready to wrap my hands around her neck and squeeze—squeeze hard and tight until I saw her eyes protrude from her face. She leaped from the bed, knowing that I was going to throw her out the window. She found the situation funny. She ran from me and locked herself in the bathroom. I banged and kicked on the door. If I had to, I was going to knock the door off the hinges and murder this bitch.

"Fuck you, Trey! Don't get mad. You got what you deserve. You shoulda finished what you started. That's why your girl is mad at you," she mocked me. "If you woulda ate pussy, then maybe I wouldn't have told her everything."

"I swear, Chica, don't come out of that bathroom," I shouted.

"What are you gonna do?" she continued to taunt me, deepening her voice and trying to sound masculine.

"I'm not fuckin' playing with you!"

"Neither am I."

Chica put me in a really tight spot with Trisha. It had to be a nightmare. I had to think, and the last thing I needed was trouble in a cheesy motel room, especially with a young girl. The damage was already done, and now it was left for me to fix it.

"Fuck you, bitch. Stay in the bathroom, and walk your ass home," I exclaimed.

I collected my things, including my car keys, and left the room. I was officially done with Chica. She was childish, and she was too many problems. I got into my Benz and started the car. I wanted to call Trisha again, but I thought against it. Tonight was the worst.

"What the fuck!" I screamed, punching the dashboard.

How in the hell did I put myself into this situation? Being stupid, that's how.

I couldn't sleep. I couldn't think straight. All I could think about was Trisha. I wanted to call her, and I did, but her phone was off and going directly to voicemail. I fucked up, and I didn't want to lose her. And I was desperate to do anything.

I left her a message. "Trisha, pick up, baby. It's me, Trey. Please answer my calls. I'm sorry, baby, and I'm missing you so much. I love you so much. Call me."

I wanted to drive to Long Island and see her in person. I was ready to get down on my knees and beg for my woman to stay with me. I messed up bad. How was I going to fix this one? Chica called her, and God knows what she told her. She said, "Everything," and that haunted me. *Everything*.

I went into the bathroom to take a piss, but when I heard my phone ringing, I damn near peed on myself, leaping from the toilet and hurrying to answer the phone. Quickly, I spoke, "Trisha?" believing it was her.

"The wrong person," Ash said.

"Oh, what's up?"

"Damn, nigga, you sound out of it. I caught you at a bad time?"

"Nah. I thought you were Trish."

"Damn, it's that serious? Don't tell me you're whipped too."

"Yo, what's up?" I asked. I wasn't in the mood for any foolishness.

"Tonight, Club Suction. I got these sisters I'm gonna meet there, and homegirl told me to bring a cute friend. So you rolling or what?"

"Nah, not tonight. I got things to do."

"C'mon, Trey, her sister is fuckin' fine. You won't regret it. This bitch is in a different category."

"I'm gonna pass tonight, Ash. I got a lot of work to do."

"Work can wait. You gotta see shorty. She models like wit' a big booty. But you a'ight, nigga?" Ash said.

"I'm good," I lied.

"So what's good for the weekend?"

"I don't know. I gotta get back with you," I replied tersely.

"You sound dry, but anyway, I'm gonna let you be. One," he said.

"One."

Our call ended, and immediately I redialed Trisha's phone. I knew that she was ignoring me. She needed to pick up, and she needed to hear my side of the story. And when I thought her cell phone was about to go to voicemail again, I unexpectedly heard, "What?" with a severe attitude.

"Trisha," I started.

"What do you want, Trey?"

"Baby, listen, let me explain—" I started.

But she quickly ran interference on my apology by exclaiming, "You know what's fucked up, Trey, is that I still love you. I do. But for some girl to call me last night and tell me everything, that you were at a motel with her and that you were ignoring my calls because you were too busy getting your dick sucked, I swear, that shit hurt me to my core. Oh, my God!"

"Trisha, I can explain."

"What is there to explain, Trey? Huh? How you gonna lie your way out of this one? The bitch called my phone, Trey! She told me a lot of shit about you and her. So what fucking lie do you gotta tell me now? What explanation? And the fact that her name was Chica, the same bitch you lied to me about."

"Trisha, when I met her, we were separated," I said.

"So when we got back together, you continued fucking her," she retorted.

"It ain't even like that," I sadly defended myself.

"You caught, nigga, with your fuckin' pants down and your dick in the next bitch. I swear, Trey, everybody told me not to fuck with you, but I was calling you last night to see you because I missed you. I wanted us to work. And now you got me out here looking so fucking stupid!"

I could hear her crying through the phone. She was extremely upset. And I never heard Trisha this mad and upset before.

"Baby, I'm sorry," I cried out sincerely. "I fucked up! I know I fucked up. But I promise you, I'm changing, baby, for us. I swear to you, I'm done."

"You're changing and you're done. How many times have I heard that before? And the fact that I had to find out by some cheap-ass bitch who called my phone." She chuckled, but it wasn't a good laugh. "I swear if she didn't call me, you would have kept on doing it."

The thing that hurt the most for me was that I found my way, and I didn't want to have sex with Chica anymore. I finally came to my senses, and this was all before I knew she had called Trisha. But karma was a bitch, and it came biting me back with the teeth of Jaws.

"Trisha—"

"Fuck you, Trey! And I mean that shit for real. Do not call me or come see me. I'm so done with you. So you can go and continue to fuck your whores because you won't be touching me anymore. You're a liar and a cheater! And I don't need a nigga like you in my life. I can find better!"

She ended the call abruptly. I was speechless, and I was crushed and seriously hurt. I just dropped into a chair and felt deflated. What I wanted to do was break Chica's neck in so many different places. But I couldn't get mad at her, because she didn't control me. I did what I wanted to do. And as a result of that, I might have lost the best thing that ever happened to me.

Chapter Twenty-one

Sophia

Love is . . . when the two of y'all become a single soul dwelling in two bodies, y'all become so close that it becomes hard to tell y'all apart . . .

"What's on your mind, girl?" Yasmin asked me. We were standing by the bar and getting our party and drink on at this club called Vertigo located in lower Manhattan.

"Nothing," I responded. I took a sip of my wine.

"Too many cuties up in here for your mind to be wandering," she said.

I chuckled. "I know."

It was a Saturday night, and Yasmin and I looked like real divas up in the place. Yasmin was in her red sleeveless mock neck and a tight, short miniskirt stopping at mid-thigh. She had on a pair of knee-high boots and looked like a cute, sexy Puerto Rican slut.

I was wearing an animal-print miniskirt with a black top and sandals. It was something simple but still sexy, showing off my beautiful legs and figure.

"How are things going between you and Terrance?" she asked.

I sighed. "Ain't nothing changed."

"What about Eric?"

"I'm still seeing him."

Yasmin already knew that I'd had sex with Eric. I filled her in on all the details about our previous night together. She was my alibi.

"Excuse me, ladies, but can I buy both of y'all a drink?" this guy asked out of the blue. He was a handsome guy with his bald head and dark skin.

Yasmin and I smiled.

"The both of you are looking too sexy. Y'all here with anybody?" he asked.

"That's our business," Yasmin said.

"Oh, it's like that, beautiful?"

"If I want it to be," she continued to flirt.

"I see."

"You're too cute," she said to him. "I'll have a cranberry and Hennessy.'"

"What about you, beautiful?" he asked me.

"I'm okay," I said.

"You sure?"

I nodded.

He bought Yasmin her drink, and they started to talk at the bar. I simply stood around, staring at the crowd and occasionally at those two. I figured Yasmin was about to get her groove on with him. He was fine. And he was dressed nicely, too.

I needed some time to myself, a break from all the drama. Terrance and I were at war with each other. The night he walked out on me after he'd locked himself in the bathroom, I cried for hours. Things were difficult. I didn't want it to be hard, but he was making it so.

I gulped down my wine and noticed that I was receiving quite a lot of attention from the opposite sex. They looked my way, smiled, and flirted. I smiled and then faced the opposite way. I didn't want the attention, not tonight. I had all the attention I needed from Eric. I thought about him a lot. And I missed him.

Hours passed. The night went well. I danced, I drank, and I mingled with a few cute men, and my mind was on Eric. If I could see him tonight and get mine, it would definitely scal the deal on a beautiful evening.

It was soon three in the morning, and I was ready to leave. Yasmin was still with the man who bought her drinks earlier. His name was Desman, and he was in real estate. They hit it off quite well. She danced with him, and I could see him in her life. She was single, beautiful, and friendly. I wanted to see my best friend happy with someone.

I watched the two of them dance closely on the dance floor. Desman had his arms around my friend intimately, and it looked like the two of them had known each other forever. Yasmin was all smiles. She was definitely having a better time than I was.

I tapped Yasmin on her shoulder and asked, "You ready to go? Because I am."

"Already?" she replied.

"It's late. It's three in the morning," I said.

"Oh, wow. Damn, time flies when you're having fun."

"It does."

"Y'all need a ride home?" Desman asked us.

"No, I'm driving," Yasmin said.

"Okay."

"But you can pass me your number, handsome," Yasmin said.

He smiled, and the two of them exchanged numbers. "Call me," he told her.

"I will."

We left the club giggling and a bit tipsy. We walked to Yasmin's car arm in arm, supporting each other. She couldn't stop talking about Desman.

"I'm gonna call him, girl," she said.

"You'd better. He was cute," I said.

We finally made it to her Honda Civic. Yasmin slid her tipsy self into the driver's seat, and I got into the passenger seat.

"Girl, you okay to drive?" I asked her.

"I'm perfect. I'm not drunk," she said.

She started the car, and the moment she drove off, I found myself dozing off. And it seemed like we teleported to my place. The next thing I knew, Yasmin was nudging my side and saying, "Sophia, we're here."

I opened my eyes, and I was home already. "Damn, girl, what did you do, Mach 3?" I joked.

"I got a heavy foot, okay?" she joked. "Is Terrance home?"

"I don't know. I hope not," I said. I didn't see his Expedition in the driveway. I opened the door and slowly climbed out of her car. "See you, girl," I said.

"Bye, bitch," she joked.

I entered my quiet home and started to undress. I simply wanted to climb into my bed and sleep forever. Terrance wasn't home, thank God, and Zaire was at his mother's for the night.

I got a few hours of sleep until I heard movement inside the house. I knew it was Terrance coming home from wherever he was. I heard him enter the bedroom, and I felt him flop down on the bed next to me.

Surprisingly, he started to rub my leg and touch me closely.

"Terrance, you okay?" I asked him.

"I'm fine. I miss you," he said.

I felt his touch moving upward, going for my ass and other places, and I slightly moved away from his wandering hands. I rolled my eyes, knowing he wanted sex. And I could smell the alcohol on his breath. "You were drinking."

"I'm not drunk," he said defensively.

His body moved closer to mine, his arms were around me, and he started to touch me sexually again. He grabbed my ass and cupped my breast roughly, and then he kissed the back of my neck. I felt his erection behind me.

"Terrance, it's not that type of party," I said quickly. I drew away, trying to elude his lecherous hands and unwanted kisses against me.

"What the fuck? I can't get any pussy now?" he said.

"No!" I exclaimed.

I turned around, and we locked eyes, and he was someplace else. His pupils were intensely fixated on me, and his look quickly scared me. It was like he wasn't taking no for an answer.

"You're my fuckin' wife, and you are denying a husband his needs," he cried out.

Once again, he forced himself on top of me. He physically grabbed my legs and desperately tried to pry them open.

"Terrance, stop! Stop it," I shouted.

"You're my fuckin' wife. You owe this to me. You gonna fuck another man and not me, your fucking husband?" he hollered.

I wrestled with him on the bed, but he was stronger than me and outweighed me by at least a hundred pounds. He was determined to put himself inside of me. I resisted a great deal, but his hands and the weight of him was profoundly against me. He kissed me wildly, and he wasn't letting up. I could feel his strength compressing me against the bed and simultaneously trying to undress me quickly. He tore my panties off and hurriedly shimmed out of his jeans, all while controlling me with what felt like dozens of hands on top of me. He was soon naked below, and he maneuvered between my thighs. One hand was around my neck, and the other pinned my arm against the bed. I wasn't going anywhere. And he was hurting me.

"Terrance, stop it! Get the fuck off me!" I screamed.

He wasn't listening, and he wasn't stopping at all. His aggressive physical attack continued. His erection was nearing my treasure, and I had to embrace myself for impact.

"I can't live without you, Sophia," he growled into my ear. "I fuckin' need you, baby. I need this."

"Terrance, no. Stop it, please."

But my cries fell on deaf ears, and he hastily thrust his erection inside of me. It was grueling and uncomfortable. My body jolted from the rough entry, and he started to fuck me with brute force. My body was pinned underneath him, my arms were restrained, and he continued to slam into me. He panted and grunted in my ear, so close against me and enjoying me thoroughly. It was rape. After a moment of him inside of me, I relented and let him have his way.

"You're my fucking wife! My wife!" he cried out emotionally.

I was emotional. As Terrance was on top of me, doing his thing, a few tears escaped from my eyes and trickled down my face. My body was physically being violated with him on top of me, penetrating me with callous might. He fucked me like a possessed fiend. I felt nothing but pain and rape. I went dead inside at the audacity of him taking something that didn't belong to him. Yes, we were married, but I still had a choice. And he took that from me.

It felt like forever as he plundered my body and tried to kiss me intimately. I didn't kiss him back. He already had me below.

"I'm coming!" he announced.

I lay there still underneath him, like a log, like his prostitute, and soon I felt him coming inside of me. He shuddered and grunted on top of me, releasing his seed into me, and then he collapsed against me, spent. He huffed and looked completely satisfied, and I wanted him off of me. I wanted him gone, and I continued to cry. I was hurt, and I was raped by him—my husband.

While still on top of me, he said, "I'm sorry, Sophia. I can't let another man come in between us that easily. Until death does us part, remember? I can't live without you. I love you too much."

I didn't say anything. Silence overcame me. He finally was out of me, and he rolled off of me, lying on his side near me. He looked at me intently and asked, "You love me, right?"

I couldn't even look at him. I rapidly removed myself from the bed and hurried into the bathroom. I was in tears. I was wounded by what he just did to me. *Oh, my God. My own husband raped me. Is that even possible?*

Chapter Twenty-two

Ash

The dick got her lookin' so crazy, hair is disarray cuz the sex is gettn' ugly . . .

It was Sunday night, and I didn't have anything to do. I was with Chanel and my daughter most of the weekend. We made up. We had reconciled from our fight the other day, subsequently having some of the best sex we'd ever had. But I still had an issue with Keith, her son's father. I was a jealous man, and I didn't want him anywhere near Chanel and my daughter. Whatever interest my baby mama had in him, I wanted it gone completely.

It was a dull moment. Trey was going through something, Devin was with his fiancée like always, but Terrance was down for whatever. It was a beautiful night, and I wanted to get into something.

Terrance and I both decided to hit the strip club. He was upset with his wife and wanted to get away. It got even better—he expressed to me that he strongly felt his wife was cheating on him. I said that we could get payback one of two ways: either he could go fuck another bitch, or he could find out who Sophia was seeing and beat that fool down. I was down for whatever.

Terrance opted for the first choice—to enjoy the strip club and free his mind from the drama.

It was getting late, and before the strip club, I had to swing by Chanel's place to collect some money from her. She'd promised me $100. She had gotten her unemployment check a few days ago, and she wanted to look out for me.

Terrance was coming by my mom's place to pick me up soon. I got dressed, looking fabulous in my black-and-white Enyce sweatsuit and cotton white Air Force Ones. My long gold chain was swinging and gleaming, and I boasted my big-face watch. I was ready to have a good time tonight. And by eight thirty, I got a call from Terrance telling me that he was outside.

Walking out my front door, I got a page from Shannon and another page from this new girl named Cherry I'd met the other day. I hadn't spoken to Shannon since she cursed me out and let me take the bus home. I smiled. They were mad one day and craving you the next.

I slid into the passenger seat of my friend's Expedition, greeted him with the glad hands, and hollered, "What up, my nigga? You ready for tonight?"

"No doubt," he greeted me.

"But yo, I need to stop by Chanel's place real fast and collect this money from her."

"What, are you her pimp now?" Terrance joked.

I laughed. "You know it."

We laughed.

I arrived at Chanel's place and saw Peanut standing outside. I had to holler at him. He was a cool dude, and we spoke while Terrance stayed parked and idling on the block. Afterward, I rang Chanel's doorbell and waited. It felt like it took Chanel forever to answer her door, and

I was growing impatient. I repeatedly rang her doorbell and banged on her door. Finally she swung open the door with an attitude and said, "Damn, Ash, what the fuck? Why you gotta be banging on my damn door so fuckin' hard?"

"You takin' too long," I said. "Where the money at?"

She sucked her teeth and replied, "How you know I got it?"

"Because you got paid the other day. Don't front on me now, Chanel. I'm 'bout to go out tonight."

"Who that, Terrance in that truck?" she said, looking past me. "Nice ride."

"Don't worry about who that is. Just give me my money," I said boorishly.

"You are so rude."

"Whatever!"

She started to walk back up the steps, and I followed her. Seeing that I was going upstairs with her, she turned around and said, "Where you going?"

"Upstairs," I said.

"You can't wait down here?"

"Nah, I wanna see my daughter before I leave."

"And you gonna have Terrance sitting in the truck?" she said.

"He can wait. I ain't gonna be long. What's wrong wit' you?"

"Nothing," she replied with an attitude.

She pivoted and continued to march up the stairs. But she was acting strange. And I just wanted to enjoy my night out with Terrance. And with Chanel's $100, it was going to be a much better night.

I followed Chanel and noticed that she was in a house robe and her feet were bare. Her hair looked crazy. I walked inside and saw my daughter in the kitchen seated at the table and eating cold cereal.

"Daddy," she called out, and immediately she ran to me to give me a hug and kiss.

I picked her up in my arms and hugged her lovingly. "You miss me?" I said.

She nodded. "Daddy, you stayin' the night?" my daughter said.

"Next time, sweetie. I promise."

Patrice sucked her teeth, upset with me, and Chanel went into her bedroom and closed the door behind her. I gawked at the bedroom door with my daughter still in my arms. Unexpectedly, I felt something wasn't right. It felt like Chanel was trying to hide something from me.

And then, my daughter said it all. "Daddy, how come Keith gets to stay da night, and you can't?" she said.

"What? That nigga's here?" I said, my face instantly tightening with rage.

Patrice nodded and pointed to Chanel's bedroom. I put my daughter down. "Where's your little brother?" I asked her.

"He's in Grandma's room, sleeping."

"A'ight, you go into Grandma's room too, and stay there," I told her.

She did what I said and ran into her grandmother's room. The door closed. Now I was in battle mode. I was heated. I frowned with my fists clenched and marched toward Chanel's bedroom, ready for war with whomever. And the moment I stepped up to her door, Chanel loomed from the room, closing her door with the money in her hand.

"Here," she said hastily, rushing me away.

"Who is in the bedroom, Chanel?" I said, not beating around the bush.

"What?" She was playing stupid with me.

"You heard what the fuck I said. Who you got in your bedroom?"

"Nobody, Ash. You fuckin' bugging out."

"Oh, I'm bugging, huh? Open the fuckin' door," I exclaimed.

"No! You got your money. Leave!" she spat at me.

"Nah, open the fuckin' door before I kick it open."

"Why you always starting shit? Don't you got someplace to go?" she argued.

And she stood between me and her bedroom door like a brick wall, definitely trying to prevent me from entering her room. But she wasn't going to stop me from going inside. I attempted to kick open the door, but Chanel got between me and the door and grabbed at me desperately.

"Get the fuck out, Ash!" she shouted.

She wrestled with me, but I jerked my arm free from her grip and forcefully shoved her away from the door. Subsequently, I kicked the door opened and charged into the bedroom like a blast of hell. I at once saw Keith in the room looking at me. He was shirtless and glaring at me with both shock and ferocity.

"What the fuck, nigga? Get the fuck outta here!" Keith growled at me.

"What, muthafucka?" I shouted.

"Chanel's my bitch! You a washed-up convict, muthafucka," he insulted me. "Yeah, she and your daughter be calling me Daddy!"

His words further uncoiled me with rage. I was fuming. He was in the same room where my daughter slept, and Chanel was fucking him. She lied to me. I wanted to tear him apart and then knock Chanel's head off. And he put my daughter's name in his mouth. I'd heard enough.

So I charged at him like a bull seeing red and crashed into him. My fist slammed into the side of his face, and he quickly countered with a punch to my right jaw. I wasn't fazed by it. Immediately, we came to blows inside the bedroom, rooted in violence. I smashed my elbow into the side of his skull and physically grabbed him into a chokehold. He resisted. He was stronger than I expected, but I was fiercer. I punched him again and again. We slammed into the wall, and his knuckles sank into my ribs.

"Oomph," I bellowed.

I attacked him with everything I had, striking him with a series of blows to his face and body. He couldn't hold on and physically grabbed me with everything he had. Tussling, we toppled to the floor and broke up furniture. I quickly rebounded and kicked him in the mouth so hard that I knocked out two of his teeth. His mouth spewed blood, and he was severely hurt and defeated. But I wasn't done with him yet. I wanted to take his damn head off.

"What now, nigga?" I heatedly shouted. My breathing was heavy, and I was injured too.

Chanel ran into the room and came in between us. She was upset and cursing at me. For some reason, she was defending him. "Get out of here, Ash!" she screamed at me.

Keith's mouth was coated with blood. He glared at me with disdain. He wanted more, and I was ready to give him some more. Chanel was between us, angry and furious with me. She tried to protect him, but it was a feeble attempt, and seeing that, my blood boiled. I charged at him, ready to give him more than a bloody mouth. I wanted to put him in the hospital. And quickly,

I thumped him in the eye and felt the side of his face collapse. He couldn't handle me and quickly realized that after his face started to look like hamburger meat.

"Huh, nigga? What, muthafucka?" I growled in his face.

He managed to break away from my intense grip and flee the room, retreating. The chaos brought my daughter and her grandmother out of the other bedroom. My daughter was crying and shocked.

"Daddy, stop it. Daddy! No!" Patrice cried at me.

But I was possessed. Something came over me. I smelled blood, and I wanted more of it.

I chased after Keith. He ran out of the house shirtless and a bloody mess. He stumbled down the front steps, and I was right behind him. The hood was about to get a front-row seat to an ass whooping. Keith got to the sidewalk and fell over. I was a second away from being on top of him again and implementing more damage when Terrance suddenly came in between us and quickly grabbed me.

"Yo. Yo, what the fuck, Ash?" he uttered quickly.

"Get off me, T. I'ma kill this nigga," I shouted.

A small crowd started to gather around us. Keith was a bloody mess, and I was seething.

"Yo, Ash, you just got home," Terrance said. "Fuck him. You did enough."

Terrance was my voice of reason. Keith got the message. Keith picked himself up from the concrete, and he still had some fire in him. He had enough fire that he started to spew out threats.

"Yo, it's on! Watch your back, nigga. Watch your fuckin' back!"

"Nigga, what? You throwing threats?" I shouted. "Come back around here and I'm gonna body ya ass."

He ran off, and Chanel stood near her front door. My anger homed in on her. She was next. I started for her, but Terrance quickly grabbed me.

"Yo, get the fuck off me!" I yelled his way.

"Nah! Chill out," he yelled back.

"She was fuckin' that nigga in her crib and around my daughter," I shouted.

"Fuck you!" Chanel shouted.

"What, bitch?"

"I'ma get you fucked up, nigga!" Chanel threatened me.

"You gonna what, bitch?"

I tried to charge at her again, but Terrance continued to hold me back. He was determined not to let me spill that bitch across the ground. "C'mon, we gotta go," Terrance said.

"Let him go, Terrance. Fuck him," Chanel said.

I was seeing red. And I felt like a magnet being pulled toward her with rage. But as a friend, Terrance did his best to prevent me from making the biggest mistake of my life. If he had let me go, I definitely would have seen jail tonight.

Chanel and I continued to curse and throw threats at each other, but it was from Terrance's truck. She threatened to have me jumped, and I threatened to break her neck. I was fuming. I couldn't rest. Terrance drove away, and I wanted to put my fist through his window.

"Just calm down," he said.

It almost felt impossible to calm down when the woman I loved was fucking some clown-ass nigga.

"Yo, just take me back home," I said.

"You sure?"

"Yeah, I'm sure."

He drove me home as I asked. And when I arrived there, I changed my mind. I wanted to continue with our night at the strip club, but I needed to change clothes. I ran into the house with Terrance waiting in his truck, changed clothes, and removed my pistol from underneath my mattress. It was a Glock 19, and I should have brought it with me in the first place. I stuffed it into my waistband after changing outfits and rejoined Terrance outside.

"We good?" he asked me.

"Yeah, we good."

It was my first day of work. My alarm went off at five in the morning. I hadn't been up this early since my days in prison. But what inspired me to go to work was thinking about that new girl I'd met during my interview. So you could say that pussy motivated me.

I didn't want to think about Chanel or my fight with Keith. Several days had passed, and the small marks on my face from the fight had healed.

I rummaged through my closet and removed a pair of black overalls and a pair of old Timberland boots for work. I styled my long dreads underneath a doo-rag, left the house, and climbed into a cab I'd called earlier. It took me to the nearest train station on Sutphin Boulevard, and I caught the F train going to Brooklyn. I was among the hundreds of passengers on the train during rush hour, and it wasn't a good feeling. But I survived the train ride into Brooklyn.

The Park Slope stop in Brooklyn came a little over an hour later. With dozens of other passengers, I departed onto the elevated train platform. I followed everyone and descended onto the street below. I showed up to work in the nick of time. UV Repairs was already loud and full of mechanics working on cars and trucks. I was the new guy on the team. I moved by the heap of cars in the front lot and into the garage.

"Wow, you're actually on time," she said to me, glancing at her watch.

"What, were you waiting for me?" I teased.

"Don't flatter yourself," she said sharply.

"So what's good wit' you?" I asked her.

"You need to start working instead of trying to flirt with me."

"I can do both."

"But don't," she said.

She was playing hard to get. But I never gave up on something that I liked. I went into Jim Jackson's office to see what he had assigned for me today. He was happy to see me there on time. It was a good start. I followed him out the door, and he introduced me to my coworkers. The majority of the guys in the shop were Latino, and a handful were black. Jackson introduced me to everyone as Kirkland, but I wanted to be called Ash, and I quickly corrected everyone.

This Puerto Rican named Jose was going to train me on the job. He was a pleasant middle-aged guy who was married with five kids. I liked him. We connected like Legos, and he started showing me the ropes. We started working on this crashed-up Chevy Impala. It had severe front-end damage. I helped Jose strip the front of the car, including the bumper, the hood, the headlights, and everything else. It was grunt work, but Jose made it bearable with his stories about his family and country and his dirty jokes. He made me laugh.

By noon I'd become a grease monkey like everyone else. My overalls and hands were stained with a hard morning's work. It was my first day of doing a real job.

We ate lunch together at this local diner a block away. We talked, and Jose informed me of the good and the bad about the job. Pretty much everyone was okay except for a few rotten apples. And Jim Jackson was an okay guy. As long as you came to work on time and did your job, he didn't bother you at all.

I asked Jose about the secretary, or whatever her job was. She'd never told me her name. But she was in charge of bookkeeping, ordering parts for vehicles, managing payroll, and other things. He told me her name was Kenya. She was a flirt with everyone in the shop. And many had tried, but none had conquered her. Of course, I was up for the challenge.

I did another hour's work, and it was my time to punch out. After my shift, I lingered around the workplace. My motive was Kenya. I wanted to know more about her.

She stood at the lot's entrance smoking a cigarette. She was pretty in her short skirt, white top, and black Nikes. It was causal, yet it was sexy.

"Haven't you heard? Smoking is bad for you," I said.

"Who are you, the surgeon general?" she quipped. She took another pull from the Newport and blew the smoke in my direction.

"Oh, so you just gonna blow smoke on me like that?"

"You can move," she said.

"You're lucky I like you."

"I'm not asking you to like me," she countered.

She continued to smoke, and I continued to try. She was on a quick break, so I had to talk fast. "How long have you been working here?" I asked her.

"Three years."

"You like it here?"

"It pays the bills."

Her replies were short with no embellishment. And she enjoyed her cigarette more than she did talking to me.

But then the questions shifted toward me, and she said, "Why are you here? You on parole? You in trouble?"

"Oh, so you judging me already? Why I gotta be on parole or in trouble?" I said.

She looked me up and down, sizing me up, and said, "I know your type—smooth hands, nice long hair, likes to dress, and you think that you're God's gift to women. You used to be a hustler."

"Nah, I'm just a squirrel tryin' to get a nut," I said.

"Yeah, I bet you are."

I laughed. She didn't.

"So where you from?" I asked her.

"Don't worry about that." She was soon finishing her cigarette.

"Damn, shorty, why you so mean?"

"I'm not mean. I just don't like people being in my business."

"I can respect that."

"Then please do."

Kenya was a piece of work. She was like a concrete wall I was trying to knock down with a spoon. I wasn't leaving a crack so far. So I had to change the tool in my hand.

"How can I get you to like me?" I said.

"Just leave me alone," she said.

"That's not happening," I replied.

"Wow, you're really an asshole."

"If an asshole is someone who goes after something he likes, then I'll be your asshole, baby," I said.

She managed to smile and chuckle. Finally, there was a minor crack in her concrete foundation. "You are relentless," she said.

"That I can be. But I think you're worth chasing."

She took her final pull from the cigarette, flicked it away, and was ready to go back to work. "It's catching me that's the problem," Kenya said.

With that said, she pivoted and walked away. I lingered and admired everything about her. From head to toe, she was right and definitely my type.

Chapter Twenty-three

Terrance

What is love . . . love can be a challenging thing, but once you start doing it right, guarantee it's something everlasting, cuz she's worth it to keep . . .

My own wife tried to accuse me of rape. Was that even possible? We were married, and I knew she was cheating on me. It truly bothered me that she was denying my needs but probably satisfying someone else's. But it seemed like the drama was everywhere, and that crazy incident with Ash was like the icing on the cake. There was too much going on, and I just wanted to escape it all. I wanted peace of mind, but that was hard to get when I was swallowed up into the storm. And I tried to drink my problems away.

I sat alone in my home with no wife and no child. It was merely me with a bottle of E&J brandy. Being alone was haunting. Hordes of emotions crowded me. I had been yearning to feel the love and affection from my wife again. I attacked her in the bedroom. I took it from her because I was hurting and horny. It was a senseless act, but damn it, it was needed at the time.

The brandy went down my throat smoothly, the bottle partially consumed. And as I drank, I gazed at old pictures of Sophia and me from our wedding day and the additional happier times we had together.

What now? Where do we go from here? Am I supposed to move out and start all over again? What about Zaire? Who will she live with? My life had been turned upside down overnight, and the thought of moving out and starting over was unbelievable.

I remained slouched in my chair and listened to R&B slow jams. Each song put me more into a funk, but this one particular song, Jermaine Jackson's "Don't Take It Personal," caught my attention. It felt like this artist was singing directly to me and trying to comfort me at the same time. The song was about a breakup. I listened to the lyrics.

> *The time has come in my life for me to move on*
> *And get on with my life, my life*
> *Oh, but I don't regret no,*
> *Every precious moment that we spent*

I listened attentively, and it was my first time ever paying attention to the song. I wiped away a few tears and downed another glass of brandy. I released a deep sigh and continued to slouch and mope.

> *Love was here, now it's gone*
> *So it's time you keep moving on*
> *Don't take it personal*
> *Take the bitter with the sweet*
> *Easy come easy go*

How couldn't I take it personally? I was married. I was in love. And how could I not see it coming? I was sucker punched from behind, knocked on my ass, and was failing to get up. And Jackson's lyrics were trying to sugarcoat a fucked-up situation and put some comfort behind a bad breakup. He sang, "No blame, no shame. It was nice, but sometimes things do change."

I didn't change. Sophia changed. And there was blame and shame, and it wasn't nice. I had a life, a wonderful life, with my family, and I thought we were having great sex and had magnificent humor. So the blindside was devastating. And I was taking it personal.

Fuck Jermaine Jackson and his song!

I downed another glass of brandy. I was looking for some escapism. I was desperately looking for something to ease this pain, if not erase it. Forced sex with Sophia the other night was like a quick high that I immediately came down from. She became furious with me, even threatened to call the cops about it. I felt she was out of her damn mind.

For an hour, I sat in my living room drinking. I wasn't drunk yet, but I was on my way there. I wanted to finish off the E&J by night's end.

The doorbell ringing was a disruption from my escapism. I didn't want to get up. I wanted to wallow in the darkness and swim in nostalgia. But whoever it was at the door was relentless. The doorbell echoed inside of my head, and it removed me from my seat with a frown. I opened the front door to find Yasmin and Zaire, rapidly forgetting she was bringing my daughter by.

"Hey, Terrance," Yasmin greeted me.

"Hey," I said.

I immediately smiled at my baby girl in Yasmin's arms. She was asleep. It was late. No matter what I was going through, she was always a delight. I stepped aside so she could come inside with my daughter.

"How long has she been asleep?"

"For about twenty minutes."

Yasmin took Zaire straight to her bedroom and placed her into her bed. She was a great godmother to our child. She was always a big help when it came to babysitting, clothes, and schooling. Whatever Zaire needed, Yasmin was there.

I sat back down in my chair and replayed the song. Why listen to it twice when I hated it? Maybe I was trying to find comfort in his words. Perhaps I was reaching for something that wasn't there.

Yasmin came out of Zaire's room. She was ready to leave, but I wanted answers. So my eyes fixated on her, and I quickly asked her, "Who is he?"

"Excuse me, Terrance?" she said.

"The nigga my wife is fucking. I know you know who it is. She tells you everything."

"Terrance . . ." she started with her excuse.

"You know who, so don't bullshit me. I need to know who my wife is leaving me for. She's lying to me. I know it," I interrupted her.

"I don't get involved with y'all relationship. You know this." She stood there, defending her friend's secret, probably justifying my wife's affair.

"I can't take this shit. I love Sophia too much to lose her," I admitted wholeheartedly, followed by a profound sigh.

"Are you going to be okay?" she said.

"Do I look like I'm gonna be okay?" I snapped at her.

She lingered near me, looking heartbroken by my words. But I didn't want her to feel sorry for me.

"What happened, Yasmin?" I blurted out. "Why doesn't she want me anymore?"

"Terrance, y'all need to talk."

"I'm trying to talk. What does she want from me?"

"Honestly, I don't know."

I poured more brown juice into my glass and continued to drink.

"Maybe you need to slow down on the liquor," she suggested.

"I'm a grown man, Yasmin, and this is my only cure for the pain she put on me," I returned edgily.

"Maybe you'll be happier without her," she had the nerve to say.

My eyes shot up at her, and my stare was cutting deep into her flesh. She couldn't take back her words. "I'm happy with her," I exclaimed.

"Look, I always felt that y'all got married too young, and a year after y'all met—"

"If you think our marriage was a mistake—"

"I'm not saying that, Terrance. But maybe the two of you should have waited. I introduced the two of you, remember?"

"We were in love. Well, at least I was."

She came closer and sat nearby, halting her departure. I guessed she felt that I needed someone to talk to. And liquor, heartbreak, slow jams, and my daughter in the next room wasn't the appropriate mixture for me to be alone.

She released a deep sigh and looked at me. "If I could change her mind, Terrance, I would. But Sophia's going through something. I don't know what it is exactly, but she has to go through it herself. Maybe a separation is for the best."

"You really feel that way?"

"Just give her some space," she suggested.

Space or separation, I found it the catalyst for divorce and for another man or woman to come into your world. It was hard to give her the space she wanted when I saw her daily. I just couldn't walk out of her life altogether, especially since we had a child together.

"You're a handsome man, Terrance. And you are a great father. Any woman would be lucky to have you in their life," she said.

"Too bad Sophia doesn't feel that way."

"She's my best friend, but I don't always agree with everything she does," Yasmin said. "Yes, we talk, but it's her life and her mistakes. I'm just a friend helping her through whatever storm she's bearing. And I don't wanna get too much in y'all business."

Yasmin was prepared to leave, but I took her by the hand and said, "Have a drink with me, Yasmin. I just need the company. I just need someone to talk to. Please."

She looked reluctant. She looked at me with some uneasiness.

"Just one drink," I pleaded slightly.

She sighed. "One drink. And I need to go."

I removed another glass from the china cabinet and poured her a half glass of brown juice. She sat near me and took a few sips. The slow jams continued to play, and Yasmin and I continued to talk.

During the conversation and a few sips later, Yasmin said to me, "Can I be honest with you, Terrance?"

"Someone needs to start being honest, because it damn sure isn't my wife," I uttered.

"I sometimes envied Sophia and what the two of y'all have or had. Watching the two of y'all together, being there for each other, I think it's what every woman wants."

"A beautiful woman like yourself, single and lonely? Why?"

"Have you seen what's out there lately? You'll understand why. And your friend, Ash, no offense, but he's the archetype of why I'm still single. He's a nightmare with an STD waiting to happen. Every year the choices become slimmer and slimmer. Today, these men are either incarcerated, uneducated, unemployed, or already married or gay."

She said a mouthful.

"Just keep your fishing line in the pond or try the sea. You'll soon come up with something nice."

"I can move from the pond to the sea and still catch the same thing," she said.

"Then change your bait."

She laughed. She finished off her glass, and I poured her another.

"You're beautiful, Yasmin, and whatever guy finally gets to snatch you up, it's gonna be one lucky dude," I proclaimed.

She smiled. "Hopefully sometime soon."

"I know plenty of dudes who would marry you right now, and I'm not including Ash," I laughed.

"Most men are scared of success and intelligence," she said.

"And those are the fools you need to stay away from. I think success and intelligence are sexy, and if a man is intimidated by that, then he's not the one."

"Tell me about it," she agreed.

"Cheers," I blurted out, lifting my glass.

"Cheers to what?"

"To our friendship, to you being a wonderful god-mother, and to the future, wherever that's leading us. Maybe down better roads."

She cheered along, and we clinked glasses. I admit I was a bit drunk. But my chatter with Yasmin was flowing, and it was helpful. I no longer was thinking about Sophia, but getting to know Yasmin better. She was a good listener and a great supporter, and I saw why she was best friends with Sophia.

"What's your ideal guy, Yasmin? Maybe I can hook you up with a friend. Shit, if I can't find love, then maybe someone can," I said.

"You have love, and you found love, Terrance. Sophia still loves you. It just a bumpy road right now."

"Please, it feels like I'm sliding down a razor and a steep mountain naked and shit, and Sophia's the one who pushed me."

She chuckled. "You're so silly. But my ideal guy is someone I can grow old with. Someone who is not afraid of commitment and will always put me first, and some-one who's not afraid to help me raise a family. I want kids."

"How many?"

"Four."

"Damn, you want close to *The Brady Bunch,*" I joked.

"I like kids."

"They're a beautiful thing," I said.

"They are. And you and Sophia are blessed to have Zaire."

I smiled. We were.

There was more drinking and more conversation, and together we finished off the bottle. It all came naturally. I found myself talking freely to her and laughing. An hour went by, and that night I learned so much about her. She spoke about Puerto Rico, where her parents were from, and her love for cooking and arts. She was in school for culinary arts. Her goals were to open her own restaurant one day and become a master chef. I found that interesting.

We locked eyes, smiled, and laughed, and then there was a moment of silence between us as we continued to lock eyes. Yasmin was stunning with green eyes and long hair. The smell of her perfume was suddenly alluring to me. There was a moment between us that made my heart beat a little faster. Her hand was against my forearm, just slightly. Her attire was simple—a skirt, blouse, and some sandals—but put together stylishly. I peered down at her long legs crossed in my direction.

The look we both shared toward one another was a chancy gaze, one that could lead to vulnerable moments. And once the lengthy conversation stopped, the lingering admiration started. Somehow, a spark ignited, and it was leading to fireworks. Maybe it was the alcohol, and perhaps it wasn't. A sudden desire for her stirred inside of me. It came out of nowhere, or maybe it had been there simmering and slumbering for some time now.

I leaned closer first. And Yasmin right away followed my action. Our mouths were only a breath away from each other. And then, like magnets, our lips came together compactly and connected. A passionate kiss ensued. I embraced her intimately as my tongue arrowed into her mouth, and our tongues grappled. There was an intense minute or so of passion before she finally pulled herself away from me and looked winded.

"What just happened?" she blurted out, looking shocked.

"I don't know," I said, but I'd enjoyed it.

That minute of kissing had me intensely aroused. Yasmin leaped from her seat and rushed toward the door. It was like she committed murder and wanted to flee frantically from the crime scene.

"Yasmin," I called out.

She stopped and pivoted. We stared at each other. I knew she didn't want to leave, because she wouldn't have stopped so quickly if she did. I went toward her, and I took her hand into mine. I wanted whatever had started to continue.

"We can't do this," she apprehensively expressed.

"Why not?" I said.

"Sophia's my best friend. It's not right."

But it felt right. Now I had both her hands in mine, and I stared at Yasmin intently. I was looking for some reassurance in her gaze. She resisted somewhat, but it wasn't relentlessly. Her look was of yearning and acceptance hidden behind guilt and remorse.

I didn't say a word and pressed my lips against hers again. For a split second, there was opposition, a feeble tug away from me, but it was fast consumed by lust and desire. And another passionate kiss followed. I lifted Yasmin into my arms, with her legs straddling me. I carried her off into our bedroom, the same place where Sophia and I had sex plenty of times and a place that was supposed to be forbidden from infidelity.

Our clothes peeled off, decorating the floor, my mouth latched on to her nipples, and my hands were exploring her body. Every part of her was soft, like a peach. I rapidly thrust myself inside of her, and she immediately fastened against me with a satisfying groan and sucked on the side of my neck. Her glorious insides instantaneously addicted me as I spewed out, "Oh, shit!"

Her breathing was brisk as she continued to moan and say my name. She panted with each thrust.

She didn't need to announce that she was coming. Her body and eyes clearly spoke to me. We transitioned from missionary to her riding me. I cupped her breasts and palmed her ass. Our lips continued to lock, and our bodies were entwining underneath the sheets completely.

And when she finally came, I felt her. Her breathing intensified, and the rapid movement of her body underneath me, her legs quivering, felt like a bell ringing. And right after her orgasm, I too relieved myself inside of her, panting heavily against her smile.

Subsequently, it felt so surreal. We lingered on the bedsheets, nestled intimately. With Yasmin in my arms, I peered up at the ceiling.

"Oh, God, Terrance, what did we just do?" she said with abrupt remorse.

"Had sex," I said quietly.

I could tell that our postcoital moment was starting to eat her up inside.

"She's my best friend," she said.

"And she's my wife," I said casually.

"And y'all are married." A strong huff came from her, and her eyes were becoming distant with a thought.

"I won't tell if you don't tell," I said.

It was replied by silence from her. Her mind had journeyed somewhere, and there was shame there. I could see it on her face. And then lying against me had suddenly become bothersome to her. She removed herself from my grasp and sat up and removed herself from the bed.

"You okay?" I asked.

"I'm not, Terrance." She started to dress. And she said, "I'm Zaire's godmother, Sophia and I have been friends forever, and I just fucked her husband. So no, I'm not okay, Terrance."

I sat up too. I looked at her. What words could I say to her? I didn't know. So I said the first thing in my mind. "So what now?"

She was almost dressed, and then she stopped and looked my way. Her eyes were filled with confusion and embarrassment. Still, there was something else that I saw—hesitation in saying what she truly felt.

"I don't know," she replied. "I need to go. I need to think."

She retrieved her shoes and started for the bedroom exit. She propelled herself into the hallway, and I was right behind her. Yasmin couldn't leave my place fast enough, looking like she was being chased by something. And she was gone, running away from what just happened.

I sighed. It had been one helluva night. The sex was impulsive, and the truth was that I enjoyed every minute of it. And the sad thing about it was that a part of me had hoped Sophia would walk in on us and catch us having sex. I wanted to be vindictive, and I wanted to really hurt her emotionally like she had hurt me. And what better way of distributing that hurt than being with her best friend?

However, my feelings for Yasmin were genuine, and I didn't want her to feel used, like she was some ploy for my revenge. Yasmin gave me needed companionship that night. And as a man, it was wanted.

Chapter Twenty-four

Devin

Love . . . it's seeing her at her worst, and you're still ready to hold her close, telling her that she's beautiful; saying that will never get tiring, because it's the truth . . .

Love was trust, right? And I trusted Danielle because I loved her so much. But could my woman be pushing the limits? It was her second night out with her friend, her ex-boyfriend, and I wasn't trying to get jealous or become insecure. I had every reason to trust my fiancée. I was a good man to her, and we had so much invested in each other.

But the hour was growing later. I glanced at the time for the umpteenth time, and it was nearing midnight. I continued to lie in bed and read this book by Carl Weber called *Married Men*. But I couldn't focus entirely on the book. I was continually thinking about Danielle and worried about why she wasn't home yet.

I picked up the phone and was going to call her. But I didn't. Was it fear, thinking the worst? I went back to bed and continued reading. And then I fell asleep.

When my eyes opened again, it was daylight, and it was 8:30 in the morning. I looked to my side, and Danielle wasn't home yet. Now I was worried, nearly panicking. Where was she? I didn't hesitate to call her phone this time. I dialed and it rang. I listened to each ring, worrying. There was no answer. It went straight to her voicemail. But immediately my phone rang, and I knew it was her.

"Hello?" I answered right away.

"Hey, baby, good morning," Danielle said. "I'm sorry I missed your call."

"Where are you? I'm worried sick about you," I said.

"I'm still with Jonathan."

"You're what?" I couldn't believe she was still with him—and why? "Where are you?"

"I'm in his hotel room."

My heart dropped into my chest, and my worry went to anger. I gripped the phone tightly and tried to hold back the tears. "What are you doing in his hotel room?" I exclaimed.

"Baby, nothing happened, believe me. We went out drinking last night, and I got too drunk. You know how I can get sometimes. I overdid it. So Jonathan offered to let me stay the night. I slept on the bed, and he slept on the floor. Honestly, baby."

"Danielle . . ." I started. It was hard for me to believe that nothing happened. I mean, liquor, a beautiful woman, and her ex-boyfriend. Those ingredients created a disaster, and I started to hate myself for allowing her to see him.

"Devin, I know what you're thinking, and believe me, nothing happened. I love you too much, baby, and I was being safe. And Jonathan was a complete gentleman."

I sighed. "When are you coming home?"

"In a few, baby. I can drive now. I love you."

"I love you too."

She gave me a kiss over the phone and ended the call. I felt apprehension. Why did she have to stay the night with him? She could have called me, and I would have picked her up from wherever. And she said nothing happened, but did I believe her?

Danielle came home an hour before noon. I was sitting on the couch watching TV. When she walked in, she was smiling at me, looking cheery. Now how was I supposed to take that?

"Hey, baby," she greeted me, coming close and placing a kiss on my lips.

I kissed back halfheartedly and said, "So how did things go last night?"

"It went okay. We went bowling, talked, and had dinner, and we went to the club, and I overdid it at the club. He wants to meet you," she said.

"Sound like y'all had a wonderful date," I said.

"It wasn't a date, Devin. We were just two old friends hanging out and having fun. Baby, I know you aren't jealous."

"I didn't expect you to stay out all night and wake up at his hotel room and come home right before noon," I said.

"I'm sorry, Devin. But would you rather have had me drink and drive and get arrested, or worse, get into a car accident? Jonathan was kind enough to have me sleep in his bed, and he took the floor. Nothing happened between us, baby, nothing!" she said with conviction.

She came closer to me. Her eyes were apologetic. She took my hands into hers, showing me closeness as she continued with, "Baby, I love you too much, and you know I'm always honest with you. You are the one I want to be with, who I'm going to marry and live the rest of my life with. Jonathan means nothing to me. You do. And if you don't like it, I won't ever see him again. Ever. You're more important to me than keeping friends with him."

We hugged each other tightly, and she kissed my lips spicy. Then she continued with, "You're smart, caring, understanding, and so damn handsome, and you're my man, and I'm your woman. This is us, and it will always be us."

I smiled. I loved Danielle too much. "I believe you, baby," I said.

We kissed passionately. And soon after, our clothes came off, and we ended up on the floor, making love.

Everything was cool and calm with me. I believed Danielle, and then I started hanging around my boys. They started telling me a different story, filling my mind with doubt.

It was a Sunday night, and I was with Terrance and Ash. Danielle encouraged me to go out, and I did. I rode in the back seat of Terrance's truck, and Ash rode shotgun. We were on our way to the bar to have a few drinks and watch some sports. Hot 97 was playing, and I was chilling. And then, out of the blue, Terrance said the unthinkable. "I fucked Yasmin the other day."

Ash and I looked at Terrance like, "What the fuck?"

"What, you fo' real?" Ash hollered.

He nodded. "Yeah, it just happened."

"Now, that's what up. Now that's my fuckin' nigga! That's how you do it, T. What! That's how you get back on a bitch, with someone close to her." Ash was all praising and glorifying the man's infidelity, and worse, with his wife's best friend.

"Yo, how was that pussy?" he continued. "Got you some of that good Spanish *mamacita?*"

Me, I wasn't so excited about it. "How did that happen?" I said.

"It just happened. She came by to drop my daughter off. We started talking, had a few drinks, one thing led to another, and we had sex."

"Hold up, you fucked her in your bed?" Ash asked.

"Yeah," he replied faintly.

"My nigga." Ash continued to praise the situation. "You are making me look bad," he joked.

"But I felt that it was more than just sex with her," said Terrance.

"What? You got feelings for her now?" Ash said.

"I don't know. Everything's moving too fast," he replied.

"Yo, you shoulda recorded that shit. Damn, what I would do to see that ass naked. Shit, I wanna fuck her too," Ash commented vulgarly.

"What is wrong with you, Ash?" I said.

"What's wrong wit' me? What's wrong wit' y'all niggas? That monogamous shit doesn't play anymore. Terrance's marriage is proof of that. It's an age where you need to get all the pussy you can," Ash proclaimed.

Ash was a hopeless cause. But I was surprised that Terrance would stoop to the level of having sex with his wife's best friend. Was he that mad at Sophia? Was there such a thing as a monogamous relationship in this century? Everywhere I turned, people were cheating and having casual sex. I didn't want that in my life. I wanted a relationship where it would be my wife and me for-ever, happy, and in love. But was that uphill and far-fetched thinking? Would my woman cheat on me? Had she cheated on me? And would I too, one day, become corrupted with infidelity?

It was an age where women could become just as grimy, disloyal, and manipulative as men. They could have multiple partners like men. I'd heard nightmarish stories about cheating and affairs. And it wasn't just the men who were doing wrong, but some females.

A month ago, an employee of mine at the Brooklyn location, after being married for five years, found out that his 4-year-old son was not his. His half brother confessed to having an ongoing affair with his wife. It was *Jerry Springer* up close.

And then I heard about a situation where a woman gave her man gonorrhea. It was revealed that she was an undercover whore, dancing in strip clubs and taking money to have sex with men. Her boyfriend was clueless.

It was a new generation. It was scary times. Was love still a real thing, or did people use it to take advantage of each other? It was a generation where roles were reversed, and some of the ladies were worse than the men when it came to cheating, lies, and deceit. And it was becoming a generation where divorce was on the rise, and some-thing else was climbing even higher—HIV/AIDS. And it was the highest among African Americans. There were so many sexually transmitted diseases out there, why cheat and why sleep around? Why risk your health? And it bothered me to hear Ash boast about his sex life. How he fucked this bitch and that bitch, he had two children out of wedlock, and he wasn't slowing down anytime soon. He was gambling with his health and safety, and he thought it was so glorious to do so that he should be cele-brated for it. I didn't condone his promiscuous lifestyle. I frowned on it, and he was my friend, but sometimes peo-ple needed to learn the hard way.

Suppose Ash saw what I saw when I used to work as an orderly in the AIDS unit at the hospital—seeing the rapid destruction and decay of a human body that was suffering from that sickness. In that case, he might have second thoughts about his wild sex life. It was a temporary job for me, but it changed me a lot.

My mind shifted to Danielle. I wasn't promiscu-ous. Yes, I'd had my share of partners, but I could count on one hand how many girlfriends I'd had. I was al-ways careful, and I still got tested. In fact, Danielle, and I both were tested for HIV early in our relationship. We both came back negative, and I was ecstatic.

I wanted children. I wanted a family, and I didn't want to risk that by catching an STD. And I knew Danielle was the right woman to have a family with. But her time with Jonathan, although I said that I believed her, I couldn't get it out of my mind. What if she lied to me? What if she put our relationship at risk?

Terrance and Ash were talking. I had zoned out for a minute. I needed to talk about my own issues.

"Terrance, I need to ask you a question," I said.

"What up?" he said.

"What, your girl ain't sucking dick right?" Ash chimed.

I glared at him and uttered, "Fuck you!

"Damn, I was just joking. Don't take it personally," Ash replied.

"I don't joke like that," I said.

"A'ight, my bad. I know how sensitive you are with your woman."

"What's on your mind, Devin?" Terrance said.

I said, "If your woman tells you that her ex-boyfriend is in town and she tells you that this man wants her to show him around town, and she told you that they were just friends, what would you say or do?"

"Fuck outta here!" Ash immediately shouted out. "That bitch better stay her ass home. Ain't no nigga my girl used to fuck wit' gonna come in town and take my woman anywhere."

I already knew what Ash was going to say. He was predictable.

"Why you asking this?" said Terrance.

"Because Danielle's ex-boyfriend came into town a few days ago."

"Don't tell me you let her go and chill wit' him. Nah, Devin, you ain't that stupid," said Ash. "C'mon, my dude. Wake up!"

"I trust her," I defended myself.

"You trust her? Nah, you lock her down. That's the worst thing you could have done. You gave some fool an easy opening to the pussy," Ash continued.

I swear, I asked Terrance the question, and Ash took charge. "It's not like that," I said.

"Honestly, I couldn't do it," Terrance said. "It would be awkward to allow Sophia to hang out with an old boyfriend of hers."

"What did she tell you?" Ash asked.

"That they were cool. That they're just friends."

"Fuck that, Devin. I'm gonna tell you like this—you can't let these bitches get away with so much shit, especially shit like that. Yo, let me ask you something. You think Danielle is gonna let you go hang out with an old girlfriend of yours, huh? If some ex-bitch of yours just suddenly came into town and you wanted to go and hang out with her, how the fuck you think she gonna feel? Watch that bitch get jealous and start acting stupid on your ass. Watch she be like, 'Go,' catch an attitude, and then when you come back home your shit be all broken up and out the door because she thinks you're cheating on her ass. I'm telling you, son, bitches are funny like that."

"How long is this dude in town for?" Terrance asked.

"I don't know. She told me a few weeks."

"Yo, you think that dude came into town to just chill and act like they're friends? Yo, let me tell you something—that nigga came into town because he was missing your bitch, thinking about that old pussy he used to hit. Now that muthafucka pulling game over her eyes. He ain't trying to be friends with your girl. Yo, you wanna go see this fool?" said Ash excitedly.

"Nah, it ain't even like that."

"What the fuck you mean it ain't even like that? Yo, Devin, you need to go handle that on the real. Don't let this fool come into town and try to handle your bitch like you invisible. Go see that fool, and let that nigga know who he fuckin' with, yo."

"I'm saying—"

"Let me ask you something—how did her ex-boyfriend get her number in the first place?"

"She ran into him in the streets," I said.

"Bullshit. Yo, make sure your girl ain't scheming," Ash said.

I kept hearing Ash's mouth move. He was acting like it was his woman we were talking about.

"Devin, I don't know what to tell you. I kind of agree with Ash. A man ain't just gonna come up in town and want to remain friends with his ex, especially as fine as Danielle is. Be careful with that one."

"I hear you."

"Word, some fool trying to fuck your woman," Ash said. "Yo, you coming home one night and see this dude fucking your bitch on your muthafuckin' bed, I would kill her and that nigga, no lie. These bitches think shit is a joke out in this muthafucka, especially wifey. Chanel gonna catch it. Son, don't let that nigga get up in your bitch. You handle that, Devin. You know I got your back. I'll handle that shit for you if you want."

"Nah, I got it," I said.

Ash was hyped. Terrance had already told me what had happened between him and Chanel. But what was bugging me out was why he was so upset with Chanel when he was no better. He wasn't committed or faithful to her at all.

My conversation with my friends about my issues didn't put me into a better spin with Danielle and her male friend. In fact, Ash somewhat made it worse for me.

The three of us went to the Bronx BBQ in Valley Stream, Long Island. We took a seat in one of the booths, and when our waitress came up to take our orders, all of us were stunned. She was beautiful.

Of course, Ash immediately tried to hit on her, doing what he did best—the three Fs, and that was find 'em, fuck 'em, and then forget about 'em. He flirted with the waitress. She smiled and was falling for his charm. He thought that he could have every woman in the world.

"See that?" Ash said. "She wanna holler at me."

I just ignored it. It was his life and his health.

"She is cute," Terrance said.

"Yes, she is. That bitch is definitely fuckable."

"How do you know that?" I asked.

"I know," Ash replied.

"Why, because y'all were flirting?"

"Devin, I know I can fuck her. I see it in her eyes, the way she looks at me," he said, so sure of himself. "Man, let me tell y'all clowns something. A bitch is gonna know after a few days with you—shit, even after a few hours with you—if she's gonna fuck you. And some niggas got it like that, and some don't."

Terrance and I sat quietly, waiting for our food, while Ash preached to us about nonsense. To him, a woman was a piece of meat, nothing else, and sex with them was simply another notch on his belt. He had no respect at all for them. So why did they love him back so much? It was a mindboggling question.

Ash continued his assault on the beautiful brunette with a slim waist and brown eyes when our food came. He wasn't going to change. But I was a one-woman man with a great woman in my life.

Chapter Twenty-five

Trey

*What is love, love is time . . . because only time
is capable of understanding how valuable love is . . .*

I had a late night that led to a late morning. I had a
few drinks and thought about Trisha, and I missed her
deeply. It had been a week since she cursed me out, and
it felt like it was definitely over between us. She wasn't
accepting any of my calls, and I'd left her over a dozen
messages.

My cell phone started to ring. I looked at the caller
ID, and it was an unknown caller. I ignored it. My phone
rang again, and it was the same unknown caller. Whoever
it was, they were very persistent about reaching me. I
sighed and reluctantly answered the caller.

"Hello," I dragged out.

"Trey, I'm pregnant," she said out of the blue.

"What? Who this, and who pregnant?" I said, not
taking it seriously.

She said, "It's Chica, and I'm pregnant wit' your baby."

Immediately I perked up and felt this wave of a panic
slice through me like a samurai sword. The news of her

being pregnant cut me in half. But I wasn't going to accept it.

"What?" I uttered. "You're fuckin' lying."

"Why would I lie about this?" she rebuked.

"Because you're a scandalous bitch! You like to play games, and I'm not with it." I was ready to hang up on her.

She uttered, "I'm so serious, Trey. I'm pregnant and it's your baby."

I hung up on her. It was too early for her nonsense. I was done with Chica, and I didn't want anything to do with her. Her stupidity cost me my relationship with Trisha. And if the bitch thought that she was pinning a baby on me, she had another think coming.

My cell phone rang again, and I knew it was her calling me back. I frowned and answered her call with anger. "Look, bitch, that's not my baby," I exclaimed.

"It is your baby because you were the only man I was fuckin'!" she hollered. "And my grandmother is pissed off. She knows, and she's ready to come after you wit' her shotgun!"

"She gotta find me first," I countered brusquely. I'd never brought Chica to my place, and I was glad she didn't know where I lived.

"Trey, why you dissin' me?"

"You're a damn ho!"

We went back and forth, and my last words to her were, "Don't call me anymore!"

I hung up on her again. She called back right away, and I ignored the phone. I'd had enough of her drama, and I was going to block her number or change mine.

The thought of her actually being pregnant by me terrified me. If she was, then I broke a cardinal rule, and that was getting my side bitch pregnant. It wasn't supposed to happen. But I knew that I wasn't the only man in her life. Chica liked dick too much to remain monogamous with me. She thought I was a fool. I had no sympathy for her.

My day was about to start, and I wanted to erase Chica's phone call from my mind. The sun was bright, and the day was warm. But I was still in a funk about losing Trisha. I took a shit, shaved, and showered. It was the weekend, and I had nothing to do. I didn't even feel like hanging out with my boys. I didn't want them to see me losing it over a woman. So staying home was my only option.

I put my phone on silent and lingered in the bedroom. I smoked a cigarette and thought about some things. But my solitude was soon interrupted by the sound of the doorbell chiming. I had company. I trekked downstairs and took a look out the window. It was Janice at my door. I had no idea what she wanted. I sighed and opened the door.

"Hey, Janice," I spoke.

She smiled and said, "Hey, I saw your car parked out front and thought that you might want some company."

I hesitated for a moment and said, "Come inside."

She proudly entered my home, and I closed the door behind her. I quickly eyed her attire: white shorts showing off her meaty thighs, sandals, and a blue T-shirt. She was cute and simple.

"You want breakfast?" she said.

"You gonna cook?"

"Yes. I wouldn't ask if I wasn't. And you need to try my omelets and pancakes," she said.

"I am hungry."

"So is that a yes?"

"I guess so," I said.

She smiled.

Early afternoon was spent with Janice in the kitchen putting together an excellent breakfast for me on a whim. She had my kitchen smelling like a five-star restaurant, and my nose was enticed by the aroma.

"So how are things with you and your girlfriend?" she asked loudly from the kitchen.

"She's out of town," I lied.

"Oh, where did she go?"

"She's away on business," was what I felt like telling her.

She chuckled. "I guess it's personal."

"I don't wanna think about her right now."

"Well, I have the perfect remedy to get her out of your mind."

The smell of her cooking was turning me on. It smelled like paradise in my kitchen. It never smelled that good from a home-cooked meal. I mean, Trisha did her thing, but she wasn't the best cook. But Janice definitely knew her way around the kitchen. And when she was done, my kitchen table looked picture perfect with two omelets stuffed with diced ham, a creamy cheese sauce, and jack and cheddar cheeses. Her pancakes looked buttery and fluffy, and her bacon looked crisp. One look at everything and my mouth watered.

"Damn! Everything looks delicious," I expressed.

"Wait until you taste it," she said.

She poured orange juice into the cups, and we both took a seat at the table. I at once started stuffing my face with her cooking. Everything was delicious. I mean, it felt like her food was making love to my mouth. I devoured it all and licked my plate clean.

"Was it good?" she asked.

I let out a massive burp as my answer.

She laughed and said, "I guess so."

I said, "Yo, you're the bomb in the kitchen."

"Thank you."

"Why did you volunteer to come over and cook?"

"I'm just neighborly, I guess."

I smiled. My belly was happy. They say that the way to a man's heart is through his stomach. Janice was the epitome of that saying. With cooking like hers, it was easy to make anyone fall in love with her.

I started to remove the dishes from the table, but Janice quickly stopped me and said, "No, Trey, I got this. Go relax."

"You sure?"

"Yes. I'll clean up." She started taking the dishes and placing them into the sink. She took charge, and I didn't dispute it. I wobbled my stuffed ass back into the living room, sank my ass into the couch, and turned on the TV.

Fifteen minutes later, Janice joined me on the couch after doing the dishes and cleaning up my kitchen. She sat close to me and said, "What are you watching?"

"Nothing now, just channel surfing."

The TV soon rested on one of my favorite movies, *Poetic Justice.* I was lucky to catch it from the beginning, where Q-Tip was about to get his head blown off by L.A. gangbangers. Unfortunate for his character, he was about to get some from Janet Jackson, and violence put an end to that. Janet Jackson, now I loved her.

"Trey, can I be honest with you?" Janice said all of a sudden.

"Yeah, of course."

She propped up from leaning against me and looked at me seriously. "I was thinking about our last encounter, and I had a really good time with you. I came by because I wanted round two with you. And I know you have a woman, but I really want to have sex with you right now. I'm a divorced woman with needs, and I enjoy everything about you. But if you don't want to, I understand," she proclaimed to me.

Her hand found its way on my thigh, and she was waiting for my reply. Her touch was desirable, and her presence created my arousal. It was her cooking that ignited it. My day had started out stressful, but Janice wanted to relieve me of my pain. With food and pussy, what man could resist the urge? I could feel that animal instinct to conquer bubbling inside of me.

I placed my lips against hers, and a passionate kiss ensued. It was my cool reply. Our tongues locked into one, and her hand reached for my crotch. She gently squeezed and massaged my manhood to a full erection. It didn't take long for her to unbuckle my pants and pull out my dick. She dropped her face into my lap and started to suck me off. Her full lips around my dick made my head go back, and my eyes rolled around in my head. Up and down her lips went, putting me into absolute bliss.

She gave me a long blow job, and afterward our clothes came off and were on the floor. Her naked flesh straddled me against the couch, and she quickly descended on top of me and evenly put me inside of herself. I felt her weight on my hips as she straddled me against the couch and rested her naked tits on my chest, mashing them into me as she sucked the side of my neck.

The power of p-u-s-s-y was crippling and overwhelming. I moaned as we both got our rhythm going, entwined on the couch, huffing and puffing like we were marathon runners.

I was an educated fool. But one moment I was griping and crying over Trisha, and the next I was having sex with my neighbor. *Damn, where do I go from here?*

Chapter Twenty-six

Sophia

Love is putting time and effort into your relationship and practicing unconditional love . . .

"Pass me the onions," I said to Yasmin.

We were in my kitchen, and I was cooking up some soup and cornbread for the night. This was like our girls' night out. Zaire was in her bedroom watching cartoons, and Yasmin and I were going to enjoy a wonderful dinner together.

She reached into the bottom of the fridge and passed me the onions.

"Why you so quiet tonight?" I asked her. Usually, Yasmin was talkative, telling me about her business or asking me about mine.

"Nothing," she quietly responded.

"So what happened between you and that fine-looking brotha you met at the club the other night?" I said, waiting for the juicy details.

"Nothing. He's really boring."

"Damn, he was cute, though."

"That's all. He's not spontaneous enough for me."

I chuckled. "I see, you like 'em like Indiana Jones."

"No, that's too much for me. Too old, anyway."

I laughed. "Girl, you're crazy."

I started stirring my soup. We had some ol'-school jams playing on the stereo. My soup was cooking, and I felt terrific tonight because I spent all day yesterday with Eric. We had a fantastic night together. In fact, these past few days, I'd been spending a lot of time with Eric. We'd been talking, chilling, having fun, and also fuckin' our brains out. We were having so much sex that it felt like I was a teenager again. It felt like I was sneaking out after curfew to be with the one I loved. Eric made me feel so alive.

"Where's Terrance?" Yasmin asked.

I sighed. "I have no idea. He's probably out there hanging with his knucklehead buddies."

"Mommy, Mommy, look," Zaire said as she came running into the kitchen, showing me a picture that she drew with the crayons I'd bought her today.

"I see. Who is it?" I asked, looking at the child's drawing of four colored stick figures.

"That's you, Mommy, and that's me, and that's Daddy and Auntie Yasmin," she pointed out.

"Oh, it's nice, sweetie."

"I want Daddy to see it too."

"I know, sweetie. Daddy's going to see it," I said.

"Auntie Yasmin, look. That's you, see? Next to Daddy and Mommy."

"I love it, Zaire. You're so talented," Yasmin said.

"That's nice, Zaire. Now go finish coloring while Yasmin and I finish making dinner, okay?"

"Okay, Mommy." She ran back into her bedroom.

I saw Yasmin smiling. "She's so sweet."

"I know, that's my heart," I said.

I then noticed Yasmin's smile transform into a frown. "What's wrong?" I asked.

"Are you sure, Sophia?"

"Sure about what?"

"About you and Terrance?" she abruptly asked.

"Yasmin, do I have to keep explaining myself over and over again?"

"I understand your feelings, but you have everything going for you—a beautiful daughter and a wonderful husband. How can you just give up everything so easily?"

"My feelings have changed, Yasmin. I want to move on. I need to move on," I explained to her.

"I envy you, Sophia. You stand here in front of me with everything I always dreamed of having. You have a family, a caring husband, and you're willing to throw everything away that you and your husband built together for a booty call."

"It's not the same anymore. Things changed. And why the change of heart now, Yasmin? Before, you were supportive of my decision, and now you actin' like my mother."

She sighed. "Marriage isn't always easy, Sophia. You have to take the good along with the bad. Terrance has his flaws, and so do you."

"Well, his flaws are really starting to piss me off."

"What if you found out that Terrance was with another woman, maybe he was in love with another woman? How would you feel about that?" she asked.

I thought about it. "Honestly, it wouldn't bother me. I will probably be happy for him, as long as the woman he's with treats my daughter right, and then we won't have any problems."

I started preparing my cornbread, mixing my ingredients into a bowl. Yasmin just sat in a chair. I was wondering what was going through her head. Why was she suddenly so concerned about my relationship with Terrance? She knew everything. She was my best friend. I told her everything.

I heard her sigh, so I glanced over at her. "What's wrong, girl?" I asked.

I noticed a few tears trickled from her eyes. Something was going on with her. Was it a man? Was it work? I was ready to listen and help Yasmin with whatever problems she had.

"Sophia, I have to tell you something. I gotta be honest with you," she said.

"Honest about what?"

She paused for a minute and then went on with, "I had sex with Terrance the other day."

"Girl, stop lying," I quickly reacted.

Her look toward me said that she wasn't joking. Her eyes were sad and showed guilt. What she said, it felt like I just fell into a hornet's nest and was promptly attacked. What I felt was a shock. I stopped what I was doing in the kitchen and looked at her.

"Wh . . . what?" I stammered.

"I'm sorry, Sophia," she said remorsefully.

"You're damn right you're sorry," I shouted. "What the fuck were you thinking? You had sex with Terrance?"

"It just happened," she tried to explain.

"What the fuck do you mean it just happened? How does fucking my husband just happen? Huh? Yasmin, explain that!" I yelled, coming toward her. I wanted to punch her in the face.

She quickly rose from the chair, standing there, staring at me like a deer caught in headlights. "Terrance and I just had this thing."

"Mommy, Mommy," I heard my daughter call out.

"Zaire, not now. Go back into your room," I yelled and saw my daughter suddenly turn around and run back in the opposite direction. "I thought you were my friend, Yasmin. How could you do this to me?"

"Wait a minute, Sophia. You're the one who doesn't want to be with him anymore. You're the one who keeps telling Terrance to move on with his life. You're the one who just said you wouldn't care if he was with another woman. You're the one who doesn't want him anymore," Yasmin hollered.

"So? That doesn't give my best friend the right to go out and fuck him behind my back!" I screamed heatedly. "When did this happen?"

"The night I had Zaire and dropped her off. The night you were supposed to be home but stayed the night with Eric."

"I can't believe this. You bitch!" I shouted.

"Wait for a second, Sophia. I understand that you're upset, but don't come out of your mouth."

"I'll call you whatever I want to call you. You always have been a fuckin' slut, Yasmin. I swear. How dare you fuck Terrance? Do you have to fuck every man you're around?"

"Fuck you, Sophia, fuck you!" she shouted.

"It seems you've been doing that a lot lately."

"You know what, Sophia? At least you have someone who loves and cares for you. You got a man who's supportive and loyal and takes care of his family, yet you don't see that. You're a selfish bitch. You're just thinking about yourself, not this family, talking about you want your freedom. Bitch, you know how many women would love to be with a man like Terrance? But you're the ho who wants to go and fuck another man. I know you might hate to hear this, but I'm in love with your husband. I've been in love with him for the longest time, and I always envy you, and now that you're willing to let him go, I want him."

"Get the fuck out of my house!" I yelled.

"I'm gone, Sophia. Kiss Zaire good night for me."

"Fuck you!"

As soon as Yasmin left, I just dropped down on my knees and started crying. I couldn't believe that shit. My best friend and Terrance, the man who was still my husband, had sex with each other. Why was that bothering me? I mean, I couldn't accept the fact that out of all the women Terrance could be with, he had to go and fuck Yasmin. We'd been friends for years. Was he doing this just to spite me? *That muthafucka!* I had a few words to say to him when he brought his black ass home.

I couldn't even finish cooking dinner. I just shut everything down, made Zaire a snack, and went into my bedroom, furious. *How could he do this to me?* He didn't love her. Terrance just fucked Yasmin out of spite. He wanted to get even with me. I know he did. I was sitting on my bed, and then I had this appalling thought, thinking that the two of them probably fucked on this bed. My bed! I quickly got up, glared down at the sheets and mattress, and then promptly removed the sheets and covers from my fuckin' bed and tossed them against the wall. I was disgusted.

How could he? I thought, having tears flood down my face.

Chapter Twenty-seven

Terrance

Promise to love and promise to progress . . . for united together in love and there isn't anything y'all can't conquer, for love is might and love is power . . .

I pulled into my driveway with a smile on my face. Today had been one of my better days. Work was good, and I'd had a fantastic night out with my friends. Day by day I was trying to heal from my upset with Sophia, and I was trying to forgive my wife. I started to think that maybe it was for the better. Perhaps it was time to move on. And I couldn't stop thinking about that night with Yasmin.

I walked into the house, and it was dark and quiet. I figured Sophia and Zaire were sleeping. So I tiptoed through the house in the dark, and I nearly tripped over something in the living room. I stumbled and hit my leg against the coffee table.

"Shit!" I grumbled.

I turned on the lights and saw the disaster. My stuff was everywhere. My clothes were bleached, cut up, shredded, and scattered all over the living room. My

PlayStation was destroyed, and all my games were broken in half. My sneakers and shoes were damaged to the point of no return. I was wide-eyed at the tragedy of my shit.

"What the fuck!" I exclaimed, tightening my face. I became furious. "Sophia!" I shouted.

I ran to the bedroom and forced open the door. Sophia was awake and lying in bed casually. She looked at me with this wicked grin.

"Yo, what the fuck did you do to my shit? What the fuck is wrong with you?" I screamed at her.

I got no immediate response from her. Her chilling look and wicked grin continued on her face. She removed herself from the bed and approached me calmly, and she stood directly in front of me. I didn't see it coming. She slapped me so hard that my ears started ringing.

"What the fuck is your problem?" I yelled.

"How dare you? You are my fuckin' problem!"

"What the fuck did I do to you now?"

"Of all the women, Terrance, you had to go and fuck my best friend!"

"Yasmin told you?"

"Yes, that bitch told me tonight."

I smirked. I couldn't believe that Yasmin actually told her. But why was she upset? Was she jealous? "Why you trippin'? It ain't like we fuckin' anymore. You've moved on, remember?"

"That's not the point!" she screamed.

"Then what is the point?"

"She's my best friend, Terrance. You didn't have to go there. That's fucked up! On this bed, too, I bet."

"Yo, it just happened. I kind of got some feelings toward her," I proclaimed.

"Are you serious?"

"I wouldn't be telling you this if I weren't."

"I don't fuckin' believe this!" she shouted.

"Sophia, you need to calm down and be quiet before you wake up Zaire."

"Don't tell me to calm down! I want you out now, Terrance. Get the fuck out of my house!"

"Your house? Shit, I pay the bills around here too."

"Terrance, I'm so fuckin' serious."

"You're serious? You know what, Sophia? I love you, but you're acting like a straight-up bitch. You don't know what the fuck you want. Now you wanna flip because I fucked Yasmin. So what? I fucked your best friend, and I don't regret doing the shit either. In fact, I'd fuck her again. Shit, I wanna fuck her again," I let her know, being sarcastic.

"You're a fuckin' dog, Terrance. I swear you're only doing this to hurt me. Why, Terrance? That's my best friend."

"Yo, like I said before, it just happened."

"Well, you know what else just happened?" Sophia said, folding her arms across her chest and continuing to glare at me. "Me fuckin' some other nigga. That also just happened, and the dick was so good, Terrance. Really fuckin' good. And he was so big and black . . . damn. Now what?"

I didn't say a word to her. *This fuckin' bitch! I knew I was fuckin' right, and she got the nerve to flip out on me.*

"I've been with him for over a month now," she added, throwing more fuel on the fire.

"Oh, so it's like that? You just gonna throw that shit in my face, right?"

"You wanted to know the truth, so there's the fuckin' truth!"

It took every bit of strength and composure I had to keep from knocking this bitch across the damn room. "You know what, Sophia? I don't need this shit. I don't need this fuckin' shit!" I shouted.

"You mad?"

"You wanna play games? Okay. Who is he?" I asked.

"Don't worry about it. You're doing your thing, and I'm definitely doing my thing," she stated. "Right?"

"Why are you doing this to me, Sophia? I swear, you're gonna have me kill this nigga."

"Whatever!"

"Whatever? Bring this nigga around me. I swear, if I see this nigga in my home or around my daughter, I'm gonna kill both of y'all," I threatened madly.

"See, now you're acting so fuckin' stupid. You wanna threaten people now? What's the matter with you, Terrance?"

"What's wrong with me? You wanna fuck some other nigga and be out all night."

"It's my life. And why are you so worried? You got Yasmin now. Fuck that bitch!"

"Fuck you, bitch! I'll fuckin' kill you and that nigga!" I belligerently shouted out.

I was starting to lose control. That quickly, she pissed me off and threw the advantage that I had right back in my face. I was jealous. I was doing fine just a few hours ago. But now, having the image in my mind of some other man having sex with my wife, I felt immediate rage and anger.

I squeezed my hands into tight fists and was seconds away from implementing domestic abuse. I glared at

Sophia. Seven years we'd been married, and not once had I put my hands on her. But I felt that was all about to change tonight.

We cursed, and we screamed at each other. Putting on the boxing gloves, we were about ready to go pound for pound. Sophia said some nasty and hurtful things to me, and I returned the favor. Vehemently, I spewed to her words like "cunt," "whore," "filthy, ugly bitch," "fuck you," "suck my dick," blah, blah, blah!

She vehemently retorted, "I'm a nasty bitch, and I sucked his big black dick every night and had him come in my mouth. And I loved it!"

Her merciless remark threw me into a heated rage, and I exploded. I charged at her and found my hand wrapped around her neck. I threw her against the bedroom wall so hard there was a loud thump. I was ready to choke her to death or break her neck.

"You gonna kill me?" she shouted. Her eyes were fierce against me, and she dared me.

Our wild and violent commotion woke up Zaire. She came into our bedroom. Seeing my baby girl threw me back into some sanity. She was there to witness me putting my hands on her mother. And our fighting was unhealthy for her to see. I quickly released my hand from Sophia's neck.

I uttered, "Fuck this!" and I grabbed my jacket and charged toward the front door. I had to leave right away before I did something that I was going to regret. I was seeing red. I was spiraling with fury. She was about to see the devil in me tonight.

I jumped into my truck, sped out of the driveway, tires peeling, smoke thickening, and I did fifty miles per hour away from my house. I knew where to go. She was on my mind. I figured that I would be welcome there.

I arrived at Yasmin's place twenty minutes later. It was late at night when I rang her doorbell. I waited on her steps briefly, and she opened the door, tying her robe together. She looked at me. A smile loomed on her face.

"Did I wake you?" I said.

"No."

"Can I come in?"

There was a moment of hesitation. Our eyes locked and she nodded. She stepped to the side, and I slid into her home. When she closed the door, right away I pulled her into a passionate embrace, kissed her over-poweringly, and scooped her up into my arms. I had no time for words. She didn't resist and allowed me to carry her off into her bedroom.

I wanted to forget about my troubles with Sophia. I felt she was becoming a closed chapter in my life. It was time to move on to something better. I thought she forced me to be with Yasmin. Why not? Her friend was a beautiful woman.

I escaped my troubles and aches between her long legs and soft thighs. I entered her passionately, and I kissed her. I wanted this. Maybe this would work, she and I. Perhaps we were meant to be together. But was it my anger speaking? Was it fear of loneliness? Was it because I was horny? I didn't know, but I didn't want it to end. She felt so good, her kisses against me, her skin against mine, and me inside her, missionary. Her comfort and her sex were needed.

An hour after our sexual rendezvous, I held her in my arms, and we lay nestled on her bed. She started to cry against my chest. "What are we doing?" she said.

"I don't know, but I love it."

"Are you sure about this?"

I sighed, and I looked at her, and she looked at me. I nodded. "I think I want this to go somewhere," I said.

My marriage with Sophia was ending, and her friendship with Sophia was ending—and there was us.

Chapter Twenty-eight

Ash

Lies and deceit are poisonous to a relationship . . . to pretend to care is even a lot deadlier, for love should always be the truth, and love should always bring about better . . .

I was leaving work when Kenya gave me a kiss goodbye on the cheek. It was a random kiss, and it came unexpectedly. But I felt proud. I thought I was breaking that wall of hers little by little. And what made me prouder was that she did it in front of my coworkers, stirring jealousy among them. I saw the hate in their eyes, and I smiled. Where they had failed with her, I was surely conquering. I just needed to be patient.

I walked from my job to the train station on what felt like the hottest day of the year. The humidity was attacking me, and I was sweating like a runaway slave. I wanted to get home and sit in front of the air conditioner.

The moment I reached the train station, my cell phone rang. It was an unknown caller. I answered and heard her say my name.

"Is this Ash?"

I smiled. It was Monica.

"I see you decided to finally call me," I said.

She heaved a sigh and replied, "Get over yourself. The only reason I'm calling is to ask when you're coming by to see your son again."

"I'll be by there soon. I just got off work," I said.

I heard silence, and then she spoke. "Excuse me, did I hear you correctly? Did you say you were coming from work? You got the job?"

I laughed. "You sound shocked. But yeah, I took the job three weeks ago."

"Wow, I'm impressed."

"Why? I'm serious about change, Monica. I want something different."

"That is great to hear, Ash. I'm happy for you. So how's the job?"

"It's cool. I really like it. I don't mind getting my hands dirty. But how's my little soldier?"

"He's fine. You disappeared for a few weeks. I was afraid something happened to you," Monica said.

"What, you thought I got locked back up?"

"I was just concerned."

"What's going on wit' you? How's life?"

"Everything's fine. I'm a mother and a wife, and I'm in school. I'm managing things," she said.

"Monica, let me take you out. My treat," I said out of the blue.

It caught her off guard. "Excuse me?"

"You sound stressed right now, like you got a lot going on. So take a break from your world, and let me treat you to a nice dinner."

"Ash, you know I can't."

"Why not?"

"Because I'm married. I have a husband, and we've been over for years. I called about your son, and that's it."

"I know, but what's wrong wit' just dinner? I owe you, Monica."

"You don't owe me anything."

"Monica, back in the day, I was fucked up. I was a cheating dog, and I did some things that I regret. But my biggest regret is not treating you fairly and losing you. You're good people, Monica. You got me this job, you take good care of our son, and my life is changing for the better. I'm not that man I used to be," I proclaimed wholeheartedly. "But all I'm asking is to do one nice thing for you, that's it."

She was silent. I didn't hear an abrupt no from her, which was a good sign. I didn't want to keep pushing her. I tried to play my cards right.

I heard her sigh, and she replied with, "Just this one time."

Boy, I was ready to do cartwheels in the middle of the street. But I had to hold my composure. "One dinner with you and that's it. I promise."

"I'll have to find a babysitter and talk to Patrick," she said.

"My moms won't have a problem watching him. She's dying to see her grandson."

"Okay."

"I know a very nice place."

We continued to talk for a moment. Friday was the day we chose. I felt dinner with her was a step in the right direction. She said that she would always be there for me as a friend. I was her son's father, and we had to deal with each other. But once again, before our conversation ended, she reminded me that she was a married woman.

***

I had warned Keith to stay away from Chanel and vice versa, but word on the street was that my baby mama had been seen with him recently. What, they thought that I wouldn't find out? And I guessed that first ass whooping didn't scare him off enough. But I was upset, and I was jealous. Why was she still seeing him? So hearing the news of them, I felt that I had to bring the drama. I was hyped and animated. Ain't no other man gonna outshine me, and I needed some excitement in my life.

Thursday evening, I went looking for Keith. I rode shotgun in my friend Crown's Denali truck. We were riding dirty with the gun underneath my seat. I knew that I was on parole, but Keith had me itching to fuck him up and put another serious hurting on him.

We drove by Chanel's place, and I looked for him there. I knocked on her door, but there was no answer. Either she wasn't home, or she was hiding from me.

"Yo, let's chill for a minute," I told Crown.

We stayed parked on her block, right across the street from her place. She didn't know the truck. I lit a blunt and eyed her home like a hawk. He killed the ignition, and I shared the blunt with him.

I'd met Crown a few years ago. He was a beast in these streets, and we did time together in Clinton. I had two sets of friends. Terrance, Trey, and Devin were my square friends. Then there were my grimy and "don't give a fuck" street associates/cohorts I called when shit needed to pop off and shots needed to scream out. Crown came home a few months before me, and he was back to his grimy ways. He was a stick-up kid and a wild nigga, too.

We waited a half hour, and my gut told me to try her door again. I climbed out of the truck and walked toward the door. I knocked and ranged the bell repeatedly. Her moms came to the door with a scowl and an attitude toward me.

"Why the fuck you ringin' my bell so goddamn much?" she barked.

I wasn't in the mood. "Where Chanel at?" I asked.

"You got a cigarette?"

I reached into my pack of Newports and pulled out a cigarette. She was aching to light up. She turned and marched up the stairs. I followed right behind her, an invitation in or not.

I entered the messy apartment. The place looked like a trash dump with piles of dishes in the sink, garbage piling up in the trashcan and spilling onto the floor, toys, clothes, beer cans, and everything else spewed everywhere. The place smelled like ass, eggs, and cigarettes. My daughter had to live in this mess. *Nasty bitches!* I wanted to change things for my daughter and felt guilty that she had to live under such crazy conditions.

I marched directly into Chanel's room, praying to see Keith in there with her again. This time I came with a pistol tucked into my waistband. But fortunately for her, she was alone, lying there watching TV in her T-shirt and panties and smoking a blunt. She was startled to see me in her room.

"You ain't hear me knocking on your fuckin' door earlier?" I scolded.

"No. What the fuck do you want, Ash? Why you here? Get out!" she barked my way.

"Where are the kids?" I said. "And my daughter better not be wit' that nigga."

"They somewhere," she spat with sarcasm at me.

"Don't get cute!"

"Whatever!"

"Where my daughter at?"

"She's with Tammy, okay? They went to the park."

"Yeah, a'ight. You better not be lying to me."

She sucked her teeth. "Whatever!"

I moved closer to her and sat on the edge of her bed. Chanel was looking right in her scanty garb, her ass looking like a brown bubble, and her thighs were thick and right.

"Yo, let me get a pull," I said, reaching for her blunt.

She rolled her eyes at me and still had her attitude. "You smell like weed already."

"And?"

She relented and handed me the blunt. I took a few pulls. Chanel looked at me, and her look screamed to me that she had something on her mind to say.

"Why did you do him like that? You ain't had to fuck him up, Ash. You ain't right," she griped.

"Man, fuck that fool. I know you ain't still crying about that muthafucka."

"It's my house."

"Yeah, whatever, and don't think I don't know you ain't still fuckin' wit' him. I should wild out on ya ass right now."

My eyes burned into her. She knew I wasn't someone to joke with. She rose from her lying position and looked my way intently.

"So it's okay for you to go out there and do you wit' all these bitches, but soon as I have some other man over, you wanna flip out. And he's not even some other man. That's my son's father. But you can be a fuckin' ho and fuck all theses bitches, and I'm supposed to be okay with that," she proclaimed.

"What you think? You ain't me," I replied boldly. "And I ain't fuckin' no other bitches. Ain't nobody cheatin' on you. I'm out here tryin' to do me and get this paper so we can live."

"You think I'm stupid, Ash. I got friends who talk, and they be seeing your dumb ass out there."

"Your friends don't be seeing shit! You gonna believe them bitches?"

"Yes!" she hollered.

"Them bitches are just jealous because they don't have a good man in their life," I said. "I look out for you and my daughter all the time."

"Good man," she chuckled. "Where he at?"

"You tryin' to be funny?"

"No! I'm so fuckin' serious! So where do you be at when I page you or call your house? You don't call me right back. So what am I supposed to believe?"

"Chanel, I'm not cheating on you! I ain't fuckin' wit' no other bitch. I'm out here working, got a nine-to-five and shit. That's my word. I ain't out here fuckin' these bitches. I'm working my ass off!"

I pulled out my recent paystub and tossed it at her. She picked it up and stared at it.

"You really got a job?" she said.

"Yes!"

Her eyes were glued to the paystub, probably studying my net amount. It wasn't much, but it was still something.

"Why didn't you tell me?" she said, her tone toward me somewhat changing.

"Because it's my business."

"Well, I'm happy for you," she said.

"Thanks. I'm a changed man," I said.

She laughed.

"What, you find me funny?"

"Hilarious," she replied with a grin.

"Oh, you think I'm hilarious, huh?"

"Ash, do you really care about me? Do you love me?"

"What? Yeah, I do."

"You have a funny way of showing it."

"You just insecure," I said.

"I'm not insecure. I just know you like a book. And what are you here for anyway? To check up on me. To see if he was here. Well, he ain't. You acted so stupidly that day with Keith. I swear, sometimes you just a fuckin' bully."

"You got this muthafucka naked in here and around my daughter, fuck yeah, I'm gonna see that nigga. Yo, that was disrespect right there. That fool better fuckin' respect me."

"What do you know about respect? It ain't like you give it," she countered.

"I respect you."

She laughed again. It was becoming *Def Comedy Jam* in her bedroom, and I was Martin Lawrence.

"Respect? You come into my place like you own shit, barge into my room, and do whatever you want, and you call me a bitch in front of our daughter like that's cool."

"You be wildin' out too."

"You make me wild out."

"We're two peas in a pod," I said.

She sucked her teeth. "Don't you got somewhere to be right now?"

I moved closer to her and looked at her. "What, you want me to go? You know I still love you, right?" She sighed faintly and gave no answer. So I repeated, "Right?"

She nodded.

"I'm always gonna look out for you. And I ain't fuckin' wit' no other bitches. That's my word, Chanel. I wanna come home to you and my daughter every night. And the only reason I wild out is that I care for you a lot, and my daughter. I love y'all! And I ain't tryin' to let no bitch-ass nigga come between us, you feel me?"

"Yeah," she replied halfheartedly and looked away from me.

I inched myself closer to her and pulled her into my arms. She wanted to resist, but I was determined and nestled her into my arms. Her scantily clad body had started a fire burning inside of me. I was horny, and Chanel's big booty put on view in a pair of panties was only increasing my horniness. I was ready to put another baby inside of her. I squeezed her butt and cupped her tits, clearly indicating what I wanted from her—some pussy.

"Ain't you got someone waiting outside for you?" she said.

"They can wait."

"So I'm supposed to give you some pussy after the way you have been acting?"

I didn't answer her. I already knew what the answer was—yes. So I continued to caress her body and kiss her skin affectionately. I wanted a quickie. I pushed her against the bed and pried her legs open.

"Ash," she faintly uttered. "Ash, c'mon, chill."

"I want you, baby!"

She sighed, and I roughly tore off her panties and eyed her shaved flesh. *Fuck the foreplay.* I hurriedly undressed myself below, jeans and boxers were tossed to the floor, and I had my baby mama pinned against the mattress and was ready for action. She had my erection harder than concrete and steel combined. She wanted to resist me, but she couldn't because my fond touch and lingering kisses were winning her over. I rapidly penetrated her, and whatever resistance she felt was quickly relinquished the moment my dick was deep inside of her. Instead, she cooed against my ear and gripped me tightly.

"Ooooh. Ooooh, oh, baby. I love you. Ooh, don't stop," she groaned into my ear. "Ooooh, don't stop!"

"You love me, right?"

"I fuckin' love you," she returned entirely, feeling nine inches of length profoundly inside of her.

"Say it again," I said, fucking her with authority.

She breathed out, catching her breath from the dick, and uttered proudly, "I love you, baby!"

I smiled. *That's my girl!*

That doubt and attitude of hers quickly surrendered after some sex. I made Chanel come, and it was an affecting moment for her and me. When I was done coming inside of her, I started to get dressed again. I buckled my jeans, put on my shoes, and felt lifted. I definitely needed that. Chanel always knew how to make me feel so good.

"You leaving already?" she said.

"Yeah, my nigga waiting outside."

"I love you," she said.

"I love you too."

I kissed her lips and left the bedroom.

Outside, Crown was still waiting for me. When I climbed into the passenger seat, he said, "I hope you fucked her as long as you had me waiting out here."

"What you think?"

He smiled. "You're lucky you're my nigga."

I felt good. Life was good. I had all the pussy I wanted, and there was more to come.

Chapter Twenty-nine

Ash

The kisses against her neck send shivers down her spine, your breath against her lobe sends a smile to behold . . .

It was a quarter to eight, and I was getting dressed and waiting for Monica to show up with my son. She said she would be at my mother's around nine. My mom was cool about watching Justin tonight. She was about to order pizza and watch some movies with him.

I had to look really good tonight. I threw on my best outfit, and I was looking like the honorable Mack.

The doorbell rang, and I knew it was Monica. She was early. I opened the front door, smiling. Monica had my son in her arms. He was asleep, with his head rested over her shoulder.

"Damn, my little nigga is knocked out already," I said, taking him from Monica and holding him in my arms.

"He's tired, Ash. He's been up since seven this morning, and he's not your little nigga. He's your son."

"Okay, my bad. But damn, why y'all have him up so early?"

She looked at me like, "Really?" "School!"

"Oh! Well, let me take him upstairs to my mom. I know she gonna love seeing her grandchild again. Yo, come say what's up. She ain't seen you in a minute too."

"Nah, that's okay. I'll wait down here," Monica said.

"Nah, come upstairs and say what's up to my moms. You acting like she a stranger to you. Word, stop acting like that!"

"Ash, I said that I'm fine. I'll say hi next time."

I just stared at her. "Whatever!"

I took my son upstairs to my moms, and the moment she saw Justin, she beamed and reached for him.

"There he is. Bring me my grandson!" my mother exclaimed excitedly. "He is getting so big."

She took Justin from my arms and hugged him, though he was still asleep. I knew my boy was in good hands. Since he was born, my moms only saw him a handful of times, and that was when I was locked up. Monica and my mom trooped together upstate to see me, and we had like a little family visit.

I came back downstairs, and Monica was sitting on the couch, staring at old pictures hanging on the wall. Most of 'em were of me and my younger brother, Sunny, when we were young. She took a framed picture from the coffee table and looked at it for a while. I knew what picture she picked up. It was the one with me and her together when we were at Coney Island. I had that picture professionally done and had it around ever since.

"You remember that picture?" I asked.

She smiled. "Yeah. We were so young. I was how old? Fourteen? You had me sneak out of the house, and we took a cab out there."

"Yeah, I remember," I said, smiling.

"Damn, that was fun. Even though I got caught and my mom grounded me for a month. You always had me doing crazy things."

"That's why you loved me."

She stared at the picture one last time, shaking her head, smiling, and then she placed it back down on the coffee table. "So what's up? Where are we going?" she asked.

"I know this special place for us to celebrate."

"Okay, come on, let's go. I don't want to be out too late."

"Damn, you're so beautiful, Monica. You have always been a beautiful woman. Even when you were young, you had that thing about you."

She smiled. It was hard to look at her and not stare or drool over her. She looked stunning in a pair of denim embellished jeans that highlighted her long legs, with a seamless mock-neck top and a pair of high heels. And her hair was long and black and stylish, falling down to her shoulders. Damn, I loved a woman with long and sensuous black hair.

We walked outside. Parked in front of the house was a black BMW. She hit the alarm to the car, and it chirped, indicating the alarm was being deactivated.

"Damn, Monica, you rollin' like that?" I said

"It's Patrick's car."

"Oh, and he let you push the whip like that?"

"When I need to."

I slid into the passenger seat while she climbed into the driver's seat. What I really wanted to do was drive the Beemer. It felt awkward to be out on a date and she was the one driving. But I couldn't speak on it. I was lucky to have her come tonight. She started the ignition, and

Jill Scott immediately blared throughout the car. It was a track called "A Long Walk."

> Let's take a long walk around the park after dark
> Find a spot for us to spark
> Conversation, verbal elation, stimulation

Monica always had good taste in music, and Jill Scott was right up her alley. I couldn't help myself, but I was really excited. I felt like a kid out with his long-lost crush. Monica and I were alone, and there was no telling what the night might bring.

In Valley Stream, Long Island, Bronx BBQ wasn't the romantic and classy restaurant that I told her about, but it was still polite, neat, and refined in my book, and the food was good. It was a lounge-style place with a late-night DJ on weekends. And it was the weekend.

"This is the nice place that you were telling me about?" Monica said, sneering at the location.

"Have you been here before?"

"No!"

"So give it a chance. You'll like it. They got the best cornbread and macaroni here."

She sighed, and we walked inside. I knew about the place because another girl had brought me there a few weeks ago, and I enjoyed it.

We took a seat across from each other in the padded booths near the back. Our waitress placed our menus on the table and asked for our drink orders. I ordered a rum and Coke, and she ordered lemonade.

"You're not drinking tonight?" I asked.

"No. I'm fine."

I pouted. What fun was it to drink alone? But once again, I couldn't speak my mind. I simply let it go and wanted everything to turn out perfect tonight. The DJ started to spin some R&B records: R. Kelly, Jodeci, Troop, New Edition, and so on. He was jamming, and I was feeling his vibe. We had small talk at first. I talked about my job, spoke about our son, and waited for our meals to arrive. I ordered the baby back ribs, macaroni and cheese, and rice. Monica ordered the roasted chicken, a salad, and the cornbread.

The night was going right. We were two beautiful people having a nice night out with each other, and I wanted time to go really, really slowly.

"So can I ask you a question?" I said.

"What is it that you want to know?"

"How did you meet him, your husband?"

"We met at school. He taught English and American history. I was a student in one of his classes. He's a brilliant guy. Long story short, I started lingering around after class, we started talking, then dating, and then we got married."

"Wow, just like that, huh?"

She nodded.

"He's different from your regular type," I said.

"And what is my regular type? You?"

"I'm just sayin', are you physically attracted to him?"

"He's a good man, Ash. He treats your son and me very well. That's all you need to know."

She didn't answer my question. I knew there was a weakness in the chain somewhere.

"I was just curious," I said.

"It's not always about physical appearance. I like Patrick's personality and mind. I like the way he treats Justin and me. To me, that's very attractive."

I chuckled. "He's a lucky guy."

"He is."

It felt like I hit a small nerve with her. Monica was speaking on it, but I thought she wasn't feeling it.

"Does he know that you're out wit' me tonight?"

"Yes. He trusts me, Ash. That's what I love about him. We trust each other, and we don't keep secrets from each other."

"I respect that."

I took a sip of my drink and devoured one of my ribs, and then I said, "So what were some of the things that you used to love about me?"

"You really want to know, do you?"

"Yes!"

She chuckled. "You're a trip, Ash."

"Is that one of the things you used to love about me? Because I'm curious, that's all."

She smiled. I liked the direction it was going.

She sighed. "Well, one of the things I loved about you was your craziness. You were never boring. You were definitely something else. Even my mother thought that you were intriguing. She hated you, but she did find you intriguing."

I smiled. "Go on."

"You made me enjoy life and have fun. But you were unpredictable, always doing something dumb, fighting or selling drugs. But you did know how to make a girl have fun. That night you made me sneak out of the house and we took the cab to Coney Island, you argued with the cab driver."

"Yeah, I wasn't paying that fool no full thirty dollars. I needed some money left over to enjoy the park."

"It was stupid. He could have shot you."

"That fool wasn't gonna shoot anyone. He knew better."

"And that will always be you, Ash—a thug."

"But you used to have a good time wit' this thug. You remember how that night in Coney Island ended. We were underneath the boardwalk gettin' it in. Damn, that shit was fun," I said, feeling nostalgic over how good that pussy felt that night.

"I was young and dumb back then."

"No, you weren't. You were a pretty girl, still are, just having fun and enjoying your life."

"You almost got me kicked out of the house a few times. I don't know why I was always following your crazy ass around. The things you had me doing, getting me in trouble and almost getting me arrested . . ."

"I know. I'm sorry for putting you in a lot of risky situations," I said.

"It's in the past."

"But if it weren't for all the crazy fun, then we wouldn't have Justin."

"I think you got me pregnant on purpose. I was so scared. I thought my mother was going to kill me."

"I remember the night you found out. You kept blowing up my pager with 911. I thought you had beef or something. I was ready to wild out for you. And then you told me the news."

"Yes, and then to find out that I wasn't the only one you got pregnant . . . How's your daughter doing anyway?" Monica asked me coolly, but her eyes became hard on me.

"She's fine."

She shook her head from side to side and said, "I swear, you hurt me so much with that one, Ash. I used to cry every night over you."

"I know and I'm sorry. I was young, stupid, and naive back then."

"Do you still see her?"

"Who?"

She sucked her teeth. "Chanel, stupid."

"I do, but only for my daughter. We been done. She got a man now, some nigga named Keith. And she had another baby by him."

"Oh."

"I love both my kids. That's why I'm working and getting my act together. I want my kids to have a better life. And I want a family."

"A family? Ash, I know you. You're probably still out there and being a male whore, fucking everything that moves," she said.

"You still think that about me? That's sad, Monica. I've changed. I haven't had sex in a minute. I ain't tryin' to get caught up out there," I lied.

"And you expect me to believe that?"

"Believe what you want, but I'm different."

It was wrong of me to lie to her, but I wanted to do whatever it took to be with her. Sitting there with her, she was the only woman I saw myself settling down with and having more kids with, and it hurt me to know that she was married and had moved on with her life.

We continued to dine and chat. The DJ transitioned the music to some old-school songs by Earth, Wind & Fire, Stephanie Mills, Anita Baker, The Temptations, et cetera. It was a great atmosphere with great food. What was even better was seeing Monica laughing and smiling. The night was going smoothly. I couldn't take my eyes off her. She was perfect!

I ordered another rum and Coke, and I made Monica take a few sips. At first she resisted, but I had the gift of persuasion. I wanted her to loosen up more. Our meals were almost finished. I wanted our night together to linger.

"Monica, can I ask you a question?" I said.

"What you want to know, Ash, who got a bigger dick, you or my husband?"

I laughed and arrogantly replied, "I know it's me. That's not even my question. No comparison."

She chuckled. "You're so cocky."

"Yeah, I am," I laughed. "I'm all cocky!"

She smiled and took another sip of my drink. It was about time she started to loosen the tie and lose the attitude.

"But I wanna be serious for a minute," I uttered.

"About what?"

"Hypothetically, if I never got locked up, would you still be wit' me?"

"But you did, so there's no changing that, and you cheated on me and had another baby the same age as your son."

"I made a mistake. And I love my daughter, and I wouldn't change that in the world. But I love you. I really do. You are the one who got away, and I hated it. When I was locked up, you were always on my mind, all I could think about. I yearned for your visits. And the day I found out about your marriage, yo, I wanted to kill myself."

"Ash, why are you overreacting? You expect me to believe that?"

"Yes! Believe that because it's the truth," I replied wholeheartedly, locking eyes with her. "I'm still in love with you, girl. Shit, that same day, I got into it with another inmate and broke his damn jaw. You were my world, Monica."

"Well, it's seven years later, and things did change," she replied aloofly.

I sighed. Monica was always a hard nut to crack, but that didn't stop me from trying to break it.

"I know I was wild back then, we were young and voracious, but you can't tell me we didn't have fun. But you were that one to always calm me down when I got violent with something. You were the one who was always there for me. And I wish I could get a second chance wit' you, make things right."

"This was supposed to be a friendly dinner, Ash, not a chance for you to try to serenade me and try to fuck me. I knew we couldn't be friends or civilized. And you know my situation. I'm married."

I felt Monica was naive if she thought that we would simply have a private dinner together and I wasn't going to try to get back into her good graces, to try to spark or rekindle something between us. I felt that her accepting my dinner invitation was a slight opening into her life, and I wasn't going to allow the door to close back in my face.

In fact, I removed myself from my side of the booth and joined her on her side. Monica looked at me, astonished, and uttered, "Ash, what are you doing? Go sit back over there."

But I wasn't budging. I looked at Monica intently and said, "I just wanna be closer to you."

"You need to be closer to your son. He's what matters, not pussy."

I laughed.

"You find that funny?"

"No, and I do want to be closer to Justin, and you too. If I could rewind time, I would and make things right between us."

The smell of her sweet perfume flooding my nostrils was enticing me entirely. Being that close to Monica, I felt an erection growing inside my jeans. I wanted her badly, and I was going at full-throttle, top speed, and not veering off course.

"Ash, you're starting to make me feel uncomfortable. Please move to the other side," she said.

"Can I ask you something, Monica? Real talk?" I said.

"What?" she replied apathetically.

"Do you really love your husband?"

"I do!" she answered quickly.

I didn't believe her. I didn't see that same fierce and fanatic love that she had with me. In fact, she looked bored, and her life looked like it was mundane. Yes, she was comfortable and well-off, but I knew Monica like a book. What attracted her were random things like aggressive lovemaking and authentic excitement. If she were thrilled with her marriage, she wouldn't have agreed to have dinner with me. She was putting up a front.

"You can love him, but are you truly in love with him? Does he give you that same thrill and excitement like how I used to? We were something else back in the day, remember? Damn, the way you used to make me feel and how I used to make you feel, remember that?"

My heart was pounding heavily being so close to her. I was ready to tear myself apart with my fervent eagerness to have her right now. I couldn't control myself any longer. The smell of her, the closeness of her, the look of her—it was utterly crippling me with lust. I wanted to go to the extreme. I wanted to go in for the kill, and either

her reaction was going to be a harsh rejection with egg on my face or a slow but sure surrender. I took her hand out of the blue, and I placed it against my crotch underneath the table. She was shocked, and she resisted me entirely, but I wasn't letting her hand go. I made her feel how hard my dick was for her.

"Ash, what the fuck are you doing? Let go of my hand," she gruffly said to me.

But I didn't. I kept it there and felt her touch against me, and I said, "You remember that, baby? You remember how it used to make you feel?"

"Ash!"

She attempted to pull it away, but I firmly held it there. My dick grew more rigid in my jeans with her touch alone.

"I would do anything right now to just kiss your lips and touch you the way I want to touch you. I still love you so much. I just want a night wit' you, fo' real," I proclaimed sincerely.

"Ash, I'm a married woman," she replied feebly.

"Stop telling yourself that," I countered. "I know it's not that happy."

With her hand still forced on my crotch, I did the unthinkable. I forcefully grabbed between her legs and started to massage her crotch through the fabric. Monica sat rigidly, stunned by my action. I knew how she liked it, and I doubted that her husband was forceful, impulsive, and spontaneous like me. He seemed more of a by-the-book lovemaker—simple in the bedroom, boring missionary, no passion, and below-average muthafucka. I was a man who was batting it out of the ballpark with every hit.

"Be honest with yourself. This is what you miss," I continued to influence her.

My fingers continued to massage her crotch, and I no longer had to force her touch against me. I let go of her hand, and she continued to squeeze my hard dick cleverly on her own. It was crazy, us right there in the restaurant caressing each other underneath the table. In fact, I took things a step further and undid my jeans and pulled it out, and Monica wrapped her manicured hand around it and started to jerk me off slowly. It was exciting and bold, the two ingredients Monica always loved when it came to sex.

I looked at her intently, ready to tear her clothes off right there and fuck her on that table, but I had to control myself. Her hand went up and down my hard dick. This was my dessert. This was living. This was fun. We came this far, and I wasn't about to turn back.

"I wanna fuck you!" I growled hungrily in her ear.

"I knew this was going to be a mistake."

I couldn't let her relent to guilt and change her mind. Her door opened wider, and I was pushing myself further and further into her room.

"One night, who's gonna know? Treat yourself tonight," I said.

I had to move swiftly and subtly. I signaled for our waitress and asked for the bill. I wanted to pay for our meal and leave the place. I wanted to take her somewhere and fuck her. I had to have her tonight. I was going to explode if I didn't.

She continued to jerk me off nice and slow underneath the table. Her touch was so enticing that it was thrusting me into paradise, and she was going to make me come.

She huffed and replied, "Just one night."

***

The cheap motel on Rockaway Boulevard charged $10 an hour, and all we needed was about four hours. I paid for the room, and inside that cheesy, cheap room, I fucked Monica porn style. I had her buck-naked against the bed, legs and ass cheeks spread, and I impaled her from the back with my big fuckin' dick. As my dick went in and out of her like a piston, she grunted, cooed, and squirmed while pinned underneath me. Her face was buried into the pillow, and her hands stretched out and clutched the bedsheets tightly.

"Umm, umm. Oh, God. Umm," she moaned. "Ooooh, it feels so good."

I knew it did. I was like a jackhammer inside of her, grinding my hips against Monica's plump backside. I made sure she felt every inch of me nice and slow, and then I sped up inside of her. I was in perfect form and had my rhythm going. Her moans and cries were honest. There was nothing fake when it came to me. The pussy was so good, better than before, like it had been marinating over the years and became ripe just for my own pleasure. The only thing I hated was she made me wear a condom. I wanted to feel her raw, but she wasn't having it. No glove, no love. So I relented and pulled back the latex Magnum on my large endowment.

For four hours straight, we went at it like two horny, young teenagers. We sucked and fucked each other in every right area. We left nothing untouched. She gave me a blowjob so good that it nearly made my heart stop. That was the Monica I knew and fell in love with. We fucked in every position and in every square inch of that room, even in the shower. I brought that freak out in her. If her husband could see her now, how his wife did me so nasty, I swear, he would've blown his brains out.

I heard the magic words, "I'm gonna come!" for the umpteenth time tonight. And when she did, Monica was all over the place. Her body squirmed uncontrollably, and her moaning echoed so piercingly it could break a glass. Her body would go rigid, and her hands would tense into tight fists during her orgasm. Then she would go as limp as a wet noodle, and she would lie there spent, knowing it was that excellent dick that made her contort like a pretzel.

She did me justice too. Monica always made me come like a geyser, and tonight was no different. In truth, after my second time inside of her, the condom was no longer relevant. Monica was so horny and open, and that pussy felt so wet, that I purposely came inside her. When it neared the fourth hour inside the motel room, and it was time to check out of the room, I felt like a fat kid coming out of a giant candy store. I was delighted and overfed from the pussy. But Monica had a different look, almost like regret for what she did. She lay there naked and brooding.

"You good?" I asked her.

"I need to get home," she replied. "I need to get my son."

She started to get dressed, and even though I'd had her from top to bottom, mouth to below, I still stood there in awe at her curvy and soft body. It was perfection, better than I remembered it. And there was a part of me that wanted to get her pregnant again with my baby. It was foul thinking, but I wanted Monica to leave her husband, or vice versa, and have to come running back to me.

I wanted her back in my life.

Chapter Thirty

Devin

What is love? It's you and her, forever solid and vast, like heaven and space—an overwhelming entity, you're his sky and he's the rocket, soaring above to connect what is limitless . . .

Love starts with a smile, grows with a kiss, and then ends in tears. My mother used to tell me that when I was young, when I had my first girlfriend. I was 13. I was in love with this girl named Melanie. She was my first crush. I wanted to marry this girl.

Every day after summer school, Melanie came over to my house, and we did homework together. Afterward, we would play video games. She gave me my first kiss, and at the time, it meant the world to me.

We were boyfriend and girlfriend for nine weeks, summer love, and when you're young, you think that's a relationship. You think love is going to last forever. You think everything is perfect. But you're just a virgin to love. You don't expect the hard aches and pain that love will bring to you. You're not prepared for it.

But I remembered the first day that I ever got my heart broken. It was a week after our first day of school on a sunny September day. All summer, it was Melanie and I going to the beach and park, hanging out at each other's houses, and sneaking in kisses when our parents weren't around.

Melanie and I went to different schools. I came home from school one afternoon and saw her holding hands and kissing some guy. I was stunned. I always thought that she was my girlfriend, so why was she with this guy?

I ran up to Melanie, and I asked her if she was coming over to my place to do homework together. She told me no. She explained that she couldn't come over anymore. When I asked her why, she said to me that she was with Anthony now. Anthony was the new kid around the way. He was like the neighborhood jock. He was into basketball and football. He was taller than me, and all the girls had a crush on him.

She told Anthony to wait in front of her home while we went for a walk to talk. I begged her not to do this. I told her that I loved her. I didn't want to break up with her. I told her I would do anything. Melanie had me in tears. What she told me completely broke my heart. She said that I wasn't her type anymore. Anthony was now her type.

I went home in tears, crying my eyes out. I'd just had my heart broken. To this day, it felt like it was yesterday. I cried, and I didn't leave my room. My mother came into my room to comfort me.

"There will be others," she had said. "What you experienced was real life, Devin. You're young, and you need to move on. But one thing is for certain—this won't be the last time you'll feel lost and heartbroken. It comes with the territory in finding love."

She'd liked Melanie.

I never wanted to feel that pain ever again. My mother always gave me words of wisdom and encouragement. I would always remember what she'd told me. "Love starts with a smile, grows with a kiss, and ends in tears." I always thought that if that were true with everyone's relationship, that being in love would always end up having you in tears, then why do we fall in love in the first place?

However, that's just the tip of the iceberg. When you get older, you go through more drama, more pain, and headaches. When you become an adult, you see that love is a dangerous thing.

It was after 1:00 a.m. I was sleeping in my bed. But when I opened my eyes, Danielle wasn't in bed next to me. I knew we went to bed together, so where was she? I got up out of bed and headed to the living room, where I noticed Danielle talking to someone on the phone at this time of the morning. At first, I hesitated, listening to her on the phone, and then once again, this surge of jealousy just bled through me when I heard her say, "I miss you too."

Nah, I just didn't hear her say that. Who was she talking to so incredibly late at night? I stood in the middle of my home in my boxers. I listened to my woman chat with probably another man, and that Jonathan fellow was the first person who came to my mind.

"Danielle," I called out, looming from the darkness. I startled her.

"Devin, shit, you scared me!"

"Who are you talking to so late?" I asked.

"Oh. Jonathan. I was just calling to tell him goodbye before he leaves tomorrow," she said.

"Oh, he's leaving tomorrow? I thought he was gonna be here for three weeks."

"Nah, plans changed. He's flying out tomorrow."

"But damn, why so late at night? You couldn't tell him goodbye earlier?"

"He was busy. This was the best time to catch him," she said while covering the phone's mouthpiece. "Hold on, baby. Jonathan, I must go, but you have a safe trip back to Chicago, okay? Call me."

She hung up the phone and stood up. I didn't know what to think. I felt something wasn't right. She came up to me in her long white sleeper T-shirt.

"Let's go back to bed, baby. I'm sorry I woke you." She placed her arms around me and kissed me.

I didn't return the kiss. I was upset and I was jealous. Coming out of my bedroom to see my woman chatting with her ex-boyfriend in the middle of the night put a bad taste in my mouth. Was I supposed to forget about the whole thing?

"You okay, baby?" Danielle asked me.

"What time is his flight tomorrow?"

"Early in the morning."

"You sure that y'all are still just friends?"

She sighed. "Devin, I keep telling you this. Jonathan and I are friends, nothing else. Believe me. He's leaving tomorrow anyway. So you don't have to worry about him. Now let's go back to bed and let me give you a massage."

She took me by my hand, leading me to the bedroom, trying to become seductive, thinking that by giving me sex I'd forget about her little late-night talk with her ex.

I was quiet, allowing her to lead me into the bedroom, where she continued to kiss me all over.

"What's wrong?" she asked like she didn't know.

"You know what? Nothing!" I dryly said to her.

"Devin, please don't let this upset you. I'm sorry, okay, if that makes you feel any better."

What the hell did she mean, if it made me feel any better? I just looked at my woman, and for the first time, I had my doubts.

"Look, let's just both go to bed, okay?" I said.

She sighed. "Okay."

I just jumped into bed, throwing the sheets over me, and tried real hard to forget about this night. I wanted to believe her. He was leaving tomorrow. That was a good thing. He would be miles away from my woman, back in Chicago, and I wouldn't have to worry about him being around Danielle anymore. That was the best news I'd heard so far.

Danielle climbed into bed and tried to cuddle next to me. But I wasn't in the cuddling mood. I just turned around and had my back facing her, inching myself away from her. I heard her sigh, getting upset, but I paid her no attention for the rest of the night. I was very adamant in ignoring Danielle.

The next morning, Danielle went to work. I called in sick and stayed home. I couldn't stop thinking about this Jonathan fellow and wondering if Danielle had fucked him while he was here in New York. I didn't even know what the guy looked like. He could be some pretty boy with money trying to persuade Danielle back into his life. He was probably flossing his charm and his wealth to impress her.

But at least it was safe to say that he was on a plane to Chicago by now.

I linked up with Terrance and Trey that evening. They wanted to go out to the park and play a little basketball since it was eighty-five degrees out. I wasn't into sports like Terrance and Trey were. I'd just shoot my jump shots and make a few baskets, but as for balling and dunking, I wasn't athletic like that.

We all had on our basketball shorts, sporting our team jerseys. Terrance and I had on Knicks jerseys—33 Patrick Ewing—and Trey had on a Nets jersey. The park wasn't that crowded, so we took the nearest court.

Terrance had the ball, dribbling it between his legs, and then he went up for a layup, making the basket. Trey took the ball and shot a jump shot, making the basket, and then he passed the ball to me. I shot my jumper, and I missed, so Trey gave me the ball again, and I shot another jumper, making the second shot.

"It's about time," Terrance joked.

We continued to shoot around for about twenty minutes, each taking turns making our baskets by either taking a shot or laying it up. Terrance went that extra mile and started to dunk it. He could do that because he had ups and skills like that. But then he started getting to the point where he was showing off, repeatedly dunking the ball whenever he got his hands on the rock.

"You a fuckin' showoff!" Trey hollered at his cousin.

"Don't hate," Terrance responded, throwing another dunk into the rim. "Yo, let's get a game or something."

"There's only three of us, stupid!" Trey said.

"Twenty-one then. Devin, you start it off," Terrance said, tossing me the basketball.

We started to play Twenty-one. Terrance was winning. He was up by like ten points, and it was getting to the point where Trey and I were getting tired of playing with him. He was cocky on the courts, sometimes a little too cocky.

"Why you so fuckin' jolly all of a sudden?" Trey asked, throwing the ball hard and fast at Terrance's chest.

Terrance caught the ball, smiling. "Yo, I'm getting mine again," he said.

"Getting what? You jerking off?" Trey joked.

"Nah, I'm getting mine again," Terrance happily repeated.

"Word. You and Sophia got back together?" I asked.

"Nah, Devin. Yasmin, yo."

"Yasmin? Yo, you fucked her?" Trey asked.

"Oh, I forgot he doesn't know," Terrance said.

"Know what?"

"I've been fuckin' her."

"Say word!" Trey shouted, smiling hard. "Damn, son. Yo, get the fuck outta here! How you hittin' that, yo? That's your wife's best friend. Damn, you doing Sophia grimy like that?"

"Yo, it just happened."

"So y'all like official now?" I asked.

"Maybe," Terrance replied.

"Damn, that's a fine piece of ass," Trey proclaimed.

"I know, son. Believe me, I know," Terrance said.

"Yo, Sophia know?" Trey asked.

"Yeah, she found out. Yasmin told her."

"Oh, shit. Yo, how that shit went down?" Trey asked.

"Yo, I don't get these females. Sophia says she doesn't wanna be with me, but now she is getting all upset, trippin' out when she finds out that I fucked Yasmin, trying to kick me out of my own home. Yo, that's my word. I was about to kill her the other night."

"What happened?" I asked.

"She gonna bring up some nigga she's been fuckin'."

"Say word!" Trey uttered.

"Yeah. Yo, she finds out about Yasmin and me, so she gonna blow that shit up in my face. Yo, I was about to smack that bitch, disrespecting me like that."

"Yo, that's just hate right there," Trey said. "You doing your thang right though, damn, moving on from one piece of ass to the other."

"Man, I'm just doing me. Yasmin is cool peoples. She be making me feel really good. She mad cool."

"Terrance, that shit is good, though, right?" Trey asked.

"Yo, you see me still smiling, right? Her shit is . . . Damn, I'm catching shivers just thinking about that pussy!" Terrance said, quivering with the basketball in his hand as a joke to us.

We both laughed.

"Just don't rush out and marry her like you did Sophia," Trey told him.

"Ah, man, you ain't got to worry about that. I ain't getting married again for a minute now."

"Yeah, a'ight. You and Devin gonna end up on the same boat. So Sophia fuckin' somebody else, huh?" said Trey.

"Fuck her!" Terrance cursed.

Trey chuckled.

"What's so funny?" Terrance asked.

"You! A few weeks ago, you were all crying and shit, beating your meat, stressing about Sophia. Now you are in bed with her best friend. Yo, now that's doing a bitch dirty."

"Whatever, yo," Terrance spat. "Yo, let's get another game or something."

Terrance and Trey soon joined a full-court game with some other players in the park. I sat nearby and watched them play. My mind was on Danielle. I couldn't stop thinking about her and asking myself, was she honest with me? Was she being real with me?

I loved that woman so much, and I really wanted this. I wanted us to be together. I wanted to marry her. But if she was becoming dishonest with me, what was going to happen when we got married? *What if she doesn't want to get married?*

I was thinking crazy. Of course Danielle wanted to get married. I was just thinking negatively because of that little conversation she had last night. I probably was just blowing that shit out of proportion. I mean, she wouldn't have been stupid enough to have a conversation in my house and on my phone with some other man unless he was really just a friend to her.

All I kept thinking about was trust.

I picked up my cell phone and called Danielle's number. I knew she was still at work, and I got her voice mail.

"Danielle, hey, sweetie, it's Devin. Listen, I'm so sorry about last night and the way I acted toward you. I admit that I was a little jealous, but I love you so much. So can you accept my apology? I promise to make it up to you when I get home tonight, okay? I love you. Bye, sweetie."

I quickly hung up, seeing Trey and Terrance coming my way. They were both sweating hard, winded from the pickup game. Terrance went straight to the water fountain, saving not a drop for the fishes as he gulped down tremendous amounts of water.

"Save some for a shower, damn," Trey said to him.

"Shut up!"

I gathered my things. We were about ready to go. The sun was hot, we were sweaty and stinky, and I needed a shower. We hopped in Terrance's truck, and we all went back over to my place for the remainder of the day.

Back at my place, I took a quick shower and put on something fresh and clean. We all ordered pizza and watched ESPN and then a movie. It was a little after five, and Danielle didn't arrive home from work sometimes until after six. So I had a short time more to chill with the fellows before I had to kick 'em out and have my time with Danielle. I wanted to apologize to her, and then I wanted to make love to her.

Is it a crime to love your woman too much? Because I did. I lived every day of my life to be with Danielle. I wanted her to have my children. I wanted us to one day have a fiftieth anniversary. I wanted us to grow old together.

"Yo, Devin, you sure your woman ain't gonna flip out when she comes home and sees us sitting here? Because we all know who is in charge in this relationship," Trey joked.

"Y'all won't be here when she gets home," I told them.

"Oh, so it's like that?" Trey said.

"I was with y'all all day. Now I gotta spend some time with my woman."

Trey chuckled. "Hey. Do you!"

Before six, the guys left. And I cleaned up the mess that they left behind, and then I prepared a little something delicious on the stove for Danielle.

When she got home, she was ecstatic about the message I'd left and that I had dinner ready, because she was hungry and she was tired. She gave me a hug and then had something nice to eat.

Afterward, I pulled Danielle into my arms and grabbed her butt. I kissed her. I wanted some and said, "C'mon, let's have sex right now."

"Babe, I would love to, but I'm just too tired right now," she said. "I want to get undressed, relax, and watch some TV."

I understood. I sighed, let my woman rest, and went outside for a walk.

I felt that everything was going to be okay between us. We were young, and our relationship wasn't always going to be perfect. You're going to have arguments and quarrels with your significant other once in a while. Sometimes there's bickering, but that's just love and life, right?

Chapter Thirty-one

Trey

> *Love . . . unconditional love is truly a godsend, and priceless, worth more than any earthly currency . . .*

As much as I teased Devin about spending too much time with his woman, I envied him. He believed in fidelity wholeheartedly, and sometimes I wished I could be as strong as him. I always asked myself, *how does he do it? How does he stay faithful to one woman and not veer off course with his dick?* I told myself that if I were like Devin, then I would still have Trisha in my life.

It'd been two weeks since I'd heard or seen Trisha. She still wasn't excepting any of my calls. So I just decided to stop by her place unannounced and see how she was doing. I had Chica continually calling me up, talking about I was her baby's father and that her grandmother was really pissed off at me. If that indeed was my baby, I knew that I had to be a man and become a father. I never knew my father when I was growing up. He abandoned his family when I was 2 years old. And I'd always told myself that I wasn't going to be like him. It was going to be difficult because I didn't want a family at the moment, and I didn't want to be with Chica at all.

I parked outside of Trisha's place and sat in my car, contemplating if I should approach her door and confront our situation. How would she react? Was she still angry at me? I wanted to confess to her that I'd changed, but would she believe it? Did I believe it myself? Had I actually changed? It started to drizzle. I sighed. I climbed out of my car and slowly approached her front door. I rang the bell and waited. I deeply missed her. I couldn't stop thinking about her. I wanted her back in my life, and I was willing to do anything.

Her cousin opened the door. I wasn't expecting her. With her hand on her hip and a scowl and attitude on her face, she exclaimed, "What do you want?"

"Is Trisha here?" I asked.

"She doesn't wanna see you. She hates you! You got some nerve to show up at her door asking for her. Don't play yourself!"

"I just want to talk to her. I don't need the attitude from you, Candace."

"Well, you got one. And besides, she ain't home. She's out on a date right now."

I was taken aback by the news. She was on a date with another man. Candace saw the look on my face, and she continued with, "Yeah, she's over you."

"You're lying!"

"Why I gotta lie? She's not here."

"I'm not leaving here until I see Trisha. I'll pitch a tent right here outside. I don't care," I said seriously.

"Trey, she doesn't wanna see you."

"I don't care. I gotta make things right with her," I replied, not taking no for an answer. "I fucked up. I know I did. Your cousin is a good woman."

"Damn right she is!" Candace agreed.

"But I need to talk to her. I need to see her face-to-face and say my piece, and I promise you I'll move on. I'll go my way, and you and she will never have to see my face again. But I need to apologize to her. I really need to get this off my chest. Please tell me where she is."

Candace looked at me intently, not replying right away. I was damn near on my knees begging her. She sighed heavily and said, "You better not do anything stupid, Trey. I swear."

"I'm not. I love her so much that I'm willing to let her go."

"She's over at the restaurant on Queens Boulevard, the Royal Blue."

I smiled and quickly uttered, "Thank you!" and I sprang and leaped toward my car.

It started to rain heavier, becoming a torrential downpour. I hurriedly drove to Queens Boulevard, wipers on full blast, headlights on, and trying not to crash in the rain. It looked like a river outside, and I went through several deep puddles. But I didn't care about the weather. It could have been a snowstorm, and I still would have pushed on.

I made it to the restaurant Royal Blue and double-parked outside, not caring about parking or anything else. Trisha was my only priority. I dashed from my car and into the restaurant. A few seconds out, I was already soaked. I clashed with the maître d' at the entrance.

"Sir, do you have a reservation?" he asked.

"No! I'm here to see someone," I replied. I tried to hurry by him, but he stood in my way.

"Sir, you can't just walk inside," he exclaimed.

"Fuck I can. My woman is in there." I shoved him out of my way and hurried into the restaurant.

This was important, and nobody was going to stop me. Immediately, my eyes danced around the crowded room, looking for Trisha. I was dripping wet and quickly became the anomaly inside the restaurant. I spotted Trisha seated at a corner table near the back. Sitting across from her was a tall, dark-skinned man with a full, trimmed beard, neatly dressed in a black suit. I approached them quickly, like I was the Terminator looking for Sarah Connor. The man with Trisha noticed me first, and then Trisha turned her head and saw me coming. Her eyes went wide, and she was stunned by my sudden presence.

"Trey, what are you doing here?"

"I'm here to see you."

"What? Why?"

"You've been avoiding my phone calls too long now. I need to talk to you."

"How did you know I was here?"

"Your cousin told me."

"Well, we don't have anything to talk about. I'm done with you," she said.

"Excuse me, but we're trying to have dinner here," her supposed date chimed at me.

"Yo, this isn't your fuckin' business, so shut the fuck up!" I cursed at him.

"Trey!" Trisha exclaimed.

"She doesn't wanna see you, so leave," he said harshly and stood up from his chair. "I'll make you leave!"

I was ready to make a scene. I was prepared to fight. I exclaimed, "You better sit your punk ass down!"

"Trey, can you please leave? You're making a scene in here."

"Not until I talk to you in private!" I uttered, glaring at her friend.

"She's with me, and you're rudely interrupting our meal," he said.

"What the fuck you gonna do? That's my woman!" I shouted.

"Trey, you're embarrassing me," Trisha barked at me.

"Gentlemen!" A lean white man dressed in a fancy three-piece suit interrupted our clash. He looked like he was the manager of the place. "This is a restaurant, not a cage match. I would appreciate it if the two of you would take your quarrel outside."

I ignored him and looked over at Trisha and said, "Trisha, all I want to do is talk to you, that's all. Five minutes."

She looked embarrassed and hesitant. She continued to sit there. I added, "I'm not leaving here until you talk to me."

"Fine!" she exclaimed, upset. She pushed back her chair and stood up. "Let's talk! Outside!"

I smirked at her male friend. *Fuckin' asshole!* He couldn't have her.

Trisha and I walked toward the exit. She looked great in a black sheath dress and her high heels. She'd gotten spruced up for her date, and I was upset. But at least she agreed to talk to me. And fortunately for us, it had stopped raining, so that gave us a chance to sit in my car and talk.

I didn't beat around the bush. Immediately, I said, "Trisha, I'm sorry. I am. I did so much to you, and I fucked up. I hate myself every day for what I did to you, taking you for granted. And I miss you. You're a great woman, and I fucked that up! But I'm tired of fuckin' it up. I just want you, baby. You mean the world to me."

"I'm tired of hearing your damn excuses, Trey. I'm tired of the same apologies. You're never gonna change, and I can't wait forever," she said.

I looked at her seriously and asked, "What is it going to take for you to forgive me? I'll do anything."

"Nothing! I'm done with you."

"I love you!"

"No, you don't!" she screamed at me. "If you love someone, you don't treat them the way you treated me, Trey. That is not loving. You don't even know what love is." She started to cry.

"I just want another chance," I begged.

She fumed.

I had to pull out my secret weapon. I reached below my seat, grabbed the velvet ring box, opened it, and showed her the two-carat engagement ring.

"I do know what love is, and I want you to marry me. Become my wife, Trisha?" I proposed wholeheartedly to her.

She looked at me for a moment, speechless and shocked, I guessed. But what came next totally caught me off guard.

Smack!

My face pivoted sharply from the blow, and she exclaimed, "Fuck you, Trey! No, I'm tired of you! I'm tired of your empty promises. First you embarrass me in the restaurant and in front of my date, and now you expect me to marry you? You want me to believe that you just changed overnight? No!"

Her rejection was unequivocal.

"Trish—"

"Trey, shut up, please," she uttered with teary eyes and wet cheeks. "I loved you so much. But you continue to hurt me over and over again. You had some whore call my phone and tell me things that I can't forget. You come with risks, and I don't need any risks in my life. So please just leave me alone," she proclaimed clearly.

I groaned profoundly with my heart fluttering. I never felt so nervous. I looked at Trisha, and now my eyes were watering.

"So this is it?" I said faintly, taken aback by everything.

"Goodbye, Trey," she said right away. "You have a nice life, but it won't be with me."

Goodbye? I couldn't believe it. Her eyes spoke volumes to me. She was utterly fed up. She opened the car door and climbed out. I felt frozen to my seat with utter shock and sadness. The door slammed, and she went back into the restaurant to be with that nigga.

My tears started to fall. My heart dropped into my stomach like cement. I felt grief. There was this pain that felt like someone had hit me in the face and chest with a brick. I sat there and watched her walk out of my life. It was definitely over. I knew it was. Her eyes didn't lie to me. But who could I blame but myself? I couldn't hate Trisha for her decision. I wanted to play around, be that player, have my fun, and I lost the best thing in my life. There were consequences for my foolish choices, and losing Trisha was a disaster.

She was right, though—I couldn't keep apologizing for the same mistakes. And the chances of Chica being pregnant by me were favorable. The only thing I could do was wipe my tears and drive away. I couldn't fix things with Trisha, but maybe there was something else I could fix in my life.

That same night, I stopped my car in front of Chica's place. I had to make things right. That meant taking a paternity test when the baby was born. If the child was mine, then I was going to take care of my responsibilities.

I'd treated Chica like my own personal sex object, coming and going when I pleased. She made me feel good, and I took advantage of her. I used her. There was never going to be a relationship with her, no future. She was simply enjoyment, and now she was pregnant. The funny thing was, the same thing that makes you laugh will make you cry.

I went up to her door and rang the bell. I prayed that her grandmother wouldn't answer with her shotgun. I saw the curtain move at the side window, someone looking to see who it was. The door opened, and Chica loomed into my view.

"What do you want, Trey? You here to beat me up?" she said with sarcasm.

"I came here to talk. That's it."

She paused for a moment, her eyes on me, and said, "We can talk."

She stepped aside, allowing me into the house. The moment I was inside, her grandmother trotted down the stairs. She looked at me fiercely, angry that I was in her home. I was nervous.

"Muthafucka! Where's my damn shotgun? I warned you, nigga, not to bring my granddaughter back here pregnant, didn't I?" she cursed at me.

"I'm sorry, ma'am. I just came to talk," I said.

"You are sorry! You're lucky I don't blow your damn dick off."

"Grandma, please. He just came here to talk," said Chica.

"I did, ma'am. I didn't mean any disrespect to your home," I said.

"You talked enough with your dick!" she retorted.

Chica sighed and said, "Let's go talk outside."

We stepped outside on the porch, leaving her fuming grandmother inside. Chica closed the door behind her, turned to look at me with attitude, crossed her arms over her chest, and said, "What do you need to talk to me about?"

"Look, I'm sorry about the other night," I started. "I lost control and I was upset."

"It's forgotten."

"And you're sure you're pregnant?"

She sucked her teeth. "Yes! I went to the doctor the other day, and I'm six weeks. And yes, it's your baby. You were the only man I've been fuckin'. So don't try to play me like that."

"I'm not."

"See, you think I'm this ho, but I'm not. Yeah, I like sex, but don't get it twisted. I don't fuck every man I see or like. I liked you a lot, Trey. I thought you were special. So when I really like someone, I go all out to please them—and yes, sexually."

She was emotional and upset. The way she looked at me was heartfelt. Her eyes diverted from mine temporarily, and she sighed. She looked back at me just in time to wipe away the tears from her eyes.

"But I knew what it was between us, Trey. I was never gonna be ya girl. I was never gonna be Trisha, right? I was just that rebound bitch who got your dick hard and made you come nice. We had fun, right? And now I'm carrying your baby. But you ain't gotta worry about me. I'll be a'ight."

"So you're serious about having this baby?"

"Yes! At least someone's gonna love me, right? What, you worried about child support?"

"I just wanna do the right thing," I said.

She laughed. "And what's the right thing, trying to persuade me to get an abortion?"

"No, just—"

"Trey, you good. Just continue being an asshole and find some bitch to fuck wit'. I'm just tired of being your little whore."

I sighed. "I'm gonna be there for that baby."

"Don't make broken promises."

"I'm for real."

She looked at me doubtfully and rolled her eyes. "What, because you heard pregnant pussy is the best pussy, huh?"

"No, because I wanna change. I need to start by doing right by you."

I needed to grow up. We'd both made mistakes, and I wanted to learn from mine. I didn't want a baby by Chica, but I had to accept it. We both laughed together, and we needed to cry together. And this was my reality, and there was no alternative.

I saw the sadness in Chica's eyes. She admitted to me, "I'm scared, Trey. I don't know anything about raising a baby, but I'm gonna try. But the last thing I need from you is false hope. So if you're not serious about this shit, then step off and leave. I don't need you. We don't need you."

"Chica, I'm here. Not in a relationship, but being a father to that baby. That's all I can give you right now."

She smiled, and her eyes smiled. "Thank you," she said.

I pulled her into my arms, and I hugged her tightly and securely. She held on to me, and it was like a breath of fresh air. A different chapter was starting in my life, and I had no idea how my story was going to end.

I got home around midnight. I was tired, and I just wanted to hit the sack and sleep for hours and forget about everything that had happened tonight. But then my doorbell rang. I had no idea who was at my door after midnight. I was hoping it was Trisha coming over to reconcile and rethink my proposal, but that probably was wishful thinking.

I donned a robe and marched toward the door. I looked outside, and it was Janice. I opened the door.

"Hey, Trey," she greeted me.

"Hey."

"I just thought that you might need some company tonight."

I smiled. "Yeah. Come in."

Hey, what the heck. I lost the best thing that ever happened to me, but that didn't mean I had to sit around every night and cry about it. I was a free and single man again, and it was time for me to start over, but also to learn from my mistakes. And Janice was great company. Who knew what the future held for me? But I wanted to be happy.

Chapter Thirty-two

Ash

His tongue and hands taking her to so many places, the seduction is near . . . but be aware . . .

I couldn't stop thinking about Monica, but it was evident that she wasn't thinking about me. She wasn't returning my phone calls. I figured she must have felt guilty about that night. But I didn't. I loved every minute of it, and I wanted a round two with her. But I had other cities to conquer, and one of those cities was Kenya. After weeks and weeks of hard work with her, I finally got an invitation over to her place. She wanted to cook me dinner, and after dinner, there was going to be dessert, and I couldn't wait for my dessert.

I took a cab to her apartment in Bay Ridge, Brooklyn, and arrived late that evening at her four-story walk-up. It was a nice area, with 66 percent of the population white. And I was that black man climbing out of a cab dressed like I was going to do a rap video. But I came for a lovely evening and some pussy, and her neighbors' lingering stares weren't going to prevent that.

I rang her buzzer, and she buzzed me up. I climbed the stairs to the fourth floor and knocked on her apartment door. I couldn't wait to see her. I was excited. It felt like it was going to be an unforgettable night. She opened the door and looked stunning in a pink velvet robe tied around her waist, and I could only imagine what it looked like underneath—pure glory.

I smiled.

"Come in," she said.

I stepped into her neatly furnished apartment and gave her a hug. I wanted to give her a lot more right away, but she wanted to play this flirtatious game with me. It was cool as long as I got some tonight.

She already had dinner cooking in the kitchen, and it smelled tasty.

"Did you have trouble finding my place?" she asked.

"Nah, it was easy. I took a cab. What are you cooking?"

"Some cabbage, rice, and chicken," she said.

"Damn, you know how to burn too in the kitchen. You ain't no joke, I see. The wifey type and shit."

She giggled.

I watched her walk into the kitchen, and my eyes lingered on her little backside, and I felt a rise growing in my jeans. She was too pretty, and she was neat. Her place was well put together and organized, and it smelled garden fresh and clean. I loved a clean and organized woman.

"Dinner will be ready soon," she said, coming out of the kitchen.

"No rush."

"I know you must be hungry."

"Yeah, I'm hungry, all right, but it ain't for what's in the kitchen," I hinted.

"Oh, really, and what are you hungry for?" She flashed a rude-boy smile and took a seat on my lap with her arms around me.

"I'm hungry for some pussy right now." I was candid. I hated to beat around the bush, because a closed mouth doesn't get fed.

We started to passionately kiss, and I began to grope her body, fondling her soft breasts and ready to skip dinner and feast on my dessert.

"I wanna suck your dick," she uttered.

She descended onto her knees and positioned herself between my legs. She undid my jeans and pulled out my big black dick. It was still growing hard in her hand, and I was looking forward to a skillful blowjob. First she admired it and then jerked me off, and I moaned. I wanted to feel her soft, wet lips around it. I wanted to feel paradise tonight, and I was well on my way.

"Umm, that feels good," I groaned softly.

"It does?"

"Yeah. Keep doing that."

I knew if her hand job felt this good, I could only imagine what her lips were going to feel like. She continued with the hand job for a moment, enticing me entirely, and she had my dick so hard it was definitely like I was carrying a third leg.

"You want me to suck your dick now?" she teased.

"Hells yeah." I had my eyes closed and was sinking deeply into her rapture.

I soon felt her moist and full lips around my hard cock and her tongue against my skin. I was entirely inside her mouth, and her head bobbed up and down, up and down, nice and slow. She took complete control of me below, no gagging, deep-throating me like a professional, licking and massaging my balls. I gripped the couch cushion tightly, and my eyes rolled to the back of my head.

"Oh, shit!" I moaned. "Oh, shit. Damn, ma."

Already, she'd received an A-plus for her superb head game. She went for five minutes and then ten minutes, continuing to please me nonstop. I was ready to blow by then.

"That's good to you, baby?" she said, taking a quick breather from her oral action.

"Fuck yeah!"

She went back down on me for another ten minutes, and I was like, *whoa, this is the one.* She was definitely the one. She had my legs quivering like they were cold.

"Yo, I wanna fuck you right now," I said.

She lifted her face from my dick, her mouth coated with some pre-cum, and she grinned. "You wanna fuck me?"

I nodded. If her blowjob was this good, I could only imagine how good the pussy was. She straddled me on the couch, and my hands started to roam across her body. I undid her robe and explored underneath it, and she was soft and curvy. This was a fine-tuned woman from head to toe. I wanted to finger her. I knew she was wet, and I loved a wet woman. My touch continued to travel deeper between her thighs, and I wanted to grab a fistful of her prize. She touched me and kissed me. I wanted to fuck her so badly that my dick started to hurt. She giggled in my ear. I went for her pussy like a kid to his gifts on Christmas Day. And then it happened—something strange and unfamiliar to the female anatomy. What I felt below was a dick. I was taken aback, completely shocked. I pushed her off my lap and jumped to my feet.

"Yo, what the fuck was that?" I shouted.

Kenya was on the floor, looking up at me with a sneaky grin. She giggled and said, "Oh, you didn't know? What do you think it is?"

"Yo, that shit felt like a dick."

"That's because it is a dick."

"You a fuckin' dude?"

"We like to be called transsexuals."

I couldn't believe this shit. Kenya was a guy. She was too damn pretty to be a guy. She had tits and ass, but I'd inadvertently felt her package with my own hands, and it was almost as big as mine, so it was definitely real. I felt disgusted and lied to. She stood up and opened her robe and pulled it out—her dick.

"You knew what I was, so don't act all surprised," she said smugly.

"Fuck you! You lying freak!"

"Yeah, you weren't mad when I was sucking your dick for a half hour and you were kissing these lips."

"Yo, I ain't no fuckin' faggot!"

"You could have fooled me. You must be a faggot if you got that hard for me. I bet you're still hard for me right now."

I fumed and clenched my fists. This freak bitch was trying the wrong man. "Yo, I ain't no fuckin' faggot, you fuckin' freak!" I yelled.

"C'mon, fuck me in the ass, Ash. Or how about I fuck you in the ass and make you come from the back like a bitch?" she taunted me.

I'd had enough. I burst out in rage and charged at her heatedly, throwing a stinging punch to her face and knocking her down to the floor, bruising the side of her face. Kenya didn't stay down long though. She sprang to her feet and yelled at me, "You wanna hit a bitch?" She started to throw blows at me.

A fistfight ensued in the living room, and we belliger-ently tore into each other. But I was madder. Fuck that. I was livid. This freak bitch tricked me into a sexual liai-son, and I hated she did that to me. I became the aggres-sor and two-pieced Kenya with my fists. I then elbowed the side of her eye. I punched her in the stomach, grabbed her roughly, and madly threw her into the glass coffee ta-ble. She violently fell into the table, on her back, and it shattered entirely with shards of glass cutting into her skin.

She was dazed. I stood over her, I was possessed with rage, and I felt no other emotions. Glaring at her, I lifted my Timberland boot knee-high and slammed the bottom of it against her face, and something cracked. I continued to stomp this faggot bitch with my boots repeatedly, all while screaming insanely, "I ain't no fuckin' faggot! You fuckin' hear me? You fuckin' ugly freak bitch! Fuck you! Fuck you! I ain't no fuckin' faggot!"

I stomped her head and face until her/his face looked like it had exploded. I was breathing heavily, winded. My clothing had blood on it, and my construction boots were almost crimson. Kenya lay there unmoving, beaten, cut up, and bloody. I thought I went overboard and killed her or him. I was still on parole. I'd fucked up. Coming back to my senses, I grabbed my shit and hurried from the apartment. I just wanted to get as far away from her and Brooklyn as possible. I felt I had just murdered this muthafucka, and I had the right to do so.

I wasn't a faggot.

I arrived back in Queens hours later. I was home and walking toward my mother's place, being a block away. I wanted to take a long shower and chill out for a moment. I tried not to panic. I tried to reason. They couldn't prove I was there. I'd never told anyone about Kenya, so there couldn't be a link to me—hopefully. *First, go back to work as if nothing happened.* If I stopped coming to work, it would bring about suspicion, and if the police came by to ask questions, I didn't know a damn thing.

I strutted toward my mother's place with my mind spinning. But when it rains, it pours. The closer I came to the house, the sick and nervous feeling in my stomach started to churn faster and faster. I saw a black Lexus with tinted windows and chrome rims parked in front of my house, and it immediately told me that something wasn't right. I'd seen that car before, but I couldn't place it. It was new on my mother's block. I slowed my pace and was fixated on the vehicle. A few houses down, I stopped entirely and gawked at the car. I didn't have my gun on me. *Shit!*

I stood there, watching or waiting, fight or flight, either one, but I knew that Lexus was trouble for me. I couldn't picture the driver of that car right away. It wasn't coming to me. It was idling, though. They had to see me. I was right there in front of their view—no hiding. And then it came to me prompt like a flash of lightning. Andre was the Lexus owner, and Andre was Keith's cousin. Now Keith may have been a flower-puff girl in my eyes, but his cousin Andre was hardcore and a heavy hitter from Far Rockaway. He was a heartless killer. And he was definitely there for me. There was no denying that. It was revenge for that fight with Keith a few weeks ago. And my decision was to take flight instead of fighting. I pivoted and ran off, and the car chased my way. Behind me, I heard the rapid gunshots. Bak! Bak! Bak! Bak! Bak!

I ran so fast that I became the Flash. I didn't turn around. I was being shot at, and I was running for my damn life. I zigzagged through parked cars on the block and promptly dipped right, dashing into a neighbor's yard and scaling the fence like a track star. I tried to disappear in the dark. I was sweating like a slave. I could hear the car screeching and felt them nearby hunting me like I had a bounty on my head. I then heard someone yell, "Yo, you pussy nigga! I'm gonna body you. Yeah, run, muthafucka! Run!"

They didn't stay long. The car drove off, leaving me hiding in someone's backyard and shocked by everything. It felt like I was about to have a heart attack. My heart was racing. They wanted me dead. I knew one thing for sure—I couldn't go home. I was expected there. I needed to get to the phone.

I stayed hidden for a few hours, knowing the attention the gunshots were going to bring and knowing that Andre and his cousin weren't going to stop looking for me. And the cops came to inspect, but I kept in the dark and alert.

In the early morning, I called Terrance's cell phone, but he didn't answer. I called Trey with the same results. I was running out of options. My last phone call was to Monica, and I prayed she picked up.

"Hello?" she answered.

"Monica, please, it's me, Ash. Don't hang up," I pleaded.

"Ash, what do you want?"

"I just got shot at tonight. I need help."

"Oh, my God. Are you okay?"

"I just need to get out of Queens for a night or two," I said.

"What do you want from me?"

"Can I come by there?"

"What? No! Are you crazy?"

"They're gonna kill me, Monica!" I uttered fearfully. "I can't go back home."

"Ash, you can't come here."

"Monica, you all I got right now. Please, just for a night or two. Ask your husband. He seems to be an understanding man."

"You're putting me in an awkward position."

"I'm not tryin' to, but if I don't, I'm dead out here."

"When are you gonna change, Ash?" she cried out.

"I just need your help. That's all I'm asking," I begged and moaned.

There was a long pause from her. I knew she was considering it. And then I heard her say, "I'll see what I can do. Call me back in an hour."

She hung up. I sighed. *An hour. In an hour, I might be dead.* What I needed was my gun and a safe place to lay my head. The fact that they came to my mother's home and put her in danger made me heated. I wanted to clap back, but I was vulnerable right now. I had to watch my surroundings entirely.

I waited nearly an hour and called Monica back via the pay phone. She answered, and I asked, "What's the deal?"

"Two nights, Ash. That's it," she said.

I breathed a sigh of relief. "Oh, thank you, Monica, you're the best."

"Don't thank me. You need to thank my husband."

"I will definitely!"

I showed up at their brownstone early in the morning. Monica's husband answered the door. He looked at me, and I looked at him. I didn't feel any tension from him. He asked if I was okay. I replied, "I'm fine." I came with just the shirt on my back, and he allowed me into his home. Monica stood in the living room quietly. It was definitely an awkward situation, especially since we shared a dirty little secret. Having her husband and her son's father staying under the same roof for forty-eight hours was definitely nerve-racking.

"You can sleep on the couch, but only for two nights, and then you need to go," her husband said.

"I really do appreciate this," I said.

"The only reason I'm allowing this is because you're Justin's father, and I trust my wife," he said.

I nodded. "Thanks."

He trusted his wife. I laughed and smiled inwardly. If only he knew what his wife and I had done a few nights ago, how nasty and freaky she'd treated my dick. But I had to humble myself.

"And there are rules here. You're not allowed to be here alone, and you must spend some quality time with Justin," he said.

"I have to work in the day. And I never got to thank you for the job."

"I've heard that you made quite the impression there."

"It's a good job. I like it."

"I'm glad to hear it."

He was dressed neatly in khakis, a white shirt, and a tie, and he was ready to leave for work. His briefcase was on the table, and he was having his morning coffee and a bagel. Our conversation was brief, and he was soon off to work, leaving me alone with Monica. The door closed, and I smiled her way. But her look was the complete opposite.

"You are a piece of work, Ash, seriously," she proclaimed. "I can't believe you. You get yourself into trouble, and you decide to call me."

"I had no one else to call."

"I'm not accessible like that. I have a life with my husband, your son, and a career."

"I'm not tryin' to hinder you, Monica."

"Please don't, because whatever we had the other night, it's forgotten, and I don't want to remember it. And my husband is a good man with a good heart. He wants nothing better than to see you in Justin's life having a relationship with your son and doing well."

"What did you tell him?"

"I had to lie, okay? I couldn't tell him the truth."

I was grateful. It was like back in the day when Monica used to look out for me. Monica was getting herself and my son ready for the day. She was going to work, and Justin was going to school. I had to leave when Monica left, but it was cool. I planned on going to work and acting like nothing had happened between me and Kenya. I wanted to keep a low profile, and I wanted to keep things regular.

Chapter Thirty-three

Ash

Got him hooked on how she affects her style, got to admit her type is just right, the one he'll soon to make become his wife . . .

The next morning while I lay on the couch, Monica's husband was leaving for work as usual. He was an early bird, out the front door before 6:00 a.m. I was glad that he was gone. Tonight was my last night in his home, and I was horny, and I couldn't stop thinking about Monica. I needed to escape from my troubles.

Kenya hadn't shown up at work yesterday as I predicted, and I had no idea if that freak was alive or dead. No cops came to the job. That was a good sign, I assumed. And I couldn't go back to Queens right away. I'd made a few phone calls and reached out to a few friends. I was ready to go handle my beef.

But this morning, I lay there on the couch with my hand down my pants, touching myself. I couldn't stop thinking about Monica. I glanced at the time, and it was a quarter to seven. I stood up and started to explore the house. I went into my son's room, and he was still sleeping. I went into the hallway and heard the shower running. I knew it was Monica in the bathroom showering. I felt this lustful fire stir inside of me. Just the thought of her naked and in the shower was making my dick hard. It was a mistake on her husband's behalf to have me here, because I wanted his wife. Her husband was too naive to see it. He trusted Monica, and that was his curse and my blessing.

Shirtless, I strolled to the bathroom and saw the door ajar. Monica was still in the shower, so I lingered outside the bathroom and silently peered inside. Soon she was done, stepping out of the shower and toweling off. My eyes were fixated on her wet and teasing flesh from my careful position. I gazed attentively. Her leaving the door ajar, was it a mistake or a subtle invitation to me? I wanted it to be an invitation. So I pushed opened the door and startled her completely.

"Oh, my God, Ash, what are you doing in here?" she exclaimed, immediately covering her nakedness with the towel.

"Good morning, beautiful," I said.

"Get out! Get the fuck out!" she shouted.

Of course, I ignored her demand and approached her coolly. "You left the door open. I didn't know you were here. But now that I see you are, you wanna start round two with us?"

"You need to leave!"

"I need you."

I was intimately against her, pulling her into my arms, and of course she resisted me. She fought. I was turned on.

"Are you crazy? This is my fuckin' husband's home!"

"Please, that fool is like twice your age, and I know you ain't happy with him. Besides, he's gone, and our son is asleep," I said, forcing myself on her.

"Ash, no!"

"C'mon, I need a quickie."

She tried to keep herself covered with the towel, but she soon lost that fight. I snatched it away from her and tossed it to the side. Now her nakedness was transparent, and I leaned forward and immediately clamped my mouth around her left nipple and sucked, tugged, and bit it. She continued to resist, and I continued to seduce. I opened her thighs, and I drove two fingers into her as I continued to suck on her nipple. She cooed and moaned from the feeling. She could no longer resist it. She wanted me here. I knew that for a fact. Her fight against me was only a facade. Her husband was in his mid-thirties, and Monica was 23 years old. Why would she marry a fool like him, being so young? Simple, for security, that's why. What else did he have to offer her? She was in her sexual prime, and she liked the thrill I was giving her.

Coolly, I pulled out my hard, big black dick and made her get down on her knees. Truth, that incident with Kenya made me need to be with a real damn woman. It bothered me deeply that I got off from this faggot sucking my dick, that a transsexual made me that hard, although I didn't know she was one, and I was tricked.

My hard dick throbbed, and Monica opened her mouth. I watched the head of my cock disappear into her mouth. She gratifyingly went to work on me, proving to me that she'd wanted this from the beginning. I closed my eyes and enjoyed it, fighting that image of Kenya doing the same thing to me. I needed this from Monica. For a moment, she pleased me orally, and I wanted to return the favor. I picked her up into my arms and placed her naked ass on the bathroom countertop, and I crouched between her spread legs and went to work on her. I drove my tongue inside of her and licked her clit and fingered her G-spot. She whimpered and squirmed, definitely forgetting that we were inside her husband's home.

"Oh, God. Umm, umm, umm." Her moaning was like music to my ears.

Her hands clasped the back of my head, and she held me there as I sucked, licked, nibbled, bit, and tugged at her pussy. Then our oral relations with each other transitioned into hardcore intercourse. She clamped her thighs around me and rocked her hips against my hard dick. I was inside of her and felt every bit of her contraction. I groaned. It was bliss. And I went from fucking her propped against the countertop to her curved over doggie style, legs spread in a downward V and her grasping the sink tightly. It felt so good inside of her. Sheer euphoria overwhelmed me. I didn't want the morning to end.

"I'm coming," I cried out.

I wanted to get her pregnant this morning. I wanted to put another baby inside of her, and my strokes were deep and fierce enough to let it happen.

"Umm. Ooooh."

I felt my nut brewing. I knew she did too. But then the unexpected happened and we both heard Justin say, "Mommy, what you doing?"

There Justin was, standing in the bathroom doorway with a direct view of my dick inside his mother. We were literally caught with our pants down. Monica quickly panicked, and she scrambled to cover her nakedness. She reached for that towel with lightning speed, all the while shouting out, "Oh, my God. Oh, my God. Justin, go to your room!"

I covered myself too. Justin stood there with his innocence, his eyes wide with curiosity.

Our son pivoted and ran back to his bedroom, probably more scared than upset. It was clear that our playtime was over. We'd never locked the bathroom door. Monica turned to me and glared at me with an evil eye.

"This is all your damn fault! Our son caught us fucking!" she exclaimed.

"The boy gotta learn someday," I joked.

She pushed me and retorted, "This isn't funny, Ash! He saw us! He saw us in my husband's home. Oh, my God!"

"Monica, just chill."

"Get out!" she screamed.

"What?"

"I said get the fuck out!" she yelled. "I'm so stupid! I should have never gone there with you. You're trouble, and you always will be trouble. Now I have to fix this."

"Yo, Monica, you trippin'."

"Ash, get the fuck out of my house now before I throw you out and call the police," she threatened me with her brow furrowed.

"Police? You serious?"

The intense look on her face told me that she was serious. I didn't have a choice. I reluctantly collected my things and went for the door. Monica was still furious. She had nothing to say to me. I just said, "Tell my son I said bye."

I marched out of her home. The spark that was starting between us suddenly felt extinguished. There would be no reconciliation. I kept saying to myself, *damn, I should have locked the door.*

***

I decided not to go to work today. Instead, I continued to reach out to my friends, including Terrance. I needed a favor from him. I asked to borrow his gun. It was a .45 I gave to him before my incarceration. I knew he still had it, and it was clean. Terrance had no use for it. He wasn't about that life, which was a good thing. We talked, and I told him my dilemma. He couldn't believe it.

But the day was young, and I needed to kill some time, so I called up this young thing I met a few days back and had her come get me. I spent the day at her place—having sex, of course. It was always good to have a piece of pussy on reserve.

That evening, I met Terrance in Brooklyn, but he didn't have my gun. He came to talk. Of course, I was upset.

"What the fuck, Terrance? I need that shit!" I griped.

"Yo, this shit needs to stop, Ash. You just got home, and look at your life, man. You're wilding out right now," he preached to me.

"What? What the fuck do you mean? This fool came at me and shot at me, and I'm supposed to let that shit slide? Fuck outta here!"

"You came at him first. And for what? For Chanel, someone you don't even care for like that. You do worse to her."

I shook my head at Terrance, feeling disgusted. Never in a million years would I have thought I would see the day that Terrance would take Chanel's side, and Keith's. I felt betrayed.

"I'm gonna do worse to that fool!" I retorted.

"You're still on parole."

"I don't give a fuck!" I was angry at the world. I wanted justice . . . or revenge. Kenya, Chanel, Keith, Monica, and her husband—I was mad at all of them.

"Ash, I'm trying to be your friend," he said.

"You tryin' to fuck wit' me. I don't need a fuckin' friend. I need someone who's gonna have my back. What, you got Yasmin now and now you happy at the world?"

"It's not even like that. I'm trying to be there for you and prevent you from doing something stupid. You need to stop this shit."

"Stop what?"

"This gangster and stupid shit! You got two kids who are gonna need you in their life, and all this fuckin' around with different women is gonna catch up with you," he proclaimed.

"What, you preaching to me now? You Devin now, huh?"

"Let this shit be, Ash. Just let it go."

But I couldn't just let it go. I felt disrespected and threatened. What I wanted was Monica, but I couldn't wholly have her. And I still couldn't get the images of a man sucking my dick out of my head. I was heated over that, and then niggas tried to take my life in front of my mother's place, so I was supposed to run and hide like a scared bitch? It wasn't happening.

"Fuck that. Ain't no bitch or nigga gonna disrespect me out here on these streets. You fuckin' hear me? Fuck you! Go be wit' your new bitch. I don't need you! I got this on my own. Fuck you!" I cursed him angrily. I spun around and marched away from him.

"Ash! C'mon, man, don't do this. Just chill, man. I'm worried about you," he shouted.

I ignored him. I kept on walking. I had other people to call and have my back, and one of those people was Crown. He was definitely about that life.

Chapter Thirty-four

Terrance

What is love . . . love is togetherness, you and she, God, and we, bringing love, peace, and tranquility.

I couldn't stop him, but I couldn't babysit him either. It was Ash's life, and he was a grown man. But I was truly worried about him. The way he was moving, he was going to end up in one of two places: back in jail or dead.

We all had our trials and tribulations to go through. I was damn sure going through mine at the moment. My quarrel and breakup with Sophia still hurt, but being with Yasmin helped ease some of that pain. Love could be a compressing feeling. It could make you act out, do things that you wouldn't normally do, either from being in love or having your heart broken from it. We all were men, and we all were hurting, from my cousin to Ash and me.

We tried to act like it, but we weren't Superman with love. There wasn't a big S on our chests that made us invincible to all pain, and our kryptonite was pussy and love. Sometimes we ended up hurting ourselves and others during the outcome of a failed relationship, or jealously, or a broken heart. Sometimes we wanted to fight or act suicidal or have sex with everyone to forget about that one. But I had to overcome my pain and the squeezing feeling of uncertainty and jealousy.

I started to pray more, asking God to heal me and forgive me, because I too was on that suicidal path of self-destruction and acting out. It felt like the tears wouldn't stop falling and the pain would never go away. It felt like I was in quicksand, and no matter how much I struggled and tried to fight it, I continued to sink deeper and deeper. But it felt like I wanted to decline because I didn't want to go on. And I tried to pull Sophia into the quicksand with me, let us both sink together.

But I had to say to myself that I was selfish. Why? Because it wasn't just about me. I had Zaire, my beautiful daughter, to live for and to raise and take care of. She was going to need her father in her life, despite what her mother and I were going through. We couldn't sink together.

So I thanked God for His healing and redemption. Finally, it felt like I could breathe again and pull myself from that vile pit of sadness and emptiness, and of anger and pain, and move on with my life and to someone else. Maybe we did marry too young.

Yasmin and I definitely had a connection, more so than I'd had with Sophia. It seemed ugly, hooking up with your wife's best friend, but I couldn't resist the feelings I felt for her. Yasmin and I were taking things slow, and Sophia and I were separated, and our divorce was coming next. She was seeing this Eric guy, and I had to accept that. I had to let that past and pain go.

Funny thing, Yasmin and I ran into Sophia and Eric one day on the street.

"Hey," I greeted Sophia.

"Hey," Sophia greeted me back.

It was awkward between us. I was holding hands with Yasmin, and she was holding hands with Eric. It felt like we were all in an episode of *The Twilight Zone.*

"This is Eric," she introduced us.

It was my first time meeting him. We only exchanged nods. There was no handshake between us, just this weird exchange. And all those things were copasetic with us. There were still some ill feelings between Sophia and Yasmin. Best friends again? I didn't think so. And Eric, I didn't know the dude, but that was Sophia's new man, I assumed, and I had to wish them the best.

"Well, later," I said.

"Later," Sophia replied.

We all had to get back to us, God willing.

Chapter Thirty-five

Sophia

What is love . . . to live and breathe, to heal and need, to exhale and succeed . . . love is time and we . . .

"Ooooh, umm. Umm," I moaned and groaned, feeling Eric's erection deep inside of me as I straddled him against the bed, riding his big dick. I leaned forward and pressed my hands against his broad chest, and he cupped my ass cheeks strongly, thrusting upward into me and enjoying all of me as I did him.

It was a blissful night with us, but that awkward exchange with my soon-to-be ex-husband and my former best friend was stuck inside my head. I couldn't stop thinking about it. Suddenly, I didn't feel right. It wasn't the sex. It was something that I couldn't fully explain.

I heard my man moaning underneath me. I was milking his big dick to come, and he was squeezing my breast and ass simultaneously. But I had to put a damper on his enjoyment because my mind unexpectedly went someplace else. I stopped suddenly, mid-thrust, and climbed off his dick. He was bewildered by my abrupt movement.

"What's wrong, baby? Why did you stop?" he asked me. "I was about to come."

I sighed. "I can't anymore."

"What do you mean? What's going on?"

I removed myself from the bed and donned a robe, and he propped himself up against the headboard. I knew he was somewhat upset with me. I was wasting an entirely hard and thick erection.

"We need to talk," I said.

He looked at me critically. And then he said, "It's about the other night, right? When we ran into your husband and your friend?"

It was. I nodded.

He then asked me, "Are you still in love with him?"

"I'm not."

"So what's bothering you? Talk to me."

It was seeing Terrance with Yasmin, and it made me somewhat jealous. He used to be mine, and now he was hers. Were there still some feelings for him? I doubted it.

"I just need to think," I said.

"About what?"

I gazed at Eric's handsome features—his hard masculine body and healthy-looking dick. Everything was picture perfect about him, and he treated me nicely, placed me on a pedestal. He was the maintenance man for my daily needs, but something was missing. I wasn't in love with him. I was more in lust with him. Also, I wasn't rushing to be in another relationship, and we'd started to have unprotected sex. I wasn't on any birth control, and there was the fear of an unwanted pregnancy. It was the last thing I needed.

I needed a break—a break from everything and everyone, even sex. Though Eric felt so good, it felt wrong at the time. I needed some time to myself to heal, to think, and to recover. I wanted to get my life back on track. I wanted to go back to school and attain my bachelor's degree in maybe financing or business. I wanted to completely start over and work on a career. I was still young and motivated. I wanted to live my youthful life to the fullest. I knew I'd gotten married too young, and everything had been a rush for me—the marriage, the pregnancy, motherhood, my job, and Terrance. It was time to take a deep and lengthy breather and exhale. And being with Eric, it suddenly felt like it was happening again. I was moving too fast with him. I did not want to end up where I'd left off with Terrance—pregnant, loving, and trapped again.

It was time to start doing me again.

"Eric, I'm sorry, but I can't continue to do this."

"What are you talking about, Sophia?"

"I can't do this, us, anymore. I need a break."

"A break? Are you dumping me?"

I sighed. "Yes."

"You sure this isn't about Terrance?"

"No. It's about me and my life. You're a fine and wonderful man, Eric. But this can't happen anymore."

He looked saddened by my words, and he was hurt. But I couldn't worry about his feelings. I needed to start worrying about my own.

"Wow!" he uttered. "I thought we had something special."

"It was special, Eric. But I'm just not ready to take this further. I need some time for myself."

"I'm falling in love with you," he admitted.

I felt flattered, but I wished he weren't. I sighed. "We need to move on."

"I wanted to do that together. I want a life with you."

"Eric, I need to move on. I just came out of a marriage to get some space, and I met you. And you're great. God, you're great, but I need some time to myself. I'm sorry."

He stood up, and he sighed deeply. He was hurt. There was no doubt that he was a good man, and many may have thought that I was crazy to let him go, to give it up, but I had to.

He came up to me, and he wrapped his arms around me. His hold felt secure and manly. "I understand," he said.

I smiled. "Thank you."

We kissed each other, and it was going to be our last kiss. I pulled away from his deep affection and took a deep breath. Yes, child, I was going to miss him. I got dressed and left his place. I knew what I wanted. I was going to enroll in college this fall and take up finance and business. I was going to continue to work at the bank and maybe move up into management. But I was doing me. I finally had my own car, and I was looking at some new places.

With a deep breath and pure focus, I was going to live my life. I wasn't trying to become anyone's housewife, wife, or baby mama again—not for a while, and not until I had my own priorities situated.

Chapter Thirty-six

Ash

What is love . . . love is the beginning of something beautiful and the end of selfishness, love is forgiveness and change . . . love is you, and me and we . . . love is harmony . . . to agree or disagree, but it's still we . . . love is, We!

I rode shotgun in Crown's truck, and my head was constantly on a swivel. We were driving around the neighborhood looking for Keith and his cousin. I had a .45 on my lap, and it was loaded completely. I had a beef to settle via violence. We drove around the hood all day, searching from Chanel's place to everywhere else, but so far these clowns were MIA, and I was irritated.

For a moment, we took a time-out to eat at the Rockaway Fish House on Rockaway Boulevard. We smoked a cigarette, and an hour later, we were back on the hunt. I was determined to find Keith and deal with him. I couldn't let that night they shot at me slide. If I did, I would be considered a punk, a bitch-ass nigga, and that couldn't go down. But the day grew long looking for these fools, and Crown and I grew tired.

"Yo, take me back to Chanel's. I'm gonna chill there for the night," I said to Crown.

Crown nodded. Tomorrow was a new day, and they couldn't run and hide forever. Crown navigated his truck to Chanel's place. At least I could get some pussy tonight. I needed it.

Shortly after, we arrived at Chanel's place and were taken aback. Andre's black Lexus was parked outside the home. I knew he and Keith were inside my baby mama's place.

"That's them right there, right?" Crown said, pointing to the Lexus.

"Yeah," I said.

I grew excited and anxious. They had no idea we were outside. Crown reached for his gun, a 9 mm, and he was itching to create some drama on the block.

"Yo, let me borrow your cell phone," I said.

He removed the phone from his hip and handed it to me. I dialed Chanel's number. She answered right away. "Hello?"

"Hey, what's up?" I said coolly.

"Ash, hey. Where you at?"

"Don't worry 'bout that. Yo, your boy tried to pop me the other night."

"Who?" She was playing dumb.

"Bitch, don't fuckin' play stupid wit' me. You know who. How the fuck did he know where I live?" I exclaimed.

"I don't know."

"You gave that pussy nigga my address."

"No!" she hollered. "I would never do that."

"Don't fuckin' lie to me."

"I'm not lying!"

"Yo, my daughter in there with you?"

"Yes."

Shit! I couldn't just run up there and confront these fools that quickly. I didn't want my daughter to see any violence or get caught up in the melee that would ensue. So I came up with a different game plan.

"Yo, I'll be over there in a few minutes," I said. I hung up.

Crown looked at me and asked, "What now?"

"My daughter's in there, but I got somethin' for these niggas," I said.

I got out of the truck with my gun tucked into my waistband, picked up a giant rock, and went toward Andre's Lexus. I smashed his front windshield with the rock, spider-glassing the window, which caused the alarm to go off and echo. I knew it was going to get their attention. Crown and I were posted right by the doorway, and we were waiting for them to take the bait.

Just as I predicted, the first muthafucka to rush out the front door was Andre, worried about his ride. Keith followed right behind him. I sprang out on them, shouting, "What now, nigga! Huh, muthafucka?"

My .45 was aimed at Keith's head, and Crown had my back, training his gun on Andre. Both men stood stunned at the sight of us. They didn't move. They frowned and knew what time it was.

"Y'all niggas tried to shoot me!" I shouted.

"What the fuck you gonna do wit' that, pussy?" Andre barked at me. "You a bitch-ass nigga. You shoot me and my peoples are gonna fuck you up."

He had clout in Queens and Brooklyn, but this was about respect and comeback. I couldn't allow this drug-dealing fool to punk me. Crown and I held them at gunpoint. It was intense. Keith looked scared, but Andre was defiant, not giving a fuck that we had guns.

"You and your boy, y'all fucked up!" he griped through his clenched teeth. "I'm gonna fuck y'all niggas up! If you were a real nigga, you woulda been pulled the trigger, pussy!"

I admit I hesitated. I noticed the gun underneath Andre's shirt. He was carrying, but I had the advantage. He wasn't the Flash, and if he moved wrong, I was going to kill him.

"What, nigga? What you gonna do, pussy?" Andre continued to taunt me.

"Oh, my God, Ash, what are you fuckin' doin'?" Chanel screamed out, seeing me pointing guns at Keith and Andre.

"Daddy!" I heard my daughter shout next.

They both were standing on the front steps, and I was quickly distracted by their presence. And that quick distraction was all it took for chaos to ensue. Andre immediately reached for his pistol, and Keith reacted. Maybe he tried to run, but I shot him in the chest twice. Pop! Pop!

Crown shot multiple times at Andre. Bang! Bang! Bang! Bang! He went ferociously down in a hail of bullets. When the smoked cleared, both men were sprawled out on the concrete in their blood. I knew they were dead.

I'd never killed a man before. I stood there, smoking gun still in my hand, and was in awe. It was payback, but at what cost? I turned to see Chanel and my daughter standing only a few feet away from the murders. They'd witnessed the entire thing. They were utterly distraught. Chanel cried out in tears, and my daughter was also in tears.

"Let's go!" Crown shouted at me.

I'd killed a man in front of them. It was something they were never going to forget. One baby father killed the other baby father. I took off running with Crown. I couldn't even comfort my daughter. I'd become a murderer, and my life shifted for the worse.

"Fuck!" I uttered, still in disbelief that it had happened just that fast.

Chapter Thirty-seven

Terrance

What is love . . . love is sometimes the harder you try, the harder you cry, but you continue to try harder, because you love . . .

I got the call early that morning from Trey, once again informing me about Ash.

"He's locked up again," said Trey.

I wasn't shocked about it. He led to that predicament again and wouldn't listen, but I was sad for him. Then Trey said, "He killed two people, right in front of his daughter and Chanel."

"Shit."

I knew that, this time, Ash was going away for a very long time.

Two weeks later, I went to visit him on Rikers Island. I sat inside the visiting room among dozens of other visitors and waited for his arrival into the room. I watched Ash come into the room with several other inmates, escorted by a correction officer. He was clad in a gray jumpsuit and looked almost like a broken man. He slowly walked toward the table I sat at, and we dapped each other up. He took a seat across from me.

"T, what's up?" he greeted me. "I know you ain't shocked to see me back in here."

"Yeah, I am."

"Shit happens, right?" he said.

"Murder, yo. What the fuck?"

"I couldn't let that shit be, Terrance. This is who I am—a thug. They came for me, so I came for them."

"But your daughter witnessed it. How do you think that's gonna affect her life? And now you're in here."

It was a harsh blow to him, knowing I was right. I saw the tears welling up in his eyes. "She gonna be a'ight," he replied.

It was sad that he believed that. Or maybe he didn't.

"What are you looking at?" I asked.

"Twenty-five to life."

I sighed. "Damn!"

"I'm good, though. I've accepted my fate."

Ash had two murder charges and an attempted murder charge, and the attempted murder charge puzzled me.

"Who did you tried to kill?" I said.

"Some other shit happened that came back on me. I got caught up wit' this dumb bitch in Bay Ridge, and ended up fucking her up pretty bad that night."

"Man, you wildin' the fuck out," I said. "When the fuck are you gonna calm down?"

He chuckled out of the blue. Did he find his situation funny? I sure didn't.

"Guess what. Monica's pregnant," he mentioned.

"What, by you? Isn't she married?"

"Yeah, but that still ain't stop a nigga from fuckin' her. She came to see me the other day, told me the news. She was upset and crying. She can't get an abortion. Her husband knows and thinks the baby is his."

"So it's definitely your baby?"

"Yeah, she believes so. I put another baby into that good-ass pussy. Yeah, it was worth it," he laughed.

What a life he'd lived. He'd killed Chanel's son's father and ruined Monica's marriage. *The same things that make you laugh will make you cry.* Though Ash seemed in high spirits, I knew he was crying inside. But he couldn't show his pain or his regrets or any contrition at all. He had to remain a thug. He was a pain to everyone's world.

Funny thing though, he apologized to me. "Yo, I'm sorry about that day I screamed at you. I knew you were only tryin' to look out for me, keep me out of trouble. I was too heated and upset to listen. But I guess this is fate, right?"

"Nah, we cool. It's been forgotten."

It was a short visit, and it went by quickly. Before we knew it, the guard was interrupting us, telling us that our time was up. We both stood up. I gave him a hug and dap. It was a sad day, a depressing moment. But he smiled at me and said, "You be good, my nigga."

"You too," I replied.

"I'll be a'ight."

After a lingering moment between us, I pivoted and started toward the exit. It was sad to leave Ash behind, locked up like that, but he chose his life, and I chose mine. We all had to take responsibility for our actions and grow up someday. I had to thank God for every breath I took and every step that led forward.

Chapter Thirty-eight

Devin

Love . . . now the sensation of her love covers his heart, the look in her innocent eyes, her innocent face; he sees his world . . . his all, the one he will always love . . . ?

I thought about my fiancée all morning. She woke up sick this morning and had to call out sick from work. I was willing to stay home with her and take care of her, make her some soup, and help nurse her back to health, but she insisted that I go to work today and make that paycheck. I left her home alone, reluctantly though.

It was early in the afternoon, and I wasn't entirely focused on my job. So I decided to leave work early and go home to be with Danielle. We'd reconciled from our fight, and our lives were back to normal, back to lengthy lovemaking and caring for each other. I didn't have to worry about no ex-boyfriend in town. I picked up a few movies she would like, her dry cleaning, and some things from the grocery store to make her some soup. I was feeling good. It was Friday. The sun was shining brightly, and it was a warm and beautiful day. I wanted to surprise my fiancée today.

I steered my car into the driveway and removed everything from the back seat, carrying an armful of things. I smiled, greeted my neighbors with cheer, and walked into my home. But the moment I stepped inside I heard music playing from the stereo. It was R. Kelly's "Bump n' Grind."

See I know just what you want and I know just what you need girl
So baby bring your body to me (bring your body here)
I'm not fooling around with you
Baby, my love is true, with you
(With you is where I want to be) Is where, I wanna be

I was taken aback by the song. Why was it playing? But I thought nothing of it. Danielle loved music, and she loved R. Kelly. I placed the groceries in the kitchen and set her dry cleaning and the movies I'd rented on the couch. I approached the bedroom, thinking Danielle was lying down and relaxing. The door was ajar. I wanted to hug her and kiss her. I was excited to be in love and to be engaged. I approached the bedroom. However, I saw a slight movement happening on the bed from the hallway, and it was strange to me. I halted right there and carefully peeked into my room and was shocked and utterly traumatized by what I saw and what I was hearing.

Danielle panted out, "Ooooh, fuck me, Jonathan. Yes, just like that. Like that, nigga. Fuck me!"

I stood there, shocked and dumbfounded at the sight of my fiancée having sex in the missionary position in our bedroom. I wanted it to be a bad dream, but it wasn't. Her legs were wrapped around him, and his hairy ass bounced between her thighs. Danielle was consumed by him. In fact, they were fucking so hard that they didn't notice me watching them from the doorway. She had her eyes closed, and his back was to me.

"Damn, baby, you always had some good pussy," this muthafucka uttered.

"It's your pussy, baby. Umm, umm. Aaaah!" she moaned and groaned underneath him.

The tears trickled from my eyes, and I stood there, fuming for a short moment. I couldn't watch it anymore. I moved away from the door. I couldn't believe it, but I saw it with my own two eyes. This bitch was cheating on me, and with the same man who was supposed to be back in Chicago.

She fuckin' lied to me! I gave her everything. I asked her to become my wife, and she does this to me? She fucks another man, and on our bed in our home. It all consumed me at once: betrayal, hatred, anger, jealousy, and revenge. My chest heaved up and down with wrath. I was dumbfounded. I slithered back into the living room and marched out the back door. The pain I felt was terrible. It felt like I couldn't breathe. I wanted to collapse and cry. I had to talk to someone. I had to let someone know what was happening to me.

Terrance answered his phone with, "Devin, what's good?"

"I'm about to kill this fuckin' bitch!" I belligerently shouted. The tone was unexpected for me.

"Whoa, what's going on? You mean Danielle?"

The tears flowed heavier and heavier from my eyes, washing my face with profound grief. It felt like a nightmare, but this was real life. "She's in our bedroom right now fuckin' her ex-boyfriend . . . on our bed!" I cried out to him.

"Oh, shit, you serious?"

"Yes! I'm gonna kill this fuckin' bitch!"

"Devin, just chill and calm down."

"Fuck calming down. How she gonna do me like this? After everything I did for her. How she gonna do me like this? Yo, it hurts so bad," I cried.

"You confronted her?"

"No, she's still in there having sex with him."

"Devin, stay outside and chill. I'll be over there in a minute."

"Fuck that, Terrance, it's too late," I exclaimed.

"Yo, don't do anything stupid. I'm on my way there."

"I loved her, Terrance. I fuckin' loved her with all my heart, and she does me dirty like this. She lied and cheated. I'm going to kill her and him, Terrance. They're dead," I stated absently.

"Devin, chill with that talk. I know you got better sense than that," he shouted. "Believe me, it's not worth it. I'm on my way now."

"I'm tired. I'm tired of always having my heart broken by a woman, and I'm tired of having my feelings toyed with. I thought she was the one. I believed it! I fuckin' believed it! I can't take this anymore."

"I'll be there in five minutes. Just hold on and stay outside, Devin. Stay outside and talk to me."

I ended the call. I was done talking. I always wore my heart on my sleeve, and it never failed to backfire on me. It was still the same thing with a different woman. First there was Melanie, and then in high school was Camilla. She dumped me for another man a day before the prom, so I didn't have a date. Then there was Rhea after high school. I loved her and we got engaged, but I soon caught her sucking some niggas dick in his car one night. She didn't see me, but I saw her. She punk'd me and kept the ring.

Then there was Cindy, the woman I loved before Danielle, and it didn't work out. She left me and said I was boring. And now it was Danielle. Why? Why did women fall for the bad boys like Ash, give them their heart, commitment, and everything else, including kids, but they continued to dog me out? Why? What was wrong with me? Was I too nice, too clingy, or needy? Did I love too much? I worked hard, was educated, loving, and romantic, and I owned my own home. But it felt like the more I did for my woman, the more they continued to hurt me. I was always willing to give love a chance, but love didn't love me back. It continued to hurt and taunt me. It would show me something believable, something worth caring for, and then, bang, it was snatched away from me. And I was tired of the hurt. I wanted it to go away. I was tired of being that sucker for love, man.

Enough was enough!

I spun around and marched back into my home. My tears continued to fall. I went into the hallway closet and removed a .380 pistol from the small gun safe on the top shelf. I'd had it hidden there for so long that I almost forgot I had it in the house. The gun was loaded. I gripped it tightly in my hand and marched toward the bedroom. I still heard them fucking, and the R&B music was still playing.

They were so caught up in each other that I could have stood there forever and they still wouldn't have seen me. I was about to give them a surefire reason to stop fucking.

I glared at them, and the sad thing was, I still loved her. I gathered the strength to do the unthinkable. I stretched out my arm and aimed the gun at her infidelity, her lies, my hurt and pain, and so much more.

God, forgive me, please, I said to myself.

I then caught their attention with a loud, "I loved you!"

What I heard next were my mother's words. *"Love starts with a smile, grows with a kiss, and ends in tears."* She forgot to mention one more thing—love could also end in murder.

Chapter Thirty-nine

Terrance

What is love . . . you tell me?

I did ninety miles per hour on the city streets. I pushed the pedal to the metal, hurrying to catch Devin in time before he did something stupid. I blew through two red lights and caught the attention of an NYPD car with my erratic driving. But I refused to stop, and a police chase ensued. Three blocks in, I had three police cars pursuing me. I felt like a fugitive. But I had my reasons and would risk going to jail to save my friend's life. I had to get to Devin no matter what it took.

Our conversation was ten minutes ago, and ten minutes felt like a lifetime. I hit corners sharply, nearly crashing my SUV, and I continued to race to his home. I finally arrived at Devin's place. I had almost the entire NYPD surrounding me with their lights and police sirens blaring. It looked like a scene from *Set It Off*.

I raced from my truck and suddenly heard, "Get down! Get down now!"

I was lucky they didn't shoot me. Several officers charged at me, believing I was leaving my vehicle to flee them. Still, in actuality, I was running to Devin's front door. Their guns were drawn on me, and they were angry and excited. I was tackled to the ground and roughed up. I felt the barrel of a gun to the back of my head. I didn't struggle with them. But I pleaded with them.

"Officers, let me explain. It's my friend. He's in that house—"

"Shut the fuck up!" one cop yelled at me.

I was quickly put into handcuffs and arrested. There was chaos on the block. I felt like a criminal. But I couldn't give up. I couldn't leave there without finding out about my friend.

"Officers, please, my friend's name is Devin, and he lives in that house right there. I think he's about to commit murder. That's why I rushed over here without stopping. Please, Officers!" I begged them

"Shut up!" one cop yelled.

"Officers, I'm telling you the truth. My name is Terrance, and he just called me on my cell phone. Can one of you just run in and see if he's okay? I'm begging you."

A female cop took to my story. She asked what house I meant, and I nodded with my chin to Devin's place. She told me to hold on. She and another tall and lanky cop approached Devin's house cautiously with their hands against their guns. They knocked on the front door and rang the bell, but there was no answer. They continued to try to attract the home occupants, but still there was no answer. I was apprehensive.

"You have to go in," I shouted while they had my face down against the squad car.

"Devin, this is the NYPD. Can you please open the door?" the female cop shouted.

I just remained there, feeling my heart pounding harder and faster, continually thinking the worst. The female officer called out for Devin to open his door again, but he didn't comply.

"Devin, I repeat, this is the NYPD. Can you please open up?" she sternly repeated.

She looked back at her fellow officers and me and shrugged her shoulders. She then reached for the doorknob and slowly turned it, seeing that his front door was already open. Bizarre. She removed her gun from its holster. She and that skinny cop entered with caution.

I remained there in handcuffs, not being able to do anything. I couldn't take my eyes off the place. They were in there for about five minutes, and everything felt too still. I couldn't breathe. Subsequently, the lady cop hurried from the house, and by the look on her face, I knew something wasn't right.

"Call in a homicide. We have a situation," she said.

"A situation? What the fuck happened in there?" I frantically asked.

She looked at me, and I already knew what happened. She didn't need to tell me.

"We may have a murder-suicide inside the home," she said.

"Oh, my God!" I cried out. I was dismayed by the news. It felt like my knees were going to buckle. I started to cry like a baby. I couldn't believe it. Devin had killed his fiancée, her lover, and himself. I was crushed.

"This shit ain't happening." I continued to cry out. *Damn, Devin, I thought that you were smarter than that. It ain't worth it. Life goes on. Life goes on.*

End

Acknowledgments

First, I'd like to thank the Lord, and my personal Savior, for what He has done for me. I know without Him I am nothing, and I give all my glory to Him. I endured the trials and tribulations that made me bend but not break. That made me bruised but not broken. That made me frown but not give up. But with faith, I will always thrive and soar high to achieve my dreams. Never give up, no matter what, because the beginning is always the hardest. And everything you ever wanted is on the other side of fear. It doesn't matter how many times you fail because, at the end of the day, a single win can last you a lifetime. So, let your dreams be big and your worries be small. Visualize who you want to be, then work for it because I guarantee once you start seeing the results of your hard work, it will become an addiction. So, continue to do what you love, and love what you do. Focus on the process rather than the outcome because I believe you are one decision away from a totally different life. Just keep showing up every day, no matter what. And win through your actions, not your words. Nothing ever just happens. You have to make it happen. There are builders and great people all around us. All you have to do is find them.

I would like to say thank you to the following people: first and foremost, my parents, Alinda and Spencer Gray; my beautiful kids, Emari, Bella, Sodaytra, and Jeremy Green, and my wife, Sophia Green; my sisters, Latanya and Terri; my older brother Pat, along with my nieces and nephews. And shout out to my cousin and business partner of CGD Productions, Jamel Johnson, and my next business partner, Eric Cook, along with Anthony Whyte and Andre Thorne. I also want to give thanks and a shoutout to my southern family, my cousin and supporter, Homando Goldsmith, J.D., J.R., Chico, Derrick, Benjamin Jones, Terrance Wright, Wakesha, and Emmanuel Fogle, and their families. To Deatria, Lonnie, Quinn, and Boss Oglesby and Jessica, thank you for taking me in and making me family. Thanks to my agent, N'TYSE, for helping to take me to the next level. Thanks to my Intellectual Ink magazine family and my Philadelphia family.

Gone, but not forgotten . . .
and until we meet again . . .

Timia L. Williams,
February 1984 – August 2018

Rashad Forward,
June 1990 – March 2020

Raymond Chamble, Jr.
March 1973 – February 2021

Earl Henderson Cartwright Moses,
December 1949 – January 2021